It All Begins With Goodbye

Patricia J Parsons

MOONLIGHT PRESS | TORONTO

For information or permissions:

Visit www.moonlightpresstoronto.com

Or email moonlightpressinfo@gmail.com

With Gratitude & Love

WHEN A WRITER WRITES A BOOK from the soul, it's clear to her that her characters are more than names on pages. They are living, breathing aspects of her life. And if she's lucky, those lives are embodied in a single person with whom she shares her life. I am lucky. Art is my Tom, my Patrick, my Auguste, my Tim. He is also the only person in the world who understands this. It's not enough to simply dedicate this book to Art. I dedicate all my books to him in one way or another. And I will spend the rest of my life trying to make sure he understands how grateful I am for his support and encouragement (and often prodding), his editing prowess (I may argue, but he's right in almost every instance), his reminders when I have forgotten something. With love.

Author's Note

THIS IS THE SIXTH BOOK in a row where Charlotte "Charlie" Hudson shows up. I never intended to write a series, and the truth is that each book stands on its own. But Charlie first appears in *The Year I Made 12 Dresses*, a single, wannabe writer without a penny to her name and ends up here—in book number six.

If you haven't been introduced to Charlie yet, you might want to go back to see how she got where she is now. But even if you don't, please enjoy this book!

Some Other Books by
Patricia J. Parsons

The "almost-but-not-quite-true" stories
[aka The Charlie Hudson Books]

The Year I Made Twelve Dresses (Book 1)
Kat's Kosmic Blues (Book 2)
The Inscrutable Life of Frannie Phillips (Book 3)
Something I'm Supposed to Do (Book 4)
This is the Way the Story Ends (Book 5)

Plan B (lit-for-intelligent-chicks)
Confessions of a Failed Yuppie (lit-for-intelligent-chicks)
Something More Than Love (historical fiction)
Grace Note: In Hildegard's Shadow (historical fiction)

"If our mind is empty, it is always ready for anything. It is open to everything. In the beginner's mind, there are many possibilities, but in the expert's mind, there are few."
~ Shunryu Suzuki

"It's not a story until something happens."
~ CK Hudson

Widow

I DON'T KNOW WHY I WAS SO SURPRISED that Saturday afternoon when Frankie appeared in the doorway of my office on the second floor of our house, hands on her hips, her toe tapping impatiently, saying, "Mom, Aunt Evelyn is here."

Frankie—known to her teachers and anyone else who doesn't know her well as Francesca—is my daughter who stood there eyeing me as if I were the recalcitrant teenager and she the exasperated parent.

I was sitting on the small sofa facing my desk with my feet up under me, my iPad in my hand, while I scrolled through one vintage handbag site or another, searching for the perfect Chanel Vintage Black Patent Square Mini Flap Bag. I wasn't sure why I thought I needed a black patent handbag, Chanel or not. I didn't have anywhere to go to show it off.

"Mom? Did you hear me?" Frankie was getting even more exasperated if that were possible. "Aunt Evelyn is here?"

My head jerked up. This time the meaning of her words sank in. "What's your aunt doing here?" Had I forgotten that Evelyn was coming? Surely not. But neither could I imagine what could have brought my sister Evelyn halfway across the country to arrive unannounced. As I stared at my precocious daughter, Evelyn appeared beside her in the doorway, her eyes popping.

"What in god's name are you wearing, Charlie?"

"Well, hello to you, too, Evelyn, sister dear. What brings you to Halifax?"

"Never mind that yet. What are you wearing?"

I looked down at my outfit. It seemed perfectly fine to me.

"I told you the situation is dire, Aunt Evelyn," Frankie said, rolling her eyes. "I have homework to finish. Call me when dinner's ready. Good luck." Frankie popped her AirPods back in her ears and turned on her heel, leaving me alone with my sister.

"What am I wearing?" I said as I put my iPad down on the sofa beside me. I looked down. "I suppose I'm wearing a tracksuit of sorts—the perfect attire for a Saturday afternoon at home."

Evelyn heaved a sigh and plopped herself into my desk chair so that she was staring at me across the expanse of desk. "Charlie, dear sister, you look like you're wearing a cone of cotton candy. What's going on?" She looked around. "And why is it so cold in here?"

I was, in fact, wearing a pink cashmere tracksuit I'd bought from a luxury online shopping aggregator a month or so earlier. It was exceptionally comfortable, but I had to admit it did get a bit itchy in the warm June weather, which is why the air conditioning was blasting. I watched Evelyn as she got up to look at the thermostat on the wall near the door. She clicked it up a few degrees and returned to sit at my desk. I unzipped my fuzzy pink jacket.

"Frankie tells me you haven't worn anything but a tracksuit for months. Is that true?"

Geesh. You couldn't even get a bit of loyalty from your daughter these days. I shrugged. "I don't go anywhere."

"My point exactly. Charlie, I'm here—"

I held up my hand to silence her. "Don't say another word, Evelyn. If you say you're here to stage an intervention, so help me, I'll throttle you. And I suppose Frankie called you and asked you to fly all the way from Toronto to talk some sense into her mother."

"I couldn't have said it better myself," Evelyn said, getting up. "I'm going to settle myself into your lovely guest room if that's all right with madame. We'll talk over drinks later. You still like martinis?"

I nodded enthusiastically. Maybe this wouldn't be so bad after all. Evelyn made the best martinis on the continent.

~

No, none of this should have surprised me. Tom had been dead for just over a year, and I'd managed to alienate just about everyone I'd known before the moment he died—the moment that was seared into my memory like a brand on cattle. It was a memory that blinded me from seeing the rest of my life. I had been with Tom until the final moment and walked away from that moment in my new role—widow. The word consumes itself, or so said Sylvia Plath, who knew a thing or two about being consumed—Sylvia Plath, who ultimately stuck her head in an oven and turned on the gas. She was only thirty years old. Tom was only forty-eight.

The first few weeks after Tom died were nothing more than a blur. There was so much paperwork made all the more tedious because of Tom's real estate business and cumbersome investment portfolio. He had a lot of money—money I didn't need since my great-grandmother had left me a significant inheritance years ago, my late mother had left her wildly successful business to Evelyn and me, and Tom had invested my money well. And that didn't even count the royalties from the two bestselling books I'd had and the acquisition fee Netflix had sent me just before Tom died. One of my books was now in development as a series. All the money in the world didn't change anything. Tom was gone, and I was still here. Then there was Frankie.

I had been a good, supportive mother for the first few months after that fateful day, even hiding my grief from my young daughter, thinking she had enough grief of her own. But it seems children are far more resilient than we think. Frankie mourned her father deeply, then returned to school and got on with her life. I was stuck.

I shuddered as I thought back about all those well-meaning people who drop things off after a death in a family. The house smelled like a funeral parlour for two weeks until I threw a fit one afternoon and stuffed every last one of them into the compost bin. And flowers aren't all they dropped off.

What's the deal with the casseroles? Forgive me for sounding ungrateful, but who eats casseroles under the best of circumstances in the twenty-first century, and in what world does having to face a plate of gelatinous cheese-smothered canned tuna assist one in overcoming loss?

One morning three weeks after the funeral, Frankie stood in the kitchen with the refrigerator door ajar, sighing loudly. "Where is the orange juice, Mom?" she whined. "I can't even find it because of all these stupid containers. What's even in them?" Frankie turned to look at me where I was sitting at the kitchen island, a half-full cup of cold coffee sitting in front of me while I stared at the wall. "Earth to Mom. Are you even listening?"

I looked up. "Oh, yes," I said. "Those are casseroles."

"We don't eat casseroles, Mom."

"I know, honey, and to tell you the god's honest truth, after seeing what people put in them these days, I can't see us changing that behaviour any time soon."

Frankie started pulling them out one by one, opening the lids slightly and gagging—I think the gagging was a bit of a performance, but it was the first time I'd managed half a smile in weeks, maybe even months. Tom had been sick for months before he died.

"This one has a label on it," Frankie said, turning her head to read the letters meticulously written in black marker on a piece of masking tape lest the container be permanently marked. "It says 'Funeral Potatoes.' What the fuck—"

"Frankie!"

"Sorry, Mom. It's just that…"

"I know, honey. I know."

Frankie lifted the lid and sniffed. She made another face and looked like she was about to puke. "Oh my god, Mom. They smell like dirty socks. Can we throw them out?"

And so, we started clearing out the refrigerator. That was how I began widowhood.

~

I was slowly puttering around the kitchen, thinking about what to make for dinner for my older, big-city sister and my thirteen-going-on-thirty-five-year-old daughter, when Evelyn bounced in through the door.

"I've always loved this kitchen, you know, Charlie," she said, taking a seat at the large, marble-topped breakfast bar. "Hey, don't bother making anything for dinner. On my way downstairs, I popped into Frankie's room, and we agreed to order pizza."

"You've agreed, have you?" Why was I being so obnoxious when ordering a pizza seemed like the best idea I'd heard all day—probably all week.

"Yes, Charlie, we have. Now, let's get to the bar in that den of yours and get started on those martinis." She stood up.

Twenty minutes later, Evelyn and I were sitting companionably in two over-stuffed chairs facing one another across a small coffee table in front of the fireplace. I was waiting for the onslaught of advice to begin. We chatted about her work—Evelyn is a high-priced litigation lawyer in downtown Toronto—and her husband's work. Michael Jason Campbell-Watson III, my brother-in-law, is a stockbroker. I have no real idea what a stockbroker does all day. Tom had done his best to teach me about our investment portfolio before he got too sick, and I think I did an admirable job finally understanding our various types of investments.

Still, I never did figure out how stockbrokers made money, although clearly, they made a lot of it.

Then I asked Evelyn about her two children—fifteen-year-old Katie and ten-year-old Lucas—and she asked me about what Frankie was up to these days, and we talked about the house. She commented on how lovely the gardens were looking so early in the year—it was early June. It was no thanks to me, I told her. Although I used to love to do some gardening, I had hired gardeners to do all the work this year. We pointedly avoided talking about me. She didn't ask me a single question. Not even how are you doing? *No, I mean, really doing?* Thank god for that, but I was waiting for the second shoe to fall.

I waited through a second martini and the arrival of the pizza delivery person. I waited through the three of us sitting on the floor around the coffee table instead of eating at the big dining room table. I waited through the chewing, swallowing, and drinking of a glass of Valpolicella—one of my favourite Italian wines—and on to when Frankie offered to clean up. I knew that when Frankie offered to clean up the detritus without even being asked, the end of the world was approaching, and it would be now or never.

"Okay, Evelyn. Let's get this over with. You didn't come to Halifax to sit around and eat pizza with your sister and niece. And," I said as Frankie returned with a tray carrying a glass of water for each of us, "I know that Frankie must have called you to ask you to come. But before you tell me why you're really here, just know that I'm perfectly fine. Or as perfectly fine as a widow my age can be."

"And there it is." Evelyn sat up and took the water Frankie was offering her. "There it is, little sister. Widow."

"Well, it's the truth."

"The truth, Charlie, is that you have to start living again. It's been over a year, and the widow's weeds you're wearing are starting to overtake you. I don't even recognize you. You have to start getting out."

I sat up straight, or as straight as I could, given how much booze we'd just inhaled. I was starting to get my back up, both literally and figuratively. "I went out—for those first few months. You know I did. I told you about it during one of our phone conversations. I went to a few dinner parties hosted by friends, but I couldn't stand it, so I stopped."

"She did go out a few times, Aunt Evelyn. I helped her with her hair."

I put my hand up to touch my hair, another topic I hoped Evelyn would avoid since I hadn't had a proper cut in too long. "People stare, Evelyn, and they say the most appallingly idiotic things to widows."

"I remember you telling me you'd gone out, Charlie," Evelyn said. "But it's time you pulled yourself together."

I started laughing—one of those hollow laughs where you can hear yourself, but you're not even sure what you're laughing about. "That, sis, is one of those fatuous things people say. I didn't realize widows were fair game for everyone's platitudes and ill-conceived advice. I mean, seriously, if someone tells me that *time heals everything* one more time, or god help me, tells me that *it could be worse*, I can't be held responsible for what I might do." I was warming to my topic now. I pulled myself up from the floor where I was still sitting and sat back in the chair, picking up my empty wine glass because I could see a tiny drop of fluid remaining. I sucked in every last drop. "I even read an article by a young widow who gave a few pieces of advice. She said to wear sensible shoes because then people won't be wondering what I'm up to, and she also said not to spend too much time talking to other people's husbands. Dear god! As far as I'm concerned, if my presence makes other people so damn uncomfortable, I might as well stay home. No one knows what to say to me anyway, so I just stopped going out. I'm sure it was a relief to everyone. I know it was to me."

Evelyn sat there, sipping on the last of her wine as she got up and sat in the chair opposite me. Frankie sank into the sofa.

Evelyn was quieter and more deliberate as she spoke this time. "Okay, Charlie. I hear you. And I'm sorry for everyone's insensitivity—especially mine. But I'm worried about you, and I truly believe that the longer you take in this phase—or whatever it is—the harder it's going to be for you to get out of it."

"What the hell am I supposed to do?" I was afraid I might start crying, and I didn't want to do that. Not again. "I shop for new clothes online…" I could see Evelyn's eyes begin to roll, "…and I give money to charities I like."

"So, you spend your time in the house, spending money on things you don't plan to use and giving money to charities whose events you never attend. Is that right?"

I shrugged.

"Well, Frankie and I have an idea."

It was my turn to roll my eyes, but I thought it would be best to keep quiet and get this over with as soon as possible.

"You know I've never really understood your infatuation with making your own clothes, particularly because you can afford to buy anything you want, but I accept that you love it. And Frankie tells me you've stopped doing even that. Anyway, a few years ago, you told me about some couture person who teaches classes on making French jackets or something."

It had been so long since I'd even thought about sewing, the one activity I had found incredibly meditative the year after Mom died so long ago. "That was a long time ago, Evelyn."

"Well, I asked my assistant to do some digging. As it turns out, along with her design business in Paris, that woman is also still teaching people how to make replicas of Chanel jackets, which it seems her colleagues in the Parisian design community find distasteful, I gather. Anyway, it's something you once said you'd like to do, though it never made any sense to me."

"That's not the point, Evelyn. Just imagine the sense of accomplishment from learning haute couture techniques—to make one yourself." I was starting to remember how I'd felt about wanting to learn to create one of those jackets for myself.

Evelyn shook her head. "Well, as I said, I don't get the appeal, but clearly, you do, and this is what I'm talking about. This," she said, waving her hand over me like a wand at Hogwort's, "is the most animated I've seen you since long before Tom died."

Frankie was nodding wildly—almost smiling.

"I suppose it might be something I might be interested in," I said distractedly. I thought about it for a moment. "I suppose it might be nice to take an online course to focus my attention."

"Mom," Frankie said, "Aunt Evelyn isn't talking about an online course. She's talking about taking the course in person with this woman. What's her name again?"

"It's Genevieve LaChapelle," Evelyn said. Frankie handed her a piece of paper she'd picked from the sheaf Evelyn had placed on a table by the door when she came in. I'd noticed Evelyn placing them there at the time, but I hadn't even taken the time to wonder what it was. "Here." She handed the page to me.

I took the page. "Couture Techniques and the Little French Jacket with Mademoiselle LaChapelle." That was the heading on the page she had printed from a website. I was confused. "I don't understand. Why would someone like Genevieve LaChapelle be doing a course in Halifax? I can't imagine there would be enough people here with that kind of money and the interest in her classes." I knew her classes were exorbitantly expensive, and she was based in Paris.

"No, Mom, you don't understand. You'd have to go away to take the course."

"Away? Where? To Paris?" Truth be told, I owned a Paris flat—a bequest from my great-grandmother—but it was leased out. I wasn't in any frame of mind to go to Paris, anyway.

Evelyn chimed in. "Mallorca, Charlie. The course is in Mallorca. Can you imagine?" Her eyes were shining.

"Mallorca? I've heard of it, but I can't put my finger on its exact location."

Evelyn pulled out another page containing a map. "It's one of Spain's Balearic Islands in the Mediterranean. Look." She pointed to the tiny dot off the east coast of Spain, just off Barcelona.

"Spain? I can't go to Spain," I said. This intervention wasn't going at all how I expected it to go.

"Of course, you can," Evelyn said. "Frankie and I have it all worked out. The course takes place over three weeks in August. Frankie will come to Toronto to spend some quality time with her cousins—and her fabulous aunt—and you'll jet off to Mallorca and stay in a villa or something. It talks about villas for rent for students in the course."

My head was spinning. I couldn't go to Mallorca to take a course. Or could I?

Preparation

EVELYN HAD TAKEN THE LIBERTY OF PRE-REGISTERING me for the course. Liberty, indeed. As I lay in bed that night, staring up at the ceiling, for the first time in over a year, my mind wandered to something other than the empty space beside me in the bed. I could feel a tiny spark of something. It was still deeply buried, but I could feel the flicker.

I had taught myself to sew the year after Mom died, after finding Mom's old sewing machine in her basement when I was clearing out her house. Sewing seemed like such an odd diversion for someone my age, or at least that's what Evelyn seemed to think. I distinctly remembered her arriving from Toronto to check on the progress of clearing out the house, only to find me wearing my very first creation. I smiled when I remembered her exact words. "What the actual fuck are you wearing?" she had said. Then she added that it looked like I was wearing a shower curtain. Bravo to my sister with the keen observational skills of the practiced lawyer she was. I *was* wearing a shower curtain—but an upcycled one, to be precise. She didn't think the cycling was so much "up." I made a lot of progress that year.

I was single and thirty-two years old then, with no one in my life except a writing group and a part-time job stacking books at the university library. The other part of the time, I struggled with writing a novel. After all, I'd finished my MFA some years earlier, and apart from a few magazine pieces, I hadn't had much success. As Evelyn had said to me more than once, "If a writer

11

isn't writing, is she even a writer?" Her words had made me think, that's for sure.

In the intervening years, I'd occasionally bought myself a length of fabric and spent a few happy hours creating a dress or a T-shirt. But I never seemed to progress. I often felt I was destined to remain a beginner all my life. And besides, who needed handmade clothes when you could afford to shop in the best boutiques in town? There was a project, though, that I had often dreamed about accomplishing. It was that coveted Chanel-esque jacket Evelyn had reminded me about. I'd always wanted one. She was right, of course. I could walk into a Chanel boutique anywhere in the world and buy myself one of their jackets. I could even consider upping the ante and having a custom couture one done—but it wouldn't be the same.

I awoke the following morning feeling oddly energized. I was still skeptical about the notion of going to Mallorca, of all places, to take a course, leaving my daughter with my sister. Heaven knows what kinds of things would fill Frankie's mind when she returned from Evelyn's. Although I was unconvinced that this suggestion of Evelyn's was sound, I could feel something tugging me from within. And I was also very curious about this Mademoiselle Genevieve LaChapelle.

It was Sunday morning. On most Sundays, I found myself alone in the kitchen drinking coffee until after ten, when Frankie would finally emerge, phone in hand, yawning and asking what was for breakfast. Today was different. When I arrived in my sun-filled kitchen, Evelyn and Frankie were already there, huddled at the breakfast bar, staring into Evelyn's laptop.

"What are you two up to?" I said, reaching for a cup to put under the nozzle of my espresso maker.

Evelyn and Frankie looked up at once. Was that guilt I detected on their faces?

"We're looking at airline flights."

"For where?" I said as the noise of the coffee grinder made conversation difficult for a moment.

"Well, sis, if you're going to Mallorca, you're going to have to get there, and I can't see you flying to Spain without spending a few days in Madrid on the way. It's such a wonderful city. You've been?"

"Whoa, you two. I have not been to Madrid, but let's just back up for a moment, shall we? I said nothing about actually going on this junket. It's a great idea in theory, but I don't think I can make it work."

"Why?" Evelyn said, reaching for her own cup of coffee beside her on the counter. "Oh, I'm sorry. You must be too busy to get away. Am I right?" Evelyn had that sarcasm thing down to a science.

I turned away from them and took my time stirring milk into my coffee. I had to figure out a graceful way to get out of this—intervention or no intervention. There was no way I could go to Mallorca for three weeks with a bunch of strangers to do something as frivolous as learn to make a Chanel-style jacket, no matter how much I wanted to do it or how intriguing it might be to meet the famed Mademoiselle Genevieve. It was absurd. I sipped my coffee and turned around. Evelyn and Frankie were both staring at me.

"It's just that it doesn't make sense," I said, not knowing where I was heading with this argument. "My life is here."

"OMG, Mom, that is so lame," Frankie said, rolling her eyes. "It's not like you actually have a life these days, you know."

"Frankie!"

"Okay," Evelyn said, "calm down, everyone. First, Charlie, Frankie has a point. You seem to have given up so many things you used to like to do. I know it's been hard for you to get back into things, and we're not suggesting this so that you can spend time with other people. We're suggesting this because it's time you did something for yourself—something you've always wanted to do. And something that will give you some reason to get back into life. " Evelyn sipped her coffee. "No matter how crackpot I think it is."

She just couldn't help herself. Evelyn had opinions about everything, and my sewing ventures were high on her list of things she was opinionated about. I have to admit her characterization of how crackpot this idea was made me smile a bit.

"There, Mom," Frankie said, catching me in a half-smile. "I knew you'd want to go if you really thought about it."

"Katie and Lucas are so excited they've already started making lists of the things they want to do when Frankie is in Toronto with us—Ripley's Aquarium, the Royal Ontario Museum, the Science Centre, the zoo. I don't know how we'll get it all in, but we'll try," Evelyn said.

So, my niece and nephew, Frankie's cousins, were also in on it. I guess I was the last to know about the plans. As I considered this, I realized I *could* let Frankie go to Toronto for a week or two, but that didn't mean I'd have to go to Mallorca. I could just stay home.

"And don't even think about just sending Frankie to Toronto while you stay here, Charlie. That's not how this works. And you know it." It seemed Evelyn could even read my mind.

I pulled an empty stool over to the counter opposite my two interventionists and sat down.

"Here, Mom," Frankie said, turning the laptop toward me. "You and I can fly to Toronto together, and then you can connect on this flight to Madrid." She pointed to the screen. "You can spend a few days in Madrid and then fly to Mallorca."

"Flights go all day every day from Madrid to Mallorca," Evelyn said as Frankie turned the laptop back to her aunt. "And since you're already pre-registered for the course, the arrangements should be simple."

"Where would I stay?"

"The students stay in villas. Look at this one. It's gorgeous. I'm sure you'd have a wonderful time just sitting there beside that pool."

I peered at the screen. I had to admit it did look enticing with its brilliant blue pool overlooking a vast expanse of what had to be the Mediterranean with a view of a small island off on the horizon. Then she pointed to the biggest of the villas—a gated one with palm trees surrounding it—and told me it was where the course would take place. It was Mademoiselle Genevieve LaChapelle's vacation home, or so it seemed. As Evelyn clicked through the pages describing the course with the photos of all the jackets that students had made in the past, I could feel my pulse quickening just slightly.

"You know you want to go, Mom."

I looked at Frankie and saw the ache in her eyes. I suddenly realized my mood and lack of engagement with the world were having perhaps the biggest effect on the one person who should not have to suffer because of me—my daughter. It would be selfish of me not to go. All at once, it was clear to me. I would have to go. Evelyn and Frankie did a little happy dance the moment the words were out of my mouth.

~

There was homework to do and little time left to get it done. There were seven weeks to the start of the course. The following day, after Evelyn headed to the airport to fly back home to Toronto and Frankie left for school, I sat at my computer and opened the course website. Evelyn gave me the login for my registration that I could now complete. I took a deep breath and started.

Before long, I was immersed in the whole idea of spending three weeks focusing on an activity I'd thought about so often over the years. I paid the (exorbitant) tuition upfront, which opened up another part of the website. There were forms to fill out, materials to download and activities to accomplish in advance. The first thing was the questionnaire.

It took me almost an hour to complete the most bizarre questionnaire I'd ever seen. There were dozens of odd questions about food, wine, books, movies, shopping. I had no idea why they needed to know the answers to these questions (well, the food and wine ones seemed at least relevant!). Anyway, I decided that if I were going to do this, I would give it my all. Then I downloaded the list of materials I had to acquire and bring to the course.

I was excited about the prospect of a jacket made from Linton Tweeds. I'd read about them when I first stumbled upon a kind of online subculture of people who sewed these replica jackets. I remember thinking that these jackets represented a whole lot of history. This company, located in the lake district in the north of England, seemed to have been around since 1912. The founder, a William Linton, had a friend named Captain Edward Molyneux, a Parisian fashion illustrator and eventual couturier who played a pivotal role in the company's fortunes. Sometime in the 1920s, he introduced Mr. Linton to a certain young woman by the name of Coco Chanel. She was soon their biggest customer. I remember those photographs I'd seen online of a Chanel jacket from 1925, the first year she designed them. Can you imagine a style that is a hundred years old that someone could still wear today and feel modern? But I also wondered what Mademoiselle Chanel would have thought about all of us obsessing about copying her style. Then I remembered something.

Gabriel Chanel once said that imitation is the greatest form of flattery. If that's so, then she must be the most flattered woman who has ever lived since there seemed to be so many people copying her designs.

I was excited at the prospect of having fabric that the best design houses in Paris might have considered. I had no idea it would be so hard to choose.

Once I found the website, I was stunned at the selection. The array of fabrics was almost overwhelming. As I clicked along through the offerings, I recognized some designs similar to those

I'd seen on runways in recent years. I could hear Evelyn's voice in my head telling me that I didn't have to make my own, but I mentally swatted her away like an annoying housefly. I was going to do this.

~

The next few weeks flew by in a blur as Frankie finished her school year, and we prepared for our trip.

First, we had to finalize our airline bookings. As Frankie had suggested, we bought tickets on a flight to Toronto so that we could fly together. I would then leave her, make my way to the international departures at Pearson International Airport, and take the overnight, nonstop flight to Madrid. I hadn't been this excited in a very long time. However, mixed in with that excitement was pure, unadulterated fear. I wasn't at all sure I was ready for this. Several times, I'd woken up in the middle of the night sweating, wondering what in the world I was doing. Okay, the sweating might have been for another reason—I was past forty-five, after all. But there was still that undercurrent of apprehension.

Finally, departure day arrived.

Madrid

FRANKIE AND I FLEW TO TORONTO FROM HALIFAX in early August as planned. Evelyn was there at the airport with Katie and Lucas to meet Frankie while I made my way back through security to the international departures area.

It had been a long time since I'd flown anywhere by myself. It was years ago, long before I had money. I remembered that the last time I'd been alone in an airport, I'd been sitting in a crowded departure lounge, trying desperately to tune out the crying baby sitting on her mother's lap at my elbow. This time, I was greeted in a sumptuous lounge—the Air Canada Signature Class Lounge, to be precise—by a staff member who showed me to the restaurant, where a server handed me a menu and asked me if I'd like a glass of champagne. I sat there sipping champagne, waiting for my dinner to arrive, looking around at the couples quietly talking and sipping various libations. There was something to be said for flying in style.

By the time I finished my dinner (and a second glass of champagne), it was almost time to board my plane and really get this adventure started. It wasn't long before I was settled into my pod at the front of the plane, sipping on yet another glass of champagne and trying to figure out what movie I'd watch before I tried to get some sleep. I had never been able to sleep well on a plane, and I was so keyed up this time that I wondered if I'd even close an eye.

For the next few hours, I watched movies, then I put my seat back flat, donned my eye mask, plumped my pillow, pulled up my blanket and closed my eyes. The next thing I knew, the flight attendant was asking me if I would like breakfast before we landed. Yes, I told her, and bring on the coffee.

The airport in Madrid was big and busy. I waited in the immigration line for fifteen minutes and then found my luggage. I made my way out of the luggage area and began looking for the taxi sign. When I finally found it out on the curb, there was, of course, another line. I waited patiently until a driver pulled up.

I got in the back while he put my luggage in the trunk. "*Voy al hotel Palace, por favor,*" I said in my best Spanish. I'd been practicing. This was probably as much Spanish as I could manage other than *una copa de vino blanco, por favor*. One needs to be able to order wine in any language, as far as I'm concerned.

Anyway, the driver looked at me as if I had three heads. Was my Spanish that bad? "Ya might want to consider practising your accent," he said in the most British of British accents I'd heard since the last time I was in London. It might even have been just the slightest bit Cockney. Then he laughed.

I slunk down in the seat in linguistically induced embarrassment as he began to pull away from the curb.

"The Palace Hotel, you say?" he said.

"Yes, please."

"Don't worry. Everyone there speaks English. Staying in Madrid long?"

"Only until Monday, I'm afraid." It was Saturday morning.

"Well, you're in luck," he said as he maneuvered onto the highway heading for the city. "Tomorrow is Sunday, and Sunday is flea market day, so don't miss the El Rastro flea market. Biggest one in Europe."

"Thanks for the tip," I said, wondering if I had ever been a flea market kind of person. "Have you lived in Madrid long?"

The driver then told me his story. He was living in London, working as an accountant, and happily married to his Spanish wife. She'd lived in the UK for twenty-five years when talk of Brexit began. Finally, when it happened, she was so incensed that they would lose their ease of movement back and forth to visit her extended family in Spain (she had never become a British citizen) that she insisted they pull up stakes and move. As it turned out, he was sick of working with numbers every day and agreed. Now he drove a taxi around Madrid, gave tourists tips and loved every minute of his Spanish life—or so he said. It was a great story.

"And you?" he said when he'd finished his tale. "What's a nice woman like you doing in Madrid alone?"

I wasn't sure how I felt about telling my story to a stranger, so I just said, "I'm going to be taking a course." I hesitated. "But I should probably be at home, not traipsing off halfway across the world." Why did I say that? Probably because that's how I felt.

"Is it a course you *want* to take?" he said.

I told him it was.

"Well then, I have a wee bit of advice for you. Don't risk spending your life doing what everybody else wants. That's what I've learned, ma'am. An adventure is just what we all need to find out where we should end up. That's my life mantra." He turned the car off the circle surrounding an enormous fountain. "Well, this is it. I'll just drive around the block so I can drop you off at the door."

~

It wasn't quite noon when I made my way to the front of the short check-in line at The Madrid Palace Hotel. I was pleasantly surprised when the young woman at the reception desk, whose English was impeccable, told me my room was ready. "And how many keys would you like, *Señora* Hudson?" she said.

I was abruptly overcome with sadness and felt a tiny tear forming in my eye. Was it because I suddenly realized I was alone in this lovely hotel? That Tom wouldn't appear at any moment, smiling the way he always did when we checked into a new hotel to begin a new adventure? That I needed only one key? Or was it that I hadn't thought about Tom for at least the past hour and a half since I landed in Madrid? It was the longest time in the past year that I'd gone without thinking about him, and I realized I felt guilty.

I quickly wiped away the unwelcome tear and told the young woman that one key would be sufficient. She then pointed toward the back of the small lobby, where a wide staircase led to the elevators. I thanked her, picked up my carry-on bag and walked up the steps. At the top of the staircase, I was standing in an impressive lobby, gazing into the main dining room, whose soaring ceiling was capped with a magnificent round, stained glass cupola. I gasped as a chill ran down my spine. The atmospheric space exuded its historical pedigree. If I guessed correctly, it looked like it dated to the 1920s. I could clearly picture silk and satin-clad women strolling under that dome, arm-in-arm with men in custom-made suits. The tableau made me smile as I turned toward the elevators to find my room on the fourth floor.

The room was a reasonably good size by European standards, with gold embossed wallpaper everywhere and crisp white linens. The bathroom was clad in a well-patinaed marble that seemed to have stood the test of time. I dropped my case on the bed and noticed that my suitcase had arrived in the room even before I had. *How wonderfully efficient!* I thought. I walked over to the tall window with a white balustrade outside, giving it the sense of a Juliet balcony, which I suppose it was. I looked down into the street and watched the pedestrians strolling along the sidewalk. Although I realized that jet lag would probably overtake me at any moment now, I knew from past experience that the only way to overcome it was to keep moving. So, I unpacked a few things, slung my trusty Tumi nylon bag over my shoulder and headed out to find the hotel bar. I was starving.

Once downstairs, I walked into the dining room I'd noticed before. It was called La Rotunda, for obvious reasons. I stood in the doorway and was filled with a sense of history—and something else. I couldn't put my finger on the feeling, but it was almost a feeling of having been here before, although I had not. I shook it off and continued my perusal. In the middle of the restaurant, directly under the centre of the massive glass-domed ceiling, was a colossal planter surrounded by rounded sofas upholstered in velvet. From the centre of the planter rose an enormous fern, reaching toward the glass ceiling. In front of each sofa was a drinks table and several plush chairs. More tables were in the circle surrounding the centrepiece and beyond a series of massive columns. After snapping a few photos, I turned to find the bar.

Next to the La Rotunda Restaurant was the 1912 Museo Bar. As I walked into this dark, wood-panelled space, I was overcome with a feeling that I'd just stepped back in time. The green leather tub chairs snuggled up to the mahogany tables lining the edges of the small space. I noticed a fireplace straight ahead of me and decided to head toward the table directly in front of it. But along the way, my attention was drawn to the black and white photographs on the panelled walls, each telling a story about the historical past of the magnificent hotel.

I was right—the hotel had opened in the 1920s and, ever since, had been a central gathering place for the glitterati of Madrid. According to one of the stories, even Ernest Hemingway had sipped a few cocktails here. I could feel my creative juices flowing and couldn't wait to settle in and make a few notes.

After a glass of excellent Spanish wine and a plate of tapas, I was ready to continue my afternoon exploring a bit of territory close to the hotel to keep me awake. It was hot. I mean, it was sizzling hot. The moment I stepped outside, I realized I would be too hot on this Spanish junket if I didn't get a few new clothes. I managed to find my way to a shopping area near the hotel and found El Corte Inglese, a Spanish department store. After finding a few whisper-light linen pieces, I took my purchases, checked my map on my phone and headed toward the Retiro Park, which looked like a vast green space in the middle of the city. I wasn't disappointed.

I spent an hour exploring the park that boasted kilometres of walking paths, statues, a formal French garden, masses of trees and a lake. Once I had walked as far as I dared in the heat, I sank onto a bench and pulled out my phone to learn more about the park. According to my reading, the park was formerly royal grounds and had been only for the aristocracy in the eighteenth and much of the nineteenth century but was now a popular space for *Madrileños*, as residents of Madrid call themselves, on the weekends. It was extraordinary.

I finally returned to the hotel, cooled off, had another glass of wine, and fell into bed at nine o'clock. It felt peculiar to be here in a hotel room alone. I lay in the billowing comfort of the luxurious bed and felt utterly alone. I knew that life must go on — hadn't people been saying that to me for a year? But I could still long for just one more night, couldn't I? Then, it was almost as if Tom were in that room with me, standing at the end of the bed with his hands on his hips (that's where Frankie had learned that position). I was so startled that I sat up abruptly. I could feel his smile, but there was something else. I could hear his voice, although lately, I had begun to forget its sound. After Tom died, I found myself doing what I'd seen people on television doing. I called his cell phone every day just to hear his voicemail message until the day Frankie told me she thought that was creepy. I finally cancelled Tom's account. But now, I could hear him again. *Charlie*, he seemed to be saying, *you've got this*. And I realized I did.

"Pull yourself together, girl," I said out loud to the empty space. Then I thought, *What were all those things people said to me over the past year? Time heals? Maybe they meant well. Or maybe they know something I don't.*

I turned off the light and remembered I had somewhere to be in the morning. After all, who wouldn't listen to a local cabbie? I had to go to a flea market. This time, when I thought of Tom as I fell asleep, I thought of how proud he would be of me for doing all this by myself instead of feeling so sad he wasn't here. Then I wondered if this feeling of lead in my heart would ever lift a bit.

~

Would I be safe at Europe's largest outdoor flea market by myself? I was thinking about this as I ate breakfast the following morning under the magnificent stained glass dome. The sun was pouring in on the guidebook I had open on the table beside me, where I was reading the article about the El Rastro flea market the English cab driver had recommended. However, I had learned that it was a place to watch out for pickpockets. At least, that's what the guidebook said. *The hell with it*, I thought. *I'm going.*

I wasn't sure what I'd find once I walked the fifteen minutes toward the market. As I approached the place noted on Google Maps, I noticed that the streets were closed off, and crowds were heading in the same direction. I was swept up in the throng.

Just past a beautiful flower market where I stopped to take a picture of the colourful display (who can pass by a flower market without stopping to admire it?), I found myself at the top of a wide street that rolled down a gentle hill. I had arrived. I began my descent.

I passed stall after stall, stopping briefly to look at the macrame plant hangers. How many years had it been since I'd seen a macrame plant hanger? Were they making a comeback? I snapped a photo. I walked along, happy I'd come early since the crowd was growing. There were stalls selling jewellery of all kinds—handmade, antique-looking and the ubiquitous made-in-China stuff that fills the cheap and cheerful shops in so many parts of the world. I passed piles of purses, colourful scarves, and mounds of new and used clothing on tables where eager shoppers picked through to find hidden treasures. Then, passing a long line of hungry shoppers waiting to buy hot churros from what appeared to be a favourite outlet, I turned into a side street.

I could smell the sweet aroma of the churros wafting into the warm morning air. (You know churros? Those long, deep-fried donuts covered with sugar, served hot with chocolate dipping sauce here.) It seemed as if I could even taste them, although I'd never eaten a churro as far as I could remember. The side street was filled with antique shops whose owners were displaying their wares on tarps laid on the sidewalks or on the bare pavement.

The crowd was thinner here, so I could slow down and really get a sense of the history on display. It was fascinating. I could almost feel the decades of people who had owned and used these objects.

I stopped in front of a particularly diverse group of antique-looking objects and stared for a few moments. I wondered about their provenance. There was a rusty old menorah, old china cups and saucers, a group of four figurines that looked slightly Japanese in origin, a chipped bust of what appeared to be Beethoven, a jumble of costume jewellery in a cookie tin and an ancient kitchen pot full of old watches. I was thinking about how all of these represented lives that had likely come to an end, and I suddenly felt a peculiar melancholy descend on me. It didn't feel like the grief I'd felt for the past year. It was more like a detached sadness. Then, among the disparate items, I saw a black object in the middle, which seemed to be an antique sewing machine. I bent down to take a closer look. I hadn't noticed the old woman staring at me from the antique shop doorway.

She said something to me in Spanish. I stood up and told her—in my very best Spanish—that I didn't speak the language. She crossed her arms across her ample mid-section and spoke once again in rapid Spanish.

"Excuse me, *Señora*, but my grandmother wishes to show you something."

I looked around to find the source of this new voice in beautifully Spanish-accented English. A young woman—perhaps no more than twenty with long, shining black hair and dazzling dark eyes—nodded toward the old woman in the doorway.

"*Abuelita* has noticed your interest in the old sewing machine and wants you to know that it does not work, but she would like you to follow her so she can show you something else."

I nodded and looked toward the doorway to the shop into which the young woman's grandmother had just retreated.

"I am Martine," the young woman said, extending her hand. "You must forgive my grandmother's impertinence, but she is very good at finding objects that are the best fit for her customers."

I took Martine's hand and introduced myself. "Should I follow her inside?"

"Please," Martine said, gesturing to me to enter the shop. "My grandmother has also said something else," she said quietly as we entered. "She says that you have sad eyes."

I said nothing as I stood in the small shop surrounded by a jumble of objects, much like the group on the pavement outside but even more chaotic and immense. I could smell that distinctive odour of mustiness that permeated the space. Martine's grandmother was now at the back of the shop in front of a glass-covered showcase. It was the tidiest part of the entire space, and I wondered if it was where she kept the real treasures.

I watched as she lifted the glass top and removed a specific object. She held it in the palm of her hand and nodded her head to beckon me over. When I got to where she was standing, I noticed that the case did, indeed, contain several of what appeared to be higher-quality objects, all of them tiny porcelain figurines.

"They are all French Limoges porcelain," Martine said as I gazed with genuine interest.

Martine's grandmother then took my hand, placed the tiny object into my palm, and began speaking in Spanish. As my fingers closed around the object, I could feel a slight vibration that startled me. Then I opened my hand to look at it.

The tiny object—no more than two inches long and perhaps less than two inches high—was an exquisitely hand-painted sewing machine fashioned from porcelain. It was black with gold details. Martine leaned over. "May I?" she said as she reached toward the piece. I watched as she opened it, and I discovered that the tiny-detailed gold scissors on the side were a clasp that, when opened, revealed that it was a trinket box. Baked into the shiny porcelain bottom of the tiny compartment was a miniature painting of a spool of thread. I had no idea how much such a thing would cost. I only knew I had to have it. Martine was right. Her grandmother did have an uncanny ability to match customers with treasures.

Martine's *abuelita* began speaking again, taking my hand as she did so. Martine translated. "She is saying she knew it was yours the minute she saw you. She is also saying that we should not grieve so much—that anything we lose in any lifetime comes around again in another form." Martine furrowed her brow. "I believe my old grandmother is quoting the poet Rumi." She laughed. "Who knew!" Martine then said something to her grandmother, who pointed to a small plaque on the wall. It said, *Do not grieve. Anything you lose comes round in another form. ~ Rumi.*

Then Martine's grandmother leaned toward me and whispered as Martine leaned in to translate. "I see a sadness in your eyes, *Señora*. But when you opened the box, it was as if something flew out of it and into your heart. It has found you once again. You will not drown in your sadness if you learn to shine."

~

As I boarded my plane to Mallorca the following morning, I kept the tiny sewing machine in my carry-on bag, not wishing to risk its loss or damage. I had never had a talisman before, but now I did. Sitting in my seat in the first row of the Iberian Airlines flight, surrounded by happy vacationers, I allowed myself a moment of excited anticipation. I hadn't felt that in far too long.

Mallorca

"Some people think luxury is the opposite of poverty. It is not. It is the opposite of vulgarity."
~ Gabriel "Coco" Chanel

I HAD INSTRUCTIONS TO WAIT BY THE GIANT PILLAR with the sign that clearly said (in English), "Waiting Area." So, I collected my baggage and waited. I had an email on my phone, which I had clutched in my hand with the arrival instructions and the driver's name: Marco. As I stood there, my eyes continually scanned the crowded arrivals area where masses of drivers holding signs and tablets awaited their assigned fares. The airport in Palma de Mallorca, the island's capital, was much larger and busier than I had anticipated. I don't know what I had thought. Perhaps I thought it would be like a Caribbean Island, where Tom and I had spent many wonderful winter vacations. They all had small, sleepy airports that were only busy when a flight from the far north was delayed by bad weather, and returning travellers had to wait in sad little groups until they could get home. I hadn't realized that Palma was a thriving international metropolis and the island was a mecca for British and German tourists.

I was listening to a group of British tourists as they tried in vain to find their driver when I was startled by a voice behind me. "*Señora* Hudson?"

I turned. The young man standing in front of me with a nametag that said, "Marco," was over six feet tall with a mass of dark hair and that dark facial stubble that was so popular among European men. As he looked at me, his head cocked slightly to the side, a small smile playing about his handsome face, I could see why. I hadn't felt a jolt like that since—dear god, since Tom walked into my mother's house in preparation for selling it for

29

me. I shook myself. *This one is far too young*. What in the world made me think that? I gave myself a mental slap.

"Yes, I'm Charlotte Hudson," I said when I finally found my tongue. "You must be Marco." How stupid. Of course, he was Marco. I would enjoy this ride to Cala Pi, the town where the course would take place.

"We await two more passengers," he said, taking my large suitcase from me and causing me great disappointment. I would have to share him. "I trust the flight was pleasant." Was he leering? Surely not. My imagination. What did they put in that Spanish drink I'd had on the plane?

"Very pleasant, thank you." I started scanning for anyone I thought might be a likely candidate for this course. I saw only vacationers. "Where are the two passengers coming from?"

"We await the British Airways flight from London. I believe it has already landed. It should not be long." Marco leaned back against the pillar, one hand on the handle of my large suitcase, the other in his pocket. Was he actively trying to get my attention, or was it just that he couldn't help it? "Your husband permits such a trip for you all alone?"

"I'm a widow," I said. "*Una viuda*." It was the one Spanish word I had been determined to remember.

"*Señora* Hudson, I am so sorry for your loss. Has it been long?"

Why did I start this conversation? I was spared from answering when a tall blonde woman approached us.

"What the bloody hell?" she said, dropping her two huge suitcases on the floor. "I cannot believe there was no porter waiting. Marco? You're Marco?" She stared at his nametag.

Both Marco and I were also staring—at her. She was at least a decade older than I was, with bright blonde hair piled up on top of her head, bright red lipstick and was wearing the most enormous gold hoop earrings I'd ever seen—they were so large, they grazed her shoulders. But it was the voice—loud and slightly raspy as if she might have smoked one too many cigarettes.

"I hope there's a drink in that van or whatever contraption we're meant to be transported in. There was a bloody baby beside me on the plane and not nearly enough alcohol."

Marco stared.

The woman then turned to me. "I am so sorry," she said. "I do presume you're on this course as well." I nodded, and she continued. "I'm Mathilde Foster-Matthews, but please call me Tilly. And you are?"

"I'm Charlotte Hudson, but everyone calls me Charlie."

Tilly smiled slightly enigmatically. "Yes, of course."

Just then, a short man who had been hidden behind Tilly all this time poked his head around her and said, "And I'm Ronald Corbyn. Also, on the course."

Ronald stepped out from behind Tilly, and I shook his hand. He was several inches shorter than Tilly and of indeterminate middle age. His bald head shone in the bright overhead airport lights. For a moment, I wondered if they were together.

Tilly looked at Ronald and then at me. It was as if she could read my mind. "Ronald and I have only just met," she said. "This minute." It was clear she didn't want anyone to conclude they were together.

I looked at Ronald and wondered why I was so surprised to see a man on the course. Men were often the best tailors, after all.

"Well, *señoras y señore*, we go to the *car*." Marco seemed to give Tilly the evil eye. She shrugged amiably.

The car was something of a cross between a van and a limousine. It was a large, shiny, black Mercedes thing with three layers of black leather seats and a large compartment in the back for luggage. I sat behind Marco with Ronald, and Tilly sat alone in the third row. Well, she wasn't really alone. She had an immense carry-on case to keep her company.

"It will be forty-five minutes to the villas," Marco said. "It will be a pretty drive once we remove ourselves from the city limits."

"I don't bloody see any drinks back here," Tilly said.

"There is water, *Señora*," Marco said. I could see his smile in the rear-view mirror. I couldn't help myself—I was smiling, too.

I heard Tilly mutter, "Bloody hell." Oh, this was going to be interesting.

"Marco," I said, "you mentioned villas. Will there be more than one for the students?"

"*Sí*. Yes, of course. There are two villas for the students on each course, and, naturally, Mademoiselle's villa, the most magnificent of the three, will be the location of your classes. She also invites students to take dinner with her every Monday to Thursday evening."

"So, how do you decide which villas each student stays in?" Tilly almost had to shout since she was so far back. "Can we decide who we want to bunk with?"

"Mademoiselle is quite particular, *Señora*. She makes all the decisions. I will drop both you and *Señora* Hudson at one of the villas and take *Señor* Corbyn to the other. I will then return to the airport to meet the flight, which will carry the remaining two students."

"Where does that plane originate?" Tilly was just full of questions.

"It originates in New York, *Señora*."

"Well, well, the Yanks really are joining us. How fun!"

Tilly asked a few more questions about the route, and it occurred to me that she should have been the one sitting closer to Marco, who had to raise his voice to be heard in the back. After leaving the city environs, we drove smoothly along a narrow road that wound along the coast. I caught a glimpse of the Mediterranean Sea every once in a while. Finally, we turned down a side road where the small road sign pointed the way to "Cala Pi."

The car clunked over three large speed bumps that Marco said had been placed there after locals complained about the tourists speeding along toward the centre of the village. Then we passed by a stretch of attached two-story apartments that Marco informed us were vacation rentals. I could see towels of various colours waving in the breeze as they hung on balcony railings. Marco had to tell us when we were in the centre of the village since if any one of us had blinked at that moment, we would likely have missed it. There was one hotel, several restaurants, which he pointed out to us, two small grocery stores and lots of cars parked along the streets.

"Many cars? There are not so many today," Marco said when Tilly asked why they were there, although it seemed to me there were many cars—far too many for such a small village. "It is Monday. There will be more as the week progresses."

"Where are all the people from the cars?" I said.

Marco looked at me in the rear-view mirror, his eyebrows arching in surprise. "But they are at the beach, *Señora*. We have a magnificent beach, and we love our beaches."

I had been told. The number of cars on the side of the street decreased to nothing as we drove the final two minutes to our accommodation. Marco pulled the Mercedes up in front of a two-story villa with a bright blue fence and gate. "We have arrived."

~

I wasn't sure what I had expected. Tom and I had spent our share of vacation time in marvellous venues, from luxury cruise ships to five-star hotels. This villa was a whole new level of luxury. It wasn't so much that it was more sumptuous than what I'd become accustomed to; rather, it was the fact that it was private. I could almost see the two of us here—alone— luxuriating in the sheer seclusion of the massive pool that shimmered in the blinding sunshine. All that was missing was the private pool butler. And Tom.

I was assigned to the suite on the main floor, while Tilly had to trudge up the stairs to the second floor to find hers. She dragged one suitcase while Marco followed her upstairs with the second one. He grumbled something about this not being in his job description, but he did her bidding anyway. I smiled as I watched.

Before Marco left, he told us Mademoiselle's property manager, Martin, would be along to explain to us all the villa's amenities but that Martin would wait until Marco returned from the airport with the third student who would be sharing our villa. He said he would be about two hours. In the meantime, he invited us to unpack, have a glass of wine from the stocked refrigerator and take a dip in the pool.

"First, to the wine!" Tilly said the moment the door closed behind Marco.

I completely agreed. Then, I couldn't wait to get outside and have a closer look at the magnificent view across the Mediterranean Sea. We were right at the edge.

~

After a glass of wine, a dip in the pool and a shower, two hours had passed, and Marco returned. I heard the car pull up in front, but since all the windows were on the back of the house facing the sea rather than facing the street, I didn't have a chance to see who was coming. Having met Tilly and Ronald, I was more than a bit curious about who else might be forming a part of this contingent of students. I didn't have to wait long. I heard her before I saw her.

"Wow, wow, wow," the voice exclaimed. "This is beyond awesome! OMG, I need to take photos!"

I rolled my eyes. Dear god, we had been invaded by Gen Z! If I thought that was horrifying, I hadn't seen anything yet. I emerged from my suite down the hall from the foyer and headed toward the sound of the voice. When I turned into the living room, I was further amazed.

Standing with her back to the view in front of the floor-to-ceiling window that looked out onto the pool and the sea beyond was a blonde goddess of a woman no more than twenty-five years old, holding a smartphone on an extender with a ring light attached. She was smiling and gesturing and talking. Talking. Talking.

The young woman turned off the camera as Marco came in through the front door juggling three large suitcases. He didn't look thrilled.

"*Señorita* Butler," he said, "are you certain you have everything?" Marco handed her what looked like another small piece of technology. I couldn't tell what it was from where I was standing.

"Oh, Mr. Marco, thank you so much for collecting me at the airport. I am so pumped about gaining a whole new fam here! You're the first one in my new tribe."

I saw Marco roll his eyes as he turned and saw me standing in the doorway. The young woman followed his eyes, and she caught sight of me.

"OMG! Are you going to be my roomie?"

I shrugged and walked toward her. "We all have our own rooms, but yes, we'll be sharing this villa. I'm Charlie Hudson."

The young woman smiled so broadly I thought her face might break in half. She had the most perfect, dazzlingly white teeth I'd ever seen. Then the penny dropped. I knew exactly who she was. I did a quick internal debate about whether it was better to tell her I recognized her or let her introduce herself. I was spared when she moved in for the hug. "I'm Bella," she said, "Bella Butler, but you probably know me as @bellastyleNYC."

"I think my daughter does," I said, recognizing the name and the face as I extricated myself.

"What the bloody hell is going on down here?" Tilly had arrived.

"OMG! Another roomie!" Bella squealed yet again. "We need to have a selfie. Right. This. Minute!"

And before either Tilly or I could demur, there was Bella, snapping selfies as if her life depended on it.

Bella then explained to us that she was a "lifestyle influencer." A lifestyle blogger. A lifestyle Instagrammer. With twenty million followers. And I was about to be featured on her newest Instagram posts. I could feel it. But the single question in my mind was this: Why was a twenty-something style influencer here in Mallorca with the older set taking a course on how to sew a Chanel-style jacket? Wasn't sewing an antiquated activity scorned by anyone under middle age? Perhaps I could stand to be corrected.

~

Marco had left us again, with instructions to be at the main villa at seven pm sharp for drinks and dinner with Mademoiselle. Our destination was a short five-minute walk up the street. He said we couldn't miss it.

As Marco had promised, Mademoiselle's property manager arrived a few minutes later to familiarize us with the villa and its amenities.

Martin Engel turned out to be an affable, middle-aged German ex-pat who told us he managed all Mademoiselle's properties on the island. When Tilly asked him how many there were, he was non-committal and then turned our attention to the villa. He toured us through the kitchen and its amenities, taught us how to use the coffee maker, and explained that the pool boy would come each week while we were there and that we should just ignore him. That prompted Tilly to dig me in the ribs and say, "Pool boy, eh? Sounds divine."

Martin ignored her. As soon as his heels cleared the door, we rushed off to our respective rooms to dress. An hour later, I walked out onto the back patio, ready for whatever the evening held for us. At least, that's what I thought at the time. Tilly was already there, a glass of wine in her hand and a bottle and two empty glasses on the dining table. Bella was nowhere in sight.

"Come, Charlie," she said. "Let's you and I have a bit of a chin wag before the younger generation arrives, camera in hand." She poured me a glass of wine as I sat down at the end of the table so I could talk to her and see the pool and the view beyond at the same time. "I know who you are, Charlie Hudson."

I almost spilled the wine that was halfway to my lips. "Who I am? Whatever are you talking about? What do you mean you know who I am?"

"I know you're CK Hudson, the bestselling writer. And I cannot tell a lie. I have read your books."

I was taken completely by surprise. My writing identity was something I'd decided to keep to myself for the duration of the course. I wanted to be Charlie Hudson, a woman who loved to learn new things. For three weeks, I didn't want to be CK Hudson, the bestselling author. I just wanted to be Charlie. I said nothing.

"No point in denying it. I do my homework. When I saw your face, I experienced a whiff of familiarity. I still do love a real book as opposed to those electronic monstrosities, so, of course, I saw your face on the back cover of your most recent one." She stopped for a moment and tapped her finger against the side of her head as if she might be trying to remember something. "Something tells me your most recent book was not so recent." She shook her head. "In any case, that does not matter. What matters is that after I saw you, I naturally spent a few moments in my room just now consulting Mr. Google. So, as I said, there's no point in denying it. But I do want to know why you're really here on this course." Was she looking at me accusingly?

I could not imagine what she thought I was up to. "Tilly, I have no idea what you're talking about. I'm here to learn to make a French jacket from one of the foremost experts in the world. End of story. Isn't that why you're here?" I looked carefully at Tilly, who seemed to be considering her next words.

"So, you're not planning to write a book about Mademoiselle Genevieve LaChapelle?"

"Why would I want to do that?" I was honestly puzzled. "Tilly, I hope you don't find me rude, but why are *you* here?"

"Anyway, I also wanted to tell you something interesting about one of your books. You wrote that novel based on the lives of some real people," she said, ignoring my question. I nodded, and she continued. "I actually met that character you called Tim Sinclair."

My eyes widened. This could not be possible. Tilly looked at my face and nodded.

"Yes, darling, I did. I was in Antigua many years ago on my honeymoon." Again, my face must have held a measure of disbelief. "Yes, indeed, I was married a long time ago, the thought of which simply gives me shivers up my spine as I look back. That was something of a mistake, but I digress. Yes, I had tea with him one afternoon on the patio at the St. James's Club while my erstwhile husband was playing a silly game of golf or something equally mind-numbing. What I most remembered was that Mr. Sinclair was beyond flattering in his observations about the British parents versus the American ones based on his observations of their respective children's behaviour. A lovely man he was, I must say."

What Tilly was saying was outrageous. How could she have met the real person I had based my character on? Even I hadn't had that opportunity. Tim Sinclair had died before I began the book—with his daughter's blessing.

"As you know, he was there for his mother's marriage—or rather remarriage, to be precise. As it turns out, I was even on the beach the next day, observing the festivities. I must say you captured it well in your book."

Before I could say anything more, Bella appeared in the doorway.

"Oooh, wine. I'll just pour myself a glass. What are we talking about?" she said, taking a seat at the table.

The three of us found ourselves attired in almost identical outfits. We were all dressed in some version of a white cotton sundress. I was wearing mine with wedge espadrilles; Tilly had chosen white leather Birkenstocks (a particular aversion of mine), and Bella—who might be the only person in the world able to pull this off—was wearing high-top sneakers like the ones basketball players wear.

"OMG! We need a shoefie!" Bella said, noticing our disparate footwear.

"A what?" Tilly said as she drained her wine glass and poured herself another.

"A shoefie," I said. "You know, Tilly. A selfie but only of shoes."

Tilly grunted and poured another glass of wine. "And how might someone as cultured as you are, Charlie, know such a factoid?"

"I may be older," I said, "but I live with a thirteen-year-old girl."

"Say no more," Tilly said as she gulped the wine.

Bella had popped her ring light on her phone, attaching it with a contraption I'd never seen before. "Over here," she said. "The light is fab."

Tilly and I both shrugged. "At least no one will see our faces in this one," I whispered as we did as Bella asked. Tilly laughed.

We finished our wine, locked the door and the front gate behind us as Martin had instructed us, and turned right as we made our way onto the sidewalk.

"Isn't this exciting?" Bella said as she filmed the walk down the street.

Tilly stopped stock still. "Bella, my darling girl," she said in such a high-brow British accent that she sounded like a member of the royal family, "are we to be treated to continuous filming for the next three weeks?"

Bella looked puzzled as if such a question had never entered her mind. "I don't exactly know what you mean."

"I mean, will you continue to film and photograph everything we do for the next three weeks?"

"Why are you asking?"

I could see steam about to billow from Tilly's ears. Given my recent experience with young women, I felt it was my duty to intervene. "What Tilly means, Bella, is that continually filming might interfere with your ability to garner the most from the experience and that she worries that you might miss out on things your audience might find riveting eventually."

Tilly started to protest. I held up my hand behind Bella to silence Tilly. Bella considered this for a moment.

"But I'm here to document this for my followers. I share everything. It's part of my brand."

"Everything?" Tilly said, greatly exaggerating the "every" bit.

I shook my head at Tilly. I had this. "Why don't we give it a try putting the camera away this evening, Bella? It might inspire you even more."

"Inspo," she said. "Yes, inspo. I like that." She (slightly reluctantly, I thought) slid her phone into her Louis Vuitton clutch, and the three of us continued on our way until we reached the gate.

It was every bit as impressive as Marco had implied. As we approached, I noticed the villa was surrounded by a stone wall, yet you could see it up on a hill. *The views of the Mediterranean must be outstanding,* I was thinking as we approached the gate.

As I reached for the bell, the gates suddenly slid open, and a slightly husky, deeply female and highly accented voice said, "Welcome to Villa LaChapelle."

Here we go, I thought.

Mademoiselle

"A woman does not become interesting until she is over 40."
~ Gabriel "Coco" Chanel

W‍HY WAS I SO NERVOUS? It wasn't like I hadn't met many interesting and accomplished people in my life, and Genevieve LaChapelle was just one more. Nevertheless, I could hear my heart pounding in my ears. Perhaps I wasn't so much nervous about meeting this woman as I was to meet anyone at all. I had already met more new people today than in the past year. I was a bit rusty. There was, however, no time to dwell on that thought.

When the gate opened, Tilly, Bella and I began our walk up the driveway toward the villa. As we walked along the driveway, past the palm trees lining each side, toward the front door, I could see someone who appeared to be a butler standing rigidly, holding a tray of glasses. *A butler?* I thought. *Now, this is interesting.*

"It looks exactly as I had expected," Tilly said as we walked.

"What did you expect?" I said. I had no expectations.

"Well, I have done my homework on this one," she said. "It was supposedly designed to be a replica of Coco Chanel's villa on the French Riviera."

Bella and I both stopped for a moment and looked at the mansion we were now approaching. It was three stories of yellow stucco with a red-tiled roof, rounded archways resembling cloisters, and many small windows. It was surrounded by trees and shrubs, including tall palm trees, oleander shrubs dripping in fuschia-coloured flowers and a lemon grove.

"It looks a bit like a convent," I said. "A very prosperous convent."

"Precisely," Tilly said as we continued up the hill. "Chanel's inspiration for her own villa near Monte Carlo was the convent where she grew up."

"I didn't know Coco Chanel grew up in a convent," Bella said.

I did, in fact, know this piece of Chanel trivia.

"Indeed," Tilly said. "Mademoiselle Chanel concocted all kinds of stories about her childhood, not one of them approaching the truth. In any case, at the end of the 1920s, one of her wealthy lovers gave her the gift of a piece of property on the Riviera, and she had a villa built. I have read it was over ten thousand square feet, and this one looks at least as large."

Bella and I both nodded. It did look huge. "Nice lover to have," Bella said.

"Isn't it interesting," Tilly continued, "that this Genevieve LaChapelle should live in a villa that resembles one owned by Coco herself?"

"And teaches courses on making Chanel-style jackets," I said. Interesting indeed.

~

We arrived at the vast, double-doored entrance, where the white-haired butler offered each of us a glass of champagne as we passed him and entered the massive foyer.

A young man clad entirely in black was waiting for us in the foyer. He was almost six feet tall with dark, curly hair and looked to me to be about thirty. He stared into a tablet and appeared to be making mad notes with a digital pencil. When he looked up, Tilly, Bella and I were standing in a row in front of him.

"Oh, hello. I see you all have champagne. *Merci*, Gervais," the young man said to the butler, who silently disappeared into a hallway with his empty tray. "*S'il vous plaît, pardonnez mes manières*," the young man said to us. "Where are my manners? I am Maxence Simard, assistant to Mademoiselle Genevieve LaChapelle. You must be Charlotte, Mathilde and Bella. Ronald and Abigail are already here." Maxence's English was impeccable, if heavy on the French pronunciation, some of which sounded strange to my ear.

"Dear god, boy. Please do not call me Mathilde," Tilly said with some alarm. "I am Tilly."

"*Je suis vraiment désolé*. I am so sorry. Tilly, of course." He practically bowed.

"And you can call me Charlie," I said.

"And I'm Bella," Bella said quite unnecessarily.

Maxence's eyes started to crinkle at the corners, and a smile began playing about his lips. "And," he said, "you can call me Max. But not in the presence of Mademoiselle, please. Always Maxence for her."

We all nodded like schoolchildren, then followed him through a large archway into an enormous two-story living room. Seated on a circular sofa upholstered in fuchsia velvet was Ronald. He was holding an empty champagne glass and talking to a dour-looking woman holding a full champagne glass.

Max scuttled over toward the sofa and stood beside them, introducing us all around. The grim woman was Abigail Murdock. When introduced to us, she stared, nodded slightly and said, "Charmed, I'm sure."

"Don't tell me. Let me guess," Tilly said. "American. Southern US. I have it. Texas. Tell me I'm right."

Abigail nodded.

"OMG, I'm American, too," Bella said excitedly. It turned out that they had not been on the same plane after all.

Bella was looking around nervously, almost twitching. I sat beside her and leaned to whisper. "Are you all right?"

Bella looked around and kept trying to hold her hand away from her handbag. "It's just that I've never had my phone out of my hand for this long," she whispered.

I realized she was trying to keep herself from slipping it out of her purse. It would have been comical if it weren't so sad.

"Will we meet the famed Ms. LaChapelle before dinner?" Tilly said.

Maxence looked at Tilly and smiled. "She awaits you in the dining room as we speak," he said.

~

Mademoiselle Genevieve LaChapelle was indeed waiting in the dining room. She remained in the shadows until we had all taken our seats at the places indicated by the place cards in their silver holders. Finally, she emerged into the light, and we all gasped in unison. Were we looking at Coco Chanel? Or merely her doppelganger?

Genevieve LaChapelle wasn't a tall woman, but she had what can only be described as "presence." Her dark hair curled softly around her face, just as I'd seen Chanel's hair in photographs from the 1950s and '60s. Genevieve wore a jersey suit—skirt and jacket—that fell in soft folds around her slight figure. And then there were the pearls—at least four strands encircled her neck. The only thing missing was Coco's cigarette. Apart from that, Mademoiselle, as Max had told us to call her (just like Coco), was Chanel. I felt a frisson of excitement rise up my spine, a feeling I'd not had in too long. It was as if we had stepped back in time, welcomed into the home of the great Coco Chanel herself. And the illusion continued.

Maxence did not introduce us. He didn't have to. As the dinner progressed, it was clear she knew exactly who each of us was.

I hoped Mademoiselle might address the events planned for the next three weeks, but it appeared that the objective of the dinner was simply to eat. She said very little unless prompted. Tilly, as I was discovering, was full of questions.

"Mademoiselle," Tilly said as we ate our main course of coq au vin with haricots verts and garlic baby potatoes, "your suit is wonderful. Is it vintage?"

Mademoiselle's eyebrows raised slightly. "But, of course," she said. "It is Chanel from the 1920s."

As I looked at her suit, I wondered where I'd seen it before. I guessed it might have been a photograph online, but that didn't seem right. I couldn't put my finger on it, but the odd feeling persisted.

"It's magnificent," Tilly said. "Isn't it wonderful that a style can be so timeless? Can you imagine wearing some of today's fast fashion a hundred years from now? It makes one absolutely cringe."

"It is unthinkable," Mademoiselle said. "As you know, fashion comes and goes, but style lasts forever."

My brow furrowed. I had heard that before somewhere. Then from the other end of the table came a voice. "Chanel said that first." It was Abigail, and she sounded slightly irritated. I was beginning to wonder why she was even here.

"*Mais bien sûr.* But of course. Chanel was the first to acknowledge that fashion is a fleeting thing, Abigail. Gabriel Chanel continues to be the epitome of what style embodies. Indeed, she herself embodied a timelessness that transcends the decades and will continue to endure throughout the centuries. Of this, I have no doubt." Mademoiselle gently patted her mouth with her white napkin, not dislodging even a molecule of her bright red lipstick and continued. "The fact that each of you has chosen to spend the next three weeks here, learning to recreate something that was once only in the imagination of our mentor, suggests to me that you are devotees. Now let us chat. Tell me, Mademoiselle Bella, why you are here."

Bella's fork stopped halfway between her plate and her mouth. Although most of us had been staring raptly at Gabrielle LaChapelle, Bella had continued eating as Mademoiselle spoke. Bella's eyes registered surprise—perhaps even shock—at being singled out. She put her fork back on her plate and wiped her hands on the napkin on her lap.

"Well," Bella began, looking around to where Max was sitting at the end of the table opposite Mademoiselle. "I figure you already know that, Ma'am. I mean, my sponsors were in touch with Max—Maxence. I have a challenge to complete."

"Hmm. Yes, a challenge." Mademoiselle grunted slightly. "And you sew?"

"Well, my followers were kind of vibing on my reel where I filmed my visit to the Chanel boutique in Manhattan, and someone said you could make one of these jackets for way less than they cost. So, we joked a bit, and the next thing I know, my manager is on the phone with Maxence over there, and I'm here." She smiled brightly as if she might be relieved to get that off her back. "I hope to slay this project," she said, looking around at the rest of us. "You know, I *can* sew a bit."

"Slay?" Tilly said. "As in a dragon?"

Bella shrugged. Did Mademoiselle roll her eyes? Surely not. That was reserved for thirteen-year-old girls—and often their mothers.

Mademoiselle then turned her attention to Ronald. "Why are you here, Ronald?"

"I, well, I like to sew. There, I've said it. I realize that blokes aren't supposed to like sewing, but…"

"Why on earth not, Ronald? Many of the most famous couturiers were and are men. And many of them do know how to sew. As it happens, I am acquainted with that lovely Marc Jacobs. He sews, you know."

Ronald's eyes darted around the table. "I sew lingerie." I heard a slight snicker escape Tilly's lips. "For my wife—and some of her friends."

"In fact, Ronald, is it not true that you have a business selling bespoke lingerie?"

Ronald's face turned beet red. "Yes, Mademoiselle," he said. "I do. But I want to branch out."

"Well, sir," Mademoiselle said, "then own your passions. Be proud, and welcome to branching out." Ronald looked just slightly mortified. She continued her perusal of her dining companions.

"And you, Tilly. Why are you here?"

"Well, as it turns out, Mademoiselle, I have been a sewist all my life. And, as you know, I write a sewing blog. *Dead Ringer Design*, it's called."

I was impressed. I had read that blog occasionally and had no idea that Tilly was the blogger. She reproduced just what the blog name suggested: dead ringers for designer pieces.

"Yes, of course," Mademoiselle said, "and you are self-taught, are you not?"

"I am," Tilly said proudly.

"Do you consider yourself an expert?"

Tilly thought for a moment. "I don't suppose I do."

"Good. Then you, like me, are a believer in what the Zen teacher Shunryu Suzuki has said. *In the beginner's mind, there are many possibilities, but in the expert's mind, there are few.* I shall look for the expansion of possibilities."

"Sounds bloody terrific," Tilly said, raising her wine glass. "Possibilities, indeed." She stared hard at Mademoiselle and gulped her wine.

Mademoiselle turned to Abigail. "Abigail, what is it you would like to get out of these three weeks?" She stared down the table at Abigail, her eyes practically boring into her.

Abigail sat up straighter. "I believe we discover the truth about ourselves when we come face to face with a challenge." She did not look at Mademoiselle as she spoke.

"So, like young Bella, you are seeking a challenge?"

"Something like that," Abigail said.

Mademoiselle looked at Abigail for a moment. I expected her to say something in response, but she remained silent. Mademoiselle turned to me instead. "Charlotte, you were the last to register for the course. I feel it was done on the spur of the moment. Am I correct?"

"Sort of," I said. I wasn't sure how much of myself I was willing to reveal.

"Sort of," Mademoiselle repeated. "And what is your particular objective in being here with us?"

I felt like I was on the spot here. I hadn't thought much about my objective beyond doing what Evelyn and Frankie wanted me to do."I guess I'm here for the challenge like everyone else seems to be. And I suppose I want to learn something new."

"About what?"

Well, we're here for a sewing course, I thought. *Why wouldn't it be sewing? Seems like a no-brainer to me.* But I didn't say that aloud. Instead, I said, "Myself, I think."

~

When I returned to my room at the villa later, I was ready to flop into bed. I was exhausted—physically and mentally. It had been a long day with so many new people that my mind was buzzing. Before I could pull down the covers, I noticed someone had left a single, long-stemmed red rose in the middle of the bed. *Oh, how lovely,* I thought. *Mademoiselle has thought of everything.* I smiled and felt a bit of renewed energy.

I checked the time and realized it was only six pm in Toronto, so I picked up my phone and called Frankie.

"Hey, Mom! It's you! You on that island yet? Have you met anyone new? Are you learning anything?"

I told her to slow down and answered all her questions. Yes, yes and yes—despite the course not having started yet, I felt I was learning already.

When I'd given Frankie the answers, she said, "Look, Mom. I'm kind of in the middle of something with Katie and Lucas. We're making pizza, so here's Aunt Evelyn. Love you!" And she was gone.

"Hi, little sister," Evelyn said when she took the phone. "Met anyone interesting yet?"

"Interesting? Yes, everyone's interesting."

"You know what I mean."

"What? Did you send me here to meet a man? Evelyn, how would I meet a man on a sewing course?" I felt Ronald didn't count.

"Well, I saw those pictures of the villas, and there must be a pool boy."

I think I actually blushed. I was happy Evelyn couldn't see me. If she had, I would never have heard the end of it.

"No pool boy yet," I said. "But the driver is cute." I could at least play along. "Too bad he's so young."

"Unless he's under eighteen, he's not too young," Evely said with evident glee.

"If you were here, you'd be able to see my eyes rolling," I said.

Evelyn then asked me how everything else was going, and she gave me a rundown of what the kids had been doing for the past few days. That's when the serious yawning started. It was time for bed. Tomorrow promised to be a very full day.

Atelier

"It's not the appearance; it's the essence. It's not the money; it's the education. It's not the clothes; it's the class."
~ Gabriel "Coco" Chanel

THE FOLLOWING MORNING, TILLY, BELLA AND I met in the front yard at eight-thirty and headed to Mademoiselle's villa.

"Wasn't that rose on the bed last evening a nice touch?" I said as we walked.

"Rose? What rose?" Tilly said.

"Didn't you both get a rose on your bed?"

"I know I didn't," Bella said.

"Nor did I," Tilly said, eyeing me suspiciously. "An admirer, perhaps?"

I looked straight ahead and didn't say another word.

~

I had been curious about where within Genevieve's villa her workspace could be. When we arrived, Max ushered us up three flights of stairs to the top floor with its massive floor-to-ceiling windows and breathtaking view of the Mediterranean. We had arrived.

"One tiny thing I must ask of you this morning," Max said before Mademoiselle arrived. "Do not, under any circumstances, refer to this space by any other term than The Atelier."

"Doesn't that just mean workshop?" Abigail said. She and Ronald had once again arrived before the rest of us.

"Yes, of course, in direct translation," Max said, "but there is a world of difference for Mademoiselle."

"Seems a little highfalutin to me." Abigail sniffed.

Max shrugged. "*C'est comme ça*, Abigail. And Mademoiselle—she is who she is."

I was beginning to wonder if Abigail was always this sour. It occurred to me that perhaps once we got sewing, she would have a come-to-Jesus moment, and we might see her smile. Then I focused on the interior of the atelier.

We stood near the doorway and stared. The room had six long tables, each with a sewing machine on a smaller table behind it. Beside each large table was a mannequin, and unless I missed my guess, each was a different size. Had they created one for each of us? Then I noticed bundles of fabric on each of the tables.

There was a bundle of what appeared to be unbleached cotton muslin fabric—no doubt we would use this material to create mock-ups, variously called muslins or toiles, before cutting into the expensive fabric. The other bundle on each table was Chanel-style bouclé tweed, each a different colour—the colours we had each chosen for our projects.

"Please, take your places," Max said as he consulted his tablet. "I can presume you each know your own fabric?"

I tried to swallow my mounting insecurity about whether my skills were up to the challenge and walked toward the table holding my fabric. I immediately ran my hand over the soft tweedy black material to feel its texture, a satisfying mixture of velvety and pebbly.

I looked around at my classmates, who were all now standing behind their respective tables. Bella's table was directly in front of mine, and I watched her as she, too, caressed her fabric. Maybe there was more to her than met the eye. As I considered this possibility, Mademoiselle Genevieve LaChapelle entered the room. It felt as if royalty had just arrived.

Today, Mademoiselle was wearing another suit, but it was not just any suit. It was a cream-coloured tweed jacket shot through with gold that twinkled, catching the light from the vast windows every time she moved. There was a matching skirt, and under the jacket was what appeared to be a silk blouse with a soft bow at the neck. Then there were the strands of pearls—masses of them. She was Gabrielle Chanel reincarnated. The effect was stunning.

She stood there for a moment in silence, looking from one to another of us. Finally, she spoke. We listened.

"Bienvenue à votre atelier."

Welcome to *your* workshop, she was saying. *Our* workshop. I felt a quiver of excitement. She continued.

"You believe you are here to learn to make a jacket. And yet, who would travel this distance from their homes and families for a simple jacket? You have the opportunity to simply read about this process online or watch a video. And yet, here you are because it is so much more than a simple jacket. And I believe each of you is here for a reason that goes far beyond learning where to place each stitch." She looked around, catching each of our eyes as she did so. Only Abigail did not meet her gaze. "This process is like life. Life requires a gentle hand and attention to detail. Life requires ensuring a perfect fit. Life requires your full awareness. All these things you will bring to creating your jacket—for your life is also your creation."

I was trying to take in her words when Max rolled a mannequin over beside his boss. It was wearing a jacket that looked like a vintage Chanel original if my eye didn't deceive me. Mademoiselle nodded to Max, who slipped back to his spot near the door and then placed her hand on the shoulder of the mannequin.

"But, of course, you will recognize this as Chanel, will you not?" She looked around as we all nodded. Then she laughed lightly. "And yet, you would be wrong. It is but a replica, an homage to Coco herself. It remains true to her vision, but I created it myself. Coco herself once said, *The right ingredients can create a legend.* A legend, as you will know, is a story that comes down through the ages and yet remains. So, I will be your guide to selecting the right ingredients, and you will create your own legend. *Nous commençons.* We begin."

~

By the time the end of each day rolled around, any thought of seeing this Spanish island as a tourist was lost in the exhaustion that came from the meticulous focus that Mademoiselle expected of each of us as we toiled on our test jackets. We spent the first few days cutting, marking and sewing up these unsightly little cotton muslin jackets, covered with markings of all sorts as we inched toward perfection in fit. As I stood back at the end of the third day, looking at my "creation," I thought about Mademoiselle's words likening life to making this jacket. I could feel a tear forming in my eye as I thought about how I had thought I'd found the perfect fit in my life when I met Tom. But now that part of my life was over. Perhaps she was right. Maybe it was time for me to begin looking closely at the details to see if there wasn't another perfectly fitted life ahead of me.

"A penny for your thoughts."

I looked up from where I was examining the location of the waistline of my toile—as Mademoiselle preferred to call these ugly creations—to see Max standing beside me as my classmates filed out of the atelier to enjoy their Friday evening.

"Oh, hello, Max," I said. "I was thinking about details and perfection."

"Ah, yes, Mademoiselle does inspire such thoughts, *n'est-ce pas*?" Max gestured toward the door. "Shall we?"

I picked up my tote bag and followed Max toward the door. "So, Max, where are you from?"

"I have studied for three years at LISAA in Paris. You know of it?"

"Something to do with fashion, I presume?"

"L'Institut Supérieur des Arts Appliqués. It is, of course, the principal school for applied arts in France. I have acquired the BA in Fashion Design and Patternmaking."

"Wow," I said, impressed by the credentials held by someone in Max's position. "So, I presume you're much more than Mademoiselle's assistant. You're an aspiring fashion designer, of course."

"But of course. Yet one must…how do you say it in English? Pay one's dues?"

"Max, I hope you don't think me overly curious, and I don't mean to pry, but I was actually wondering where you're from. Where did you live before Paris?"

"Oh, here and there," Max said, his eyes darting around. "Charlie, you are a Canadian, are you not?"

"Guilty as charged. Why?"

"Then I fear I know the source of your curiosity. It is something I had hoped was gone completely."

I smiled. "Your accent?"

"*Mon dieu*, Charlie, you do know, don't you?"

"So, Maxence Simard, you're not Parisian at all, are you?" Max shook his head. "You're Québécois. How wonderful! Montréal?"

Max hung his head. "Yes. I am, as you say, guilty as charged."

"I'm surprised you didn't mention it when we first met. I love Montréal."

Max and I had stopped just outside the door to the atelier. Everyone else had already gone down the stairs. We were alone. "The truth is that Mademoiselle does not know."

I was puzzled. Why would Mademoiselle care if Max was from Montréal and not Paris? I expressed this to Max.

"Mademoiselle is a bit of a Parisian snob, you could say. I fear she would not be happy to find that her assistant is not Parisian."

"But surely she must have noticed your accent if I did."

Max shook his head forcefully. "No, she has never noticed. Mademoiselle prefers to speak English at every opportunity. She says it is the language of business, while French is the language of love. So, no, she has never seemed to notice and speaks to me as if I might have been brought up in Paris. I have never corrected her assumption, although I have never lied. And Mademoiselle is unwavering in her belief in authenticity. If she thought I was inauthentic, well, then the consequences do not bear contemplating." Max's furrowed brow deepened.

I thought about this for a moment. "But, Max, what about creating these replica jackets? Mademoiselle has her own couture line but seems fixated on Chanel and these jackets. Are they not in some way inauthentic?"

"I suppose some might think this, Charlie, but not Mademoiselle. She has quoted the great Chanel on so many occasions when someone has had the audacity to suggest such a thing. You may have read that Chanel herself has said that imitation is the greatest form of flattery. That is our motto."

I'd reminded myself of that exact Chanel phrase before I'd even decided to take this course. I thought about it again as I hurried to catch up with Tilly and Bella. Perhaps there was something authentic in imitation. That would remain to be seen.

Toile

"If you were not born with wings, do nothing to impede their growth."
~ Gabriel "Coco" Chanel

AS I SAID, IN COUTURE PARLANCE, A TOILE IS A TEST GARMENT. It is that ugly little cotton muslin jacket covered now with myriad temporary stitch lines, red-pen measurements and other markings I had created, now hanging on my mannequin. Unsightly though it might have been, there was something charming about it, too. And as I pinned and cut and sewed and pinned again, it edged closer to perfection, clearly Mademoiselle's objective. She came along several times a day to each of us, removing the jacket from the mannequin and demanding we try it on. She then worked a bit more magic, and when she was finished, it was inevitably better. It was, indeed, now a mini-me to the last centimetre. I had never truly appreciated how experimenting with something, trying different ways of approaching a problem, could achieve such beautiful results. But time would tell if these tweaks translated into the real thing. Was it that way with life?

What a week it was! When Tilly, Bella, and I opened our villa door after five that Friday afternoon, I felt like I had lived through a year. I could tell by the looks on their faces that they felt much the same way.

"Drinks, ladies?" Tilly said, heading toward the kitchen. "Anyone like a martini this evening?"

Bella looked at me, her eyes wide. We'd been drinking wine all week. "You in, Charlie?" she said. It was Friday evening, and we were not expected to dine with Mademoiselle again until Monday evening, as Marco had told us.

"I certainly am," I said, flopping into a dining room chair. I looked out the window toward the pool. "But I think I might have a dip in the pool first."

"Wonderful idea," Tilly said. "I'll get things ready, and we can drink by the pool."

Forty-five minutes later, I'd finished my dip, Bella had returned from her room where she had been doing god knows what, and Tilly, true to her word, had prepared martinis for three and a lavish charcuterie spread. This woman was undoubtedly someone with secret talents. I had no idea.

After a few sips of the fantastic martini, I sat back on my lounge chair, watching the slight breeze create tiny ripples on the aquamarine blue water in the pool, whose underwater lights were just beginning to come on. I was thinking about roses. After that first unexpected rose, another long-stemmed rose had appeared on Tuesday, Wednesday and Thursday evenings.

"You know, ladies, there's been a rose on my bed every evening. You're not just joking when you say neither of you got one?"

They both shook their heads. I was baffled.

Tilly cocked her head slightly and said, "Aha. You do have an admirer. I was right!" She smiled.

"Oh my god, Charlie, do you think it's Marco?" Bella looked slightly stricken, causing me to wonder if she had a crush on our handsome driver, who was undoubtedly more her age than mine.

"Why in the world would you think it's Marco who's been leaving me roses?"

"Well," Bella said, placing her martini glass on the cocktail table at the side of her lounge chair, "you remember when I left the dinner early on Wednesday night to come back here to take a call from my manager? I saw Marco leaving the villa, but he didn't see me."

I didn't know what to say. The possibility that Marco might leave me roses made me a bit short of breath. How would I ever deal with this?

"Dear god, this is a disaster."

Tilly looked puzzled. "Whatever do you mean, girl? Of course, it's not a disaster. It's simply someone's way of telling you he's interested. And he is rather dishy into the bargain."

"That can't be. I'm a widow." Dear god, what had I done, blurting out the very thing I thought I'd keep to myself for the duration of the course?

Tilly and Bella were silent for a moment as if taking in this new information.

"Oh, Charlie, I'm so sorry for your loss," Bella said. It was what people said.

"Me as well," Tilly said, "but that does make you rather eligible in my books. And why didn't you mention his before? How long has it been?"

I sat with my head in my hands for a moment before looking up. "I'm so sorry for this. I know it's too much information, and I hadn't planned on mentioning it to anyone." However, at that moment, I did remember mentioning it to Marco. That might have been a tactical error. I decided not to mention this to Tilly and Bella. "Tom died over a year ago, and this trip was supposed to be my way of testing out a new life alone."

"Like the toiles we're making," Bella said, surprising me with her ability to create such an interesting comparison.

"Yes, I suppose it is a bit like those toiles," I said. "But any kind of involvement with anyone like Marco is out of the question. Anyway, maybe I have his intentions wrong."

Tilly looked pensive. "Perhaps, but I wouldn't rule out his interest. Roses, after all."

Bella nodded in agreement.

Tilly emptied the cocktail shaker into her glass and raised it in a toast. "Well, ladies, here's to new adventures and trying new things. And," she continued, "who's coming with me to the famous Cala Pi beach tomorrow?"

New things, indeed.

~

The following day dawned sunny and hot like the weather had been from the moment I'd set foot on the island. When I woke up, I opened the automatic blinds and took in the view from the little main-floor balcony off my room. The pool looked inviting, and the sea beyond was sparkling in the early morning sun. I sat on the beanbag chair outside for a few moments until I began sweating. It was the perfect weather for a beach day.

I showered, slathered myself with sunscreen, dressed and joined Bella and Tilly, who were already moving about the kitchen making breakfast. Tilly had decided it was time for a full English breakfast—she had sausages and bacon in one frying pan and mushrooms and tomatoes in the other. She was getting ready to break a few eggs into the mushrooms while at the same time putting bread in the toaster. Bacon *and* sausages? And then I noticed beans in the saucepan. My stomach would not be able to handle this. Oh dear. Such a lot of food.

Bella was pouring orange juice into glasses on a tray to take outside to the table on the back deck. I made myself a cup of coffee and followed her outside.

"Charlie, do you eat that much food for breakfast in Canada?" she whispered.

I shook my head. "We can pick at it, though, Bella. I think Tilly is doing this more for herself anyway."

We managed somehow to get through breakfast without offending Tilly. To tell the truth, she didn't seem like the sort who offended easily. When we had finished, and the dishwasher had been filled, Bella said, "I think I'm going to stay here by the pool this morning. Maybe I'll go with you to the beach another time." So, Tilly and I set off for the beach by ourselves.

The Cala Pi beach was a fifteen-minute walk back into the heart of the tiny village. We found the old cement steps and stared down, down, down. What we hadn't bargained on was that many of the beaches on the island of Mallorca are at the bottom of cliffs, accessed only by steep steps or perhaps in more remote places, even by picking one's way down a steep bluff. Cala Pi beach was one of them.

Tilly stood at the top before we began our descent. "You realize, Charlie, that what goes down must come up."

That had already occurred to me.

"Well," she said, "in for a penny and all the rest." Then she started down, carefully taking one step at a time.

The beach at Cala Pi was a crescent of sand that was deeper than it was long, lying in an inlet carved into the cliff. It was early, and sunseekers had already begun marking their territory with brightly striped beach towels and umbrellas. There were teenagers, children, parents, young lovers. The sunbathers were in all shapes and sizes, and everyone seemed to be there to worship one thing—the sun.

Tilly and I found a spot near the water's edge where the tiny waves lapped the shore. I could feel a breeze making its way into the cove, and for this, I was grateful. When I had looked down at the beach from the top, I feared it might be like an oven down there, the hot air trapped between the bluffs.

We had brought bottles of water and beer and some snacks— mainly potato chips because they were a particular favourite of mine. Tilly said she'd probably just drink.

We'd been sitting side-by-side on our towels in amiable silence for a while when I remembered our conversation about my real identity as a bestselling writer. She wasn't the only one who had done some research. I'd been online the next day. I was reasonably sure I now knew a few things about her, but I wanted her to tell me herself.

"Tilly, you remember that conversation we had the other day about my books and my writing? I hope you don't find me rude, but you never did answer my question. Why are *you* here?"

"As I told Mademoiselle, it's all about the blog, my dear," Tilly said, sipping a beer daintily.

I stared at Tilly as she sat there looking so innocent. "Mathilde Foster-Matthews, you and I both know that's not true."

Tilly's eyes flashed for a split second. "Can you keep a secret?"

Another secret? I thought about Max and his secret. Did I dare take on another one? I nodded. "Yes, of course, I can."

"I'm a journalist."

I almost rolled my eyes. That much I had already discovered via the online research I'd done since she told me she knew who I was. I wanted to know who she was.

"I thought you said you were a blogger," I said, not yet letting her know the jig was up, as they say.

Tilly waved that thought away as if fanning herself. "No, no, no," she said. "I am not a blogger at all. I only said that so Mademoiselle and her squad wouldn't know my true identity."

I had already discovered Tilly's journalistic writing, but that still didn't explain what she was *really* doing here on this course. I wondered if it had anything to do with her paranoid accusation that I could be writing a book about Mademoiselle. "This sounds a bit like a spy novel," I said. "What are you not telling me?"

"I have a friend called Prudence who writes that blog. I convinced her to let me pretend I was the blogger, so I got her to put my picture in the bio and everything. I knew the team here always does some background checking, and I couldn't afford to let them know my real identity."

I was becoming more and more muddled with every word Tilly uttered. "Tilly, you're not making any sense. So you hid your identity. The question is why."

"I'm getting to that." Tilly opened another bottle of beer and offered it to me. It was still early in the day, but I took it gratefully. She opened another for herself and continued. "Did you know," she said, "that Mademoiselle Genevieve was born on January 10, 1971?"

"I did not know that. Is it important?" I thought Tilly was still trying to obfuscate.

"Indeed, it is important." Tilly took a long pull from her beer bottle. "At nine pm on Sunday, January 10, 1971, the original Mademoiselle took her last breath."

"The original Mademoiselle?" I was beginning to think I was too hot to think.

"Think, woman. Just think about it for a moment. Mademoiselle—departed, deceased, breathed her last—on that precise day."

"Are you talking about Coco Chanel?" My heat-addled brain was having more trouble than usual.

"Finally, she's got it."

I thought about the two events for a moment. One icon dies, and another is born. The idea beginning to form somewhere in the depths of my brain was too implausible even to consider. "Tilly, you don't mean to say you think our Mademoiselle is some kind of reincarnation of Coco Chanel?"

Tilly shrugged. "I'm not saying anything. But it is tantalizing, isn't it? You're a writer, Charlie, and although you write fiction, perhaps fact is stranger than fiction at times."

I didn't believe in reincarnation. In fact, I had often hoped it didn't exist. I had no idea who would want to take a chance on coming back. It was too risky as far as I was concerned because I was sure there wouldn't ever be a do-over like in all those movies. I didn't even believe in the hereafter, heaven, or whatever anyone called it. Tilly's notion was just too far-fetched for my logical mind.

"So, Tilly, are you here to do an investigation? Are you doing it for a specific publication?"

Tilly shook her head. "No, nothing specific. Thought I might try my hand at writing a book." She took another swig of beer. "I guess I'm a bit like you. You see, Charlie, I am trying on something new just as you are." She raised her beer bottle. "Here's to finding a new path!"

Secrets

"Elegance is when the inside is as beautiful as the outside."
~ Gabriel "Coco" Chanel

TILLY'S SECRET WAS SO ODD THAT I KNEW there was no one I could ever tell it to anyway. I could never do it justice. I was only worried about how she might go about finding the details that would support her cockamamie idea.

When we finally made it back to the top of the steps, Tilly declared that she'd had enough Mallorcan beach to last her a lifetime. I agreed with her. Once was enough—especially in this heat.

We walked back to the villa mostly in silence. I must admit I was a bit peeved. Tilly's secret would now colour every encounter I would have with Genevieve LaChapelle over the next two weeks.

When we arrived back at the villa, Bella was out by the pool. I walked through the house and out the back to say hi. If I had expected she would be on her phone or preening for a selfie, I was mistaken. She was reading—an actual book.

Bella looked up when she saw me and quickly closed the book, sliding it under the lounge chair mattress. She took a second to compose her features, then smiled. "You're back. How was the beach?"

I sat on the side of the lounger next to her and told her about the steps, people, and the heat.

"Oh, by the way," Bella said, "Marco came by to tell us that Mademoiselle wants all of us to take a field trip to something called the caves of Drach. He'll pick us up tomorrow after lunch." Bella picked up her iPad from the cocktail table beside her and clicked a few times before handing me the map of the island.

"Marco says it's about an hour's drive from here. See?" She pointed to the dropped pin on the southeast coast of the island.

I blanched slightly at the mention of Marco's name. I only hoped we were all wrong about his interest in me. And I could hardly ditch the field trip with the group.

After Evelyn and Frankie had told me about this course and its location here in Mallorca, I did some research. As far as I could tell, the Caves of Drach were something of a tourist magnet. They were supposed to be natural caves carved out over the millennia by the sea. I'd seen pictures of stalagmites and stalactites and lots of eerie lighting, and there was a large underground lake somewhere in the depths of the caves. I couldn't imagine how such a trip could be related to learning to make a Little French Jacket, but it might prove interesting anyway.

"I suppose there'll be lots of tourists," I said.

Bella shook her head. "I don't think so. Marco said Mademoiselle has arranged for the five of us to have a private tour, and Marco will drive. Anyway, it'll be nice to see another part of the island."

I totally agreed.

~

The following day was—you guessed it—once again hot and sunny. Sizzling hot and blindingly sunny.

There had been no rose on my bed on Friday or Saturday evening, and for that, I was grateful since I would be in Marco's company for some time today. Perhaps he had given up his attentiveness. When he arrived with the Mercedes van, Ronald and Abigail were already seated in the row behind Marco. Tilly got in beside him in the front, and Bella and I took the rear seat.

Marco said a pleasant good morning to all of us, but I felt he bestowed his most charming smile on me. I was grateful I hadn't been the one to have to sit next to him.

"We are all seated with seatbelts?" he said. "Well, then, *vamos*."

Marco drove us out of the village and along a small highway that took us inland through several small villages connected by flat, arid fields before returning to the coast, where the last leg of the journey allowed us glimpses of the Mediterranean. Bella took photos and a video she said she'd share with me since she had the best view.

After driving for about an hour and a quarter, we arrived in the seaside village of Porto Cristo with its hotel and marina. A sharp turn to the right, and we arrived at the enormous parking lot for the caves. We all got out and stretched, then followed Marco along a wide tree-lined path for ten minutes until we reached the entrance to the caves. Many people were milling around, waiting for their designated entry times. Marco led us directly to the front of the line, showed the attendant the tickets, and we entered. Marco stayed behind.

The five of us followed the attendant down the stairs. Waiting for us at the bottom was our guide. The attendant left us in the dim light at the bottom of the first staircase and went back up into the sunshine. The encroaching darkness made it difficult to see until my eyes adjusted to the dim light as we descended deeper and deeper into the caves on a modern-looking staircase. As we descended, the grandeur of the caves began to come into view.

When we reached what I thought were the depths of the caves, the guide stopped on a kind of bridge. We all looked in amazement at the eerie rock formations—masses of stalactites, the icicle-like spikes dripping from the cave ceilings and stalagmites, pillars of rock rising from the floor—all creatively and carefully lit. The effect was mesmerizing.

We stood in hushed silence, listening to the caves. It was almost as if I could hear the rocks breathing. Then I noticed, far below, a small lake, aquamarine blue, reflecting the rock formations on its glassy surface. The guide noticed me staring.

"That is only one of several lakes within the caves. You will see the best up ahead." Then the guide addressed the group.

"We now stand within the Caves of Drach. Drach means dragon, and legend says a treasure is buried within these four contiguous caves, guarded by a dragon in their depths. Keep an eye open."

Abigal, who was standing close beside me, now snorted. "What a load of crap," she muttered, just loud enough for me to be the only one who could hear her.

I turned to her. "Are you not enjoying this wonderful place?"

Abigail snorted again. "Don't know what this's got to do with sewing," she said derisively.

I decided my best course of action was simply to sidle away and ignore her. So I did.

The guide continued telling us about the four connected caves that extended twenty-five metres beneath the surface, running for almost two and a half kilometres. She then explained how they knew the caves had been inhabited since prehistoric times because they had found fragments of stone implements and pottery. Although they couldn't be sure exactly when the caves were later discovered, she told us that in the middle ages, around 1338, the governor of the island referred to the caves in writing. According to the guide, even Jules Verne had visited the caves before writing his book *Journey to the Centre of the Earth*. I was blown away by the thought of how this experience could inspire me. Maybe that's what Mademoiselle was thinking about, but the connection between these caves and our jacket projects was still unclear. We continued deeper into the cave.

Finally, we arrived in what I thought must be the centre of the caves. We had reached the shore of Martel Lake, one of the largest underground lakes in the world.

"This place has an interesting microclimate," the guide said as we marvelled at the way the lake seemed to emerge from the rocks on one side and disappear into more rock formations on the other. "It remains eighteen to twenty degrees Celsius all year round, regardless of the weather," she said.

I could see Bella shivering in her tiny sleeveless T-shirt. Before we left this morning, it had occurred to me that we might encounter lower temperatures inside caves today, so I had sensibly brought along a sweater which I now put on as the guide led us to bench seats.

Like in a theatre, rows of seats faced the lake, which was the stage. We were told to put all electronic devices away and remain sitting while the lights were turned off. The darkness was absolute. I couldn't even see my hand as I held it up in front of my face. Suddenly, I saw a glowing light in the opening where the lake emerged from the rocks. From out of the light floated two boats. Then the music began.

The musicians—two violinists, a cellist and a pianist—floated toward us on those boats while we listened to the strains of Vivaldi's "Four Seasons." The acoustics were magnificent, and I could feel a shiver up my spine as the strains of the music came closer with the boats passing in front of us. It was an odd experience to be surrounded by total darkness, with only the glow illuminating the music as if the light somehow made the sound.

The boats carrying their musical cargo then made their way to the other side, slowly floated by once again, and disappeared into the darkness. The lights remained off for a few seconds, and then gradually, the space became semi-light once again. The concert was over, and we were directed out and back into the real world.

I didn't know what to make of the Drach Caves and their secrets below the surface of the earth where we walked, but I was going to try to figure it out.

~

On Monday morning, Mademoiselle came into the atelier to tell us it was time to begin cutting apart our toiles. These pieces would form the pattern for our perfectly fitted jackets. As ugly as my muslin was, I was quite attached to it, and it pained me to wield my shears and begin cutting it apart at its seams. But before we were permitted to start, Mademoiselle wanted to address our field trip.

"Ladies and gentlemen, you have experienced a great wonder of the world yesterday, *n'est-ce pas*?" We all nodded. "You may be wondering why this should be part of your experience. There are two essential lessons to be learned here. First, you will remember the rock formations in the shape of pillars and columns and spikes. They are formed naturally, and we appreciate them as only human beings can do. But we must also appreciate the lines of the fabric created by other humans. We must see the wonder of the natural world, even in human creations. In this way, we shall be reverential as we cut into this fabric to mould it into something new."

I looked down at my fabric and was suddenly even more nervous about cutting into it.

"And the second lesson is this. It is perhaps even more important as we progress through the next two weeks. What you see on the surface does not prepare you for what is beneath. It is a lesson to be learned about many things in life, I think. It is perhaps the most important thing about these garments. Just as each of us holds secrets within us, so, too, will this jacket. The inside will have secrets that cannot be seen or experienced unless shared by the wearer. Coco herself was unwavering in her belief that one cannot achieve elegance and refinement if the inside is not as exquisite as the outside. *Nous commençons*. We begin."

I thought about Mademoiselle's words as I carefully cut into the muslin fabric to create the pattern. I was trying not to think about it as I cut into my jacket fabric later because I was trying to concentrate. I did have to admit that the idea that what you see on the outside of something—or someone—might not reflect what's inside was beginning to resonate with me.

~

The roses started arriving once again on Monday evening. Since I'd told Bella and Tilly about them, I decided we might as well all enjoy their beauty, so I started collecting them in a vase on the indoor dining table.

On Friday morning, as we were getting ready to leave for the atelier, Bella looked at the roses. "They really are beautiful, you know, Charlie. What are you going to do?"

"One thing I'm not going to do is mention them to Marco," I said. That was the one thing I had crystal clear in my mind. If he had something to say to me, then I figured he was the one who should initiate any conversation.

Tilly looked from the roses to me. "If I may be permitted to quote an American icon," she nodded toward Bella. *"One of the hardest things in life to learn is which bridges to cross and which bridges to burn."*

I thought about it for a moment, then said, "What American icon said that?"

Before Tilly could speak, Bella answered immediately. "Oprah."

~

As the second week drew to a close, I found myself anxious that it would soon be over. *How odd*, I thought. *I seem to want it to continue. I wonder why.*

I was sitting at my worktable, admiring the work I'd accomplished to date. It was shocking how much was invisible inside these jackets—and I don't mean just inside, where you could see it if you turned it inside out. I mean the stuff that was between the lining and the jacket. I had spent the better part of two days hand stitching stabilizing ribbon to every jacket edge— down the front, around the neckline, across the hems. And no one would ever see it or know it was there—no one but me. And yet it was essential to how the finished product would work—how it would hang and how it would fit. I was just about to begin cutting into the soft, shiny black silk charmeuse fabric to start creating the lining for my jacket when Max appeared at my elbow.

"Charlie, may I speak with you a moment?" he whispered in my ear.

I nodded and followed him out into the hall. "What's going on, Max?"

"It is about Tilly. I am wondering if *you* might know what is going on."

I had no idea what he was talking about.

"She has been asking so many questions and…" he trailed off.

"And what, Max?"

"Well, I just now found her…how do you say it…snooping in Mademoiselle's office. *Mon dieu*, if Mademoiselle herself had entered at that moment, I cannot bear to think about what might have happened. *Certainement*, Tilly would be on an airplane this afternoon heading for London." Max's eyes darted around, and seeing no one else in the vicinity, he continued. "Charlie, you are beginning to know her well. Do you have any idea what her apparent inquisitiveness is about?"

I shook my head, biting my tongue. I knew what Tilly was doing, and I was disappointed that she seemed to be doing it so clumsily.

"She does not know about me, does she?"

"Of course not, Max. You asked me to keep your secret, and I have."

"*Je suis désolé*…I am so sorry to have doubted you, Charlie. It is just that having someone creeping around Mademoiselle's office is worrisome. It is also very unusual." Max peered around the corner into the atelier, where the rest of the students were diligently preparing their linings. "Tilly has been asking many questions since she has been here. Have you also noticed?"

"Well," I said, carefully choosing my words and not wanting to lie outright, "she did tell us she was a blogger." That much was true. She had told us that even though I now knew it was a lie. "Perhaps she's gathering background."

"But what kind of background could one gather while creeping around an office where one has not been invited? Charlie, will you try to find out what is going on?"

"I'll try to pay attention, Max, but I can't promise anything. And I don't know Tilly all that well."

I wanted to blurt out Tilly's preposterous suggestion, but I promised to keep her secret, too.

~

Working with the delicate, slippery silk for the jacket's lining was challenging. The silk filaments frayed off every cut edge, floating around the atelier until we found ourselves swatting floating pieces off our noses and fingertips. By the end of the week, I had my lining quilted to the body of the jacket—it's how it was done in a Chanel jacket—and had sewn the pieces together so that it now resembled an actual jacket. I was excited, but I was also exhausted.

On Friday evening, Tilly told me she planned to go into Palma, the island's capital city the next day and wondered if Bella and I would like to come. Bella begged off, citing too much work to do. Tilly and I looked at her, no doubt both wondering just how much work was involved in being an online influencer. We had no idea.

Paradox

Beauty begins the moment you decide to be yourself."
~ Gabriel "Coco" Chanel

I BELIEVE IT'S FAIR TO SAY THAT EACH OF US human beings has our share of contradictions—those contradictory qualities that make us three-dimensional beings. At least, that's what I always thought when I was writing novels. Any heroine who was all sunshine and light and any villain who was totally evil was considered too two-dimensional to be authentic. I had always tried to make my characters three-dimensional, I think. Of course, by the time I embarked on that summer course in Mallorca, I hadn't written a word in almost two years. And before that, my writing had been sporadic, to say the least. Having a husband dying of cancer had been my excuse. And then came widowhood, which I seemed to have embraced so wholeheartedly that I had allowed it to take over my personality as if it were the only thing about me that mattered. I seemed to have turned into one of those flat cardboard characters. But that can't be true, can it? I was thinking about these things on Saturday evening after Tilly and I returned from Palma. More to the point, however, is that I was thinking about them because of Bella. Let me back up a bit.

Marco picked us up at ten am on Saturday morning and drove us the forty-five minutes into the heart of Palma de Mallorca. He dropped Tilly and me off near the cathedral and told us to give him a call and a half hour's notice, and he would pick us up at the same spot. He then gave me a heart-melting smile. I think I blushed.

We clambered out of the vehicle, and Tilly immediately wanted to find somewhere to sit in the sunshine and have a glass of wine. I wanted to walk, so we went our separate ways for an hour. Tilly drank wine while I wandered along the waterfront past the marina filled with every imaginable kind of sailing boat and a few gigantic, motorized yachts. We met later for lunch, toured the famous cathedral and then did some shopping, where I found myself a pair of handmade espadrilles, and Tilly bought a gauzy, white cotton caftan thing. Marco was in our pickup spot at precisely the right moment, and we returned to the villa.

As we walked in through the front door (i.e. the door facing the street), we could see through to the covered veranda out back by the pool, where Bella sat hunched over the table with her back facing us. She seemed so engrossed in whatever she was looking at on the table that she didn't hear or see us.

"Just look at that," Tilly said, dropping her purse and shopping bags on the floor by the door. "I will never understand the fascination those young ones have with social media. In my day, we spent time reading and thinking, then meeting with people in the real world. Do they ever see what's going on around them?"

I was about to say that I had often wondered that myself and tried to get Frankie to understand that there is more to life than social media "friends" when I noticed something. I edged closer to the back door and looked at Bella. "Tilly," I said, pointing to Bella, "I don't think she's online. Aren't those actual books beside her on the table?"

Tilly came and stood beside me. "Bloody hell," she said, "by George, I think you're right. I believe the child may be reading." She pushed the door open.

Bella didn't seem to hear the door open and then jumped as if someone had touched her with a hot poker. "Oh my god," she said. "You scared the life out of me." Then she looked around at the books and the open laptop on the table and reached out her arms as if to gather them in—as if to hide them from us.

I sat beside her in one of the vacant chairs and picked up a book. The look on Bella's face was a mix of surprise and sheer terror. What had we stumbled upon?

The book was a paperback, maybe three-hundred pages. It was called *Modern Day Man in Search of a Soul* by CG Jung. I remembered once, many years ago, when I'd been a struggling writer and belonged to a group of equally struggling writers. One evening, Karl, one of the group members, had talked about Jung and how knowing about Jung's work could help in developing characters, but the details were fuzzy. I picked up another book. It was *The Undiscovered Self,* also by CG Jung. I looked at this one more closely because it sounded familiar.

Yes, I thought, *I had to read this one way back in an undergraduate course on analytical psychology. I'd had to take it because it was the only psych course that fit into my schedule that year—and I needed one to graduate.* I vaguely remembered it as being dense and a bit beyond where I was (psychologically) at that point in my life. Why in the world did Bella have it here?

"You guys are back earlier than I thought you'd be," Bella said. "Um, how was your day?" Her eyes were darting around, not focusing on anything on the table, including an open laptop whose screen suggested she was writing a dissertation rather than posting on her Instagram account. It was as if she thought that if she didn't look at what was right in front of us, perhaps we wouldn't either.

"Perhaps not as interesting as yours," Tilly said, sinking into the seat directly across from Bella. She, too, picked up a book. "What gives, dear girl?" She looked at the cover of the book. "Dear god. You're not reading Jung, are you?"

Bella's eyes continued darting back and forth between Tilly and me, still saying nothing.

"Bella, what's going on? If you're reading about Jungian psychology, it's okay. It's just a bit surprising," I said.

Bella breathed out heavily as if she had been holding her breath. She sat back in her chair and pulled her feet up under her.

"I guess you think I'm too dumb to be interested in anything other than Instagram." Suddenly her voice didn't seem quite as high-pitched as it usually did, and her slight vocal fry had disappeared. Was that just something she put on?

"We never said anything of the sort," Tilly said. "But you do have to admit that it's a tad surprising, given what you've displayed to us over the past weeks."

We all sat there silently for a moment, then Bella spoke. "I have a secret."

Oh no, I thought. *Not another one with a secret. How many secrets can I keep?*

"But if I tell you about it, you have to promise not to tell a single soul. I mean it," Bella said. "No one."

"We certainly can keep a secret," I said. "But if you're worried about it, maybe it would be better not to tell us."

Bella sighed. "If I don't, you're both going to draw some conclusions about what you see here." She waved her hand over the books and notes on the table. "And it's likely to be wrong." She looked from Tilly to me and sighed again. "I guess I have no choice." She stopped, quickly clicked a few keys on her laptop, closed it and sat up straight. "Ladies, what you see before you is the real Bella Butler. Or, to be more precise, Elizabeth Butler, the one who made straight A's and sewed most of her own clothes. Nerdy Lizzie Butler, late of Columbia University, who, as a high school student, was voted the most likely to end up a crazy cat lady."

"Columbia University in New York?" I said. I wasn't very familiar with American universities, but I knew Columbia was a good one.

Bella nodded. "Everyone thinks I'm this dumb style influencer—and I suppose I am. At least, that's the persona I created, and it seems to have worked."

"Given your online success, I'd have to say it worked tremendously well," Tilly said. "But why all the artifice? Why not be who you are?"

Bella—Elizabeth—sat up straighter. "That's where you've drawn some wrong conclusions," she said. "That is who I am." She stopped and looked at the books on the table. "And so is this. I'm both of these personas."

"Tell us about it," I said. I was so fascinated by Bella's story. The writer in me was emerging again, and I could sense a real story here. So, she told us about it.

Elizabeth Butler grew up in Connecticut, the daughter of an accountant mom and a lawyer father. A straight-A student, Lizzie was headed to university on a full scholarship at the age of sixteen.

"I was so young when I started at Columbia. I was younger than anyone in my classes, and I had no friends. I didn't care, though, because I'd been bullied so much in high school about being smart that it was almost a relief to be left alone. I started spending more and more of my free time online and began creating a new identity for myself there. No one knew me, and it was like, freeing. I felt as if I could be anything I wanted to be. When I went home for Christmas in my third year, my parents started to worry about me, but when I showed them what I'd been doing online and how a few companies were starting to offer me sponsorships, they started to get interested. My father became my manager, and my mother kept the books. We decided together that I'd do this for a maximum of five years, make a pile of money, then get my doctorate." Bella pointed to the laptop. "There's the final draft of my Master's thesis. I start my doctoral studies full-time in January."

"So, no more @bellastyleNYC?" I was thinking about what Frankie would think of this incredible story.

"No more @bellastyleNYC. At least not after my high school reunion. I want to walk in there as Bella Butler, Instagram star, tell everyone who I really am and leave as Lizzie Butler, graduate student."

"Stick it to them, huh?" Tilly was beginning to vibrate. "Oh, Bella, that will be a sensation in the social media world, won't it? Bella, I have to tell you something."

Bella and I both looked at Tilly with anticipation. I figured I knew what was coming. Bella didn't.

"Bella, darling girl, I'm a journalist. I want to tell your story to the world. It is wonderful. You cannot keep this a secret."

Bella shook her head vehemently. "No, no, no. You can't tell anyone." She stopped and stared at Tilly. "But, Tilly, you're a sewing blogger. Sewing bloggers don't write about news stories."

Tilly smiled. "If you can trust me with your secret, I suppose I'll have to trust you with mine. Can you keep a secret?"

Bella nodded.

"I'm not a blogger at all. That blog is my cover. It belongs to a friend of mine. I'm here to uncover a story."

"What kind of story?"

"A story about Mademoiselle."

I rolled my eyes. "Tilly seems to think she's the reincarnation of Coco Chanel or something."

"Ooh, that gives me goosebumps," Bella said, hugging herself. "I want to hear all about it, but first, you must promise me. No one can know about my story. Am I making myself clear? No one. At least not yet."

"I can live with not yet," Tilly said. "When you're ready to come clean, will you let me tell it?"

"Maybe." Bella looked at me and then back at Tilly. "Are you two in this together? This story about Mademoiselle, I mean."

Tilly said, "Bella Butler, may I present CK Hudson, bestselling writer."

Bella's eyes nearly popped out of her head.

"Tilly," I hissed, "I thought we were going to keep that under wraps?"

"Well, it seems that all secrets are out on this table. So, I thought you wouldn't mind."

It was too late to mind anyway. "It's true, Bella. I'm that writer."

"I've read all your books."

"But you didn't recognize her from her photo on the back of the cover?" Tilly said.

"Photo? Oh, no. I only read eBooks when I'm reading a novel, so there's no back cover and no picture," Bella said. Then her face fell, and she turned to me. "Why hasn't there been a new one in so many years?"

"Maybe we can talk about that later." Changing the topic, I looked again at the books on the table. "What's your thesis topic?"

Bella smiled, and her face lit up. "It's an analysis of a possible new online influencer archetype using Jung's theory of the archetypes."

"And what better way to understand the influencer than to become one," Tilly said. "It's brilliant!"

"Well," Bella said, "the influencer in me came before my brilliant idea to use it as the basis for my master's research. I'd been doing the online stuff for a couple of years when I started my master's degree. My thesis supervisor is the only one on campus who knows who I am." Bella looked at us imploringly. "And no one else but you two on this course knows my secret."

When Bella talked about her studies and research, she dropped all her influencer vernacular. And I was right—the timbre of her voice had changed. She sounded—dare I say it—smarter. I was astonished at myself for the kind of prejudice I seemed to have about young influencers. I wondered if Bella's research would find that she was an outlier—or that I was truly biased.

"So, Bella dear," Tilly said, "why a course on making a Chanel-style jacket?"

Bella's eyes sparkled. "Because ever since I was that nerdy Lizzie in high school, I've had a secret passion for everything Coco Chanel."

"But I suspect you can afford to buy yourself any Chanel merchandise you'd like. Why not just go into a boutique in New York and buy a jacket?" I said.

Bella looked at me, and I could see that her eyes had changed from that sparkly-eyed young woman to something wiser beyond her years. "And I suppose you can't?" she said to me.

"*Touché*," I said.

"Charlie, I just want to be the one who makes this jacket with my own hands. Then I'll wear it proudly. One thing I've learned about myself since I started researching Jung's archetypes is that I'm what he would categorize as The Creator/Artist. Creating Bella online was part of it, but it goes deeper. I need to feel what I'm creating."

"I do so want to hear more about your archetype," Tilly said. Bella and I both looked at her. "I mean it. I do. But let us continue this after dinner and wine."

~

We ate our Monday through Thursday lunches and dinners *chez* Mademoiselle's, but we were on our own on the weekends. The three of us had planned to try one of the village restaurants on Sunday, but on that Saturday evening, we planned to barbeque. Tom had done most of the barbequing throughout our marriage, and I missed his perfectly done steaks and the way he could get barbequed asparagus just right. Tilly and I would share the work this evening.

I prepared vegetables to toss in a basket with some herbs and spices we found buried in the kitchen cupboards, and Tilly prepared the chicken. Eventually, it all came together, although I had a few moments of panic when I realized Tilly had already downed a full glass of wine before she started. Drunken barbequing was *verboten* in my view.

But we managed it without incident.

After we had finished what turned out to be a delicious dinner and demolished the cookies Tilly had found at the small market in the village, we sat back, watching the lights in the pool and the dusk settling over the island in the distance.

"Bella," I said, coming back to our previous discussion about her research. "What have you figured out about the psychology of influencers?"

"Well," she said, placing her wine glass on the table and leaning into her topic, "first, you have to understand that Jung's work suggests that there are what he called four cardinal orientations—ego, order, social, and freedom."

"Okay, I'll bite," Tilly said. "Whatever is a cardinal orientation?"

"It's simple," Bella said, warming to her subject. "Each of us has a main, kind of overall archetype—one of those four. Sometimes they're called our primary motivators—like, what makes us do what we generally do. Jung's approach to understanding personalities was that we're each primarily motivated by one of these things. It's what makes us tick."

"A bit simplistic, isn't it?" Tilly said. "I mean, aren't we all a chaotic accumulation of many motivators? I know I am."

Bella shrugged. "I suppose, in the end, we're a bit more complicated, but Jung never said we couldn't have more than one motivator for what we do. He only said that we all seem to have one that is the primary one. That's what makes the theory so interesting in trying to figure people out."

I was thinking about when I first had to take that analytical psych course where I'd read at least one of Jung's dense books and how Karl, from my writers' group, talked about using this background to create characters. At the time, I became one of those misguided writers who believed I would design the characters rather than allow them to find me and push me to tell their story as it eventually happened. We live and learn. But I did remember a few things he'd talked about. "If I remember my Jung correctly," I said, "the four motivators you mention are a bit like primary objectives that each of us has. But it seems to me that the primary motivator can change as we evolve throughout our lives." I was going out on a limb here, but I seemed to remember more of Jung's work as we talked about it.

"That's it," Bella said. "Our motivators are a bit like objectives." We had pushed her books to the side when we'd set the table for dinner, and now, she reached for a notebook, opening it to a page where she had pasted in a colour-coded wheel. "Look here," she said, pointing to the legend she had written below the wheel. "If your primary motivation is ego, you're motivated to leave a mark—kind of like someone like Bill Gates or Elon Musk. If order is your motivator, then you primarily try to provide structure to things."

I leaned over. "So, people motivated mostly by freedom want to have a spiritual journey?" I said. Bella nodded, and I continued. "So, influencers must be predominantly social, right?"

"Yeah. My research tells me that this is mostly true. People with the social archetype want to connect to others as their underlying motivation, but I found something more. I found that influencers are equally motivated by ego. It seems they want to leave a mark, too."

"Some marks are better off unleft, as it were," Tilly muttered dryly.

Bella laughed. "I totally agree, but what's been exciting for me is that I think I've kind of identified a new, twenty-first-century archetype."

"The Influencer archetype, perhaps?" Tilly said. Bella nodded happily. "Well, then, here's to uncovering more Jung!"

After toasting and laughing, Bella got serious. "Tilly, let's talk about the writing project you're working on while you're here. Is Charlie helping you? If she is, I'm in, too."

And so began our extracurricular project, which Tilly dubbed Project Coco.

Coco

"My life did not please me, so I created my life."
~ Gabriel "Coco" Chanel

GABRIELLE CHANEL WAS BORN ON AUGUST 19, 1883, in a poorhouse in a town in France on the Loire River and died on January 10, 1971, in her suite at the Ritz in Paris—at least according to her biographers. According to a maid with her at the time of her death, the great couturier's last words were, "You see, this is how you die." We were interested in how she lived. Between those bookends—the humble beginning and the opulent ending—was a story that the legendary Mademoiselle, as she preferred to be called, created herself. Tilly's question was simple: Could one woman, whose life began seemingly at the moment another died, be the embodiment of that creative energy? Was it a simple question? Perhaps, but the answer was not.

Since the three of us were now committed to this one task (in addition to the one that still hung, unfinished, on our respective mannequins), Tilly had divided up the work. I was to unearth everything I could on the life of the original Chanel and this seemingly new version who stood before us every day—anything Tilly had not already discovered. Bella was tasked with researching reincarnation phenomena (I was the resident skeptic). Tilly would observe the current Mademoiselle's every movement, every gesture and every word. Each evening, the three of us would begin to put the pieces together like a giant jigsaw puzzle.

Like Bella, I had been a massive Chanel fan since I was young. I had recently read several books about the legend herself and had come away with mixed feelings—equal measures of awe and bewilderment. I was in awe of what this woman had accomplished in her life, and yet I was bewildered by the undercurrent of arrogance I felt in almost everything she had done or was reported to have said. I wondered about how such a sense of superiority had evolved. Then I remembered something else Coco Chanel had once said. "I don't care what you think about me. I don't think about you at all." And I realized that this is where I had to begin trying to see parallels between the legendary Chanel and Genevieve LaChapelle. It was now easy to find details of Mademoiselle Coco's life in the internet search engine age. The same could not be said about Mademoiselle Genevieve. Apart from her couture house website and the online information about her various other enterprises—one of which was her couturier classes—she was something of a ghost. I would start with Chanel, but that work had to be confined to the times when I wasn't in the atelier working on the reason I was here in the first place.

As we grew closer to finalizing our masterpieces, it was now time to choose trim details for the jackets. Before the course began, as part of my preparation, I'd scoured any online photos I could find of both authentic Chanel jackets—modern and vintage—and those jackets made by people like me. Along with the particular tweed fabric that was so iconic, the trim was a crucial part of recreating the aesthetic. In fact, without the Chanel-type trim on the jacket fronts and pockets, it was just another tweed jacket, so this selection was key. On Monday morning, Mademoiselle brought out her mobile haberdashery, as Max called it. It consisted of an old Louis Vuitton steamer trunk. It looked like it could have gone aboard any early twentieth-century steamship crossing the Atlantic between London to New York.

The trunk stood almost five feet high, opening to reveal two deep sides with drawers. A lady travelling in first class would have needed many changes of clothes, with each different outfit requiring its own accessories. These drawers would have contained those accessories. Today, they held haberdashery items—ribbons, braids, buttons, silk threads, and other small items. The braids and ribbons were a veritable treasure trove.

I watched as my classmates made their selections—red braid for Ronald's jacket, black braid and blue fringe for Abigail, silver and black braid for Bella, and Tilly chose black trim for her lemon-yellow jacket. When my turn came, I looked at my black almost-finished jacket and chose black ribbon and braid and silver buttons. It occurred to me that it might look unquestionably funereal to some people, but I loved it. As I selected my materials, Mademoiselle came up behind me and whispered, "When I find a colour darker than black, I'll wear it. Until then, I'm wearing black." Coco had said that first. At least I was in good company.

After a full day of placing tiny hand-worked stitches to affix the ribbon to the jacket and the braid to the ribbon, it was almost relaxing for Tilly, Bella and me to come together on the back patio to work in silence on our laptops for a while and then talk about what we had found.

I discovered that Coco Chanel had spent her life trying to hide the fact that after her mother died when she was eleven, her father had abandoned Coco and her sister to the care of nuns in a convent. This situation may seem like a tragedy as we look back from our vantage point in the twenty-first century, but it was in that convent that the teenage Gabrielle Chanel learned to sew. She began working as a seamstress when she was eighteen while at the same time discovering cabaret. She spent her days toiling away as a seamstress and her evenings in a different world, the centre of attention on stage—singing in a cabaret.

Several of her memorable songs ("Ko Ko Ri Ko" and "Qui qu'a vu Coco dans l'Trocadéro" to be precise) had the name Coco in them. So Gabrielle became Coco—although competing evidence suggested her father might have given her the nickname. It might also have been that "Coco" was a shortened version of the term coquette, which refers to a kept woman, and no one could argue that Coco had been supported by several wealthy lovers during her life. If the shoe fits? An affluent lover financed her first foray into business—a millinery shop where she created one-of-a-kind hats for discerning socialites. Those were the early years. And what of our new Mademoiselle, Genevieve LaChapelle? Where had she begun her life?

The biography on her website vaguely referred to a Parisian upbringing and entrée into the world of fashion at age eighteen or so as a seamstress in a lesser-known fashion house, possibly in Milan. No one seemed to know for sure. Details were few and far between, and the Wikipedia entry on our Mademoiselle was riddled with notations that the content needed citations. Who had made up all these stories?

As I surfed through one fashion blog after another, each writing vague stories about Genevieve LaChapelle, I concluded that I was not the first person to wonder about her provenance. A couple of themes emerged. Several bloggers over the past few years had wondered why we didn't know more about Genevieve's upbringing in these days of too much information. It seemed that she had appeared fully formed at age eighteen. Where had she been for the previous eighteen years?

As I sat at the dining table with my laptop open in front of me on Tuesday evening of the second week of the course, I began to wonder if perhaps Genevieve, too, had spent her formative years in a convent. After all, her villa, like Coco's before her, was designed to look like nothing less than a posh convent. But that couldn't be true. Could it?

"How goes the online search?" Tilly sat down beside me, placed her open laptop on the table in front of her and started clicking.

"I think we're chasing a ghost," I said. "Genevieve LaChapelle doesn't seem to exist before the age of eighteen."

"Not a ghost at all, Charlie darling. We're chasing a soul."

I rolled my eyes. I wasn't buying into the reincarnation narrative. I was beginning to think Genevieve LaChapelle had taken a leaf from Coco Chanel's book and ignored her real past. I just wasn't sure how anyone got away with that in these days of so much interconnectedness. "Tilly, you cannot seriously think that anyone is housing a soul that once belonged to someone else?" I wasn't even sure I believed in the concept of a soul.

"Wouldn't you like to think your late husband's soul might somehow return to you?"

I could hardly express how alarming that sounded to me. "No, Tilly, I would not want Tom's soul to be reincarnated in someone else—or worse, something else. And I can't think of anything I'd like less for myself."

"I don't think people are supposed to come back as other things, only other people," Bella said as she joined us. She placed her laptop on the dining table across from me, and we all sat there like an office group having a meeting. "I've been doing some research like you asked me to do, and I've learned a lot about this idea of reincarnation." Bella clicked a few keys. "I'd heard about it, but I'd never really thought about it much before, and I have to say I didn't know half of this stuff," she said. "I thought it was kind of a religious thing, but it's more of a philosophy of life."

"Or, more to the point, death? The problem for me," I said, "is that Tilly is basing her absurd idea on one simple coincidence: Genevieve was born the day Coco Chanel died—or at least that's what she claims. There's no impartial corroboration of that either."

"Tut-tut, my dear Charlie," Tilly said. "Are you telling me that you're one of those people who put everything they cannot explain off to coincidence? Do you not believe in synchronicity?"

"Oh, I do," Bella said excitedly.

"I'm not sure I even understand the concept," I said.

"Here," Bella said, clicking a few keys on her laptop. "Here's a definition: 'the simultaneous occurrence of events which appear significantly related but have no discernible causal connection.' That's the definition right here on Google."

"No discernible causal connection," I said. "There you have it."

"Ah, Charlie, the connection may be indiscernible to you, but that doesn't mean there isn't one. It only means you cannot see it," Tilly said. "We just have to find it."

Bella nodded while I rolled my eyes again. "Charlie," Bella said. "Do you know who coined the term synchronicity?"

"Some pop psychologist from the 1960s who was on LSD at the time?"

"Nope. It was none other than Carl Jung. He talked a lot about meaningful coincidences. I guess it's just a matter of finding that meaning."

That bit of information did surprise me. "Well," I said, "Tilly's contention that the meaning of the coincidence is that Genevieve is a reincarnation of Coco is still too far-fetched. Having said that, I am very interested in Genevieve LaChapelle and how she became who she is today."

"That's a start," Tilly said, reaching for a notebook she'd placed beside her laptop on the table. "I've been observing our Mademoiselle and have noted a few things." She opened the notebook and began reading. "Genevieve LaChapelle bears a striking resemblance to Coco Chanel—with that, you cannot argue." She looked pointedly at me. "She also seems to channel the Chanel aesthetic." I was thinking that millions of women probably do the same. Tilly continued. "She seems to talk like Chanel. You have heard the various things she says."

I was getting a bit exasperated. "Tilly, you know very well that any of us could research Chanel's famous quotes and expressions and learn to mimic the things she said."

Tilly shook her head. "If it were not for the fact that we probably need a skeptic here to play devil's advocate, I'd have to say you were not the best person to assist in this search for the truth."

"Sorry, Tilly. I really do want to help."

"Of course. Now, Bella, what does one need to know about a person to confirm the existence of a reincarnated soul? If we could figure that out, it would be our ticket to proving the meaning of the so-called coincidence."

"I found a couple of online sources that give us a list of things. First is that someone left the earth before their time."

"Cross that one off the list," I said. "Chanel was eighty-seven when she died."

Bella nodded. "And I think the dying-befor-their-time thing has more to do with the reincarnation of someone you actually knew when they were alive. But there are more things on the list. The second one is language like Tilly said about the similarities between the two. Then there's the thing about mannerisms."

"Oh, yes," Tilly said, her excitement mounting. "I looked at several videos of interviews Coco gave in her later years. One was from 1959, where she stands in her office, smoking a cigarette while answering the off-screen interviewer's questions. The way she moves her head for emphasis and waves her hand—they are so like Mademoiselle LaChapelle. Except for the cigarette always between Coco's fingers, they could be one and the same person. They even use their pockets the same way."

Bella continued reading from her screen. "They have the same eyes and physical characteristics." Tilly nodded as Bella continued. "It also says that more than one person senses it. We sort of do, don't we?"

Tilly cleared her throat. "As it turns out, I asked Maxence if he'd ever thought about this connection. He said he thought she was Coco reincarnated the first moment he met her in person. So, we are not alone in our conclusion."

"It's not a conclusion yet, Tilly." I was adamant we should keep at least one foot grounded to the floor while Tilly explored her idea.

"And in case you're wondering," Tilly said, "I did not tell the dear boy we were looking into this possibility." She stared at me. "And neither *should* we."

Sin

"Sin can be forgiven, but stupid is forever."
~ Gabriel "Coco" Chanel

THE CONCEPT OF SIN IS AN INTERESTING ONE, isn't it? If you look it up, you'll find chapter and verse (literally) on how the various religions define sin. In fact, the definition of sin says something about the transgression of divine law—whatever that is. But we use the word in many different ways that have nothing at all to do with religion.

"What a sin," someone might say as another way of saying, "Too bad."

Other people think it's the same thing as a goof, a blunder, a misdeed, a mistake—all of which don't come close to the actual definition. As I researched Gabriel Chanel further, trying to find parallels between her life and Genevieve LaChapelle's life, I became increasingly troubled. Although I had fallen in love with the Chanel aesthetic as I grew up, I was falling progressively more out of love with the person behind the label. And I thought, *If Tilly is right (if that's even possible), and Genevieve is some kind of embodiment of Chanel's soul (?), then is she also the embodiment of the sins committed by the original legend?* Quite apart from the arrogance I was beginning to believe was Chanel's foundational relationship with everyone around her, I was starting to see her as someone who might not have been the sort of person I'd want to have in my circle of friends.

The more I read about Chanel, the woman, the more I realized she had to have felt inferior in some ways because of her background. That's the only reason I could think of to explain why she seemed never to care what she said about anyone or how it made them feel. According to an American newspaper article from 1967, Chanel once said about Jackie Kennedy, "She has horrible taste, and she's responsible for spreading it all over America . . . She's trying to look like her own daughter." This is about a woman wearing an American-made, authorized version of a pink bouclé Chanel suit as she cradled her dead husband's head in the back seat of an open car one November day in Dallas, Texas.

She also once opined that Bridgette Bardot's bust was "too much." I suppose there were others who agreed with her, but it seems only the great Mademoiselle dared to say it! She called miniskirts "an exhibition of meat" and declared that she didn't know any men who would like such a display. But it does have to be said that she lived by her own rules—and in my book, that's not such a bad thing.

I wondered if this might be the same for Genevieve LaChapelle. I wondered if her background, which seemed to have been wiped out of modern history, represented the same things as Chanel's—poverty, lack of family connection, a detached upbringing. But I couldn't find anything. And there were other things about Chanel that struck me as distasteful.

First, she was anti-Semitic. Of course, we always get into trouble if we try to judge people in history by current standards—how can we know what really happened? But it appeared that she tried to use her Nazi connections (and she had many) and its Aryan teachings to push her Jewish business partners out of the business they had legitimately bought from her at the start of the war. Did Genevieve LaChapelle have such things in her past that she knew would be even less tolerated in the twenty-first century? Is that why she suppressed so much about her early life and even her more recent personal life? I had no idea.

I would have to leave it up to Tilly for more information about our Mademoiselle, information I was keen to learn. I just wasn't sure why I was so fascinated by it all.

~

It was dinner at Mademoiselle's villa on Tuesday evening when I first got a glimpse of who Mademoiselle might really be. There was a guest at dinner that evening.

When we arrived for dinner that was scheduled to begin at eight pm, I was thinking—yet again—that I would never get used to the Spanish tradition of starting dinner so late. Truth be told, though, even eight pm was early by Spanish standards. I was just grateful I didn't have to wait until ten to eat! As we entered the drawing room for the usual aperitif before taking our seats in the dining room, Mademoiselle was deep in conversation with an older, well-dressed gentleman. Was that a smile I saw as she listened to him? And a laugh? I couldn't remember seeing Mademoiselle so much as smirk before this. I wondered who he was.

Tilly offered me one of the two glasses of vermouth she had just swiped from the drinks table. "Who do you suppose he is?" she whispered. "Whoever he is, he adds yet another layer of mystery to our Mademoiselle, *n'est ce pas?*"

"He does seem to bring out a different side of our Genevieve LaChapelle."

"Don't you think he looks rather aristocratic?" Tilly said, sipping daintily from the tiny glass.

"I suppose so—if there is an aristocratic look. Is there such a thing?"

"Dear Charlie, of course, there is an aristocratic look. I'm British, after all. We have a lengthy history of observing the upper crust. Let us decipher his patrician air, shall we?"

I nodded, taking a closer look at the man. First, he had a full head of silver hair, impeccably cut yet slightly dishevelled, as if saying that he cared for appearances—but not too much.

When I mentioned my conclusion to Tilly, she said, "Bravo, my dear. I will put that on the list. Now then, let us continue our examination. First, he is tall and appears to be very fit for his age, which I consider to be about sixty years."

"Are all aristocrats tall and fit?" I said, thinking about members of the British royal family. "How tall is your King Charles?"

"I believe he tops out at five feet ten inches or so," she said, "but let's leave out the British crew, shall we? They are a whole other kettle of fish, so to speak. In any event, this one certainly does not look British."

I had to agree with Tilly on that count. The white silk scarf tied artfully around his neck was a dead giveaway. Even on this scorching evening, this man was still wearing a scarf which I watched Mademoiselle touch lightly as she spoke to him.

Tilly continued. "His polo shirt is Lacoste if my eyes do not deceive me—I believe I see that tiny alligator on the left breast—and I noted that the trousers hang expensively."

"And those shoes," I said. "They're outstanding." The shoes were blue suede and looked like they sported a Gucci logo on the front. I was starting to enjoy this little game helping Tilly use her journalistic sensibility to figure out a story.

"They are indeed, but as interesting as all that makes him, he could just be an aging Lothario with bags of money, basking in Mademoiselle's glow of celebrity, couldn't he? And yet, I do not believe he is." Tilly finished her vermouth and took a step back toward the drinks table to reach for another. "It is all about his presence—how he holds himself."

"As if he were the most important person in the room?"

"Without a doubt," Tilly said, "and yet, I wonder how that makes our Mademoiselle feel."

We could ponder no longer. Mademoiselle was pulling away from the gentleman as Max announced that dinner was served.

As I entered the dining room with my classmates, I noticed an extra chair had been added beside Mademoiselle. Before we sat down, Mademoiselle indicated that she had someone to introduce. "Ladies and gentlemen, I would like to introduce to you my dear friend Jacques de Luc, Duc de l'Oiseau."

As Tilly leaned toward me, poked my shoulder and whispered, "What did I tell you? The plot thickens."

As we progressed through the starter and onto the main course, then to the salad and cheese—a nod to the French approach to having salad after the main course—then onto dessert, I watched the "Duc" as he chatted with Mademoiselle. I looked around at my classmates, who seemed to be enjoying their dessert of *tarte tatin*. She didn't see me looking, but I noticed Bella, who had yet to touch her dessert, slide her phone onto the table under the edge of her plate to keep it out of Mademoiselle's sight line. Then I noticed her tapping it as if itching to take a photo for her adoring followers. A French duke would no doubt add to her considerable reputation—and despite what I now knew about the real Bella, she was still, after all, a current influencer. Her problem, as I saw it, was that he was sitting right beside her, and unless she asked him for a selfie (which could conceivably happen), there was no way for her to take a photo.

I then turned my attention from Bella to Ronald. I watched him as he painfully tried to say something—anything, I presumed—to his hostess and to the duke. Whenever I had noticed Ronald since the beginning of the course, he always seemed to be trying to say something to someone without much success. He seemed so shy that I almost felt sorry for him. He glanced over as if he could feel me looking at him, and I smiled. He looked away quickly.

Then I looked across the table at Abigail, who seemed to be staring at me. The moment I looked at her, though, she averted her eyes. *Well, maybe I should try to get to know you*, I thought.

"So, Abigail," I said, trying to start a conversation with the terminally sour Texan, "what's Texas like?"

"Big," she said.

Okay. Canada is big, I thought. *But there seems little point in getting into an argument about which is bigger. Perhaps another foray might work.* "What's the weather like?" I said.

"Hot in the summer. Cold in the winter." Abigail stabbed her fork at the pastry on her plate and put a large chunk in her mouth.

Well, this was going well. Another direction, perhaps? "Isn't it interesting to meet a French duke?"

Abigail put her fork down and stopped chewing as she glared at the duke and Mademoiselle Genevieve before answering. "What a pile of horse manure that is. A duke. And if you believe that, I've got a swamp I'm willing to sell you."

I looked down the table toward the duke. "So, you think he's a sham?"

"Everything's a sham, Charlie. You just don't see it."

Was there something Abigail knew that I didn't? "So, what kind of work do you do, Abigail?"

Abigail stared at me. "Well, I suppose you think I don't know what kind of work you do. As a matter of fact, I do know, Ms. CK Hudson."

There was really no good reason why everyone here at the table couldn't know that I was a bestselling writer, but I could feel my face redden anyway. I felt like I'd been caught in a lie, but there had been no such thing. No one had asked. But Abigail had not answered my question.

"Guilty as charged," I said before redirecting the conversation. "And you? What kind of work do you do?"

Before she could answer, I heard Tilly's voice, loud enough to interrupt anyone else's conversation. "Tell me, *Monsieur le duc.* I find it fascinating that there are still dukes in France. I had no idea. How can that be in such a proud republic? Wasn't it Napoleon who first rid your country of the nobility, effectively stripping them of all their privileges? And yet, here you are."

The duke patted his lips with his napkin, lifted his crystal wine glass for a delicate sip, replaced it on the table and peered at Tilly. "In fact, it was the Third Republic which began in 1870, that decreed the status and privileges were no longer legally protected. But, my dear woman, it would be a grave mistake to assume that *la noblesse* no longer exists in France. *Bien sûr*, we believe there are more French aristocrats today than even before the revolution."

"I don't see how that could be possible, sir," Tilly said as Mademoiselle glared at her.

"Ah, but because you cannot see something does not mean it is not the case, Madame." The duke placed his elbows on the table, clasped his hands together, and leaned toward Tilly. Ronald moved ever so slightly back as if to get out of the line of fire—because I could see the duke gearing up to fire. "Madame, I can hear the sound of the English monarchy in your accent, so you are most aware of a history rich in nobility. It is nobility that adds that *je ne sais quoi* to a society, is it not? What would England be without its King and princes?"

"It would be a republic, sir," Tilly said.

"Ah, yes," the duke continued, "but it would be devoid of that layer of elegance. And it is this sophistication that cannot be acquired but through lineage."

"What rubbish!" Tilly said.

"I believe we must leave the duke to his dinner," Mademoiselle interjected. "This does not seem proper conversation for the dinner table."

The duke placed his hand on her arm. "I do believe, Genevieve, that this is exactly the conversation we need to be having at this moment in time. There are so many things the uninitiated cannot understand." Mademoiselle nodded her head almost imperceptibly. He removed his hand from her arm and sat back, looking around the table. "You, Madame," said, staring at Tilly, "have little regard for the kind of graciousness and civility that is lent to a society that reveres its aristocracy." Tilly rolled her eyes as he moved his gaze along the table, finally resting it on Abigail. "And you, Madame, you are an American, are you not?"

Abigail said nothing, barely acknowledging that he was speaking directly to her.

"You and this lovely young woman," he nodded slightly toward Bella, "have not had the advantages of knowing real civility, so I can hardly blame you for being skeptical, unlike Madame Tilly over here, who should know better. All you Americans have is an imitation *élite*, carved from the detritus of film and what passes for music these days."

I was sitting quietly, hoping he had little to say about Canadians.

"And so, *Monsieur le duc*, notwithstanding your clearly prejudiced notions of other cultures, I return to my original question. How can there still be what you call *la noblesse* in a country like France? What gives you the right to call yourself a duke?"

"I will tell you what gives me the right, Madame. To begin, there are, as I mentioned, more members of the aristocracy in France today than there were at the end of the revolution."

"That, despite the guillotine, I suppose you could say?" Tilly said, her voice dripping with sarcasm.

The duke nodded and continued. "There is an organization today called Association d'entraide de la noblesse française, or as you would call it, the Association for Mutual Help of the French Nobility, for which I am a director. There is a quaint story as to the origins of the organization. It is told that in the 1930s, two French nobles were travelling from a train station in Paris when they noted with some horror that the porter who had offered to assist them with their luggage was a fallen aristocrat himself. They undertook at that moment to assist their distressed brethren. From that day, this has been our mission to find and help our fellow nobles."

"And how does one know if one is a French noble these days?" Tilly said.

"We have criteria," the duke said. "There is a certification process, and there must be proof of lineage."

"But they still have no legal rights and privileges in France, so what difference does it make?" Tilly was making a few notes in the little blue notebook she carried everywhere.

I was suddenly worried that someone might ask her what the notebook was about, but everyone seemed more interested in the duke's response than what Tilly might or might not be doing.

The duke looked at her as if he were looking at a silly child. "My dear, Madame, you miss the point entirely. True nobility need not have legal rights and privileges given by a republic, as you suggest, to know who they are. It is god-given. When one is of the noble class, one knows, and that is enough."

"Wouldn't be enough for me," Abigail muttered into her napkin just loudly enough for me to hear.

~

"I wonder if he might just be our Mademoiselle's Duke of Westminster," Tilly said later as we walked home in the dark under the palm trees waving in the gentle breeze.

"Who is?" Bella said.

"That Jacques de Luc, Duc de l'Oiseau fellow," Tilly said, her nose twitching. "Chanel had her royal lovers, and perhaps Genevieve LaChapelle has hers. It does support our theory."

My first thought was to say, "*Your* theory," but I thought better of it and stayed silent.

"Oh, that *is* interesting," Bella said.

Tilly was referring to Coco Chanel's propensity to develop liaisons with rich and powerful men—or at least men she viewed that way. In his day, the Duke of Westminster had been one of the wealthiest men in the world. According to what I'd read, Chanel had met him at a dinner in Monaco—as one might expect—the playground of the rich and famous, as the two of them represented. The duke had been married when their affair began in the early 1920s.

"I wonder if he gave her the property here to build that villa," Tilly said. "That would be more than coincidental, wouldn't it, Charlie?"

Tilly was referring to the fact that Chanel's duke had given her the parcel of land in Roquebrune-Cap-Martin, the tiny French municipality that borders Monaco at its east end where she had built her villa, whose design our Mademoiselle had used to have her villa built here in Mallorca.

As we reached the gate to our villa, Bella started to put her key in the lock, then turned to us and said, "Do you think past lives are the same as reincarnation?"

"Whatever are you talking about, dear girl?" Tilly said as we walked through the gate, and I unlocked the front door.

Bella put her tiny Chanel handbag on the chest by the door and kicked off her Louboutins. "Well, it seems to me there might be more to it than the idea that someone is the simple reincarnation of another person. Have you ever met someone you thought you'd met before but know it isn't possible?"

"Whatever are you getting at?" Tilly said as she went into the kitchen to retrieve wine glasses.

My first thought was that I probably didn't need any more wine because all I could think about was that the future of a past life *would* be a reincarnation. Wouldn't it? My head was beginning to hurt.

"Well," Bella said, taking the offered wine glass and heading out to the back porch by the pool, "maybe it's not so much that one person is the reincarnation of another one but that two souls get to meet again in another life—in another place and time. Maybe Mademoiselle and the duke knew each other in a past life."

"What would make you think that, Bella?" I said, sitting down at the outside dining table.

"Maybe I'm just a romantic," Bella said, "but when they were talking before dinner, I was watching Mademoiselle and the duke. She was so different with him, as if they had some kind of deep connection from something more than the way we see them on the surface. I suppose that doesn't make a lot of sense. I don't know. I sometimes think I might have lived back in the 1920s or 1930s and had a wonderful lover I might meet again in this lifetime."

"You really are a bit of a romantic, Bella," I said.

Tilly drained her wine glass. "All I know is that whatever is going on with Mademoiselle Genevieve LaChapelle in all its true strangeness, I will find it."

I didn't doubt that for a minute.

Adornment

"Adornment is never anything but the reflection of the heart."
~ Gabrielle "Coco" Chanel

OUR JACKETS WERE FINALLY FINISHED. It was the last day of the course, and I was excited to reveal my creation to my classmates. Today's schedule included a discussion of our jackets and a photo session with Mademoiselle's photographer. Bella had also asked us if we'd pose for her so she could post our creations on her Instagram feed. All of us except Abigail had agreed.

"Such a cow," Tilly had proclaimed when Abigail refused Bella's Thursday afternoon request.

Tilly was already there when I emerged from my room for breakfast that Friday morning. She was sitting at the dining room table with a pot of tea in front of her, madly clicking away at the keys. When I asked her how she was, she told me she was writing a draft of her article.

"I thought you were writing a book," I said, stabbing at the on-switch of the espresso machine. "Anyway, are you sure there's even a story here?"

"By god, there will be a story," she said. "And yes, there will be a book, but first, I'm writing a magazine article as a teaser, then there may even be more articles for more publications if I read this situation correctly. I have this one all drafted, and at this evening's final dinner, we're going to get to the bottom of our mysterious Mademoiselle's life story. Whether or not she has a connection to Chanel, there's a story here, and I'm going to uncover it."

I wasn't sure this was how I wanted my three-week adventure to end, but I had no choice. I still had a dilemma of my own to deal with. A single rose had arrived every Monday through

Thursday since I'd been here, and I hadn't yet dared to ask Marco about it. I considered just leaving it alone and going home without a backward glance, but that didn't seem right. It appeared that it was something I was supposed to deal with, and maybe I'd even learn something from doing it. I could almost hear Tom's voice whispering in my ear, telling me to be sure to tie up my loose ends. He had always said I'd trip over my loose ends.

~

I walked into the atelier that morning with mixed feelings. It had been among the most unusual three weeks of my life, but at least I'd learned to make a Little French Jacket in homage to the great Chanel. I sat at my work table beside my mannequin and stared at my creation, assessing what I'd accomplished.

The collarless jacket was black bouclé with black trim and a black and silver printed silk charmeuse lining. I had tried to use black on black silk, but Mademoiselle had vetoed that idea, proclaiming that combination too funereal. I suppose she was right, but then again…

The jacket had a four-button front closure (each with a hand-stitched buttonhole that very nearly killed me) and four pockets, each adorned with the same trim as the front, neck and hem of the jacket. The buttons down the front were antiqued silver, resembling the ones on the online picture of the vintage jacket I had tried to recreate. Then there was the silver chain running along the hemline that I'd painstakingly hand-stitched into the jacket. It was a signature Chanel addition designed to help it to hang perfectly. But most importantly, it fit me like a glove—like it had been made for me, which, of course, it had. To my great surprise and a bit of trepidation, Mademoiselle began with me that morning.

"Charlotte," she said, "please put on your jacket and come to the window."

Beside the window, the photographer had set up a white background where we were to stand for the pictures.

I put the jacket on and at once felt connected to the past. I thought about the movie *Somewhere in Time,* where the Christopher Reeve character, who had fallen in love with the image of the beautiful actress from a century earlier, puts on his vintage jacket and pants, places his pocket watch in his front pocket and follows the old professor's instructions about how to transport himself back in time. I was suddenly back on a runway from the 1950s when Chanel first created this jacket. I was somewhere in time—just not *this* time. I had never felt this way before and instantly thought about great-grandmother Frannie's dresses. She had left me a rail of vintage designer dresses I'd examined and cared for, but I'd never tried them on. Why had I never put even one of them on? It was the first thing I'd do when I arrived back home.

"How do you feel, Charlotte?" Mademoiselle Genevieve interrupted my reverie.

I looked at her, then glanced at myself in the three-way mirror beside the photo set. How did I feel? I considered my reflection for a moment, then said, "Divine, Mademoiselle. It's so hard to believe that a jacket first designed more than six decades ago can still look so—fresh. It's astonishing."

She nodded knowingly. "It is indeed astonishing, Charlotte, but you must remember what Mademoiselle Chanel herself once said. Chanel is above style. As we have noted, fashion may pass, but style remains. Style, my dear, comes from within you and endures through the vagaries of the fashion industry. We would all be wise to remember that fashion is a fleetingly exterior manifestation of someone else's idea of who you are. Chanel understood how her pieces could make each of us feel that they are our own." She then waved for the photographer to begin. When he finished with me, it was Bella's turn.

Bella's jacket was a grey and white tweed with grey and black trim. It clung to her young figure just as I imagined Chanel expected her jackets to fit—slightly raised waist, high armholes, hanging perfectly. Bella, who was so much more experienced at being in front of the camera, immediately began posing for the photographer.

"And you, Mademoiselle Bella, how do you feel?" Mademoiselle Genevieve stood close to the edge of the photo set-up, her arms crossed over her five long strands of pearls. She was eyeing Bella critically, as was her usual stance when confronted with one of our pieces over the past weeks.

Bella stared at herself in the mirror, turning to see one side and then the other. Then she turned back on and craned her neck to see the back. Finally, she stood there silently for a moment before speaking. "You know, Mademoiselle, I think I feel grown up— like I've found myself somehow." She then whipped out her phone and started to take selfies in the mirror. Suddenly, she stopped and put her phone back in the tiny pocket that was just big enough to hold it. "I don't think I need that right now," she said, staring at herself.

Mademoiselle walked over toward Bella and circled her, staring at the jacket. "Bella, dear, you have spent much of your young lifetime becoming a commodity, but you will notice how many cares one loses when one decides not to be something but to be someone."

Bella looked at Mademoiselle, wide-eyed, as Tilly leaned over from her worktable toward me and whispered, "I'm sure Chanel said that first."

As if she might have heard her, Mademoiselle turned toward Tilly. "Madame Tilly, please." She gestured Tilly toward the photo set.

I watched Tilly as she self-consciously walked over to the photo spot. She had told me earlier that she hated having her photo taken professionally. She considered all that posing to be a bit too inauthentic. She might have had a point.

Tilly's jacket was, again, collarless, like a Chanel jacket of that design would always be, but hers was open down the front with no closures. She had made it in yellow tweed that had what you might call eyelashes all over it. It was a bit fuzzy. Instead of full-length sleeves like the jackets the rest of us had made, hers were three-quarter length. The yellow was trimmed with black braid. All in all, it was a curious combination—oddly attractive.

Tilly stood awkwardly in front of the large mirror.

"How does this jacket make you feel, Tilly?" Mademoiselle said as she walked around Tilly.

For once in her life, Tilly seemed to be at a loss for words. I had to admit that when I'd first seen the yellow fabric Tilly had chosen, I wondered why on earth she had chosen it. But now, as I looked at it, together, the colour and the style seemed to have created an aura about her. She looked slightly classier, perhaps even elegant, an adjective I would never have applied to Tilly when I first met her.

"I don't know," she said. "I suppose I feel a bit chic." She stared intensely at her image in the mirror. "I thought the colour would be a bit of a lark, you know, a bit of fun, but it seems to— lift me up. I thought you had to wear black to look chic and stylish these days." Tilly glanced over toward me.

"Indeed," Mademoiselle said. "One must consider how much one's clothing can affect one's demeanour. Perhaps it might even affect one's point of view?" Tilly looked at her, and I could almost see the wheels turning round and round in her head. Mademoiselle continued. "In any event, the best colour in the world is the one that looks best on you."

Tilly looked up from where she had been staring at her jacket. "Chanel?"

"But of course." Mademoiselle almost laughed. Almost.

When Tilly finished her awkward posing, it was Ronald's turn.

Ronald's jacket, of course, was not for him. He had made it to fit the mannequin he told us was made to fit his wife's measurements. When I first saw the mannequin, I concluded that his wife must be shaped somewhat like a box, not unlike Ronald himself, I now noted. Ronald had chosen a pink and red tweed and trimmed it with red braid in a fashion that looked slightly military. I wondered what his wife would think and how it would look on her.

He pushed his wheeled mannequin over to where the photographer could capture it.

"Well, Ronald, how do you feel now that you have overcome obstacles in completing your jacket?"

Ronald had suffered through much of the creation process. I had expected his sewing skills to be top-notch—it was an assumption based on my prejudice about why a man might attend this course and that Mademoiselle had mentioned that he created bespoke lingerie. I expected him to be terrific—he wasn't. More than once, I had wondered if his wife had insisted he take the class because she wanted the jacket. When Mademoiselle asked Ronald how he felt, I was taken aback by his response. He began crying.

"Blimey," he said, "it's awful. So many mistakes I had to correct. So many that had to be left."

From where I was sitting, the mistakes weren't visible.

"Ronald," Mademoiselle said almost soothingly, "strength is built by one's failures, not by one's successes."

I had heard that one before—and I knew it was a Chanelism. Ronald seemed heartened by it.

When Ronald's photos were completed, Mademoiselle turned to Abigail, who was slumped at her worktable beside her mannequin. "Abigail, please put on your jacket."

Of all of us, Abigail seemed the least interested in actually wearing the jacket—even less than Tilly had been. She had every appearance of reluctance as she did as Mademoiselle had directed. But when she put on the jacket, a blue tweed with fringed blue and black trim and long sleeves, each adorned with three antique silver buttons, her stout Texan figure was transformed. She was suddenly fashionable, almost refined.

"What do you think?" Mademoiselle asked.

The writer in me noticed that Mademoiselle had asked all the rest of us how we *felt,* but she had asked Abigail what she *thought.* A minor point, perhaps, but it seemed meaningful to me.

Abigail shrugged. "Don't quite know what I should think."

"I did not ask you what you *should* think. I asked what you *do* think."

"I think it's kind of weird, all of us here making an expensive jacket just to be like some dead French seamstress."

"I had hoped you might change your mind about this process—and about me—over the past three weeks. Perhaps that was too much to hope for."

"No words of wisdom for me, Mademoiselle Genevieve LaChapelle?" Abigail said as I continued to wonder why she was even here.

"Not yet, Madame Abigail Murdock, but expect something valuable for you by this evening's dinner." Mademoiselle then turned to look at each of us. "Thank you for these three weeks. I shall see you all at our final dinner this evening. Until then, *à bientôt.*"

Truth

"I invented my life by taking for granted that everything I did not
like would have an opposite, which I would like."
~ Gabriel "Coco" Chanel

I KNEW I HAD TO SPEAK TO MARCO before our final dinner. When I ran into him earlier in the day, he mentioned he'd be over to our villa at about six pm to check on our departure plans. Once back at the villa, Bella looked at me closely and said, "You haven't spoken to Marco yet, have you?"

I shook my head.

Tilly chimed in. "I don't suppose it truly matters in the grand scheme of things, but do you really want to let this go without seeing what it truly means? I mean, Charlie, darling, you're an attractive, fairly young widow. You have a whole life ahead of you."

"I can't get involved with a young man on a distant Spanish island."

"Didn't you hear Marco when he told us last week that he spends a lot of his time in Paris working for Mademoiselle there?" Bella said.

"And furthermore," Tilly said, "didn't you mention that you actually own an apartment in Paris? I mean, truly, who owns a Paris apartment without wanting a young lover in her bed once in a while?"

I could feel my face reddening—and not because this was a distant thought, but because it was something I'd thought about more than once over the past few weeks. You might call it a fantasy, but I'd been thinking about what Marco might be like. And yes, I did remember him saying he spent a lot of his time in Paris.

My face was still burning when I said, "Okay, I give up. I'll speak to Marco when he comes over before dinner, but you both have to promise me you won't be in the room—and you won't be eavesdropping."

Tilly smiled and made a small cross over her heart.

Bella said, "Of course, Charlie. You've kept my secret these weeks. Anyway, I'll be rooting for you!"

I rolled my eyes.

~

I had almost finished dressing for dinner by the time Marco arrived. I had dressed very carefully this evening because it was the last dinner. Who was I kidding? I dressed carefully for Marco. I peeked out of my room when I heard Bella let him in the front door.

"Damn it!" I said to myself, closing the door abruptly. Max was with him. I opened the door a crack and called to Bella.

Bella immediately came over. "Hey, Charlie, are you ready? Marco's here."

"I know, Bella. But so is Max. Now I can't talk to Marco," I whispered.

"Not to worry. I'll ask Max to come out by the pool and take a few pictures with me. He's a sucker for my Instagram stuff. Did you know that he follows me?" Bella shook her head. "I'm beginning to wonder why so many people follow me, but that's going to make for a whole lot of great research one day when I'm a professor!"

Professor, maybe, but I had already predicted she'd be a bestselling writer someday, penning books about her time on Instagram.

"So, I'll take Max outside and tell Marco you'll be out with your itinerary so he can plan his trips to the airport. Just give me five seconds, then come out," she said, heading back into the living room.

I did as I was told. When I arrived in the living room, Marco was standing by the window watching Max out on the pool deck, posing with Bella. He was holding a single, long-stemmed red rose.

"Charlie, you look lovely this evening." He offered the rose to me. "I hope you have enjoyed my little offering over the past weeks. One last rose for a perfect lady."

"Marco, about that. About the roses."

He cocked his head slightly as if to ask me, what about the roses?

"Well, I'm not exactly sure what they mean."

A huge smile broke over his face, and he said, "Of course, Charlie. It is too subtle, perhaps." He took my hand, and I started to sweat. "Charlie, when I first met you, you mentioned you were a widow. I could see a deep sadness behind your eyes. It is a look that I have seen so often in my life." I had no idea where he was going with this and wasn't sure I wanted to know. He continued. "It is a look that my mother has borne for so long. She, too, became a widow when my much-loved father died at age forty-seven. It seemed so like your story. I wanted to ensure you had something to smile about each evening and considered the roses a sign that life will go on perhaps even better than before."

So, I reminded him of his mother. I could feel the red creeping up my face from my collarbone again. Was I to be perpetually embarrassed this evening?

Just then, Bella and Max came in from the pool deck as Tilly came downstairs.

"Charlie," Max said, smiling broadly, "Bella has just told me that you are the proud owner of an apartment on the Left Bank. This is something we did not know. How very wonderful!" He walked over toward Marco and put his arm around him. "We, too, have an apartment near the Sorbonne, Marco and I would love to have you join us for dinner when next you visit our fair city of light. It will be a most marvellous adventure!"

"Well, I had no idea," Tilly said as everyone turned toward her. "You and Marco are a couple. How bloody brilliant." She gave me a side eye—in support, I suppose.

Just when I thought I couldn't feel any more embarrassed, I did. Dear god, how could I have gotten it so wrong? On the other hand, I was off the hook.

~

Dinner was at the usual time, and we were at the same table in Mademoiselle's dining room. But there was something different in the air. Was it the rare vintage champagne she was serving? (I recognized the label because Tom had once bought us a bottle to celebrate an anniversary. I had considered it a splurge even for us with our ample finances.) Was it the candles that lit every corner and crevice of the dining room, giving it the aura of an old film noir? Or perhaps it was the hushed voices that this muted lighting seemed to demand. Whatever it was, it was clear to me that this evening's dinner would be different from the ones we'd experienced over the past few weeks. I just had no idea how different.

Mademoiselle's duke had left, so there were the five of us students, Mademoiselle and Max, who, once again, took up the table position nearest the door dividing his roles into both guest and staff.

We had finished our Kir Royales—a particular favourite of mine with its mixture of champagne and crème de cassis—this evening's special pre-dinner drinks and were now taking our seats in the dining room. Immediately, the server arrived with a pitcher of soup. At each place, there was a soup bowl, empty except for three large croutons. The server slowly poured the soup into each bowl. Once she had finished, Mademoiselle picked up her spoon, and we followed suit.

After a few sips of the exquisite tomato basil bisque, Tilly reached down below her seat to where I'd seen her place her large purse and retrieved a notebook, the same one I'd seen her madly jotting in for the past three weeks.

"Mademoiselle," she said, opening the cover and donning her red, rhinestone-studded reading glasses, "if I might. I'd like to ask you a question."

"*Bien sûr*, but of course." Mademoiselle placed her soup spoon on the side of the plate under the bowl, dabbed at her lips with the napkin and leaned toward Tilly.

"Mademoiselle LaChapelle, I've been curious about your background, as you can imagine one might be before embarking on such a course. I have found, deeply buried in the internet archives of the first couture house where you sewed in Paris, a reference to the new hire, Genevieve LaChapelle, who came highly recommended by a reclusive couturier in Milan." Mademoiselle began to speak, but Tilly silenced her by raising her hand. "I would like to finish if I might." Mademoiselle sat back and looked at Tilly, her face a mask of indifference. "The recommendation evidently suggested that young Genevieve had been raised in Paris, educated at the Institut Français de la Mode, and then worked in Milan for several years, learning at the feet of the designer." This information was all news to me but must have been the material Tilly had found and been madly writing about earlier. I wondered why she hadn't shared it with me.

"*Félicitations*, Madame Tilly." Mademoiselle did a gentle, slow clap. "My sincerest congratulations for having discovered my history. These facts do not appear to be a question as you had suggested you might have for me."

"Facts, yes, of course. I'm getting to it," Tilly said as she peered down at her notes through the half glasses. "There is a problem with these facts—with this history, Mademoiselle. There is no record of your attendance at Institut Français de la Mode in Paris, and no one in Milan has ever heard of you. How is this possible?"

"Ah, you have been doing your research," Mademoiselle said. "You believe you have uncovered something—how does one say in English—nefarious, perhaps? There is nothing nefarious at all."

All eyes were riveted on this conversation, the delicious soup abandoned to the juicy tidbits that seemed to have started flowing.

"Mademoiselle LaChapelle, you have no evidentiary history, no apparent history at all. You have no life before your couture house. If that is the case, then I believe you are intentionally hiding something. I believe you are, in a word, a fraud, plain and simple."

Mademoiselle nodded to Maxence to summon the server to clear. Before Mademoiselle could say a word, two young women servers appeared, cleared the bowls quickly and reappeared with the main course. I was so shocked by Tilly's allegation—at least she didn't suggest the reincarnation theory—I hardly noticed the beautiful serving of coq au vin that the server had just placed before me.

Mademoiselle picked up her knife and fork, took one bite of the beautifully fragranced chicken, closed her eyes as if savouring the moment, then put her cutlery down and turned to Tilly.

"I am the fraud? Do you think that it is I who is the fraud? I must beg to disagree very vehemently. It is not I, the fraud, but you." Mademoiselle looked around the table. "All of you. I have created no deception, nor have I elevated myself to anything that I am not. I am not the imposter here. I chose to walk through a door and create a life that suited me. I chose not to look back because that was not me. Who are we, in any case? We are only the story we have told ourselves and the world. Who is to say that my life, as I have created it, is not who I really am? Who are you to question this? There is not one among you here who is not a veritable fraud. You have each created a face to show to the world," she said, looking around at each of us. "Sometimes you even give yourself a label whose characteristics are dictated by others. You begin to tell yourself a story dictated by this label that has been created by others—living a story created by someone else makes one a fraud."

I began to think about how I had labelled myself a widow. Was I a fraud?

"Be very careful," she said, continuing, "to tell yourself a story that helps you to achieve your goal rather than one that hinders you. That is what makes one authentic."

Then I noticed our mannequins wearing our jackets lined up along the far wall. I hadn't noticed them before because they'd been in darkness. Mademoiselle had nodded once to Max, who had somehow turned on the lights—a remote control, perhaps? Again, I hadn't noticed. Soft light from overhead spotlights now bathed the jackets standing in a row like sentries protecting their provenance.

"You see these jackets?" Mademoiselle said, gesturing toward the mannequins. Everyone looked. "What do they represent? Like all clothing and personal adornment, they are costumes we put on ourselves to create an aura. That aura can be authentic, or it can be fraudulent. Indeed, one might conclude that each of you is fraudulent in attempting to wear your creations, hoping others will see them as the work of haute couture—created in a Chanel atelier. You know that this is a lie, and yet you persist. I have no problem with this when it is taken as it is. There are those among you who can well afford to purchase a true Chanel." Again, she looked at Bella and then at me. "Do not try to guess how I know, but you will be surprised to understand that I know a great deal about each of you. It is my way to know about my students before they arrive. And if you can afford the real Chanel, why are you here learning to make an imitation?"

My face flushed with embarrassment. I hoped no one else knew it was me about whom Mademoiselle was now speaking. Then I realized that she was probably including Bella.

"The process of making the jacket, though, is one that transcends the authentic versus inauthentic piece. It does this by taking the creator outside herself—or himself—and into the process of creation, knowing that every stitch added to this jacket is a piece of the creator's heart. And if the creator's heart can go into each stitch, then perhaps there will be room in that heart for authenticity. Perhaps it is time to walk through that door and close it behind you, leaving your label behind." She was looking at me.

Widow. That was my label.

Then Mademoiselle looked around the room further. "Then there are those among us who derive their living from creating that inauthentic face for the world." She nodded toward Bella.

"Also, there are those who live a life only because it makes it easier to exist in the world." She looked at Ronald. "I know that you are making this jacket for yourself, Ronald. Hiding your real self is the easy way. But it has been said that the only thing positive about the easy way is that it is easy. It does nothing to bring you to peace."

Mademoiselle then stood up and walked around the table, stopping where she could face Tilly directly. "Then there are those who accuse in the hope of benefiting from that accusation." I could see Tilly bristle. "I do know why you are here, Tilly, and equally important, who you are. You have come to uncover a story that you believe will advance your career at the expense of others. Even at that, I needed to have you among us so that you could see that there is a fine line between what is authentic and what is not. A journalist must learn that lesson. But, by the way, I was, indeed, born the day the great Coco Chanel died, as you already know, and I have often allowed myself even to consider that I may be her rebirth—but that is a story for another day, *n'est ce pas?*"

Tilly said nothing. That left only one person at the table who had yet to be unmasked. Mademoiselle's eyes fluttered toward Abigail.

"But you don't know why I'm here, do you, Mademoiselle?" Abigail said.

"Indeed, you may be surprised at what I know about you, Madame Abigail Murdock. I believe that is your estranged husband's surname, is it not?" Abigail did not respond. Genevieve then looked at Abigail carefully, appearing to weigh every aspect of the woman's persona.

If I hadn't known better, I could almost have believed that Mademoiselle Genevieve LaChapelle could see inside another's soul. Abigail started squirming almost imperceptibly under the harsh scrutiny.

"To begin," Mademoiselle said, "you are, to a degree, who you say you are. You are, indeed, from Texas. That much is clear."

"Ah suppose you're fixin' to tell everyone how clever you are recognizin' my accent. Not clever by half. Miz' Tilly there heard it the first day." It was the most Texan I'd ever heard in Abigail's accent.

"*Mais, non*, my dear. Not at all. After all, you and I both know an accent can be cultivated, *n'est ce pas*, Maxence?" She glanced sideways at Max.

"What? Me?"

Maxence? She knew about Maxence?

"Oh, Maxence, you do not give me enough credit. I have always known your origin, and you might be surprised to learn that it matters not in the least to me. You are good at what you do and will be a famous designer one day. Of that, I am certain. But you might begin to use your Québécois provenance to your advantage before some investigative journalist tries to unmask you."

Now she turned back to Abigail. "*Non*, Madame. I believe your accent to be genuine. But do you not say, no retreat, no surrender in your Texas? Hmm. I believe I remember that from somewhere." Did she bat her eyes?

I was fascinated by all this since, despite my best efforts, I hadn't been able to get to know Abigail very well. I knew nothing more about her than what she had offered on the first day of the course and that she appeared terminally disagreeable. What did

Genevieve know about Abigail that the rest of us had missed? Then I remembered that I had also had a moment earlier in the course when I wondered if Abigail knew something we didn't. There was just something odd about her.

"Ya'll are just putting us on, Mademoiselle. I suppose you think you're smart. That Miss Tilly over there hasn't got your number. Well, she does, in a way, but I know something about you everyone else here doesn't. And you don't know I know it."

I was starting to get seriously confused.

"Oh, but there you are wrong, Madame Abigail. I know precisely what you are about to reveal—and reveal it you will because it is the only reason you are here."

"You're right about that. All this making French jackets is a pile of horse shit. Ya'll aren't from Paris, France, Mademoiselle. Ya'll are from Paris, all right. Paris, Texas."

There was a collective gasp echoing around the group. Maxence spilled a bit of the wine that was on the way to his lips while Ronald clutched Tilly's arm. Bella had begun filming the whole encounter.

"You are partially right, Madame. I was born there, but I'm not *from* there. I am from wherever I say I am from. That, my dear, is my story."

"That's not all," Abigail said. "I'm not finished by half."

Genevieve sighed, walked back to her seat and reached for her as yet untouched glass of wine. "And, of course, you must be the one to say it. Pardon me if I do not pay attention. Because I already know." She sat down.

Abigail looked around as if to be sure we were all listening. I was sure I could have spoken for the whole group that, yes, we were hanging on every word. "This here woman," she said, pointing to Genevieve LaChapelle, "is my sister—my little, long-lost sister, Jenny Chapel."

I nearly swallowed my tongue. Tilly had taken out her phone and was capturing an audio recording. I could feel her next to me shaking with excitement.

Tilly pushed her phone along the table to get it closer to Genevieve. "Mademoiselle Genevieve," Tilly said, "is this true? Are you from Texas? Is this sorry cow your sister?"

Abigail started to get up with her fists tightly clenched. I was sure she was planning to hit Tilly. Then Genevieve waved her hand to stop her, and she sat down. Genevieve then crossed her legs daintily and sipped her wine contemplatively. "To set the record straight," she said, dropping her clearly well-cultivated French accent for something resembling American, "I will say that I was christened with the name Jenny Chapel when I was born. But the day after my fourteenth birthday, I walked out the door of our little old Paris, Texas house and closed it behind me. I remember walking down the front steps saying goodbye to the house and everything—and everyone, including that monstrous father my sister loved so much. I never looked back. Not once in all these years." She stared at Abigail. "The moment I said goodbye was the moment everything began."

And in that moment, hearing those final words, I understood what I had to do. Then one of the housekeepers slid silently into the room and whispered into Max's ear. He immediately got up and came over to me.

Max leaned down and whispered, "There is a telephone call for you."

Paris

*"Instead of gathering knowledge, you should clear your mind. If your
mind is clear, true knowledge is already yours."*
~ Shunryu Suzuki

"CHARLIE, I'VE BEEN TRYING TO GET A HOLD OF YOU. Why aren't
you answering your phone? I even texted you, and you're not
answering."

When I heard Evelyn's voice on the other end, my mind
immediately started churning like an uncontrolled blender, one
thought after another smashing into one another. *There was
something wrong with Frankie. Frankie was sick, hurt, or worse. I
shouldn't have left her for three weeks. I should be there for her. I'm all
she's got. Or my house burned down. Or, or, or...*

"Frankie! Is she all right? What's happened? We have to turn
off our phones during dinner. I'm such a terrible mother!"

"Good lord, Charlie. Calm down. Frankie is fine. I'm fine. My
kids are fine. But we might not be able to say the same about your
Paris flat."

"My Paris flat? What's wrong with the apartment?"

"There's been a *situation*, and since I'm the second contact for
the guy managing the property when you lease it out—who, by
the way, sounds like a lovely Frenchman—and he couldn't get a
hold of you, so he called me."

I took a deep breath, seriously relieved to discover that the call
had nothing to do with Frankie (which didn't do much to assuage
my absent mother's guilt, though), and began trying to guess
what kind of situation Evelyn might be referring to. She
emphasized the word so much that I knew she had chosen it
carefully. As a lawyer, Evelyn was always judicious in her use of
terms like situation, incident and accident. Since she didn't say

there had been an incident—a term she dearly loved—I could only assume that it might well be serious because if she had used the term incident rather than situation, she would have meant the unexpected event had not resulted in serious losses or injury, to use her legalese. But she had said "situation."

"What kind of *situation*, Evelyn?"

"I don't know all the details, but it seems that the professor who was staying in your flat this semester had some party or seminar or something at the apartment, and someone had a fall as far as I can figure out from that Lucien person you have managing it. My god, Charlie, I don't think I've ever heard anyone who speaks as fast as he does. And in English!"

I felt my heart jump into my throat. If someone had fallen in my apartment, with the French approach to "situations" as I'd come to know them, I could be in serious trouble. What if something in my apartment had been deemed unsafe?

"Is the person all right?"

"That's the thing, Charlie. She's dead."

I thought I might pass out right there in the hall outside Mademoiselle's dining room. It made everything that had just happened during that dinner fade away into my past, no longer of any importance.

"I think you should go to Paris before coming home," Evelyn said. "Frankie's fine with staying here for another week or so, but school starts in two weeks, and you'll probably have to have it cleared up by then anyway."

I sighed and thought about the complications involved in taking a side trip to Paris, not to mention the potential fiasco that faced me there, but I knew I had to go. I told Evelyn I'd let her know my plans, said a quick hello to Frankie, who assured me she was just fine with staying in Toronto for another week or ten days and returned to the dining room.

~

"I suppose I've always realized that someday that other life would come calling," Genevieve was saying as I returned to the dining room as quietly as I could. "I do truly believe there has been nothing at all fraudulent about my life, but the past cannot be changed. Today is all one has. I have always believed that. In this moment, we live. What will happen tomorrow is of no importance."

I was a bit puzzled about the appearance of camaraderie that Genevieve was showing to Tilly, whose phone was still on the table, clearly recording every word. What had happened while I was out of the room?

"What's going on, Tilly?" I said quietly as I sat down.

"Mademoiselle has agreed to allow me to write her story. I'm tingling. As soon as dinner is over, I'll be off to telephone a friend who has a literary agency in London. This is going to be a bestseller!"

I looked around the table. "Where's Abigail?"

Tilly waved her hand as if to dismiss the question. "Oh, she left—flounced out of the room in a huff. I'm certain she expected Genevieve to deny everything. She's probably on her way to the airport as we speak." Tilly stopped for a moment as if this last statement might have reminded her of something. "I suppose I should try to find her. An interview wouldn't go astray. I think she expected Genevieve to give her money to keep her secret."

I gasped. "Do you really think Abigail was planning to blackmail her sister?" This was the stuff of movies, not real life.

"Well, if she did, our Mademoiselle here has turned the proverbial tables on her, hasn't she?" Tilly turned to look at me. "And where were you?" she peered at me closely. "What's happened?"

I gave her the briefest of explanations mainly because that was all I had.

"I understand that you have a real estate issue to deal with, but I'm sensing something more than that. Spill, Charlie. This is our last evening together."

I wasn't sure I could tell her what I was really feeling. I took a deep drink of my remaining wine and thought about Tom. The real problem with going to Paris wasn't about French bureaucracy or my apartment at all. It was because the last time I had been in Paris was the last trip Tom and I took together before he got too sick to travel.

~

Later that evening, after I'd managed to cancel my flight back to Madrid and onward to Toronto and book an Air France flight from Mallorca directly to Paris for late the following afternoon, I shuffled into the kitchen. I hoped there might be a drop of wine left in the villa. I found Bella and Tilly deep in conversation at the dining room table. There was an empty bottle of wine in the middle next to one that was still half full. I found a clean glass and sat down. Tilly looked up.

"Have you managed to sort out your flights for tomorrow?" she said as she poured me a glass of wine. I nodded. "Good. Well, then, Bella and I are just plotting here."

"Plotting? What kind of plotting?" I sipped the wine and let it slide down slowly, savouring the feeling and trying to capture a moment of calmness. I knew I would need this serenity if I wanted to keep it together when I got to Paris.

"I'm going to help turn Tilly into a social media sensation so she'll have an audience when her book about Mademoiselle is published. And since you're a bestselling writer, we were hoping you might join us," Bella said.

"I thought you were going back to school," I said.

"I am, but that doesn't mean I don't want to be part of this project. Imagine helping people to see how they can create their lives. The three of us together."

"Don't you see it?" Tilly said. "We are the triumvirate of women who will create a groundswell of movement toward the belief in creating one's own life. We're experts. Bella created herself, you create characters in books, and I'll be sharing Genevieve's story of creating her own life."

Where have I heard that one before? I thought wryly. My novels were almost entirely about women hell-bent on creating their own lives. The one inspired by my great-grandmother Frannie's life was almost entirely about that theme. I suppose it made some sense for me to be involved in this project, but I had so many other things on my mind.

When I told them this, Tilly said, "Fair enough, darling. You go to Paris and sort out your issues. Bella will go back to New York and get ready to return to school. I'm off to London to see my literary agent friend." She stopped for a moment. "Let's plan regular Zoom meetings until we can meet again in person."

And so, the mad triumvirate had a plan.

As I sat in my room later, finishing my packing, I picked up the tiny Limoges sewing machine I'd found in Madrid—my talisman. I held it in my hand, clasping my fingers tightly around it. Like before, it seemed to vibrate. I had the odd sensation of it comforting me—calming me. As I opened my hand to look at it, images of Paris swirled in my mind's eye. It was the Paris I knew, and yet it wasn't. What was going on?

~

The flight was just over two hours long, but when the pilot announced we were about to land at Charles de Gaulle Airport in Paris, I felt like I had just gotten on the plane. I was sitting in an aisle seat, so I didn't have that iconic first glimpse of the city as it came into view on approach—that glimpse that has always given me such a thrill on previous visits. I remembered the first time I'd seen it after I found out that Frannie had left me her Paris apartment after she died. I had been in my early thirties, but I had never been to Paris. Seeing the Eiffel Tower in the distance had brought tears to my eyes. And once again, I felt the tears pricking in my eyes as I thought about the last time I'd been here.

It had been more than a year before Tom died. He had just been diagnosed, but we still didn't fully understand how quickly his cancer might progress. We had travelled to Paris numerous times since we'd been married, but we wanted this trip to cherish in case it might be our last. As it turned out, it was. Tom's chemotherapy began shortly after our return, but his cancer didn't respond as the doctors hoped. Just over a year after his diagnosis, he was gone. And now here I was, the widow returning. God, I missed him.

As I exited the terminal to find a taxi to take me into the city, I realized that this was my first time staying at a hotel since that first visit. On subsequent trips, I always stayed at the apartment. This time, though, I had no idea what the situation was, so I'd booked a room at the same hotel where I'd stayed on my first visit to the city. On that occasion, Evelyn had used her points and gifted me a room at the Marriott on the Champs-Élysées. It now had the great advantage of being a place I'd never stayed with Tom.

Despite my melancholy, I never ceased to be amazed by Paris. As the taxi made its way along Avenue Foch toward the Arc de Triomphe, where it would join the other wild Parisian drivers around to the turn-off to the Avenue des Champs-Élysées, I couldn't help myself. I felt more alive than I thought I deserved. Paris had always had this effect on me ever since my very first visit.

Once settled in my room, I called Lucien, as I told him I'd do. Lucien Allard was one of only three people in Paris I knew. I'd briefly met my neighbours at the apartment building, but I really only knew Etienne Lemieux, his wife, Rose and Lucien. Etienne, whose publishing house Éditions Lemieux had long published my great grandmother's novels—since early in the twentieth century—now sent me royalty cheques twice a year as they created new editions and republished Frannie's classic erotica. He was the one who had contacted me after my mother died to tell me I'd inherited both the royalties and Frannie's apartment.

Etienne had also recommended Lucien to manage my flat when I decided to lease it out from time to time to visiting professors at the Sorbonne. I knew nothing about the current lessee other than he was a visiting professor who had arrived in Paris in April, staying until late August. It was now late August.

When I finally got Lucien on the phone, he prattled on in rapid-fire French. I had to ask him to slow down several times as I attempted to get the whole story. The "accident" had happened ten days ago. The police had attended the apartment. The professor and all attendees at the *soirée*, or whatever it was, had been interrogated. The police had examined the premises. The professor had moved out immediately. Lucien and I agreed to meet at the apartment on Monday morning. I would have preferred immediately or at least the next day, but it was *le weekend,* and it was sacrosanct to most Parisians, especially Lucien. That meant I would be at loose ends all day tomorrow, Sunday, and I didn't relish the freedom of the extra twenty-four hours I'd have to wait to begin clearing up this mess.

~

Sunday morning in Paris. Late August. A heatwave had gripped the city for weeks, but on that Sunday morning, a coolness that seemed to announce the impending arrival of autumn seemed to have settled in. When I walked out of the hotel in search of a café for my requisite café au lait and chocolate croissant, I could see smiles on the faces of passersby, a rarity in Paris, I have to admit. They seemed to be relishing the cooler air that permitted them to once again double-wind those ubiquitous scarves that Parisians wear so well around their necks.

I found an empty table at a café two blocks from the hotel and settled in to enjoy a continental breakfast. I had always preferred these small, carbohydrate-filled breakfasts to anything on offer in a British or American restaurant. As I sipped the perfectly balanced café au lait, I watched the people go by. Before long, the feeling that Tom ought to be with me began to settle on my shoulders. I had to shake it off. Tom was not here—at least not in the flesh. That part of my life was over. I knew that, but I also knew I wasn't ready to embrace it fully. Yes, Tom would always be with me. But he wasn't here, sitting across from me, chiding me for my love of chocolate in the morning and making me laugh with one of our inside jokes.

"I hope you're looking down, sipping your own café Americano in heaven," I whispered, realizing how odd it was for me to be thinking about heaven—a concept I'd always had trouble believing in.

I took in a deep breath and practically inhaled the remaining crumbs of my excellent croissant. I wished I could replicate these flaky pieces of heaven in my own kitchen. Perhaps I'd make that a new project for the fall and winter. Time to exorcise some ghosts, I thought as I asked for *l'addition, s'il vous plait*, and paid my bill.

I headed toward the Arc de Triomphe, where I planned to take one of the streets running in spokes from around its centre toward the bank of the Seine River. Avenue Kléber would take me directly to Trocadéro Gardens, a public green space across from the Eiffel Tower. It had been one of the first places Tom and I had visited on each of our trips to Paris. It had the best views of the tower that was, to me, quintessentially Paris. I planned to spend half an hour walking around the perimeter of the reflecting pond.

The walk from the café to the gardens took me about twenty-five minutes, and when I reached the gardens, I was nervous about just being there. As I walked around the reflecting pond, looking at the clouds on the surface of the pond, I began to feel a peacefulness settle around me, as if Tom was right here, walking with me. I slipped my hand into my pocket and felt the tiny sewing machine talisman there. I felt at home. Then I headed across the bridge, the Pont d'Iéna, and stood looking up at the tower. *Yes*, I thought, *this is Paris*. I found myself a bench and sat down, watching Parisians and tourists alike as they strolled through the lush green space, looking for a place to spread their picnic blankets on this sunny Sunday. And suddenly, I was back to the first months after Tom died.

The one thing that bothered me most about my new role as a widowed middle-aged woman was that everywhere I looked, people seemed to be paired off. Why had I never noticed this before? The world worked in pairs—or so it seemed. There were the teenagers, walking hand in hand, looking lovingly at one another every so often. Little did they know that the kind of "love" they were experiencing was almost certainly doomed to fail. Then there were the young adults who seemed to be moving tentatively toward permanence. Then there were the middle-aged couples, serene in the full knowledge that they were together. (I deliberately overlooked the ones who appeared to be spending their day wishing they were any place else but at this person's side.) Finally, there were the older couples—the ones who had been together forever. These were the ones I noticed the most. These were the ones I had always thought Tom and I would be—the ones taking a Sunday stroll together, content in the knowledge that we were friends, lovers, confidantes till the end. What I hadn't bargained for was that the end was to come so much sooner than I could ever have imagined. Today, I noticed these same couples. But I felt different.

Suddenly, I realized that maybe it was okay for me to be alone. Maybe it was okay for me to sit on a bench in a park for a few minutes just enjoying a sunny day. Maybe I would even find that I liked my solitude. Maybe I was almost ready to say goodbye to Tom. Almost.

When I had my fill of people-watching, I left the park and headed toward the Sorbonne in the direction of my apartment building. The Left Bank, home to that edifice of higher learning and the Latin Quarter, was full of buildings much like the one where Frannie's apartment—my apartment—was on the Rue de Vaurigard. Dating from the nineteenth century, the buildings were what was called Haussmann style after the man who had designed so much of what we now embrace as modern Paris. Georges-Eugène Haussmann, an architect and city official, had designed these stone buildings of various heights with their wrought iron Juliette balconies with French double doors and Mansard roofs of grey zinc. I was dizzily in love with them. But I wasn't heading to the apartment today. That would be for tomorrow. Today I was looking for another favourite haunt Tom and I had discovered on our first trip to Paris. It was a bookshop.

You might think that I'm going to tell you about Shakespeare and Company, that storied bookstore frequented by the likes of Beat Generation poet Alan Ginsberg and other literary luminaries since its birth in the early 1950s. It was a nice place to visit, but it wasn't what had captivated my imagination. The shop I was looking for was a far less well-known spot, favoured by students and faculty of the university, yet offering a wide variety of fascinating books of all genres in both English and French — both new and gently used.

La Librairie Calvetti was four blocks from my apartment, closer to the Seine River. Situated on a corner in a building reported to be over three-hundred years old, the shop was improbably owned by an Italian family who had immigrated to France in the early twentieth century. I had fallen completely in love with it at first sight. Its walls were filled from the top of the twenty-foot ceilings to the floor with wall-to-wall books. You could access the top shelves only by climbing the ladders that ran on tracks like one I'd seen in an Audrey Hepburn movie years before. Each shelf groaned under the weight of massive numbers of books with multi-coloured spines.

In the middle of the store were tables loaded with more recent titles. Once, I'd even seen one of my novels on the English book table. It had given me quite a thrill. Of course, like all writers before me, I'd spent a few minutes hiding behind a free-standing bookshelf to see if anyone picked up a copy of my book. When a woman happened along and picked one up, I almost ran over to tell her I'd be delighted to sign it for her. Alas, she put it down and moved on to the table showcasing French language books. I sighed. Perhaps I'd have to speak to my publisher about publishing a French edition of my books.

When I finally arrived at my destination, I opened the door to the familiar jangling of a bell, which always reminded me of my favourite fabric shop back home. There was an identical-sounding bell above the door of that shop where I'd first been introduced to the wonders and creative potential of fabrics. This door led to the creative wonders of generations of writers.

The moment the door closed behind me, I felt like I had come home. As much as I loved my electronic books in recent years, nothing could match the smell and atmosphere of a shop containing so many real books—books with covers that could open to reveal the wonders and curiosities of the human creative process. I breathed deeply, taking in that indescribable scent of books, and slowly made my way into the back of the shop where the English books used to be shelved. The proprietors seemed to have moved the English books because I found myself standing in front of a wall of French-language books that appeared to be about philosophy and spiritual topics as best as I could make out.

My spoken French was quite good—my oddly authentic accent often getting me into trouble with those who immediately thought I could understand every word of their rapid-fire French—and my ability to read French was passable. But I usually only tried it out on French fashion magazines.

As I turned my head slightly sideways to read a title at eye level, a hand reached out beside me and pulled a volume off the shelf. A voice from behind me said, "*Je pense que vous pourriez aimer celui-ci.*" The accent was almost perfectly Parisian—almost perfect.

Startled, I turned abruptly, almost knocking the book out of the hand of a tall, good-looking, bespectacled man with a mop of dark blonde hair shot through with grey. He was wearing a scarf (of course) and a tweed jacket. Clearly, he was a professor. Why in the world was this perfect stranger telling me that he thought I might like this particular book? But before I could get the question out of my mouth, our eyes locked, and I felt a jolt of familiarity such as I had never felt before. His forehead furrowed as if he might be thinking the same thing.

For the briefest of moments, there seemed to be an arc of electricity between us, and he didn't seem so much like a stranger. "*Madame,*" he began before I could ask where we might have met. But before either of us could say another word, I heard the door bell jangle again and an urgent voice call out, "*Professeur? Patrice? Le taxi est arrivé.*"

His eyes darted toward the door. "*Je suis vraiment désolé, Madame.*" So, he was the professor named Patrice, and his taxi had arrived. And he was sorry. So was I. He nodded and was gone.

He left so quickly that he startled me, causing me to back up into a table, knocking several books to the floor while I was left standing in front of the bookshelf holding the book he had offered. It was titled *Esprit Zen, Esprit Neuf,* by someone called Shunryu Suzuki. The name sounded familiar. Where had I heard it recently? I thought for a moment before it dawned on me. Mademoiselle Genevieve had quoted someone by that name. I looked again at the title and remembered she had said something about possibilities. I'd have to find a copy in English. I had no idea what had just happened, but it occurred to me that I probably needed to follow the metaphorical door that had just opened up to me.

Before I turned to go in search of an English-language copy of the book, I leaned down to pick up the books I'd knocked onto the floor. It was two copies of a book called *It All Begins With Goodbye.* The author was someone called Lejeune, who I'd never heard of. I stood up with them in my hand and placed them back on the table. *I wonder,* I thought, *does everything really begin with goodbye?*

~

Later that evening, when I was tucked up in bed with a glass of wine from the mini-bar, I picked up the book I had bought. I sat for a few moments looking at the cover before opening it. In English, the book was called *Zen Mind, Beginner's Mind*, and of course, the name was familiar to me even though I'd never had any occasion to read it. Zen literature had never been something I'd been drawn to, and I was beginning to wonder why I'd even bought it. It seemed that it was because some stranger (I hesitate to say random stranger because that's not how it had felt) had told me I might like this book. I once heard someone say you could open a book, any book, to any page and find the answer you're seeking. So, I thought, *why not?*

I flipped open the paperback cover and found myself on page thirteen. I started reading. "*...you may say, 'This is bad, so I should not do this.' Actually, when you say, 'I should not do this,' you are not-doing in that moment. So there is no choice for you. Not-to-do something is doing something...good and bad are only in your mind...All that we should do is just do something as it comes. Do something! Whatever it is, we should do it, even if it is not-doing something. We should live in the moment...*"

Dear god, I thought, *What does this stranger know that I don't?*

Enlightenment

"To do something new, of course, we must know our past, and this is all right. But we should not keep holding onto anything we have done; we should only reflect on it."
~ Shunryu Suzuki

I TRIED TO READ A FEW MORE CHAPTERS but found my mind wandering as this Zen teacher described aspects of meditation. Then I fell into a deep, dreamless sleep and awoke to the jangling of my cell phone.

"Madame?" It was Lucien's voice. "I just wish to reconfirm that we will meet at your apartment at ten o'clock this morning."

I glanced at the clock on the bedside table and realized I'd overslept. There would be no time for a leisurely café au lait this morning. I assured him I'd be there, then flew out of bed to shower and dress. I quickly texted Frankie so she'd have a note from Mom when she woke up in a few hours, then went downstairs to ask the bell staff to find me a taxi. Normally, I would have walked, but I'd never get there on time, and Lucien was a stickler for punctuality.

When I arrived in front of my apartment building, Lucien was getting out of his own taxi ahead of mine. I paid the driver, and Lucien and I greeted one another with the requisite double kiss. I had become less awkward with this over the years as I'd begun to feel like Paris was my second home.

Lucien Allard was probably fifty years old, with one of those long, aristocratic faces held upright on a stiff neck. I had often wondered if he had some aristocratic background. Now, from what I'd learned from Mademoiselle Genevieve's friend *le Duc*, I had more occasion to wonder, but we didn't have the kind of relationship that invited personal questions. I'd just have to keep wondering.

Together, we entered the building through the massive double doors and walked across the black and white tile floor, our heels clacking in unison as we headed up several steps to the ancient cage elevator.

When we emerged on my floor, I realized how much I'd missed this place. I had a momentary jolt of wistfulness, remembering the last visit had been with Tom. Then I brought myself back to the present moment—perhaps I had learned something from the Zen master, after all—and focused on trying to ensure that the "situation" had been resolved.

I opened the door to the apartment, unsure of what I expected to see. I had visions of a post-soirée trashed apartment or vestiges of the accident somehow. The place looked perfect. It looked as if I had just left with every piece of furniture in its place and not a soupçon of damage I could see anywhere.

"What do I have to do now?" I said to Lucien as we looked around.

"I have arranged for the officer of the *Gendarmerie* to meet with us here. He will wish to speak with you and perhaps provide some further information on when they can release your apartment."

"Police? Release my apartment? Am I in some kind of trouble?"

"I cannot comment on that, Madame. The officer will be here momentarily." Lucien glanced at his watch, then put his hands behind his back as he walked slowly around the perimeter of the living room.

I sat down on one of the sofas in front of the fireplace.

"I shall go down to the front to meet the officer," Lucien said. I nodded.

When he returned, Lucien introduced the officer of the *Gendarmerie*, and I didn't catch his name. I suppose I should have been more attentive under the circumstance—in case I needed a lawyer— but, as it turned out, that didn't matter.

"*Nous avons terminé notre enquête, Madame,*" he said. I hoped that the fact they had completed their investigation was good news. Then he continued.

It turned out that the woman in question had suffered from a massive brain aneurysm and had simply fallen dead on the sofa where she had been sitting. Further, it turned out the gathering had not been a party so much as a graduate student seminar conducted by the visiting professor as they neared the end of the term. After the incident, the professor had moved out as requested by the police, pending the investigation. The police had finished whatever they had been doing in the apartment, and the officer told me it was "released" back to me.

When he left, Lucien said, "Shall I begin the arrangements for another tenant, Madame?"

Before even thinking about it, I told him no. I would not be leasing the apartment until further notice. I wasn't sure if I planned to stay there myself at some point, but I only knew that leasing it out at this time was not going to happen.

Lucien left, and I was alone in the apartment. I wandered into the office where I'd first encountered an unfinished manuscript left by my great-grandmother, Frannie, who had been the apartment's original owner—at least in my family. I had gone ahead and finished her manuscript, and now I suddenly realized I was finishing something else. I sat in the desk chair and reached out to touch the brass unicorn on the corner of the desk. It had been a gift from Tom with a card that said, "Charlie, unicorns are magical beings that are so hard to find these days. You're my unicorn—my once-in-a-lifetime. I will be grateful for every magical moment I have you in my life, however long that is."

Perhaps it *was* time to say goodbye.

~

Frankie and I arrived back home in Halifax together three days later. I was exhausted, but there was much to be done. School started in a few days, and Frankie and I had a lot to do—shopping for clothes was the main one in her mind. As I sat outside the dressing room at Uniqlo, Frankie's current favourite, I thought about the conversation Evelyn and I had when I was in Toronto to pick up Frankie on my way back from Paris.

"Evelyn," I had said, "do you think I'm a fraud?"

She had looked at me in much the same way she had often done when we were children. As the older-by-two-years sister, Evelyn had always considered herself more worldly and sophisticated than I was. Over the years, although we loved one another as sisters do, my choices often exasperated her. Mainly, she thought my MFA had been just short of the path to perdition or, more likely, destitution. Her path to law school and beyond had led her in a very different direction and had pointed out our differences more clearly than anything else could have.

Evelyn had her feet firmly planted on the ground, while I often had my head in the clouds. Mom had always provided me with both financial and moral support for my creative dreams—I had always wanted to be a novelist. On the other hand, Evelyn thought I should get a real job. The funny thing was that it had been Mom's death and the secrets I'd discovered about her life that neither of us had known that propelled me toward the first real writing of my life and led to two bestsellers. That, coupled with the inheritance Evelyn and I both received from our great-grandmother's estate and Tom's money, meant we were now financially on equal footing. But I still had doubts about who I really was. Wasn't she the one with the real life and I the fraud—the creative one with mirages of a life that I wasn't really living, a life that lived only in the pages of a novel?

Now, faced with my question about being a fraud, Evelyn rolled her eyes. "Charlie, you're a bestselling writer and a mom. What's fraudulent about any of that?"

"But am I hiding behind this veil of widowhood? It's been well over a year, as you and Frankie so eloquently put it when you staged that intervention—"

"It wasn't an intervention, Charlie," Evelyn said, interrupting my train of thought.

"It was, and you know it. Anyway, where was I? Yes, I realize that being a widow shouldn't define my life."

"Yes," Evelyn had said, smiling. "I think you've gotten it. You're so much more than that. "

"What exactly am I? Who am I?"

"That's up to you, Charlie."

That's up to you. I was thinking about Evelyn's words when Frankie emerged from the Uniqlo dressing room in a crop top that I wouldn't be letting her wear anywhere any time soon. Anyway, the clothes were only for after-school and weekend activities since she wore a uniform to school every day.

As we headed home in the car, Frankie chattered on about the events planned for the first few weeks of school, and I pondered the question of who I really was when I remembered Tilly and Bella's project. Maybe their idea of a social media campaign to urge everyone to create their own lives wasn't as outlandish as I had initially thought. Perhaps I *could* create my own life, even at this late stage.

~

Two weeks later, I was alone in the house one Friday afternoon. I was thinking about my Friday evening glass of wine, but I checked my watch and figured three o'clock was too early to start. Frankie had an after-school activity at a friend's house, and I still had a couple of hours before we had to consider which kind of takeout we'd have this week. So, sue me if I don't do the whole mom-in-the-kitchen thing every day of the week. Friday night take-out was our tradition. It had been this way for years, even before Frankie had come into our lives. I cooked on weekdays, and Tom and I cooked together on weekends, but it was pizza, Chinese, or the occasional Mexican quesadilla on Friday night. With time on my hands, I thought it might be an excellent time to begin the fall closet review before the cooler weather really set in.

I was now one of those people. You know the ones. They have Instagram accounts where they show pictures of themselves trying on outfit after outfit inside their massive walk-in closets with built-in shelves for purses and the mirror. That was me, minus the Instagram account and the continual change of clothing. I did have lots of clothes, even if I rarely wore them anymore, but not nearly as many as all those Instagrammers. I'd often wondered what those people did with all those clothes. No one—and I mean no one—has a life that requires three or four clothing changes a day. I had always thought we'd come a long way from those years gone by when every woman of means had a morning dress, an afternoon frock, and a dinner outfit—and other bits and pieces in between. But I guess in the grand scheme of things, we hadn't come as far as I thought. I sighed as I looked at the masses of clothes hanging in the closet.

My eyes first landed on the jacket—my Little French Jacket. Mallorca now seemed a long way off, and I hadn't had a chance to wear it yet. It had been too hot. I slid it off its hanger and put it on over my white T-shirt and jeans—my regular mom-and-writer outfit.

"Not bad," I said to myself in the mirror, remembering when Mademoiselle had asked me to put it on. Then she asked me how I felt. I clearly remembered telling her I felt divine. More than that, though, I distinctly remember thinking it connected me to the past. That's when I thought about Frannie's dresses again.

My great-grandmother Frannie Phillips had lived a remarkable life. She had survived the sinking of the Titanic at the age of twelve, then went on to defy her family by pursuing a career in fashion. But that career never stuck, and she ended up something of a literary luminary of the early twentieth century.

She'd spent her young adult years in 1920s Paris, which was when she had begun amassing designer dresses, many of which she had kept. Now I had them. And, as I had recalled when I was in Mallorca trying on my finished jacket, I had never even tried them on.

At the far corner of my closet, encased in undyed cotton garment bags (I had consulted a friend at the local museum for advice on how to store vintage clothing), hung eight of the dresses. When I discovered them among my mother's belongings after she died, I had spent a year trying to figure out how they fit into my great-grandmother's life. I had even used them as the framework for a novel I'd written that had been inspired by Frannie's life. While doing that, I'd had to do a lot of research about each dress and could now store them in chronological order.

I took the eight garment bags down from the rail and placed them on my bed. I opened the first one. It contained a purple silk confection by British designer Lucille dating to sometime before World War I. I took it off the hanger and soon realized that I could never fit into this dress, so I put it back.

Then I took out the green and gold silk flapper dress by French designer Paul Poiret from around 1920 and laid it on the bed. The next one was a Jean Patou flapper dress dating from 1923—this one I'd been able to nail down during my research. There was a gold-trimmed black silk flapper dress by Madelaine Vionnet, a black Elsa Schiaparelli gown with pink and green embroidered flowers across the bodice that dated to the Second World War years, a demure black Chanel shirt-waist dress with a white silk bow at the neck from the 1940s, a Jean Muir dress from the 1970s and a St. Laurent caftan from closer to when Frannie died in the 1980s. I laid the rest of the dresses out in chronological order on my bed. Which would I try on first?

I started at the end of the line with the St. Laurent because I figured it would fit with its flowing long skirt and wide long sleeves. When I looked at myself in the mirror, I felt nothing other than it made me look older than my years. I suddenly looked like I had entered my wise woman years, perhaps without the wisdom. I took it off and put it back in the closet. Then I went back into my bedroom to look at the rest of the dresses.

There was little doubt in my mind about my great-grandmother. She had been a flapper. As I stood there staring at the dresses, I wondered what it was about the era—the jazz age, *les années folles*, the crazy years, as they called them in Paris—that so captivated me. I looked at the three silk dresses from the era and knew I'd have to try on the Patou.

I lifted it carefully to avoid snagging the diaphanous, almost filigree black lace overdress with the deep fringe at the bottom. It was designed to be worn over the slinky gold slip dress that hung underneath it so that the gold would shimmer through the black. I took a deep breath and slipped it over my head. It fit like a glove and felt divine—even more divine than the jacket. I walked back into my closet and stood in front of the mirror.

I was startled at what I saw. I was no longer me—Charlotte Hudson, Charlie, the writer, the mom, the widow. Looking back at me from the mirror was a stranger, and yet not. I knew her, but I didn't. I felt her memories, but I didn't. I moved slightly and felt the tickle of the fringe against my calves. I swivelled my hips and watched the fringe dance. Until that moment, I had never been a hip swiveller, that's for sure. But I didn't feel like me—and yet I did.

I don't know how long I stood there, staring at myself in the mirror, thoughts of soirees and champagne coupes and big bands swirling around in my head. My reverie was finally broken when I heard Frankie's voice.

"Mom? Is that really you? You look so...so different."

~

For the next few weeks, I found myself going back into the closet each day to stare at the Patou. Every time I saw it, I felt strange. As crazy as it sounds, I felt like it was trying to tell me something. Of course, as a writer, it seemed the most likely explanation was that I was supposed to write something about it—or maybe about the era, the 1920s. The roaring twenties had always fascinated me, even as a teenager. I had read F. Scott Fitzgerald and Ernest Hemingway, although Hemingway wasn't a favourite of mine. Fitzgerald's books, though, had captured my imagination with their images of glittering parties, flowing champagne and, of course, flappers. I remembered that evening in the villa in Mallorca after the dinner where we met Mademoiselle Genevieve's aristocratic friend—lover, perhaps? Bella had started talking about her romantic fantasy of having lived before back in the 1930s or 1920s.

I smiled at the thought of Bella as a flapper. *Yes*, I thought as I held the Patou up in front of me in the mirror once again. *Yes, Bella, you would have looked incredible in this dress. You would have given Zelda Fitzgerald a run for her money with Scott.*

I put the dress back in its muslin cocoon and placed it back on the rail beside Frannie's other dresses. As I headed out into the hall and across to the front of the house where my office was, I remembered a line from Fitzgerald's book *The Great Gatsby*. *"Life starts all over again when it gets crisp in the fall."*

Fall would be upon us in mere days.

Possibilities

"A mind full of preconceived ideas, subjective intentions, or habits is
not open to things as they are."
~ Shunryu Suzuki

BY THE END OF SEPTEMBER, Tilly, Bella and I had a standing Zoom conversation every Thursday afternoon at one o'clock. Of course, for Tilly in London, it was five pm and time to pour a glass of wine. It was noon for Bella in New York, and she would take a lunch break of organic salad greens, walnuts and a banana. "I'm trying to get my generation to eat better," she had said while snapping photos of her various lunches. I remembered telling her I had read that Gen-Z, her people, tended to eat more healthily than the rest of us already. "So they say," she said. Then, like the soon-to-be doctoral candidate she was, she quoted the research that had found her generation states that although 54% of her peers were quick to tell researchers that they preferred healthy snacks, only 3% admitted to including fruits, vegetables or nuts. "Not sure what they're actually eating that they consider healthy snacks," she had said. Take that, Generation Z!

Despite her continued focus on her Instagram status, Bella was, indeed, winding down her accounts to some degree. She had already met with her research supervisor in advance of beginning her studies in January, and they had decided together that because of her interest in influencers, she should keep her online presence at least as much as possible given what would likely be a demanding school schedule. Her father, who managed her account, had already lined up someone who could replace her by posting regularly. Her adoring followers would never know she had left them—at least not yet because the plan was for Bella to be featured in some, but certainly not all, the photos. She would still have to take some photographs of herself, just like most other people her age. Knowing that she could do this was more than enough corroboration of my long-held contention that social media was where truthfulness, authenticity and integrity went to die. Some day, I hoped to be able to tell Frankie this, but for now, it was confidential. Tilly was also making progress on her plan.

"My agent has just called with the most fantastic news," she said during our call the first week in October. "She has three—not one, not two, but three—publishers interested in my book! It seems our Mademoiselle Genevieve's story has legs, as they say!"

"That is wonderful news, Tilly," I said, genuinely excited for her. "Are you making much progress on the writing yet?"

"Early days, darling, early days. Now," Tilly said, "what about you? How is *your* writing going?"

I had been hoping this question wouldn't arise, but I suppose it was inevitable. I still hadn't been able to get down to writing anything substantial, but I thought I'd run my idea of a story set in the 1920s by both of them.

Immediately, Bella was excited. "Charlie, you must do it! You must! I can promote it with my followers. There will be a romantic heroine, won't there? My followers would love that. I can make sure of it!"

I laughed. I hadn't gotten that far yet.

"Charlie, darling, you aren't planning to go to the dark side, are you?" Tilly said, moving closer to her webcam so that her face filled the screen.

"Dark side?" I said.

"The dark side of literature. That wasteland of creativity. That desert of independent thought that is formula fiction." She paused for effect. "Romance novels, darling. Romance novels."

Bella and I both laughed. My laughter was, perhaps, a bit more ironic since I had wondered that exact thing myself. Was I going down the road of genre writing where I must have cookie-cutter characters and a happy ending? No, I thought, that's not what I had in mind.

"I'm going to have to miss next week's chat," I said. "Frankie and I are flying out early to Toronto for the long weekend here. We'll spend it with my sister and her family."

"Oh, it's Canadian Thanksgiving," Bella said.

"We just call it Thanksgiving," I said. I couldn't help myself. I had tired in recent years of online mentions of Thanksgiving, qualifying it as "Canadian Thanksgiving" as if, somehow, American Thanksgiving was the only *real* Thanksgiving. Anyway, Bella missed the slight cynicism in my voice. I was happy she did.

"Be sure to wear your French jacket," Tilly said. "Yours is stunning."

"You know, Tilly, I might just wear it." Evelyn would be so confused when she saw how much the jacket I made resembled that classic Chanel I knew she had hanging in her closet. This could be fun!

~

Frankie and I arrived in Toronto just after six pm on the Thursday before Thanksgiving. We had only three days to spend with Evelyn and her family since Frankie had to return to school on Tuesday morning. Evelyn told us she planned Thanksgiving dinner for Sunday rather than the actual day—Monday. I didn't know what she had arranged for this year since I had never known my sister to cook a turkey—ever—yet turkey was the tradition in our family for these holidays. She was even a Christmas take-in kind of cook. I expected nothing less on this occasion. At least in Toronto, she had lots of terrific places to choose from for a supplier!

It took us almost an hour to get into the city from the airport. There was the usual massive pre-holiday traffic and an accident. When we finally arrived at Evelyn's enormous house in

Rosedale, she immediately mixed martinis, and Frankie caught up with her cousins.

"Evelyn tells me you're starting a new book." Michael, Evelyn's stockbroker husband, who usually worked such long hours that I seldom saw him, had joined us for a drink. His poison of choice, however, was a twenty-one-year-old scotch. I only knew it was twenty-one years old because he happened to mention it when he poured himself "two fingers" and then pretentiously dropped in two whiskey rocks he had just retrieved from the freezer section of their beverage fridge. Until that moment, I hadn't been aware beverage fridges (you know—those wine fridges that have space for other things like mixes and vodka) even had freezer sections, and it wasn't that I didn't know anything about wine fridges. Tom and I had a massive wine fridge in the basement.

"Evelyn might be a bit optimistic in her interpretation of what I told her," I said, eyeing my sister suspiciously. She batted her eyes. "I have a few ideas, but I'm still at the handwritten notes-in-a-notebook stage."

"You know, I never could understand the lure of creative occupations. I mean, my work can be creative—"

"I sincerely hope not," Evelyn said, slightly alarmed. "Creativity could have serious legal consequences in your line of work, my dear husband."

I was trying to picture Michael being creative in his work. Would that mean his financial advice to his clients might be creative? The term "creative accounting" had always been a euphemism for sleight of hand—cheating, in other words.

"What I meant," Michael said, giving his wife the side eye, "was that we sometimes have to think outside the box when making recommendations to our clients. But basing a whole life on a creative occupation that succeeds or fails on the whims of a capricious audience—I don't get it."

"Sounds a lot like the stock market, if you ask me," Evelyn said dryly, sipping daintily from her crystal martini glass.

I was enjoying this. I realized that I'd missed adult conversation in the evenings, even conversations that involved people who clearly didn't understand creativity or the creative process. Perhaps I could enlighten them.

"Creativity is just turning imaginative ideas into something else," I said. As I listened to myself, I realized that this was probably true as much in life as in writing a book.

"Into reality?" Evelyn said.

I thought for a moment. "It depends on how you define reality. Scientists would define it one way; philosophers another," I said as Michael yawned. I continued. I was enjoying this. "In science, reality is defined in physical terms—which I suspect is the world you live in, Michael." He started to protest, but I stopped him. "I'm not criticizing that approach, but it doesn't tell the whole story." I didn't care if either of them—two thoroughly grounded, pragmatic, rational adults—cared about this, but I suddenly realized I did. This rumination was for me, not them. "Think about it for a minute. You both love Katie and Lucas. Would you say that love is a reality?" Michael and Evelyn both looked slightly baffled. "You can't see it or touch it or smell it in the so-called real world, but I think you'd have to agree that love is reality as much as this martini glass."

"Yes, but I don't see how this relates to the real world. You know that one? The one where things are tangible? The place we live every day?" Evelyn said.

I should have expected this. Evelyn had always been the one who told me I should stop living in my dream world and move into the *real* world. "Well, Evelyn," I said, "if your love for your children—and your husband—is real, then it's a form of reality. It's something invisible but substantial. Something felt but not seen. You can't touch it, but it's there. If I write a book about characters living in the 1920s, is that reality?"

Both Evelyn and Michael seemed to be at a loss as to how to respond in any lucid way. I was now talking entirely to myself. "Do you have to be able to touch and see the elements of your story for that story to be real? Or can a story be real even if it's inside your mind?" I wasn't sure of the answer, but I sure as hell was now determined to find out.

~

Evelyn had planned a Saturday spa day for the two of us while Michael took the kids to the Royal Ontario Museum to see the T-Rex exhibit. I had never been a big fan of spas, but Evelyn was devoted to them. It was her "self-care" time every month, she said. Oh, how I hated that self-serving term that seemed to underpin a billion-dollar industry designed to part women, in particular, from their money. Anyway, maybe I had it all wrong and needed some "self-care" for myself. Whichever way I looked at it, I couldn't get out of going to the spa.

Evelyn had mentioned it as a kind of sisterhood bonding exercise. I almost laughed. Evelyn didn't have time for a sisterhood, and we were real sisters who needed no exercise to be bonded. That had been taken care of by our parents. Anyway, I donned my self-made Little French Jacket and waited for her in her foyer.

"Oh my god, Charlie. That's a fantastic jacket!" she said, coming down the wide staircase toward me dressed in her own authentic Chanel version.

She was stunned when I told her it was the fruit of my Mallorcan labour. "Wow! I cannot believe you made this with your own hands."

"My hands, lots of silk thread and the occasional assistance of a sewing machine," I said. "Do you think I'll look like a fraud?" There was that word again.

"A fraud?" Evelyn said, picking up the hem to look inside and gazing at the hand-stitched silver chain at the bottom. "This is as real as it gets, Charlie. Let's go!"

When we came out of the spa two hours later, she told me lunch was next on the agenda.

After practically inhaling the exquisite omelette and arugula salad (where could I get the recipe for that dressing?) at Evelyn's newest favourite brunch restaurant, Sophia, we returned to Bloor Street, Toronto's mink mile. We strolled arm-in-arm, stopping every so often to gaze at the window displays in Dior, Prada and Cartier. Evelyn had her heart set on a new Cartier watch for her birthday. I made a mental note to pass this on to Michael, which, I suppose, was the reason she told me. I was nothing if not a complicit sister in this case.

"Oh, let's go into Holt's," Evelyn said as we approached the valets and doormen (door people?) on the sidewalk outside the iconic Holt Renfrew, Canada's answer to Neiman Marcus or Harrod's.

I knew Evelyn wasn't in search of designer apparel, although this was the mecca for that. She loved their two floors of cosmetics and perfumes. In the interest of further self-care, she bought herself a bottle of Creed perfume—at the eye-watering price of five-hundred-and-ninety-seven dollars for one hundred millilitres.

We then trolled the handbag department. Holt's was more fun than individual stores for that because they carried a variety of designer brands. Then Evelyn suggested we backtrack and visit Chanel, which was practically across the street from where we'd had lunch.

"Are you crazy, Evelyn? I'm not going into a Chanel boutique wearing a fake Chanel jacket!"

"Oh, Charlie," she said, waving away my concerns with her hands, "you're not wearing fake Chanel. You're wearing authentic Charlie Hudson. Weren't you the one who told me that Chanel herself said imitation is the greatest form of flattery? Anyway, it'll be fun to fool them."

"Yeah," I muttered as I considered how often this same Chanel-ism surfaced in my life. "Fun for whom?"

Evelyn wouldn't take no for an answer. She wanted to see if they had the new shoes she "needed" for work. Once inside the store, I was drawn immediately to the racks where the jackets hung in all their tweedy glory. As I caressed the silk lining of a particularly colourful bouclé jacket, I tried to conjure that Parisian feeling. Nothing. *Hmm*, I thought, *I guess modern designer clothing doesn't do it for me.*

"Wow!" I turned at the squeal emanating from one of the black-clad, severe-looking-yet-austerely-pretty Asian sales clerks. "I don't remember what collection that jacket came from, but it's fantastic on you!"

I felt oddly validated.

We finally made it back to Evelyn's house just before five, where we found Michael in the kitchen making dinner, a situation that surprised the hell out of me. The three kids were dutifully acting as multiple sous chefs when he called out to us. "Dear god, Evelyn, don't we have any of that raw basil pesto?"

"No, Michael," Evelyn said, going into the kitchen. "We don't have any of that pesto. You never mentioned that you'd be needing any. Do you need some?"

"I can't finish making this pasta sauce without it," he said. "Can you go to Harvest Wagon and get some?"

Evelyn sighed.

"I'll go, guys," I said. Harvest Wagon was a specialty store about four blocks from their house. It was part of what everyone liked to call the five thieves—five uber-high-priced specialty stores that included a fancy bakery, a seafood shop, a butcher and an expensive pizza restaurant standing side-by-side on a chichi part of Yonge Street. Harvest Wagon was the grocery store. I really needed a few minutes to myself, so I practically begged to go.

Once Michael had produced a photo of exactly what I was to look for, I put on my shoes and headed out, breathing in the relative quiet. As much as I might have missed the evening adult conversation, I was now missing the quiet, meditative parts of my life. Funny how we always want what we don't have.

When I arrived at Harvest Wagon, it was buzzing with people who seemed to be finishing their Thanksgiving grocery shopping. I slipped between the shelves past a well-dressed older couple who appeared to be arguing about the kind of organic potato chips they should buy toward where I thought the jars of pesto sauce might be. As I scrutinized the shelves, I backed up to squat and bumped into a man behind me who seemed to be doing exactly the same thing at the same time on the other side of the narrow aisle. We both stood up and immediately apologized.

"I'm so sorry," we said in unison. Then we both looked. "You?" we said.

Our eyes locked, and we were momentarily speechless until I finally broke the silence. "You speak English," I said.

"You speak English," he said.

And we both laughed.

"Paris?" I said.

He nodded. It was him. It was the man who had passed me the Zen book in that Paris bookstore and then left. It was the one someone called professor. Patrice. It was the one I felt I'd met before.

"But I thought you were French," I said, seriously confused.

He laughed. "I was only there temporarily. I live in Toronto. Teach at U of T." He was referring to the University of Toronto. "What about you? I could have sworn you were Parisian."

I was flattered. I shook my head and told him I was from Halifax, just visiting my sister for the long weekend.

"It's funny," he said. "I could swear I know you from somewhere before we bumped into one another in Paris. Do you have time for a quick coffee? Maybe we can figure it out."

Enchantment

*"As long as you have some fixed idea or are caught by some habitual
way of doing things, you cannot appreciate things in their true
sense."*
~ Shunryu Suzuki

THE PESTO SAUCE COMPLETELY FORGOTTEN, I followed this
stranger across the street to a little French bakery and café, which
seemed superbly appropriate. We took the last tiny table out on
the sidewalk since the sun was shining and the day was warm by
October standards. We ordered café au lait, and then he turned
to me. "I'm Patrick, by the way. Patrick Harrington."

"Charlotte Hudson," I said, extending my hand across the
table. "But everyone calls me Charlie."

He reached for my hand, and when it made contact, I felt a jolt
of pure energy run up my arm, finally settling in the back of my
neck where it lingered, making the hairs stand up.

We began our conversation as strangers usually do with that
kind of banal chit-chat that places each of them in a time and
place—names (Charlie and Patrick), location (Halifax and
Toronto), occupation—then we were off as if we had known one
another all our lives.

"Charlotte Hudson?" Patrick said when I told him I was a
writer. "That name seems so familiar." I didn't help him.
"Hudson, Hudson," he said, contemplating his coffee. "CK
Hudson! That's it! I knew I'd seen your photo before. I read
Something I'm Supposed to Do, and your picture was on the back
cover. You know, I loved that book. I must get you to sign it for
me."

I was flattered that he recognized my name and appreciated
my work. I was even more flattered that he'd noticed the cover. I

151

was further impressed that he'd bought a physical copy I could sign.

Then he sat back in his chair and looked at me. "No," Patrick said, "that's not it. I saw your picture on the book cover, but I'm sure that's not where I know you. When I saw the photo, I stared at it for some time, wondering where we'd met before."

I asked Patrick if he'd ever been to Halifax. He had not. "What do you teach?" I said, thinking we could figure this out if we could nail down where our paths had crossed.

"I'm a professor of art history," he said. "I wrote my doctoral dissertation on lost French models of the Impressionist era. Are you familiar with Degas' ballet works?" I was. "Have you ever seen that sculpture he did of the fourteen-year-old ballerina?"

"Yes. As a matter of fact," I said, "I saw it here in Toronto when it was on tour at the Art Gallery of Ontario some years ago. I love everything Degas ever did—sculpture and painting."

Patrick smiled. "We have something in common, then. Degas and other Impressionists of nineteenth and twentieth-century Paris used models, some of whom were ballerinas with the Paris Opera Ballet. The thing is, though, they've largely been lost to history. I traced the history of how female models were used and how male artists portrayed them."

I was fascinated. It almost seemed like the perfect springboard for a new book. I was itching to take out my notebook and interview Patrick, but that seemed a bit gauche under the circumstances. So, I resisted. "Is your work still focused in that area?"

"Not really," Patrick said. "Recently, I've been researching obscure Parisian artists of *les années folles*—jazz age Paris."

I felt another jolt of electricity. *My era*, I thought. Then I thought about Frannie's dresses and could feel the goose bumps forming up and down my arms. Now I realized I really would have to begin doing some research for a book set in 1920s Paris. All signs pointed me in that direction.

"So that's why you were in Paris in August when I bumped into you."

"Partly," he said. "I'm also the coordinator of a new program we have in my department at the university. It's a kind of exchange program with the Sorbonne for Canadian PhD students with a focus on French art history and French students whose work focuses on French-Canadian art history."

From the moment Patrick told me he was a professor who had been in Paris over the summer, I had wanted to ask him if he knew the professor who had been leasing my flat. I also wondered if he knew anything more about what happened when that woman died in my apartment. I didn't quite know how to broach the subject. Circumspection was my way in.

"How long were you in Paris?" I said as an opening gambit. He told me he had been there since April. "You must have enjoyed living so close to the heart of your research subject matter." He said he had enjoyed that very much. "Did you know many other visiting professors?"

Patrick looked at me and cocked his head to the side. "Anyone specific?"

I cleared my throat. "Well," I said, stalling, "I own a flat on the Left Bank—"

"What? You own an apartment in Paris? How wonderful!"

"Yes, well, my great-grandmother, Fran Phillips, left it to me." I stopped for a moment, wondering if perhaps he knew my great-grandmother's work. "Have you ever heard of FE de Plessis, the early twentieth-century writer?"

"Of course. Anyone who has ever seriously studied art in France has had to study literary artists as well as visual artists. Why?"

"FE de Plessis was my great-grandmother." He looked startled. "Perhaps you hadn't heard that old FE was not a man, as popular opinion would have it."

This was, indeed, news to Patrick, but it was also not getting me the information I wanted. I would have to be more direct.

"Did you hear about the woman who died in a Paris flat in August while at the apartment of a visiting professor?"

The colour drained from Patrick's face. "It was your apartment." It was both a statement and a question. "I was the visiting professor." Then, rather than continuing to tell me about the event I wanted to learn more about, he began to describe how he'd felt when he first moved into the flat.

"From the moment I walked across the threshold, I had a strange feeling. It was almost as if I'd been there before, but I realized it was probably because during all the years I spent on my doctoral research—and even now—I've been in many such apartments, at least in my head. But that first night, I could almost feel a presence."

"I've felt that, too," I said. "I always thought—and don't laugh at me for this—that Frannie was still there. That her spirit still permeated the place. You know, she wrote many of her most popular books in that apartment."

Patrick whistled softly. "Wow. Then, I guess I wasn't going crazy."

"But, Patrick, what happened at that party or whatever it was?"

Patrick sat back in his chair as if to give himself more personal space. I wondered if I'd crossed the line. Had the woman meant something more to him than simply being a student?

"Lili was my assistant while I was visiting Paris. We were hosting a final seminar for the students I'd been teaching while I was there. It wasn't strictly an administrative visit. I also had to conduct a graduate student seminar. I have to admit there was a lot of drinking. Then, suddenly, it happened. Lili simply fell over on the sofa and was gone. I was terrified that there had been something in the drinks."

"How could that have happened if you were hosting?"

"I don't know. It was just my terror, I guess." Patrick looked stricken.

I began to get the impression there was something more to the story. "What else, Patrick?"

Patrick looked down into his empty cup. "Lili and I were becoming more than friends. Nothing happened, but I was angry with myself for becoming attracted to someone working for me. I was her boss while I was there. But nothing happened," he repeated. "I guess I felt responsible."

I was floored by the apparent coincidence of literally bumping into the very person who had been living in my flat. I decided we should move on to other subjects in the interest of discovering how we might have met before.

Then Patrick asked me if I was married. As much as I willed them to stop, tears began forming in my eyes as I told him about Tom.

"The hurt never goes away completely," he said. "But I don't think you really want to erase it. It's a reminder."

"Sounds like you know what you're talking about," I said, wiping away a tear that had made its way down beside my nose.

Then Patrick told me about his wife, Alison, who had died of breast cancer at the age of thirty-nine. He had been widowed for the past ten years. His two children—a boy and a girl—were both now away at university. One was in journalism school in Ottawa, and the other, a pianist, was at Juilliard in New York. I smiled, wondering where Frankie would end up.

"Would you have dinner with me tomorrow?" he said suddenly.

"I'm sorry. I'd love to, but my sister is planning her big Thanksgiving dinner for tomorrow evening."

"Drinks after?"

As I was about to say yes, my phone dinged. It was an urgent text from Evelyn. I knew it was urgent because of the capitalization, "Where ARE you? WORRIED! Micheal improvising with the pasta sauce!" And I remembered that I had been going to bring the pesto for Michael's pasta sauce.

"I have to go, Patrick. I'm so sorry." I passed my phone to him. "Here. Put in your phone number, and I'll text you tomorrow."

He did as I asked, then said, "Life starts all over again when it gets crisp in the fall."

My head jerked up. That very Fitzgerald quote had been on my mind earlier in September. Was this life starting over?

~

We had all been in suspense. Evelyn loved springing things on people and hadn't yet told anyone—not even Michael, evidently— what she had planned for her Thanksgiving dinner. The following morning, at breakfast, Evelyn finally put us out of our misery and made the announcement. We were all expected to dress up and join her at the Royal York Hotel for dinner in their famous restaurant.

"Finally," Michael said. "And not a moment too soon. I was beginning to think we'd be having peanut butter sandwiches."

All three kids started giggling but stopped when Evelyn severely reminded them this was a very dressed-up occasion. "Reign is not a place for sweatpants," she said, giving Lucas the stink-eye. I had never seen young Lucas in anything but sweats. But of course, what can you expect of a ten-year-old whose idea of a perfect day is playing computer games and eating popcorn? I couldn't wait to see them all in their Sunday best.

Evelyn had arranged for two Town Cars to pick the lot of us up to drive us downtown to the hotel for dinner. I was impressed, but it was so Evelyn. Before I was due to meet everyone in the foyer, I texted Patrick to tell him I'd be eating dinner downtown at the restaurant at the Royal York Hotel and that maybe we could meet later.

"See you in the Library Bar at eight?"

"The Library Bar?" I texted.

"Other side of the lobby at the hotel where you're having dinner," was his reply.

I smiled. That would be convenient, and I was sure Evelyn would understand. I just wasn't sure I did. Was this another crackpot idea? I didn't know the answer.

As Evelyn and I headed toward the first car with Frankie, Michael stood by the door of the second car helping Katie and Lucas into the back.

"Oh, by the way, everyone," Evelyn said just before getting into our car in front of me, "Joel is joining us for dinner." Then she disappeared into the car.

Joel? Who was Joel? I'd never heard her even whisper that name before.

Michael, too, looked puzzled. "Joel? Joel Gluckstein? What the..."

Evelyn poked her head outside the back seat and said, "You know he's alone this year for Thanksgiving for the first time, so I invited him." Then she disappeared again.

"Who's Joel Gluckstein?" I said to Michael just before he got into the back with the kids.

Michael rolled his eyes. "A friend. I play tennis with him at the club. You better talk to your sister." And he disappeared, swallowed up by the black car.

"Evelyn," I said, arranging myself in the back seat of our car beside Frankie, who was wedged between us, "Who is Joel?" I had the disagreeable feeling he might be someone Evelyn thought I should "meet."

Evelyn just waved her hand, swatting away my question as she liked to do. "Just a friend. You'll like him." Then she turned to Frankie and started babbling about school and Christmas holidays. I figured I'd just have to wait and see.

We all arrived in convoy at the hotel's front entrance twenty minutes later. A uniformed doorman helped us alight from our chariots, and we all walked into the magnificent lobby of this storied hotel whose history was attached to Union Station directly across Front Street. I'd been in many beautiful old buildings, but this one was special. There was something about its marble floor, masses of warm wood panelling, multiple intimate seating areas and soaring ceilings with a mezzanine above that spoke of a different era.

As Evelyn had mentioned, the restaurant was called Reign, which I supposed was a nod to the "royal" part of the hotel's name. When we entered, a maitre d' led us to a large table near the back of the restaurant. The table was dressed in snow-white linen and glittering silverware and crystal glasses with massive one-page menus at every place setting. A gigantic floral arrangement in the centre of the table was reminiscent of a turkey.

As I took my seat, I looked around at the other diners and wondered what kinds of families eat their Thanksgiving dinner at a hotel. Perhaps those in from out of town, people with small kitchens as is so common in large urban areas where everyone lives in a smallish condo. Maybe they were people who needed to have their family gatherings in a public place to avoid drama. Whatever it was, the restaurant was surprisingly full.

We were just settling into our places at the table when a tall, dark-haired man with a trim beard appeared. He looked to be between fifty-five and sixty if I guessed correctly and was wearing a black suit with a pink shirt and a pink and purple bowtie. The moment he clapped eyes on Evelyn, he smiled in a kind of enigmatic way. Evelyn introduced him to me as Dr. Joel Gluckstein, but it seemed to me he was far more interested in Evelyn than he was in me. This was awkward.

As we made our way through the five-course dinner, the highlight of which was, of course, the magnificent turkey, I couldn't help myself from thinking about Patrick and the effect he seemed to be having on me. And what about that Fitzgerald quote? It was as if he could read my mind somehow. And, of course, I shouldn't even be thinking about meeting him for a drink after dinner (a situation about which I wasn't planning to tell Evelyn until we had finished dinner). I should be going directly back to Evelyn's with the family.

My reverie was broken by Evelyn, who had decided it was time Joel and I exchanged CVs. And she was the one to do it for us. She told him about me, my writing, my "loss" as if I wasn't even there. Then she started on Joel, telling me he was an American-turned-Canadian, with a medical degree from Johns Hopkins and a specialty in neurology. He was also—wait for it— divorced. Of course, he was. Otherwise, why would he be here?

I was starting to tune out until I heard Evelyn saying, "Charlie had coffee last evening with a stranger she bumped into in Paris." She gave me the side-eye as she emphasized the word *stranger*. "Charlie has that déjà vu feeling." Why had I told her that when I got back last evening? Well, I had to find some way to justify my temporary disappearance.

Joel looked at me over the top of his wine glass. "Déjà vu? What kind of déjà vu?"

"Are there different types?" I said, hoping this would go away.

"Of course," he said. He put his glass back on the table, propped his chin on his clasped hands and leaned into his topic. I could feel a lecture coming on, and I had just met the man. He continued. "Well, to begin with a broad definition, it's important to understand that déjà vu is a false sense of familiarity. Just to be clear, we must recognize that the sense of familiarity is *artificial*."

"But can't it ever mean something real?" Frankie said from down the table. I had no idea she was even listening to what the grown-ups were discussing.

Joel looked past Michael, who seemed to be zoned out on the wine he was enjoying, toward Frankie. "Of course, one would like to think it's real, but let's start by accepting that it is not."

Frankie looked disappointed, and I wondered if she'd had the feeling before. I'd have to ask her later. Joel retook the floor.

"First, there are four different sensations. *Déjà entendu*, which, if you know your French, means that you hear something you believe you have already heard. Then there is *déjà su*, which is learning again something you already know. There is *déjà senti*, the feeling that you have felt this way before, and finally, the one most people think of as déjà vu, *déjà fait*, a feeling that you have done something before often in a place you believe you have been before when you know you have not." He looked toward me. "Which of those did you feel, Charlie?"

"Does it really matter if the feeling is false anyway?" I said, a feeling of irritability growing by the minute. Evelyn gave me a sour look. Was I ruining her attempt at matchmaking?

"Perhaps not," Joel said. "But it would be interesting to consider which part of the experience resonated with you the most."

I wasn't sure I wanted to divulge anything I might have felt that was anything more than superficial. Finally, I said, "I suppose it was a feeling I thought I'd felt before."

"Ah, good," Joel said. "Because if you thought you had felt it before, you might well have, just not under the kind of circumstances you think might be the reason. If you felt you had met this person before and it evoked a particular feeling, it is because you have felt it before for someone else in your lived life experience. That's all."

Was that all there was to it? That didn't seem like a sufficient explanation. "That doesn't feel right to me," I said.

"Perhaps not, but it would then be important for you to know that, from a clinical perspective," he turned to Evelyn. "May I lapse into neurologist mode, my dear?" Evelyn smiled and nodded. I thought that was the mode he was in all along. He continued. "If I might wax a bit more professorial—there are two main types of clinical déjà vu. One is non-pathological in nature, which of course, means that there is no pathology or disease involved. The second type is pathological, which suggests underlying pathology or disease."

Dear god, this man was patronizing. Was he going to tell me I have a neurological disease just because I felt like I'd met Patrick before?

"Pathological feelings of déjà vu can suggest conditions like epilepsy of the temporal lobe or dementia, but it's safe to say that you would likely need to exhibit other symptoms." That was encouraging. "I should also say that there have been papers suggesting that déjà vu can be of a so-called para-normal type, but I don't put much stock in those. Quacks, if you ask me." He raised his wine glass to his lips and took a sip.

Evelyn seemed to be hanging on his every word. "Paranormal, you say? You mean, like ghosts?"

Joel laughed. "Not really, but the papers do suggest that the patients in question may show what they call precognitive knowledge."

"Is that like knowing something before it happens?" I said.

"Yes," Joel said. "And related to that, patients sometimes believe they are telepathic. For example, I might suddenly think something, and you would say you knew exactly what I was thinking."

"So, the bottom line for you, then, is that déjà vu is false and cannot be related to anything except coincidental memories or a disease," I said.

"That about covers it," Joel said.

"I think you're a cynic," Frankie said, clearly still following the conversation. Where was this coming from?

"I suppose I am," Joel said, "but I'd prefer to think of myself as a scientist. I prefer to look for the evidence. And there is no evidence that déjà vu means anything but what I've told you it does."

I wondered what had made Evelyn think Joel and I might get along. He was far too misanthropic for my liking. Perhaps it was because his wife left him, and he suddenly had to look after his own laundry. I knew this because he had mentioned it earlier in the dinner conversation. If I had wondered why his wife left him, knowing his most fond wish was for her to be there to do his laundry certainly answered that question.

"Well," Frankie said as the server put a big piece of pumpkin pie down in front of her, "it sucks to be you."

"Frankie!" I said. She shrugged and put a large forkful of pie into her mouth, effectively ending the conversation. Then she winked at me. My daughter winked at me!

I didn't know what to think. I couldn't shake the feeling that I'd known Patrick somewhere else. It wasn't just that I'd met him in passing. It was a profound feeling that I'd *known* him before. And it seemed to me that he felt the same way.

The words of French writer Antoine de Riverol came flooding back to me from a distant history class. *It is the dim haze of mystery that adds enchantment to pursuit.*

Resilience

*"Nothing we see or hear is perfect. But right there in the
imperfection is perfect reality."*
~ Shunryu Suzuki

As DINNER PROGRESSED, I HAD BEEN surreptitiously checking my watch to be sure I'd be able to meet Patrick across the lobby at eight o'clock as we had arranged. Finally, at seven-thirty, Evelyn got up from the table and declared it was time to call the cars back so we could make our way home. Then she turned to Joel and asked him back to the house for a drink. He agreed.

As we all edged toward the lobby, I put my arm around Frankie and whispered, "I'm planning on staying a while to have a drink with Patrick, who's meeting me here." I had let his name slip the evening before when I tried to explain (in as few words as possible) to everyone where I had been for the lost hour or more.

Frankie looked at me conspiratorially, gazed around to be sure no one was close enough to hear, and whispered, "Go for it, Mom. I have a good feeling about this person, whoever he is." She looked around again. "Besides, that'll keep you away from that gross Dr. Gluckstein."

We both laughed. What a great kid I had.

"What are you two whispering about? Conspiring against your family?" Evelyn was paying more attention to us than I had thought.

"No, just making plans," I said.

But before I could tell her I wasn't going directly home, Frankie blurted, "Mom's having a drink with Patrick, so we'll just leave her here."

Evelyn turned to me. "You're what? Charlie," she hissed, "Joel is coming home with us."

"All the more reason for her to have a drink with a mysterious stranger," Frankie said as she donned her little quilted jacket and arranged her long hair over the back collar. "Come on, Aunt Evelyn. We can amuse Dr. Joel."

Evelyn had no choice but to go along with my plan. That's how I found myself sitting in a dark corner of the Library Bar at seven-fifty-eight pm, scrolling through my phone and wondering how an almost-fifty-year-old woman could be feeling this nervous about meeting a man and what business she could have agreeing to meet a stranger—and yet he didn't feel like a stranger.

At precisely eight pm, I looked up and saw him standing there in the doorway, silhouetted against the soft light that washed the interior of the lobby after dark. I could see Patrick trying to let his eyes adjust to the darkness when a hostess asked him if she could help. She led him directly to the empty chair across the tiny bar table from me. I hadn't yet ordered.

I could feel that electricity again flowing through me as he sat down. Patrick reached across the table and squeezed my hand.

"So happy you came," he said as the feeling of familiarity returned. Where had I met him before? "What do you want to drink?" he said.

I was considering a dry martini, but that's what Evelyn and I had been drinking for the past few days. She was the best martini maker I'd ever encountered, and Tom and I had experienced quite a few during our decade and a half together. Since I often thought you could tell a lot about a person by what they chose to drink, I wanted to ask him what he wanted. On the other hand, I didn't want to appear to be the kind of woman who couldn't think for herself. Always those dilemmas!

Before I had to choose which approach to take, Patrick took me out of my misery. "I love a French 75. Are you familiar with that one?"

I thought for a moment, and although it did sound familiar, I couldn't remember where I'd heard of it, and I certainly didn't remember ever tasting one. "Not sure. What's in it?"

"There are a few variations, but the simplest one is the one I like best. It's a variation on a champagne cocktail, but this one is champagne, gin, simple syrup and lemon—sometimes they add a bit of pastis."

"Sounds interesting. Do you think the bartender here can make one? Is it old?" It occurred to me that a historian might well like historical drinks. It turned out I was right.

Patrick smiled in a way I could only describe as mysterious. "It certainly is old, if by that you mean it's been around a long time. But as far as I'm concerned, it's as contemporary as that martini I see in front of that woman over there. " He nodded toward the table next to us. "The drink is over a hundred years old," he said. "Remember I told you about my research on French art in the 1920s? Well, I know this will sound silly, but I like to immerse myself in the era I'm studying, almost as if I am living and breathing it. So, I often research specific things about life in that era, and one of the things I love to do is research popular drinks. This is one."

"The 1920s? That's fantastic. It's an odd name for a cocktail, though. How did it get its name?" I figured a historian—even if art was his specialty area—would have some sense of the drink's provenance if he learned to love it so much.

"It's an interesting story," Patrick said. "It dates from the First World War and then became very popular in Paris in the years that followed. Legend has it that it was created in the New York Bar in Paris and was considered to be so potent with such a kick that someone christened it French 75 after a 75-millimetre field gun the French used during the war. It was even mentioned in the film *Casablanca,* and since then, its popularity has endured."

"Well, then," I said, "given that I'm such a sucker for a good story, how can I resist?"

Patrick smiled and called over the server. She asked him to repeat the name and then left to put in our order. We chatted amiably for a few minutes. I told him about dinner (omitting the bits about déjà vu and the annoying Dr. Joel), and he mentioned his children were joining him for his Thanksgiving dinner the next day. Both had arrived in town on Friday evening for the weekend, and I wondered if he should be with them now instead of having a drink with a strange woman.

"Not a chance," he said. "both of them grew up here in Toronto and have lots of friends they don't see often. When I told them I was meeting a friend for a drink, they seemed more than a bit happy. When I mentioned it was a woman, they were both ecstatic. I think they're beginning to conclude their dad is a lost cause on the social front, I'm afraid."

I was happy to hear that he'd referred to me as a friend—despite the fact we'd met only yesterday! Did Paris count?

The server arrived with our drinks. "I've never heard of this one, " she said, "but our new bartender worked in Paris for a few years before coming here, and he says he's made thousands of them." She placed a small cocktail napkin in front of each of us, then placed a drink on each one. "He told me to tell you that he likes to serve it in these vintage champagne coupes, but if you'd prefer a highball glass or a flute, he'll make you another one."

Patrick shook his head. "This is perfect," he said. "Just the way it should be. Thanks."

The server nodded. "Well, then, cheers!"

And we were alone.

I sipped my drink, and images began flooding my brain. I knew I'd never had this drink before, yet it seemed to evoke a kaleidoscope of feelings. I suddenly wondered if Dr. Joel had left out another kind of déjà vu—*déjà goûté* if my French served me—already tasted.

I closed my eyes and let the delicious elixir slide down my throat as I held onto the old-fashioned coupe by its stem. I could almost feel myself wearing one of Frannie's dresses at a glittering party where everyone around me was drinking champagne cocktails from coupes and smoking cigarettes that burned at the end of long cigarette holders. When I opened my eyes, Patrick was staring at me.

"You were there, weren't you?"

"Excuse me?"

"It took you right to Paris in the 1920s, didn't it?"

How could he know this unless it had the same effect on him?

I took another tiny sip. "It's incredible how a drink I've never had before can have such an almost hallucinogenic effect on me. Does it do that to you?"

Patrick took another sip of his cocktail and then took a deep breath. "I remember the first time I ordered one of these concoctions; it was the first time I was in Paris on a semester exchange while doing my PhD. I'd looked up the drinks, and when I told the French barman at Harry's New York Bar what I wanted, he rolled his eyes and said something to the effect of *les Américains* are *fou*. Notwithstanding that I happen to be a Canadian—a fact he, of course, couldn't know despite my almost impeccable French—I probably was a bit crazy. Anyway, he made me one, and at first sip, I was captivated by a feeling of a bygone era. It was wonderful for my research."

As we continued to talk and get to know one another better, I found myself comparing him to Tom. The truth is that he was a lot like Tom. Every so often, I felt Tom was right here, almost inhabiting Patrick. There were gestures and smiles, and even how he seemed to want to make sure I was happy and enjoying myself.

Finally, the hour was late, and it was time to say goodbye. Patrick walked me through the lobby and out the front door, where he asked a bellman to call me a cab. He knew I was flying home in the morning, but he was adamant on one point. "We will see one another again," he said as we stood watching the taxi make a U-turn so it could pull up in front of the hotel. "I am sure of that."

~

At home in Halifax, Frankie and I got back into our routine of rattling around in our big house, doing the things we'd always done. Frankie had school, piano lessons, soccer practice, friends over, and her newest thing: a penchant for old movies. Frankie had announced to me when we arrived home that she planned to be a screenwriter and movie director someday. She had watched one and a half old movies on her way home on the plane—*Breakfast at Tiffany's* and part of *The Maltese Falcon*—and they had captured her imagination the way nothing ever had before as far as I could remember. As a mother, I was skeptical about the career trajectory, but what could I do? I fed her thirst for more, and we settled in a few evenings a week and streamed old movies.

One Saturday evening, about three weeks after Thanksgiving, Frankie and I popped a big bowl of popcorn, poured the Italian lemon soda (her current favourite—I had a glass of Sancerre), and clicked the television on to the 1974 version of *The Great Gatsby*. It's the one where Robert Redford brought Jay Gatsby to life among the glittering costumes of the 1920s that won the costume designer an Oscar that year—and with good reason.

I knew Frankie hadn't yet read the novel the screenplay was based on, and I thought she should. When the final credits rolled, I told her this. She nodded thoughtfully, then said, "Mom, have you ever had the feeling you've lived before?"

"What do you mean? Like past lives?" I was thinking about what Bella had said when we were in Mallorca when she asked whether we thought there was a difference between reincarnation (as if that existed) and past lives.

Frankie grabbed a cushion and held it to her chest as she curled her legs up under her on the sofa beside me. "Sometimes I think I was born in the wrong era."

I had known for years that Frankie liked vintage things—clothes, furniture, books and now movies. But I had not been aware of the intensity of her connection. Perhaps it had something to do with how teenagers considered everything intense.

"I know you like vintage things, Frankie darling, and that's how you're developing your own taste and style."

"I know, Mom," she said, "but sometimes I think I would have been better suited to someplace else—some time else."

I didn't quite know how to respond, especially given my own recent brush with déjà vu. We decided it was late and would return to the discussion over the next few weeks. Frankie yawned and agreed, then took herself off to bed, leaving me to ponder the oddity that my life was becoming.

Suddenly, that pondering led me to think about characters and stories and, most of all, places. I dropped the empty popcorn bowl in the kitchen and hurried up the stairs to my office. I turned on my computer and began typing madly. I was back. And I could feel Tom hovering over me saying, "You go, girl. Write me those pages I love to read for you." And I did.

~

November arrived cold and drizzly—typical for the Atlantic coast. I always felt just slightly melancholy at this time of year. It was the harbinger of darker days to come, and I often thought that was both literally and figuratively. Tom's pancreatic cancer diagnosis had come on a dark November day only two years earlier. I remembered the phone call from him.

"Charlie, I have news. And it's not good," were his words. I could hear the terror in his voice, and it transmitted through the telephone, sinking into my heart with a thud. He hadn't been feeling well.

I had been tapping away at my computer when the call came, working on what I thought might become a new novel. I don't think I was ever able to write another single cogent word in that manuscript since that day, and god knows I tried. It now languishes partly printed out in my desk drawer and stashed in a computer archive.

Pancreatic cancer is an insidious process because it's usually at an advanced stage before there are any other signs that the patient has it. Tom had always been healthy—disgustingly so. When I heard his diagnosis, I immediately fell down the rabbit hole that is online search engines. Just plugging in the diagnosis uncovered almost one-hundred and sixty million results. Some were from such storied, credible places like the Mayo Clinic and Johns Hopkins. Others were posts by big pharma whose only interest was to have you push your physicians to administer their drugs. Then there were the patient experience sites.

Funded mainly by drug companies, these patient-centred sites give people from all walks of life a chance to tell their wretched stories about any disease you could imagine. And wretched they certainly were. As I read through some of them, it seemed a diagnosis gave them a label to put on every ill that had ever befallen them, no matter how remote its connection to their diagnosis. The sad thing was that, under all this noise, was the stark reality that by the time it is diagnosed, pancreatic cancer is too advanced in almost all cases to be treated successfully. Tom and I soon learned this. So, we went to Paris.

From the start, it was clear to me that Tom would be much better at saying goodbye than I would be. We visited all our old haunts—museums, art galleries, churches, department stores (what's Paris without a visit to Galleries Lafayette?), bistros, cocktail bars. We did it all, and I could tell that Tom was saying a silent goodbye to each of them. Since I knew I wasn't the one who would never return to Paris, I knew I had to say goodbye to Tom. I couldn't do it.

That winter, I watched my soulmate, the love of my life, slowly deteriorate. Although I should have been ready for it, I felt utterly unprepared the day Tom asked me to begin arrangements for MAID—medical assistance in dying. He wasn't prepared to let nature take its course, effectively taking any control of his own death away from him.

Tom and I were pragmatists in addition to being lovers who lived in a cocoon of happiness we'd created since we'd met more than fifteen years earlier. When he broached the subject, he reminded me that we'd talked about this before. But that was when it was all just theoretical. You know the kind of conversation couples have about the future. "If I should become so sick that I don't want to live any longer, can I count on you to make the arrangements?" Of course, he could count on me, as I knew I could count on him. The thing is that I never thought that day would come—but it did.

How did one even go about finding information about medically assisted deaths? It had been an option in Canada for some years. Many terminally ill people had taken advantage of the opportunity to take control, not letting do-gooders who opposed such action and always thought they knew what was right for everyone else take away the dying person's autonomy. I had always believed we have the right to decide when we die, but this was too close to home now. But I had no choice. It was Tom's right, it was what he wanted, and I had vowed to do my part to help.

Before anything else, I had to talk to Frankie. Tom and I did it together. She was unsurprisingly overcome with emotion—crying like I had never seen her before—but then surprisingly supportive. In the end, I think it might have been her involvement that helped her to rebound from Tom's eventual death faster than I did. She was with us all along the way and could see how much her father would gain from taking this path.

After the lengthy discussion with Frankie, I began the legal process, filling out forms and arranging independent assessments of Tom's terminal condition and his mental state. Once we received the approval, it was up to Tom. He would let us know when he'd had enough, when he could no longer continue living (dying). When that day came, Frankie insisted on being in the room with Tom and me and the doctor, who was kindly helping. One injection helped Tom into a soothing sleep. We said goodbye as he drifted off. We watched his smooth breathing for a few minutes, realizing these were the first comfortable breaths he had experienced in months. The second injection induced a coma. Ten minutes later, while I held my hand over his heart, that wonderful heart stopped, and I felt an odd sensation of a breeze that seemed to blow through me.

Frankie must have felt it too. "That was Dad," she said as the tears streamed down her face. "He's saying goodbye." She edged herself up onto the bed beside Tom and said, "Goodbye, Dad."

All I could do was cry.

I still wondered if I'd ever have the courage to truly say goodbye. That's when the phone rang.

~

"Charlie? It's Patrick. I hope I'm not interrupting you."

"Not at all. It's lovely to hear from you. How are things back at the university in Toronto?"

Patrick and I had a few texts since Thanksgiving, but it was clear he was swamped by work, and although I'd hoped we might talk on the phone, I had to be content with getting to know this stranger slowly.

"I've been hoping to have time to at least have a Zoom call or something, but my daughter Chloe has been ill and had to leave Juilliard in New York to recuperate here at home."

"Oh, I'm so sorry, Patrick," I said, alarmed at the thought of his daughter having to leave school because of illness. "Is she going to be all right?" I didn't think it was polite to ask about the nature of the illness, but I hoped it might slip out.

"I'm happy to say she is going to be fine, but she's lost her semester. We're trying to get her some remediation from a piano tutor at the Royal Conservatory of Music here, but it's been tough. She really wants to go back to New York." It seemed he wasn't going to let it slip.

"In any case, I'm happy to hear from you," I said, hoping I didn't sound over-eager.

"Here's the thing," Patrick said. "I have a proposition for you." Was he propositioning me already? This was interesting. "I have to go back to Paris at the end of December, and I would love it if you could join me."

I felt a frisson of excitement. Paris, with a French art history professor, sounded intriguing. Then I realized I wouldn't be able to go. Frankie would be here—or maybe I could take her with me, although that might be awkward. I told him I'd have to get back to him after I checked on a few things. He told me he'd call back in a week.

~

Three days later, I still hadn't figured out what to do about Patrick's invitation. I planned to run it by Tilly and Bella when we chatted later today, but my search for answers fell into my lap as they so often do.

"Mom," Frankie said as she packed her school lunch that morning, "Ariel's parents are going to Sugarloaf to ski over New Year's, and they've asked me to come." She said this so quickly that I almost missed her meaning. After she finished, she turned and fled the room.

Sugarloaf. Carrabassett Valley, Maine. The spot where so many of the well-heeled members of Halifax society skied every winter. It was a nine-hour drive—give or take—and I knew Ariel's parents were reasonably level-headed, sane people. Ariel's father was an ophthalmologist, and her mother was a retired lawyer—retired at age forty-five if memory served. I wasn't sure how she spent her time now.

Clearly, Frankie's strategy was to drop the bomb and leave the dust to settle before picking through the debris, out of which would emerge my permission, or so she hoped. Were there any good reasons why I should say no? I could not think of a single one.

So, Frankie and I spent Christmas together in Halifax, just the two of us baking Christmas cookies and filling stockings for one another, topping off Christmas Day with a marathon of old Christmas movies, culminating in *It's a Wonderful Life*. Three days later, I packed her into Ariel's parents' Mercedes SUV beside Ariel and her younger brother, whose name escapes me, and packed my bags. I had an overnight flight to London with a connection to Paris.

Enigma

"In the end, only three things matter: how much you loved, how gently you lived, and how gracefully you let go of things not meant for you."
~ Gautama Buddha

THE OVERNIGHT FLIGHT TO LONDON was comfortable enough in business class with its lie-flat seat. Spoiled, I know. Still, instead of sleeping as I had hoped to do, I found myself thinking about the conversation I'd had with Tilly and Bella just before Christmas.

I had wondered why Genevieve's sister Abigail had never gone public, had never sold her story to the tabloids as I had expected. Tilly had the answer.

"We—meaning Genevieve and me, oh and my agent—pre-empted her. We've sold the story to every rag that counts here and abroad. It seems they prefer to hear it directly from the horse's mouth, as it were. Or at least the horse's writer's mouth! There will be January headline stories all around. She was pushed out entirely And then, of course, there will be a book, and the audience will be primed!"

Of course, I had thought, *that's what Tilly would arrange*. Then I thought about Abigail. What had she really hoped to gain? I found it hard to believe all she wanted was money. Maybe it was to reclaim her lost sister—or perhaps it was to say a proper goodbye. That thought was niggling at the back of my brain as I finally drifted off.

It seemed I had just fallen asleep when the announcement to fasten our seatbelts as we descended into Heathrow Airport came on. I shook myself and got ready for the two-hour layover to await my Air France flight into Paris. I was starting to get nervous.

~

I had decided to stay in my apartment (of course), but Patrick would be staying at an Air BnB two streets over. I didn't feel comfortable asking him to stay with me, although there were three bedrooms and plenty of space by city standards. First, there was my continuing feeling that he was a stranger that I already knew. Then there was the fact that the last time he'd been in the flat was the evening his assistant had died right there on my sofa. I figured that had to be a low point in his most recent Parisian sojourn. We planned to meet for lunch the day after I arrived.

When I finally closed the apartment door behind me, I dropped my carry-on tote bag on the floor and took a deep breath. As always, there was something about the atmosphere of the flat that seemed to whisper of earlier days. And, as always, I could almost feel my great-grandmother's presence among the beautiful pieces of art deco furniture and artwork. Tom and I had discussed taking some of the art pieces home, but we concluded (actually, it was mainly at Tom's insistence) that they belonged here. I did, however, put away the most valuable pieces whenever someone was going to lease the place. Now, I had to have them around me.

I dug the key out of my tote bag and went to the locked pantry behind the kitchen. I turned the key in the old lock and flicked on the light. The old pantry was lined with shelves, as one might expect, but I had removed the ones at the back so I could have a clothing rack and keep some of my things here all the time. Under the hanging clothes were four pieces of artwork that came off the walls when I leased it out, and on the shelves were more clothes and three sculptures. I took each one out, placing them back where they belonged.

All three were Art Deco pieces, and all three always evoked the Roaring Twenties and a luxurious lifestyle for me. Those years had been my great-grandmother's most formative years in Paris, and I liked to think about the circumstances around which she bought these pieces. And although I had read Frannie's diaries, she had never mentioned how she acquired them, so I was left to create stories. Perhaps this one, with the dancer on a glass base, was a gift from a suitor. Perhaps she had purchased the reclining nude for herself with her first royalty cheques. But my favourite was the one whose provenance fired my imagination the most.

I lifted it carefully from the shelf and carried it to its pedestal in what was once Frannie's den and where I sometimes wrote. The sculpture was called "Beloved." I knew this from my research, and it was created by Erté, who had also been a famous art designer and illustrator in the Deco years.

Once in her place, the sculpture needed only one other element. It needed the pedestal light. I flicked it on and sat down in the desk chair. I was home.

I hadn't meant to fall asleep that early, nor had I intended to fall asleep sitting up. When I woke up, it was dark, I was hungry, and my neck hurt. I shook myself and quickly got up to unpack and then find something to eat. Since there was nothing in the apartment, I had to find my shopping bags and head to the only market I knew would be open this late. On the way home, I stopped for a glass of wine and a croque monsieur at a bistro a few blocks from the apartment, then went home and fell into a deep sleep. When I finally woke up the following day, I only had time to shower and dress before meeting Patrick for lunch.

It was cold. It was too cold for me to sit outside to eat, but the Parisians didn't seem to be bothered by the cold as much as I was. Since I was a Canadian and very acclimatized to cold late-December weather, I had always found this strange. In any case, I hoped Patrick would find a table inside, which is where I found him, sitting against the back wall with a glass of wine in front of him on the table.

When he saw me, his face immediately broke into that enigmatic smile I'd noticed before. He arose to greet me with the French double kiss as I unwound my scarf and sat opposite him. I suddenly felt as if no time had passed since we'd last been together. It was as if we'd spoken yesterday and every day since our chance encounter in Toronto—but we had not.

Once I had ordered my wine, there was a question I'd been wanting to ask him since that first coffee encounter in Toronto and hadn't gotten around to after Thanksgiving dinner.

"Patrick, I've been wondering about something. When we bumped into one another at that bookshop here last summer, and you had no idea who I was, you impetuously suggested a book to me. Is that something you like to do?"

Patrick's eyebrows raised slightly. "Something I like to do? If you're asking me if it's something I do regularly, the answer is no. In fact," he said, stopping to think for a moment, "I can't remember a single time when I've ever done it before."

"Why then? Why me?" I hesitated a moment. "Not that I'm complaining."

"To tell you the truth, Charlie, I've wondered that myself. All I know is that I felt a connection to you, even before I saw your face, and something came over me. You seemed to be looking for something and were standing right in front of a book that meant a lot to me, so I offered it. Did you read it?"

I nodded. "I did. And now I want to know how you became interested in Zen Buddhism."

Patrick sipped his wine thoughtfully. "It's not something I'm devoted to if that's what you're asking. My favourite books outside of art history ones are novels from the early twentieth century—Hemingway, Fitzgerald, Steinbeck, the usuals. But after Alison died, I was searching for some kind of deeper meaning. I was angry at first and believed her death had to mean something. A colleague suggested I might find something useful in Shunryu Suzuki's writing since his approach to Zen isn't so esoteric—he's the one who managed to popularize Zen in North America back in the 1960s. Anyway, I reluctantly bought that book and found myself finally believing that nothing is meant to stay the same. When I finally realized the truth of how things aren't meant to stay the same forever, I memorized the specific quote. *When we realize the everlasting truth of "everything changes" and find our composure in it, we find ourselves in Nirvana.* That's when I knew I had to say goodbye to Alison and move on. My life as a widowed father of two young children was just another phase of life that I had to live. From one ending came another beginning. And here I am, ten years later."

I reached into my purse that I had tucked under the table and pulled out my now-tattered copy of Patrick's recommended book. I opened it to a highlighted sentence and read, *"Treat every moment as your last. It is not preparation for something else."* I closed the book and put it back.

"That's what I believed, Charlie. At least until I met you."

I stared at him. I was puzzled by his statement, and yet I seemed to have some understanding of it.

"I'm no longer so sure that some moments aren't preparation for something else, but that something else might not be in our lifetimes. What I mean to say, Charlie, is—and you're going to think I've lost my mind here—but I have a deep sense that I've known you before."

"That doesn't seem so odd, Patrick. I think we both concluded that we may have met somewhere before. We've both spent time in Paris and Toronto over the years." Even as I said this, I knew it didn't ring true. It didn't seem to ring true for Patrick, either.

He shook his head. "That's not it. At first, that's what I thought. But every time I see you, I have a feeling that goes deeper than a chance encounter with someone whose face is imprinted in your mind, and you happen it upon again. No, this is different."

I was starting to feel that frisson of the unknown beginning to creep up my back into my neck again. "How is it different, Patrick?" I could almost feel what he was about to say.

Patrick swallowed the last of his wine and signalled for two more glasses—and we hadn't even ordered our lunch yet. "Charlie, I know this sounds crazy, but have you ever given any thought to the concept of past lives?"

I was trying to digest Patrick's words when the server appeared at our table. "*Êtes-vous prêt à commander?*" She asked.

Yes, I thought, *I am more than ready to order, even if just to give me a few minutes to get my head around Patrick's words.* This was the third time in recent memory someone had mentioned the concept. First, the last week we were in Mallorca, Bella had asked Tilly and me if we thought past lives were the same as reincarnation. I hadn't given it much thought at the time since I was the resident skeptic about the whole concept of reincarnation and Tilly's bonehead idea that Genevieve was the reincarnation of Coco Chanel. Although, I occasionally allowed myself to consider that this could still be true. Then, more recently, Frankie had mentioned past lives.

Frankie's question had been more specific, more personalized. She asked me if I had ever had the feeling I'd lived before. Was this what Patrick was asking?

I told Patrick to go ahead and order first since I hadn't made up my mind and I was still stalling, hoping to have a few more moments to collect my thoughts. I heard Patrick order steak tartare—a dish I'd never been able to justify in all its raw beef glory—in perfectly accented French while I fixated on the French onion soup. Cliché, I know, but I love it, especially when it's made in an authentic Parisian bistro.

When the server left, Patrick said, "Okay, I know it's way out there, but I have to believe you've felt the same familiarity from the first moment we met. You must have thought about this."

I then related my Thanksgiving dinner story about discussing the concept of déjà vu with a neurologist. Patrick laughed. "I suppose I sound like a fool."

The truth is that he didn't sound like a fool at all, and I told him that. "It's just that this whole thing is so outside my logical self," I said.

"Mine, too," Patrick said. "You might consider an art historian to be a creative romantic with his head perpetually in the clouds, but my children would tell you a different story. My historical research borders on the obsessively didactic. My daughter, the pianist, thinks I'm suppressing an overly creative streak. According to her, I have a deep-seated fear of being a starving artist."

The moment he mentioned the starving artist, I felt a jolt of electricity run up my spine yet again. What was it about the notion of the starving artist that made me think that? *Oh, yes*, I thought, *it's because Evelyn told me I liked that persona way back in the days when I was, in fact, a starving artist trying to write my first novel.* I was sure that's why it hit me so intensely, but somewhere deep in my gut, I knew that wasn't the only reason. I just didn't know what it was.

"Okay, I'll bite," I said as the server returned with our lunch orders. "For the sake of argument, let's say there is such a thing as past lives, and we met before. How do we go about finding proof?"

"Proof? That's going to be tough, but I did do a bit of research." He wiped his mouth on his red-checkered napkin and reached for his backpack that he had slung on the back of his chair under his leather jacket. He pulled two books out and passed them across the table to me. "Here, Charlie, have a look at these."

I put my spoon down and interrupted my quiet swooning over the deliciousness of the perfectly caramelized onions under a bed of perfectly broiled Gruyère cheese. The first one was called *Beyond Past Lives: What Parallel Realities Can Teach Us about*

Relationships, Healing, and Transformation by someone called Mira Kelly. The second was *Old Souls: The Scientific Evidence for Past Lives: Compelling Evidence From Children Who Remember Past Lives* by Tom Shroder. Scientific evidence? Well, that seemed to appeal to my logical self. As was now becoming my habit, I opened the first one to a random page and read a line.

As it turned out, that page was the book's foreword—a foreword that Wayne Dyer, the late pop psychologist, had written. I refrained from rolling my eyes and read the line. He was referring back to one of his own books. *"Have a mind that is open to everything and attached to nothing."* I read it to Patrick.

He smiled. "Well, Charlie, that seems like a good place to start, doesn't it?"

I looked at Patrick thoughtfully. "Perhaps," I said. "The question is: where will it take us?"

~

Patrick and I had four days together. It was December 28, and I had to fly home on New Year's Day, so if we were going to get to know one another and figure out where we'd met before, we didn't have much time.

When we finished eating, Patrick reached into his backpack, pulled out one of those yellow, legal-size pads, and put it on the table beside his coffee cup. "Okay," he said, "let's start with this déjà vu we've both been feeling. Charlie, have you ever had this déjà vu feeling before?"

I thought about it for a moment and couldn't think of a specific time when I'd felt that way before. Suddenly, it struck me. I had, indeed, felt déjà vu before but never in the context of being with another person. "Yes," I said. "I have felt it before. I was here in Paris by myself. I had just discovered that my great-grandmother had left me money and her flat."

Patrick seemed excited. "So, you felt you'd been in the flat before." It seemed more like a statement rather than a question.

"No. That's not where I felt it." Patrick looked crestfallen. I continued. "It was when I was walking in the city."

"Where was it?"

"That's the problem," I said, sipping my coffee. "I can't remember. Is that important?"

"I think so," he said, rummaging through some papers in his backpack. He pulled out a few more yellow-lined sheets. These ones were already covered with writing. "I made a few notes on the flight over," he said. "I've been doing a bit of research."

I could see that he had. "Patrick, why did you look so disappointed when I told you I hadn't had the feeling when I first visited my apartment?"

He sighed. "Because that's where I felt it most strongly."

My eyebrows shot up. I was sincerely shocked. "My apartment? Frannie's flat?"

He nodded.

"So, you thought perhaps we'd encountered one another in a past life in that very flat?" I could hardly believe what I was hearing myself say. *I don't believe in past lives, and here I am, being sucked into this vortex. Is there a way out? Should I even be talking to this man? I really don't know him.* My mind was swirling.

Then Patrick described in detail how when he'd arrived in Paris the summer before, and Lucien Allard, my property manager, opened the door to the flat and invited him to step inside, he'd had an overwhelming feeling that he knew that apartment—that he'd been there before. But he knew this wasn't possible. He had certainly never been in the flat on previous sojourns in Paris. "I even knew the way to the kitchen. I knew there was an old German-made typewriter in the office."

I had often felt Frannie's presence but couldn't remember ever feeling like I'd been in the apartment before. It had never felt familiar in that way. In fact, I'd been fascinated to learn what I could about her from the various pieces of furniture and art, not to mention her dresses. But it seemed that Patrick had a connection to the place, even if it was only in his imagination. As much as I liked the idea of knowing someone in the past—and I couldn't shake that déjà vu experience—the skeptic in me was bubbling closer to the surface despite my agreement to keep an open mind. I decided to try.

"Patrick, through your research, were there any specifics about how we might discover this past connection?"

Patrick looked at his notes. "There are things like instant familiarity," he looked over at me. "We have that in spades, don't you think?" I couldn't disagree with that. "Then there are dubious signs like a telepathic connection and seeing the connection in Tarot cards or birth charts."

I could see he was as skeptical of those things as I was.

"There is one other one, though, that might be worth considering." He shifted in his seat. "When you walked in here today, I had the strangest feeling that no time had passed since I'd seen you. It was as if we had talked only yesterday."

I shivered a bit. I had felt exactly the same way. "Is that a sign?"

Patrick nodded. "But most of the rest just seem like pop-psych babble. I believe that Paris has something to do with our feeling of connection. I have a proposition." I was all ears. "I propose we explore Paris together to see if that feeling of déjà vu returns to either of us."

It seemed like a good suggestion, so we set up a plan. Like so many tourists before us, we decided to do Paris in four days. We had no idea where it would lead us, but of course, we would begin with the Louvre.

~

Over the next three days, Patrick and I visited museums and art galleries, including Notre Dame (still under construction as it recovered from that massive fire a few years earlier) and ate in any bistro that seemed to capture our imaginations. Both of us had visited most of the galleries before (in this lifetime), so, of course, they were familiar. But nothing seemed unusual or electrifying.

Each morning, Patrick arrived at my flat at precisely nine am bearing coffee and chocolate croissants. We sat in my living room, happily eating while Patrick reviewed our plan for the day. On the morning of the thirtieth, Patrick suggested we spend the morning strolling along the Seine, then stop for lunch at Les Deux Magots, that storied Parisian café that had hosted so many artists and literary luminaries in the 1920s and 30s. I had never been there and immediately felt sad that Tom would not experience this with me. I shook off the feeling and grabbed my coat and scarf.

"Better wear some boots," Patrick said. "It looks like it's started snowing."

Snow in Paris in December? Was that a thing? I had no idea.

"Oh, I almost forgot to mention another place I thought we might enjoy visiting."

"What would that be?" I said as I rummaged around in the wardrobe in the front hall to see if, in fact, I had a pair of boots here. *Voila!* There they were. *A bit long in the tooth for a stylish Parisian,* I thought. Then it occurred to me that I often observed that Parisian women were masters at wearing older, well-loved pieces that served them well for almost a lifetime, or so it seemed. Perhaps I could channel my inner Parisian with these old boots whose provenance was a mystery to me.

Patrick wound his own scarf more tightly around his neck, cleared his throat and said, "Tomorrow is New Year's Eve, and I hoped you might not have other plans." I hadn't given New Year's Eve a single thought and told him so. He continued. "I've taken a very great liberty. I've bought tickets for a New Year's party at the Hotel Le Meurice. Do you know it?"

I did know it. I had never darkened its door, but I knew it to be one of the swankiest hotels in all of Paris. It had a long history that included being the home of any number of artists, including Salvador Dali and Andy Warhol, not to mention Bob Dylan, for a time. The idea of New Year's Eve at Le Meurice slightly terrified me. It had to be more upscale and glamorous than I could pull off. My immediate thought was that Evelyn would never think this. Anyway, I had nothing with me to wear to a posh event. I told Patrick this.

"I thought you might say that. As it turns out, I have a meeting this afternoon at the university, and I can't get out of it. Maybe you could use the time for a bit of shopping?"

The idea was oddly captivating. "What are *you* planning to wear?"

"That's the thing. It's a theme party." I frowned. A theme party? Patrick cleared his throat again and said, "The theme is *les années folles*."

"Seriously? The Roaring Twenties?"

"I thought you might find it interesting."

Interesting didn't quite cover it. I thought about Frannie's fabulous flapper dress inside its muslin cocoon hanging in my closet at home—what I wouldn't have given for a chance to wear it if I dared. But I couldn't. I took a deep breath. "Okay, Patrick, but you didn't answer my question. What are *you* planning to wear?"

"A colleague has given me the name of a vintage rental place. He says they have lots of 20s-era formal wear for men, but their collection for women isn't great. I have the names of a few vintage shops you could visit?" It was more of a question than a statement. Then he added, "I'm sure it won't be too expensive."

I almost laughed. I hadn't yet clearly explained to Patrick just how much money wasn't an object for me. I had wondered what he might think. This moment, however, didn't seem to be the right time for that discussion. I was beginning to feel a tremor of excitement building as I considered which of the current designers was doing twenties-inspired styles. I would start at Chanel.

"Then, I guess it's a date," I said as I opened the door. But first, we had more exploring to do.

~

It was colder that day than I could ever remember it being in Paris. That being said, I rarely spent time here in the winter. We walked toward the Left Bank of the Seine, where I knew there would be artists painting outdoors. That was where they could usually be found, but today was so cold I wondered if anyone would be there.

We strolled past a few diehards and stopped to watch them paint for a few moments. I remembered the day—a bright, sunny summer day—when Tom and I strolled past the artists and vendors selling vintage postcards and magazines. We had stopped to watch an artist as she worked, and I found myself staring at one of her finished pieces. Female artists weren't that common along the banks of the Seine as far as I had observed, and her work was something different. Not quite impressionistic and not quite something else, her rendering of a view over the Paris rooftops was mesmerizing. I remember being caught up in the fantasy of standing on a rooftop somewhere, gazing out at the urban landscape that was so different from a North American city. Of course, the moment Tom noticed me staring was the moment he made the artist an offer she couldn't refuse. We rolled up the canvas, and I tucked it under my arm, then into my suitcase for the flight home. Once it was framed, we hung it in our family room, where we could both see it from the kitchen as we worked together. I hugged myself tightly to stifle a tear.

"You cold?" Patrick said, concerned for my well-being.

"A bit," I said. Perhaps I would have mentioned my thoughts if I had known him better. Another time?

"Time for lunch, then," he said, taking my arm as we made our way toward Les Deux Magots.

As we neared Boulevard St. Germain, I found myself examining every building, every storefront, every stone church, every cobblestone. I felt peaceful here. Then the café came into view.

Every picture I'd ever seen of this historic café showed only the outside. Despite the cold weather, the tables were filled with Parisians (and probably many tourists) all drinking coffee and perhaps trying to conjure days gone by when you might have run into Ernest Hemingway or Simone de Beauvoir. Patrick, however, had reserved a table inside, for which I was very grateful.

As we stepped inside the door, I wasn't sure what to expect. What greeted me was a large space with magnificent ceiling ornamentation and pillars, furnished with simple wooden tables beside red leather banquettes. It was both grand and unpretentious at the same time.

We settled ourselves at our table and perused the menu. I had heard that Les Deux Magots was famous for its hot chocolate, so I had to keep that in mind as I ordered lunch. I would certainly be having that after my main course. Once we had ordered and our wine arrived, Patrick said, "I don't want to pry, but I felt you were somehow moved by those artists along the Seine."

And I started. I told him about Tom and his illness. I told him about Frankie. I even told him about inheriting money from my great-grandmother, although I didn't tell him how many millions—yet. I was clear that Tom had left me a lot of money, but it could never make up for losing him. I told him I'd had two bestselling novels (a fact he already knew) and how I'd been having trouble writing the next one. By the time we got to hot chocolate, Patrick was telling me about how painful it had been when his wife died, and he was left a single dad for two young children. He told me about the book he was struggling to write about lost artists of the early twentieth century. We had much in common, it seemed.

When Patrick finally checked his watch, we were both startled at how much time had passed in the blink of an eye. He was late for his meeting at the university, and I had shopping to do. We said goodbye and promised to meet later at a bistro near my apartment for dinner. Although we turned in different directions at the door, I realized we both seemed to be heading the same way.

~

I pulled my coat tightly around me as I walked down Rue du Faubourg Saint-Honoré toward Rue Cambon and the Chanel boutique. Tom and I had visited it once before when he insisted I needed a pair of Chanel ballet flats—cream-coloured with the iconic black patent leather toe. That was ten years ago when I was still getting used to having money. I balked at the suggestion at first—who needs a nine-hundred-dollar pair of shoes? But after I agreed, it became a kind of game for the two of us as he would teasingly ask me, "What's the price per wearing down to now?" Quite low at this point, if you must know.

I arrived in front of the boutique's door, and the doorman opened it and saluted to welcome me inside. But something stopped me. I abruptly turned around and wandered back out into the street. I walked mindlessly for a few blocks without a clue as to a destination, and when I looked up, I was standing directly in front of a shop with a deep lavender canopy. The gold letters on the canopy said, "Maison LaChapelle." *Oh. My. God.* I thought. *It's Genevieve's boutique. Genevieve LaChapelle. Mademoiselle.* Before I knew what I was doing, I had my hand on the ornate brass doorknob that opened the massive door leading into a three-story, light-filled space that resembled nothing less than a more ornate version of the atelier in Mallorca. The only difference was that the sewing machines and cutting tables were replaced with clothing rails and tables displaying a rainbow of cashmere sweaters. And then there was the sweeping staircase that reminded me of the one in the Chanel boutique that Chanel herself used to sit on to view the models as they showed her dresses to waiting clients back in the day.

I took a deep breath and looked around. My eyes were drawn immediately to a rack at the far corner of the space. It was filled with what looked like cocktail dresses with wisps of chiffon, lace and sequins peaking out. As I made my way toward the rack, a young woman materialized out of nowhere—or perhaps from behind the screen that blended so seamlessly into the wood panelling on the wall that it seemed as if she had just appeared before me.

"*Puis-je vous aider, Madame?*" Could she help me? I wasn't sure.

Before I could say a word, I heard a familiar voice coming from the direction of the staircase.

"Charlotte! *Charlotte Hudson, c'est vous*? Is it you here in Paris, in my salon?"

I turned. It was Genevieve herself, resplendent in a tweed suit—Chanel-like right down to the five strands of pearls encircling her slender neck. As always, I looked for the cigarette, but that would have been Coco.

"Genevieve, hello. Yes, it's me." I wasn't sure how to proceed. I knew she and Tilly were still working on the book, and there had already been a series of articles. I had many questions, none of which were really any of my business. I hadn't expected to see Mademoiselle in the flesh when I walked in, but I wasn't at all sure exactly what I did expect. I took a deep breath and decided to tell her why I was browsing a boutique in Paris.

When I related my dilemma to her and its seriously short time frame (I had only two or so hours to find a dress for tomorrow evening), she seemed delighted.

"Charlotte," she said, "what a wonderful way to celebrate the beginning of a new year! It does promise to be an exciting one, *non?*" She winked. "And *les années folles*! A most wonderful theme."

I noticed that her French-accented English had returned after her momentary lapse into American-accented English at that last dinner in Mallorca. I smiled.

Then she asked me to remove my coat. She stood in front of me while her assistant, the young woman clad in head-to-toe black (as expected), ran to get Mademoiselle her tape measure, her glasses and a notebook. I remembered Genevieve's critical gaze as I stood before her in Mallorca wearing my French Jacket. Back then, she had been examining the jacket. This time she seemed to be studying me. I wondered if she thought I'd be up to carrying off one of her dresses, although I doubted whether she would have anything that could pass for flapper-era evening attire anyway. I was wrong.

The next thing I knew, her assistant shuffled me off to a dressing room and told me to undress. She returned a few minutes later with an armload of silk, chiffon and fringe. Yes, Mademoiselle loved the inspiration of the 1920s. Yes, she had current dresses that might work. But none of them did. I tried on six dresses, all resembling the 1920s but not quite capturing it.

I was about to put my clothes back on and give up when Genevieve knocked on the door of my changing room and asked if she might show me one more dress.

"Before I show it to you, Charlotte, you must answer me one question. Are you willing to wear a vintage dress?" I told her I was, at which point she lifted the dress that had been over her arm and hung it on a padded hook in the dressing room.

I stood, staring at this vision of ivory silk, speechless. It was beyond perfect. It had a back neckline that dipped low, almost to the waist, trimmed with beads and fringed tiers, The scalloped hem and tiers of silk fringe adorning the skirt suggested that it would gently brush the dance floor, and the straps and bodice were decorated with tiny silver oblong pastes and diamantés in a floral motif. In a word, it was exquisite.

As I touched the dress and checked the label, my heart began beating so fast I thought Genevieve might be able to hear it. I was beyond excited. The label announced that it was a Jean Patou, the same designer as Frannie's dress that now hung in my closet at home—the dress I wished I had with me at this very moment. But I didn't need it. Fate had stepped in.

"I'll buy it," I said even before trying it on. It was a magnificent piece of art, even if it didn't fit me.

"Non, non," Genevieve said. *"Tu ne comprends pas, ma chère.* You do not understand. It is not for sale, Charlotte, but it needs to be displayed. I wish to think of it enjoying yet one more night at the Salon Pompadour. You know, it has been there before. I know that to be true since I bought it from the grand-niece or something of the woman who wore it. It would be my great pleasure if you would wear it." She lifted it off the hook and slipped it off the hanger. "And dear Charlotte, it *will* fit you. I promise."

Of course, she was right. Who would be better at assessing bodies and garments than a couturier? I promised Genevieve it would be returned to her on January third, when the salon reopened. I would ensure that Lucien arranged it when I left.

And so, I left the salon with my dress. At least it would be mine for one night.

~

Patrick and I had dinner together that evening and also spent part of the morning of New Year's Eve sharing breakfast and our plans for when each of us returned to our respective homes—I to Halifax, and he to Toronto. We hadn't been able to determine the source of this enigma that was our deep connection, but we both hoped it would continue. Then he asked me if I'd had any luck with the dress hunt, but I refused to give him any details. He would have to wait. He left at noon so I could have the time to tidy the apartment since I was leaving the next day, and get ready for the evening's event.

As I sat at Frannie's (my) dressing table at five pm with a glass of wine in one hand and a mascara wand in the other, I looked in the mirror. I saw myself, but I also saw Tom. He was smiling at me. It would be okay.

Illusion

"I have realized that the past and future are real illusions, that they exist in the present, which is what there is and all there is."
~ Alan Watts

PATRICK ARRIVED AT EXACTLY SEVEN PM. When I opened the door, I felt swept back to *les années folles* for sure. He was wearing a black tailcoat with a white bowtie and weskit. His shoes were patent leather, and he had a white silk scarf slung jauntily around his neck. He was carrying a walking stick with a faceted crystal handle and a black top hat.

Before I could say a word, Patrick stared at me, his eyes popping. "You look…you look…exquisite. You look…."

"Very 1920s?" I laughed at his speechlessness.

"Yes, and so much more," he said. "It's as if you just walked out of 1923 and into the twenty-first century."

"Maybe I did," I said, grabbing a cashmere shawl I was using as a wrap. I held out my arm. "Shall we?"

~

I felt like a completely different person as Patrick helped me out of the taxi in front of the Hotel Le Meurice. Located opposite the Tuileries Garden, between Place de la Concorde and the Musée du Louvre on the Rue de Rivoli, Le Maurice had been there for close to two centuries. I knew the Nazis had commandeered it as a headquarters during the Second World War, but you would never have known this silent history. This evening, it was magnificent in its Louis XVI-style grandeur. I imagined this was precisely what the partygoers in Jazz Age Paris had experienced. Then we entered the Salon Pompadour.

The grand salon reminded me a bit of the hall of mirrors, the ballroom at Versailles, except that when Tom and I and Frankie visited it a few years before Tom died, it had overflowed with tourists. This magnificent, gilt-trimmed room was filled with dazzling partiers sitting at large tables dripping with crystal, silver, and magnificent candelabra while sipping champagne from coupes.

A maitre d' (one of several) led us to our table, where our six tablemates, who were already deep into the cocktails and champagne, introduced themselves. I promptly forgot every single name. As I looked around at our fellow guests, I was impressed at the extent to which they had, to a person, taken the theme seriously. If you didn't spy the odd cellphone on a table here and there, you might have believed you'd stepped back in time. The women were clad in bias-cut satin dresses, slip dresses with fringe, strings of pearls, and elbow-length gloves. The men all looked dashing in their white ties and tails. Everyone looked so comfortable in this attire that it seemed like we had all fallen through a hole in the space-time continuum and were now, at this moment, inhabiting 1923. Patrick and I didn't know a single person, and it didn't matter. Patrick and I seemed to be in a world of our own.

We ate dinner and drank champagne and danced. We danced to a jazz orchestra's sounds of the 1920s, and I had no idea how to do some of the dances so many other couples seemed to find so easy. I recognized the Charleston and the Tango, but the rest were a blur. We did our best.

Later, breathless, we went back to our table. It was still only 11:30, a half an hour to go before the countdown. I sipped my water and then reached for my champagne coupe once again. Patrick did the same.

"Do you believe in parallel realities, Charlie?"

I stopped sipping my champagne for a moment. "I thought we had been exploring the concepts of déjà vu and possibly past lives. Isn't that a different thing?"

Patrick looked slightly tortured. His brow furrowed, and his lips narrowed. He rubbed his head as if trying to figure out what was in it. "I don't know, Charlie. I really don't know. It's just that the moment I saw you in that bookstore for the first time—the moment you turned and looked at me—I felt my search for why Paris had always felt so familiar had come to an end. You were the missing piece."

"Do you still feel that way?"

"More than ever. But now it doesn't feel like the ending at all. It feels more like a beginning."

"So why the idea of parallel lives, whatever that means?"

"This will sound seriously weird, if not totally irrational, but it's more like I sometimes feel I'm living two lives simultaneously. I have my kids, my students, and my research. And that's all so real. Then there are other times when I feel like this life isn't real and I'm somewhere else."

I looked around at all the glittering people, laughing and drinking champagne as one year ended and another was about to begin. And I could feel myself drifting or maybe sinking. Just as I had experienced that very odd feeling when I entered the hotel and again when we walked through the doors into the salon, I now felt both more connected and more disconnected. This contradiction made me feel dizzy.

"What do you suppose reality is, Patrick?" I said without even thinking about my words. "Are our thoughts and experiences real, or is reality only about what we can see and touch?"

"I'm not sure anymore, Charlie," Patrick said.

I was suddenly seized by an idea. I took a very unladylike swig of champagne and gestured for the passing server for a refill. "If I write a book with characters living in the 1920s, say, is that reality?" Patrick looked baffled. I continued. "I've been thinking about this for a while now. Does a story have to be observed outside yourself to be real? Does it even matter?"

~

The countdown came and went with confetti, balloons and popping champagne corks all around—and an unexpectedly tender kiss at midnight—then it was time for us to leave. It was our last evening together, and I still had no idea where this was going. We both felt like we knew each other so well, but it wasn't so much about knowing what we'd been doing in our lives. That didn't seem to matter. It was more about already knowing who we were. And I didn't want the feeling to change—whether it was a reality or, just as likely, an illusion. Can't we just have our illusions and live them?

When the taxi dropped us outside my apartment building at one-thirty, I asked Patrick if he'd like to come in for a cup of coffee. He said yes.

Once upstairs, I went to the kitchen to make the coffee, leaving Patrick alone in the living room. When I returned with a tray, he was still standing by the fireplace, fidgeting.

"Is there something wrong?" I said as I laid the tray on the coffee table.

"I guess I'm just not sure where we go from here," he said. "I don't want this to be over."

I told him I didn't either. We sat down, and I poured the coffee from the press. Patrick took one sip and then put his cup down on the table. "Charlie," he said, "I know how odd this sounds, but may I go into your bedroom."

Well, this is unexpected, I thought. *And a strange way to ask. Could he go into my bedroom?* But how did I feel about it? Oddly, happy if I was being honest with myself.

I told him he could and wondered if he meant I was to follow. *Of course, that's what he means,* I thought. *You're just out of practice.*

Before I knew it, Patrick had already gotten up and was gone down the hall toward my bedroom. By the time I arrived at the door, Patrick was standing at the entrance to my closet, staring at…I wasn't sure what he was staring at. Then, he moved my clothes on the rail to open up a space on the wall. He got down

197

on his hands and knees and started running his hands over the baseboard. Suddenly his hands stopped, and I heard a click.

"What the hell?" I said, moving closer to the closet where Patrick was now sitting on the floor with his arm stuck inside the wall. Or at least that's how it looked to me. "How did you know that was there?" Then I remembered Patrick had spent several months living in this apartment. Of course, he knew, but why hadn't he mentioned it to me? And what was he doing now?

Patrick looked feverish as he began to pull a large, flat, muslin-wrapped package from behind the wall. "I didn't know it was here, Charlie. I didn't sleep in this bedroom when I leased the flat. In fact, tonight is the first time I ever walked inside the room. I always had a feeling that whoever owned the flat might want some privacy."

I was a bit mollified by his explanation—and I did believe him—but the whole tableau made no sense at all. "What the heck is that?" I said. "And if you didn't know it was here, how did you *seem* to know it was there?" My head was beginning to hurt either because I seemed to be facing a conundrum or because of the copious amount of champagne I'd imbibed over the course of the evening. Probably both.

Patrick finally stood up, and we both looked at the package, which was now on the floor in the middle of my bedroom. It was about three feet long by two feet wide—give or take—wrapped in muslin and tied with twine.

"What is it?" I whispered, not understanding why I thought I should speak softly.

"I have no idea," Patrick said.

"Then what made you come in here and go immediately to the specific place in my closet where it was hidden? A place I had no idea about. Patrick, I don't understand."

Patrick sank onto the side of my bed. "I have no idea, Charlie. I'm telling you honestly. I don't know what suddenly came over me that made coming into this room and finding this parcel so urgent. It was like I had no control over my actions —as if I knew just what to do and where to go, but we both know that would be impossible."

I sat down beside him, and we both looked at the parcel. "What do you suppose is in it?"

Patrick shrugged. "I don't know, but I have a strange feeling it's important."

I couldn't believe I was sitting here staring at something that looked as if it had been inside my walls for decades, believing this man had no prior knowledge that it had been there, yet was able to find a hidden door and pull this out. It made no sense. The most troubling part for me, though, was that I believed him, and I had no idea why. After a few silent moments, I said, "Well, I guess we're not going to figure out what's inside by staring at it. We need to open it."

~

We took the bundle from my bedroom down the hall to my office, where Patrick laid it on my desk. We stood for a moment, looking at the package in the pool of light cast on it from the brass goose-neck art deco desk lamp.

"Would you like to do the honours?" Patrick said.

I opened a desk drawer and withdrew the large, antique shears that Frannie had left behind all those years before. Before I cut the twine, I thought I should see if it would come loose without cutting, but it held fast. I took the shears, slid one blade under the twine and snipped.

The string fell away from the muslin, which loosened but didn't immediately open. Together Patrick and I lifted the bundle off the desk and unwrapped it. Once it was unwrapped, we placed the contents back down and just stood there staring.

On the desk in front of us were what appeared to be unframed oil paintings—canvases with frayed edges that suggested age. The top image was a well-executed landscape that appeared slightly impressionistic to my untrained eye. What was clear, however, was that they were old—very old.

"What do you think?" I said to the art history professor who was so handily in the room with me.

Patrick squinted at it. "It looks like a rendering of the French countryside."

"Any idea about the artist?"

Patrick squinted at the signature. "Dear god," he said. "It's by Auguste Vaillancourt."

"Should I know him?"

Patrick looked at me. "No, not at all. I'd be surprised if many people outside art history and art connoisseur circles know his work. He's one of the obscure French artists of the 1910s and 1920s that I've been researching." Patrick sat down heavily in the leather chair opposite the desk. "How is this possible?"

"Which part?" I said, sitting in the chair across the desk from him.

"All of it," Patrick said. "First, how did I know to look in your closet? It's impossible that I could have had any idea there was a secret door inside. And it's even more inconceivable that there was a bundle of canvases with a painting by an artist that I may be the only person in the world interested in stuffed in the space."

I lifted the top canvas revealing another landscape. Unlike the first landscape painting, this one looked to me like it was of the French Riviera. The signature was the same. The third canvas was definitely of the river Seine in Paris. The focus of the painting was four artists, all sitting at their easels working on their art. I lifted it and placed it with the other two. There was one more.

The moment I saw the last painting, I felt I could barely breathe. "It's impossible," I said.

Patrick immediately got up and came around the desk to see this one with me. "Oh my god, Charlie." He looked at me. "It's you."

~

Half an hour later, and not yet recovered from the shock of looking at a century-old painting and seeing myself, I was sitting in the living room with a glass of brandy. The portrait was now on the coffee table, where Patrick examined it closely. My mind wandered, and I stared out the window where snow flurries scurried across the window in the faint glow from the streetlights below. It must have been after three am, and I had to pack for my flight scheduled in twelve hours. I closed my eyes, and the image on the canvas burned the back of my eyelids. It was me—and it wasn't me.

The dark, kohl-lined eyes stared out uncompromisingly from the depths of history. The ruby-red lips almost pouted. She wore a wide, beaded headband and held a cigarette in a long holder. Her head was turned, and her bare shoulder and back faced me. Around her neck were three strands of pearls. Her eyes stared. But it was the back of the dress I recognized because I was still wearing it. It was the dress Genevieve had lent me. What the hell?

I got up quickly and said, "I have to change, Patrick." I had to get that dress off my back at the very instant. I had to hang it up like the art piece it was and try to figure out why it was in that portrait, how Genevieve came to own it and why on earth she thought of lending it to me.

Patrick nodded and continued examining the painting with a magnifying glass I had found in a kitchen drawer. When I returned to the living room, now clad in jeans and a sweater, Patrick had finished his examination and was sitting in a chair by the dying fire, sipping brandy. I flopped onto the sofa and grabbed a cushion to hold tightly to me as if it might help to slow my thudding heart.

"I don't know what to say, Charlie," he said. "The likeness is remarkable. And that dress? Also impossible."

"Yes, impossible…unless…"

"Unless what?"

"Well, I've seen photographs of my great-grandmother who lived in Paris in the 1920s. Didn't you say this was from the 1920s?"

"Yes, and I was right. There's a date on the back, and there's also—"

"Yes, a date," I said, interrupting Patrick's thought. "A date. Okay, so if it really is from Paris in the 1920s, and Frannie lived there at the time, and this looks like me, and I look at least somewhat like her, then maybe..."

"You think maybe it's a portrait of Frannie? Charlie, it's just that—"

"Of course." The idea that this was a portrait of my great-grandmother grabbed me and shook me awake. "She was here then, and this is her apartment. She must be the one who hid the canvases." I quickly got up and ran to the sideboard where I had left an old photo album with its faded black and white images and little corner tabs to affix them to the pages.

Beckoning Patrick to join me on the sofa, I sat down and opened it. I knew exactly what I was looking for. It was a photograph of Frannie wearing a similar outfit from back in the 1920s.

"Here it is!" I said as I turned a page. It was there, just as I remembered.

We both looked at it closely. As my eyes moved from the photo to the portrait on the coffee table and back, my excitement began to dissipate. It resembled Frannie, but it wasn't her. I had to admit it.

"I guess I was wrong, Patrick. I wanted it to be Frannie, but it's not her."

Patrick picked up the canvas and turned it over. "What I was trying to say is I think I know who it is," he said. "Well, I know the name, but I don't know who she is. Look," he said, pointing to a line of writing.

"Charlotte Broadhurst?" I said, looking from the canvas to Patrick. "Who is that?"

"I don't know, Charlie, but I intend to find out."

~

I arrived back in Halifax the day before Frankie was to return from her skiing adventure. I spent the day doing laundry and trying to make some notes about the images that swirled in my head about Paris, flappers and oil paintings. Patrick and I vowed to keep in close touch, and I had already had a text from him. He would be in Paris for another two weeks and planned to begin researching the artist and the artist's subject. I looked forward to something concrete to ground this illusion I had that somehow it was me in that portrait. It was unsettling. But then there was Tilly to keep me grounded.

The phone rang at five pm, nine pm in London. I was happy to have the distraction.

"Tell me all about it, darling girl," Tilly said, but I wanted to hear about her book about Genevieve. "I want to hear all the gory details of your dirty trip to Paris." I rolled my eyes and told her about my encounter with Genevieve in Paris. Tilly was delighted. Then she told me about the three articles appearing in the media over the next two weeks. It sounded gruesome to me, but Tilly was looking forward to it with the excitement of a small child looking forward to visiting Disney World. Of course, she and Genevieve realized there would be much attention, both good and bad (cue the online trolls), to follow. Not everyone would think it was good or even sane to create the illusion of a life for which there was no concrete evidence. According to Tilly, though, that was the point. The public would be then primed for the book that would take the world by storm later in the year — or so she hoped. I wished them well. Then I told her about the portrait.

"Dear god," Tilly said, "there's a book in that picture. You will, of course, be writing it?"

I had gotten to know how Tilly's mind worked well enough to realize what she was really saying—if I didn't write the book, she would. So I told her I was on it, and she let it go. We said good night, and I clicked off the phone.

After eating an omelet and toast for dinner (it was all I had on hand), I wandered into the den, where I had laid out the four paintings I'd brought home in cardboard cylinders with me on the plane. I sat down in Tom's favourite overstuffed chair and stared at them. I promptly fell asleep.

"Charlie." I could hear the voice in my head before I could see where it was coming from. "Charlie."

It was impossible, but it was Tom. I could see him so clearly. I wanted to say something, but no sound came.

"Charlie. The love of my life. Follow the story, my darling. Follow the story."

Finally, I found my voice. "I want to follow the story, Tom, but I can't seem to get anywhere without you."

"I'll always be with you, Charlie, but you need to follow the story. For you. It's time, my love. Just say goodbye."

When I woke up, the sun was streaming in the window, and my eyes were wet. I almost said it.

Connection

"Time goes from present to past...The world is its own magic."
~ Shunryu Suzuki

AS THE WINTER SET IN WITH A VENGEANCE, I was hoping to get back into my writing groove. My great-grandmother's diaries had inspired me in the past, so I thought I should have one more look. Now that Patrick and I had uncovered the hidden canvases in the Paris apartment, it occurred to me there might be a seed of an idea hidden between the lines—something I'd overlooked on my first reading. Had I missed a mention of her connection with Auguste Vaillancourt?

My great-grandmother Frannie Phillips had lived in Paris for some years in the 1920s and 1930s and kept the apartment there until she died at eighty-nine, although she had long since relocated to Canada. A writer to her core, she had kept meticulous diaries throughout her entire life from when she was twelve and survived the sinking of the Titanic with her family. But now, I was particularly interested to see if I'd missed anything from those roaring twenties years.

Frannie had worked as a mannequin in several couturier salons before discovering her writing passion and talent. The first time I'd read her diaries, I hadn't noticed any mention of the names Charlotte or Auguste among her many friends, but it was entirely possible that I'd missed them along the way. Frannie travelled in art circles in her early adult years, and I wondered if they had all travelled in those same circles. The first time I read her diaries, I was so focused on learning more about my great-grandmother that I may have overlooked some details that didn't seem pertinent at the time. Now they were pertinent.

For several days in late January, I poured over those old, handwritten pages between the leather covers. Frannie had attended her share of glittering parties where there would have been many people, and she often mentioned them. She had crossed paths with such luminaries as Cole Porter and Scott Fitzgerald—I already knew this—but I wondered if there were other names I'd glossed over because they had meant nothing to me then.

Of all the parties Frannie attended, there seemed to be one that had been worthy of more than a passing mention. As I reread the diary entry, I realized why I'd felt odd when I arrived at Le Meurice on New Year's Eve and why I felt even more peculiar when Patrick and I entered the Salon Pompadour. It seemed clear to me that it wasn't so much that I was experiencing déjà vu, as it was I'd read this before in Frannie's diaries, and it seemed so real I thought I'd been there before. Frannie had attended a party at Salon Pompadour—although it wasn't a New Year's party— and had written about it. *There*, I thought, *now I have a plausible explanation.*

I sat back in my desk chair, tapping a pen on the leather blotter. Yes, that was an acceptable explanation. Why didn't it seem to satisfy me? Why did I still think there was more to it than simply what I'd read in Frannie's diaries and hadn't paid attention to? I flipped back in the diary.

As I searched for any mention of Charlotte or Auguste, I wished old diaries had the benefit of today's online search engines: plug in a search term and see where it leads you. I'd even have settled for the ability to search within a document. But, of course, that wasn't possible.

After three days, I was ready to give it up. There was no connection between Frannie and these people revealed by the hidden canvases—at least nothing obvious. But there had to be. They were, after all, hidden in the walls of her apartment, although it occurred to me they might have been put there by a previous owner. I was on to something.

The date on the back of the canvas depicting Charlotte Broadhurst was 1923. I went immediately to my filing cabinet and pulled out the folder that contained all the documents I'd received when the apartment became mine. It had a deed with my name on it and all the paperwork produced by the French authorities. What I was looking for was an old document that might indicate when Frannie first bought it.

It took some digging, but I found it among the oldest papers now in an acid-free plastic sleeve. There it was: the date Frances Elizabeth Phillips had purchased the flat. It was July 23, 1923. I sat down at the desk and looked at the original bill of sale. 1923. So, in all likelihood, Frannie *was* the one who had stashed the paintings in her wall. I couldn't think of a single reason why she would have done that. And there was no mention of it anywhere in her diaries.

I opened the diary that I knew she had written in 1923. I scoured those pages and found nothing. Why would a woman who wrote down so many details of her life omit any mention of an artist who she had to have known? It was possible that she didn't know Charlotte, but I thought that unlikely. In any case, there was nothing. Zero. Zilch.

I put the diaries and the files back where they belonged and closed my laptop where I had been making notes. Perhaps Patrick had better luck.

~

Patrick and I talked on the phone or via Zoom every week. I could feel a sense of connection even at such a distance, something I thought would dissipate when we returned to our respective homes. Yet we were no closer to determining how we might have acquired this connection. So, we concentrated on our joint research project.

As an art history researcher, Patrick was more meticulous about his research than I probably was as a novelist. After all, he had much more at stake—his reputation and career being the most prominent. As a result, his methods sometimes seemed ponderous to me, but I knew he had to document every step of the process.

Before uncovering the canvases with me in Paris, as he had told me, Patrick had already been interested in Auguste Vaillancourt. When I asked Patrick where he had first discovered even the name, he didn't seem to want to tell me, but I pulled it out of him.

"I think I might have stumbled on his name in the archives at the Sorbonne when I was doing my post-doctoral work," he said vaguely one day in March when we were comparing notes via Zoom. "No, maybe I wasn't the one who tumbled on his name. I think it might have been Alison. She knew I was looking for the most obscure of the obscure." He and Alison had been newly married and spent a year in Paris, where she assisted him with his post-doctoral research because she couldn't get a work permit for the year in France. Alison had been an English professor before her children arrived, after which she had worked part-time.

"Did you both stumble on his name only or did you see some of his work?"

"The first reference to his name was related to my research on Degas and the impressionists in nineteenth-century France. Vaillancourt would have been much younger than Degas, but he seemed to have a connection to one of Degas' models."

"The little dancer," I said, recalling an earlier conversation we'd had when we first met.

"Yes, that's the one," Patrick said. "I have an old friend, Dr. Elspeth Savant, a former professor and museum curator, who's now a well-respected historical investigator. Since she retired a few years ago, she has owned a unique antique shop in Chinatown here in Toronto. Anyway, I asked Elspeth for help with my research."

"Was she able to help?"

"She was. Her work is incredible—and so is she, I might add. Elspeth knew exactly where to look for Vaillancourt's work, although there wasn't much to find. I plan to make sure you meet her. You two would get along so well." Patrick stopped his story and cleared his throat before continuing. I waited patiently. "The thing is, Charlie, Elspeth had this rare reference book from the 1930s. There was a reference to his work, but there was something else."

"Something else? A photograph of his work?"

"Yes, that, too. But it also had a picture of a grainy daguerreotype portrait of Vaillancourt. You know? Those old photographs?" I did know what a daguerreotype was. "It was his face that struck me." He stopped, and I could see him on my screen as he moved papers around on his desk, where I knew he was sitting. "I'm texting you a photo I took of the page in the book."

I picked up my cell phone and looked at the text. My hand flew to my mouth. "Oh my god, Patrick. It's you."

~

"This is far-fetched even for you," Evelyn said some months later when I finally told her about Patrick and me and our bizarre connection. Ever the pragmatist, Evelyn could not imagine anyone entertaining the idea that the portrait of Charlotte Broadhurst being my doppelganger was anything more than a coincidence. And the idea that Patrick had the same situation in the same time frame was beyond ridiculous. "If you're going to tell me that you think you knew each other in a past life, you're going to need more than an intervention, sis."

The more I told her about the story, the more she dug in her heels. I was beginning to wonder why I'd even told her—but I suppose I did need a dose of Evelyn's groundedness. Her view was that I had to get a hold of myself. Then she said, "Is this how you think you move on from your widow's weeds?"

I don't remember ever being as angry at my sister. We'd been close all our lives, especially since Mom died fifteen or so years earlier. I thought I'd been angry with her then for leaving me with all the responsibilities involved in emptying out and selling Mom's house, but that didn't compare to how I felt now. Then, as I thought about it, why was I so angry? She had a point. How could I allow myself to be so gullible? Perhaps I wasn't angry with her as much as I was angry with myself for going down this absurd road.

"Here's what we're going to do, Charlie," Evelyn said. "You and Frankie are going to come to Toronto to spend a few days in July with us. You can get together with this Patrick and visit that historian you mentioned. I remember reading an online article about this Dr. Elspeth Savant sometime over the past year or so. It seems she's something of a celebrity in history circles. And I think I know her shop in Chinatown. If you and Patrick can visit her there, you can probably get over this nonsense."

I was still fuming, but the idea of having the time to spend with Patrick to explore this bizarre idea—even if only for a few days—was very appealing. So, I agreed.

~

It was a steaming hot day in July when the taxi dropped us— Patrick and me—off at the corner of Dundas Street West and a small unprepossessing-looking lane in downtown Toronto. I was becoming increasingly excited as we exited the taxi and turned down into the lane. I hardly noticed the oppressive heat emanating from the pavement and every tall building and reflective glass surface.

We walked into the lane for about a block, then Patrick stopped and said, "Well, Charlie, here it is."

I looked around at the lane, bordered on both sides by three-story red-brick buildings making the lane seem even narrower than it was. Number 8, Lotus Lane, was directly in front of me.

I had never spent much time in Chinatown when in the city visiting Evelyn, although we had brought the kids here for dinner a few times. It was one of those places where you needed someone in the know to guide you to the best Chinese food. We had found such a place, but I'd never noticed these little lanes poking out from the main drag.

I suddenly wondered what Sherlock Holmes would notice here because lately, I'd begun to think I was in a mystery novel. First, it was the mystery of Genevieve LaChapelle; now, this. I looked at the people at the end of the block hurrying past and noticed the one most obvious thing: Patrick and I seemed to be the only non-Asian people in the district. I felt as if we'd been sucked up by some alien force and redeposited on the far side of the world. I had to shake myself to be reminded that I had, in fact, not left Toronto.

The second thing I noticed was that the street signs were all posted in both English and Chinese characters. Then I looked more closely at our destination while Patrick stood quietly, totally aware of what I was doing, or so it seemed. *The Lotus Flower Antiquarian* said the white sign hanging out into the lane on a black wrought iron arm perpendicular to the door. Below the English name were several Chinese characters—莲花古董—which presumably represented a translation.

The shop had two windows flanking double, arched, wooden doors with black wrought iron hinges, door knocker and lever. It looked as if visitors were meant to knock. Patrick had told me he'd spoken with Elspeth Savant, the proprietor, so she knew we would be arriving. Still, I suspected we should knock.

I stood there for a moment, contemplating the contents of the two windows. One was filled with the most exquisite, beaded handbags and vintage hats I had ever seen. The second window contained an array of extraordinary vintage jewellery that seemed to beckon from under the strategically placed lights that made the gold shimmer and the stones adorning many of the pieces sparkle. Finally, Patrick opened the heavy door without knocking, and we stepped across the threshold.

At once, I felt like I was dropping fast through a rabbit hole. Everywhere I looked were the most exquisite pieces: glass jewellery cases laden with sparkling diamonds and other stones, crystal goblets glittering on shelves, cases of more of the shimmering beaded bags in the window. I could hear the faint tinkling of a piano that seemed to be coming from somewhere in the back of the store, which was much larger than it appeared from the street. I could also smell the faint aroma of lavender—it was an assault on my senses. As I breathed in deeply, I felt immediately relaxed and could look around.

"It's extraordinary," I said when I could think clearly.

"Yes," Patrick said, "but wait until you meet the proprietress. She's the very personification of extraordinary."

I first noticed one security camera almost hidden in the rafters, then another, then a third. As unassuming as this shop looked from the street, it was clearly well-patrolled, and it ought to have been. The merchandise must have been worth a fortune.

Suddenly a beautiful young woman appeared silently from behind an elaborate Chinese Coromandel screen resembling one in Genevieve LaChapelle's living room in Mallorca. And that one in Mallorca was a replica of one I had seen when I visited Coco Chanel's apartment in the rue Cambon in Paris. I remembered being in Paris once and the guide telling our little tour group that Chanel was believed to have owned over thirty similar screens that decorated her apartment. For a moment, I wondered if this might be one of them—one that had been owned by Coco Chanel herself—then quickly dismissed the idea. It was ridiculous. Patrick and I looked at the young woman who had not yet said anything but had smiled at Patrick in recognition.

She was an extraordinary Asian beauty with long, glistening black hair pulled over one shoulder of her floor-length, blue silk Cheongsam dress. It wasn't easy to discern her age. She might have been thirty—or perhaps even sixty.

Finally, after a moment of mutual examination, the woman smiled and spoke to me. "You must be Charlotte," she said. Then she nodded at Patrick. "Welcome back, Dr. Harrington."

I had expected her to speak with an Asian accent, but it was clear that English was this young woman's first language. I thought she must be Elspeth Savant, although she wasn't at all what I had expected, and I had expected her to be much older.

"Dr. Savant," I said, holding out my hand, "I am so happy to make your acquaintance."

The young woman laughed. "I'm sorry, Elspeth is upstairs. I'm her assistant, Andrea. She is expecting you. Please," she said, gesturing toward the screen from which she had emerged, "come this way."

We followed Andrea in behind the screen, which hid a double door leading to the bottom of a curving staircase. I glanced over at Patrick, who seemed familiar with the way. We walked silently up the stairs, our feet sinking into the sumptuous carpet.

The top of the stairs emerged into a vast open space resembling Mademoiselle's atelier—a workshop of sorts. The high, sloping ceiling comprised three large skylights through which I could see puffy white clouds scudding across a canvas of vibrant blue. How wonderful this must be at night, I thought, forgetting for a moment that the lights of the urban landscape would be too much competition for the lights of the heavens.

Along the wall where the very best of the daylight lit up the working space was a long table with a snowy white cloth that looked as soft as the clouds above seemed to be. On the table were four handbags, each more beautiful than the last. I walked slowly along the table; neither Patrick nor Andrea hurried me along.

The first bag was rectangular, slightly narrower at the top than the bottom. It was fashioned from what appeared to be red brocade heavily embellished with beading in the shape of various flowers. The short handle was also of the same material. The second bag was large and familiar to me. It was unmistakably Louis Vuitton, but it was not a handbag, and it looked to her to be very old. It was a kind of miniature trunk fashioned of the now ubiquitous LV-monogrammed canvas with a flat leather handle on top and brass closures. The third bag looked like an evening bag I might see on the arm of a young nightclub aficionado even today (were there still such things as nightclubs? I hardly knew!), but I suspected it was a vintage piece with its shiny beading, fringe trim and kiss-lock closure—something from the 1920s perhaps.

The last one was unusual. It was a very old-looking, green-velvet portfolio-type bag with gold embossing and embroidery. I could make out a faint gold marking that looked like it said, *"Napoleon, Empereur et Roi"*—Napoleon, Emperor and King. My breath caught at this.

"Exquisite, aren't they?"

I jumped.

"I am so sorry to have startled you, my dear. Welcome to my studio. I am Elspeth Savant."

I turned to see our host. Elspeth was slightly shorter than I was but slim and regal, with pure silver hair cut into a stylish pixie. She wore a white lab coat and a massive necklace of extraordinary turquoise beads. Her face was only slightly lined, and I had a hard time determining her age as well. Seventy perhaps?

Elspeth slid off one of the white gloves she was wearing and held out her hand. "You must be Charlotte. I've been expecting you." Then she turned to Patrick. "And you, old friend. So lovely to see you, as always."

Patrick leaned in for the double kiss and said, "Elspeth, thanks so much for agreeing to see us about such a strange matter."

"You are much better acquainted with me than that, Patrick. There is no historical matter too strange for someone of my proclivities, as you know." Her eyes twinkled.

"Thank you so much for taking time for us, Dr. Savant," I said.

She shook her head. "I was Dr. Savant for too many years at the university and the museum. Now, I am simply Elspeth, historical investigator. And I would never refuse the opportunity to be a part of one of Patrick's investigations."

I looked at Patrick. This was the first I'd considered his work to consist of investigations, but perhaps I didn't know as much about historians as I thought I did.

"I have tea set out in my office. Please." She gestured toward a large, white door.

I lingered for another moment, gazing at the handbags again, wondering where they had come from.

Elspeth came to stand beside me. It was as if she could read my mind. "You see that first one? The red brocade? It is Belgian, from the 1950s. And the Louis Vuitton, I'm sure you recognize. It's a vanity case—also 1950's. And that evening bag—it is one of my favourites. It's a flapper bag from Whiting and Davis from around 1923. And then there is this." Elspeth put her glove back on and picked up the last one. "We're working on dating it, but as you can see, it once contained documents from Napoleon, so we think."

"It must be worth a fortune," I said incredulously. But I couldn't tear my eyes away from the evening bag. 1923. There it was again

"Hmm. Yes," Elspeth said, smiling. She laid the bag back onto the work table and put her gloves beside it. "But I see you are captured by the Whiting and Davis." I nodded. "This work can wait. Let's talk."

Patrick and I followed her across the workshop past two other large tables that held pieces of jewellery—necklaces, rings and pendants mainly, as far as I could determine. Andrea nodded to Elspeth and then walked back to the staircase, presumably to oversee the shop.

Elspeth's office was unexpected. In contrast to the antique vibe that both the shop downstairs and the workshop exuded, the office was Scandinavian modern. It was almost Ikea-like in an expensive kind of way. The walls were blonde wood, as was the enormous desk. The desk chair was upholstered in white leather, and the sofa on the far wall was also leather, this time dove grey. The cushions that appeared to be carelessly tossed onto the sofa were soft pink. The overall impression was one of softness and modernity.

Elspeth gestured to us to sit on the sofa across from her. "Not what you had envisaged, is it?" She laughed. "Most people expect me to be a fusty old woman, as you can imagine. I suppose someone who has spent her life around vintage objects is expected to become an antique herself."

Elspeth poured the tea and offered each of us a steaming white ceramic mug. Despite the heat outdoors, the air was cool and dry inside — almost cold — and I was grateful for the hot drink as I sat there in my lightweight linen dress.

"So, Patrick, I understand you have two portraits you wish to investigate."

"Yes," he said, pulling both his photocopy of the picture of Auguste Vaillancourt and the portrait of Charlotte Broadhurst from a portfolio he'd been clutching since we'd gotten into the taxi at Evelyn's house earlier. "One of these you've seen before. It was from a reference book you shared with me when I first began researching this French artist some years ago. But I'm not sure we looked at it as closely as I have now."

Elspeth placed her mug on the table and picked up the copy of the photograph. "Is this the artist whose work you were investigating when you were her last? Auguste something?"

"Yes, Auguste Vaillancourt. But take a closer look, Elspeth."

Elspeth looked at the photograph for a long moment. When she finally looked up, she said, "You had a beard when we first uncovered this picture, Patrick. I distinctly remember that because it did not suit you in the slightest."

Patrick chuckled a bit. "I did, indeed."

Then Elspeth picked up the copy of the photograph and looked at it again. "Yes," she said. "I can understand the need for further investigation."

"It looks exactly like Patrick, don't you think?" I said quite unnecessarily. I felt a bit out of my depth here.

"Hmm, yes," she said, her gaze moving to the portrait of Charlotte Broadhurst. When her eyes focused on it this time, I could see a slight stiffening of her back. "This is interesting." Her eyes fluttered toward me as she turned the canvas over to read the name and date on the back. "Ah, now I see."

I had no idea what she saw.

Elspeth turned the canvas back over and placed it beside the photograph. She lifted her tea mug and sipped contemplatively for a moment. Then she placed the mug back on the table and sat back, looking at us across from her, where we sat side-by-side on the sofa. The portrait of Charlotte Broadhurst lay on the table directly in front of me, and Auguste Vaillancourt's photograph was directly in front of Patrick. She looked from the table to us and back again, then started to laugh.

"As it turns out, I have a few days available. We certainly cannot let this mystery go, can we?" She looked at me. "Now, Charlotte, let me tell you a bit about myself before we begin a serious discussion of this incredible...coincidence."

It turned out that Dr. Elspeth Savant, apart from being an academic rebel, had been something of a superstar professor who had won awards for uncovering the provenance of several important historical objects, including a psaltery that had purportedly belonged to the twelfth-century mystic Hildegard of Bingen. Patrick added that detail since she seemed hesitant to talk about her awards. She had also traced the origin of several now well-known pieces of artwork and jewellery held in museum collections in Paris and Vienna. It occurred to me that we were in good hands. If anyone could find out the origin of this coincidence—and possibly connection—it would be Dr. Elspeth Savant.

Corroboration

FOR THE NEXT FEW DAYS, PATRICK AND I visited Elspeth in her
workshop every day for a full-day investigative session. Every
morning when we arrived, she and Andrea were already sitting
at a vast worktable with vintage books, notebooks and laptops
piled around them. Patrick and I would join them with our own
equipment, and Elspeth would share with us her investigative
plan for the day.

Elspeth's methods were detailed and meticulous, and her
apparent interest in the project was voracious. And not only did
she have the obvious resources like online databases and her
stock of vintage books (including ones she borrowed from the
rare books library at the university), but she also had connections
seemingly all over the world—museum curators, professors,
antique dealers, gallery owners—and she used them. Her phone
was beside her on the table, and she used it well. By noon on our
third day, I had noted at least a dozen people she had working
on the project with us—mainly located in Paris and New York. I
was curious about the New York connection.

"I began with the name Broadhurst and the hypothesis that
this was not a French name." I had to agree with that hypothesis.
Elspeth continued. "Then I added to that hypothesis that the time
period we're searching is the early 1920s." Again, I agreed. "If we
add what we know about Paris in the 1920s to this hypothesis, I
concluded that Charlotte Broadhurst must have been an
American. Thus, she has led me directly to my American

connections, many of whom are in New York." Then she smiled enigmatically but said nothing more.

Patrick cut in. "I've seen that look before, Elspeth. You've found something."

Elspeth smiled. "I have indeed. But before I tell you about what I've discovered, tell me, Patrick. When you were here a few years ago, you were researching this artist Auguste Vaillancourt." Patrick nodded. "If memory serves, we weren't able to uncover much more than this entry in the book where you copied that photographic portrait of the artist. Do you have any further information now that might enlighten this current investigation?"

Patrick shook his head. "That's the thing, Elspeth. I spent time in Paris trying to uncover more about him but ran into dead ends everywhere. Even the proprietor of the gallery where I found three of his paintings for sale didn't seem to know much more than the information on the backs of the canvases. One had 1899 written on the back. The other two had 1919. I suppose I just gave up, so I returned to my research on the Degas models. I had nothing to publish about Auguste Vaillancourt. I had concluded that he would remain in obscurity." Then he turned to Elspeth. "Now, what have you found, Elspeth?"

Elspeth checked her watch and then gathered her notes before getting up from the worktable. "Come, let's have lunch. Andrea has ordered sandwiches, and we've set the boardroom table. We can discuss it over lunch."

Until that moment, I didn't know she even had a boardroom. For the past few days, Patrick and I had left the workshop at noon for lunch and had then returned to find Elspeth and Andrea back at work.

The boardroom resembled Elspeth's office in its expensive Ikea-like furnishings and décor. Andrea had covered the table with a white tablecloth and set places for the four of us. We all sat down and enjoyed lunch. When we had finally finished eating and settled in with tea, Elspeth put on her reading glasses and looked at her notes. I could tell Patrick was as anxious as I was for her to tell us what she'd found.

"First, I was correct. Charlotte Broadhurst was, indeed, an American in Paris. And I believe the reason we were never able to find any more information about August Vaillancourt was that she—Charlotte—is the missing piece in his story."

I shivered slightly, remembering that Patrick had called *me* his missing piece.

"I don't understand," Patrick said. "From the portrait, I would guess that Charlotte was in her early twenties. By 1923, Auguste must have been much older."

"He *was* much older," she said. "In fact, in 1923, he was sixty years old—born in 1863. Charlotte was twenty-five when Auguste painted her portrait."

Patrick still looked confused.

"Elspeth," I said, "what was the connection between them? Who *was* Charlotte Broadhurst?"

Elspeth slid her glasses off and placed them on the table. Her eyes were sparkling. "That is where the story gets fascinating," she said. "Have you ever heard of Broadhurst Chemicals?"

"Yes, of course. Everyone knows the name. Didn't they play a role in creating synthetic fibres for clothing manufacture early in the 1900s?"

"They did, indeed. And the Broadhurst's were one of the wealthiest families in the United States back then, and they still are. As a matter of fact, at one time, they were among the wealthiest families in the world."

I was trying to piece the story together. Charlotte Broadhurst, who was my doppelganger (or I, hers), was living in Paris during the 1920s and was the daughter of a wealthy American family. Auguste—Patrick's twin—was an older man, a Parisian artist who painted her portrait.

"Was there any other connection between the two of them other than the fact that one was the artist and the other his model for that portrait?" I said. I had to admit that I was slightly disappointed with this conclusion. I had hoped for something more romantic.

"That is where this story becomes even more curious and a bit more difficult to tease out details." Elspeth pulled her notes toward her and put her reading glasses back on.

"My friend, Donald in New York, is a historian at Columbia University who focuses his research on newspapers of the early twentieth century. When I realized Charlotte's family connection, I suspected there would be news stories about them from time to time. It turns out I was correct. Donald found several articles that might provide a bit more illumination to our investigation." She lifted several pages that I'd seen Andrea pull off a printer just before lunch.

I marvelled at how Elspeth had managed to entice her connections to help her so quickly. It was a testament to her stature in the community of international historians that Patrick had told me about. I was also surprised to hear that her friend Donald was at Columbia, the university which, if I remembered correctly, was where Bella was planning on studying for her doctorate. Such coincidences!

Elspeth placed several news stories on the table. Patrick and I moved closer together so we could read the printouts together.

"Pierre Broadhurst and Family Survive the Titanic Disaster." It was an article from the *New York Tribune* from May 23, 1912.

I had a strange feeling as I read the article about how Mr. and Mrs. Broadhurst and their daughter Charlotte and son, Pierre Junior, had made it off the Titanic alive just as my great-grandmother and her parents had. Charlotte had been fourteen at the time; my great-grandmother Frannie had been twelve. Had they known one another? It was a tantalizing theory.

The second article was perhaps even more intriguing. It was from a 1923 issue of the *New York Morning Telegraph*. Perhaps even more interesting than the headline was the story's byline—Louella Parsons. I was baffled.

"Why would an article by Louella Parsons be of any relevance? I've always understood that she was a movie gossip columnist in the twenties and thirties." And yet, it was headlined, "Delicious news from Paris." No movie gossip there, or so I thought.

"You are absolutely correct," Elspeth said. "Louella was a gossip columnist whose columns detailed rumours and the more salacious news related to movie stars. But there is an important connection here in this story. Have you ever heard of an actor called Peter Hurst?"

"Didn't he win an academy award in the 1930s?" Patrick said. "I have a colleague who specializes in Hollywood history, and I remember a research symposium he presented a few years ago."

"He did win the Academy Award. That was in 1934, but before that, he was an up-and-coming heartthrob whose antics in Hollywood, New York and the French Riviera made attractive fodder for gossip columnists. And, as it happens, Peter Hurst was a stage name. His real name was Pierre Olivier Broadhurst III."

"He was Charlotte's brother?" I was starting to see Elspeth's connections.

"Indeed, he was," Elspeth said, pointing to the article. "But you must read the piece. It is, of course, gossip, but as we all know, there will always be a grain of truth even in rumour."

The story detailed a party Louella herself had attended in Paris in 1923. According to Louella, she had been there to see the Paris premiere of a new movie starring newcomer Peter Hurst and to do some couture shopping. The party was a wedding celebration for Mr. and Mrs. Gaston Reneau. It was held in the Salon Pompadour at Hotel Le Meurice. Peter's parents, Mr. and Mrs. Pierre Broadhurst, were in attendance, as was their daughter, Charlotte, who was then living in Paris. Other luminaries who attended included Cole Porter and Scott and Zelda Fitzgerald, among others. But that wasn't really the story Louella wanted to tell. The story she had in mind involved something a bit more dramatic. It seemed to concern an altercation—a confrontation that devolved into a quarrel that further deteriorated into blows, or so she said. The quarrel was between Pierre Broadhurst, senior, and an artist who was now teaching at École des Beaux-Arts. The artist in question was none other than Auguste Vaillancourt.

~

Later that afternoon, after pouring over Elspeth's news stories (there were many more, but none so relevant) and more material she had uncovered after that revelation, Patrick and I took copies of her materials. Then, in a daze, we found our way to the main street to hail a cab.

I called Evelyn to tell her I'd be a few more hours. Patrick and I had a lot to review. The moment we walked into Patrick's house, we opened a bottle of wine and sat together on his sofa in front of his empty fireplace.

"Where the hell do we begin?" Patrick said, running his hand through his hair.

"Right here. Right now," I said. And I really meant it.

Reality

*"The best way is to understand yourself, and then you will
understand everything."*
~ Shunryu Suzuki

Paris, 1923

KIKI AND HER NEW HUSBAND, Gaston Reneau, had been close
friends of mine since my arrival in Paris four years earlier. Kiki
was a former ballerina, and Gaston a successful banker—an
older, wealthy widower. They made a wonderful couple. They
had married impulsively while vacationing in Biarritz and had
returned to host a lavish party to celebrate their nuptials. I was
so looking forward to this party. I adored Hotel Le Meurice and
its Salon Pompadour, where it was to be held, and Kiki was such
fun that I knew the party would be memorable. I even had the
perfect dress—a Jean Patou that had not had a suitable occasion
for an outing since I'd bought it. The moment my dear brother
Pierre (I could never get used to calling him Peter as he now
wished to be addressed) let me know he would be in Paris for the
European opening of his new movie (the Americans in Paris were
numerous enough to warrant such a gala affair), I was thrilled
that it overlapped with the timing of the party, so I let Kiki know
he would be my date. My elation was, however, short-lived. As
it happened, my parents were also coming to Paris.

I had not seen my parents since their visit a year earlier. To
say that it had been an acrimonious encounter would be an
understatement. By then, I had been in Paris for several years,
defying their express wishes that I return home. My parents, who
had never understood the seductiveness of Paris, were coming

ostensibly to be with Peter for this European first for him, but the real reason was more pointed. I was well aware that their main objective was to ensure their recalcitrant daughter returned home and married some suitably rich and dull man. My father had been hostile, and my mother embittered. Hostility from my father was a reasonably new development in our relationship. Bitterness from Mother was nothing new. It had consumed her for many years—at least since that dreadful night in the bitterly cold North Atlantic on that awful trip when I was fourteen. I shuddered every time I thought of it, and I had tried very hard to forget about it. Only two years ago, I met another young American woman, Frannie Phillips, here in Paris, who had also been on that ill-fated ship in 1912. We had seen one another in passing the first-class dining room, but I had not seen her again after the catastrophe. She, too, had survived with her own family, and it was through our acquaintance all those years later here in Paris that I began to deal with my emotional reaction to that experience. Frannie and I had never really become friends; rather, we lunched together a few times. I had never been to her home, and she had never been to mine. Still, we both seemed to find solace in this shared experience. But my mother had apparently not had anyone with whom to share her feelings since my father's attitude had always been, "Just get over it." She had not.

In any case, there I was, looking forward to the party where I hoped to introduce Frannie to my brother Peter. I didn't think her current beau, whom I had met once or twice at Kiki's soirées, suited her at all—this Jean-Christophe publishing person—and I had an idea that she would make a perfect sister-in-law. I thought she would fall in love with the glitter of his Hollywood life. All of this was on my mind when I received the telegram from Father.

"Mother and I arriving in Paris two days before the premiere. Will attend premiere with you. Father."

Short and sweet and truly unwelcome. My parents didn't like anything that wasn't American, so one could only imagine how they would find the Parisian film audience. I shuddered at the thought. This attitude had always puzzled me since my great-grandfather was born in Paris, which was why my father and brother were both called Pierre after the original Pierre. I knew I could do nothing about either their dislike of Paris or their impending and wholly unwelcome arrival, so I dropped around to visit with Kiki. I had to tell her that I would likely not be able to attend her party after all.

"*Non, non, non*! You will do no such thing!" she said to me as she poured us each a glass of white wine in the sumptuous living room of the townhouse she shared with Gaston. "*Mon dieu*! I have been so looking forward to meeting the famous and most handsome brother of yours. You will come, you will bring your brother," then she peered at me closely, "and you will bring your parents."

"Oh my god," I said. "Kiki, I cannot do that. I cannot subject you to their distaste for anything that is not American. They have said such nasty things about the French. I have told you this."

Kiki sipped her wine, her eyes sparkling. "Well, then, we must prove them wrong. We must convince them of how wonderful we are here in Paris. They must come to the party with their prejudices and leave with a deep appreciation for everything French. I will make that happen!"

Even Kiki, the maestro of the dinner party and the genius of the gala, would find that an impossible task.

"Kiki, you *do* remember I told you about the last time my parents were here in Paris a year ago, do you not? Do you remember how their presence affected my life?"

Kiki looked at me sadly. "I do remember, *ma chère amie*, Charlotte and I have been heartbroken over you and Auguste. But I remember how you survived the situation and took up your life anew. You are a strong woman, Charlotte Broadhurst, and I am proud to call you my friend." Kiki grabbed my hand and squeezed. "I will be there for you, and together we will conquer your parents. The Americans will love Paris. This I promise you!"

And that is how we all came to be in the same place at the same time.

~

"Are Mother and Father really planning to attend this party this evening?"

My brother, Pierre, had arrived at my apartment for a pre-gala drink. He had mixed us each his specialty, something he called a French-75, consisting of lemon juice, gin and a hefty dose of champagne, which he was now drinking as if he hadn't had a drink in years—which would have been true if I didn't know that he frequented the Hollywood speakeasies and parties where the long arm of the prohibition laws either didn't reach or joined in the fun. I often thought this was the main reason so many Americans were living in Paris.

"Oh, Pierre, you have no idea how much I was looking forward to this party until Mother and Father said they were coming to town." I was standing beside my makeshift bar in the living room of my tiny apartment on the Left Bank, sipping my drink. "Do you like my dress?" Dear god, I was shallow, wasn't I? But I had bought this couturier dress with money Father had sent me for rent, and it seemed oddly important to me that the dress be perfect—Father would, after all, be seeing where his rent money went.

"Yes, of course," he said rather offhandedly, then promptly changed the subject. "Why on earth are they coming to this party? And by the way, I'm Peter, now, as you well know—Lottie."

How I hated it when he called me Lottie, and he knew it. As a child, I had asked everyone to call me Charlie, something my mother expressly forbade, but Pierre had settled on Lottie mainly because I hated it.

"May we have an agreement on names, then?" I said. "I will try to call you Peter on every possible occasion if I never hear that dreadful name from your lips again."

Pierre looked at me and raised his glass. "We have a deal. Now, I say again, why are Mother and Father attending, and how are we going to deal with them?"

"That, dear brother, is the unanswerable question." I drained my glass, then put it down on my coffee table, feeling slightly fortified by its fizz. I lifted my fur wrap and said, "Shall we?"

~

As I stepped through the door of the salon, I was at once swept up into Kiki's glamorous life. Her two-hundred and fifty or so guests (the number she had shared with me) mingled, drank, laughed, and generally looked like they owned the world—and perhaps many of them did. Gaston had numerous rich friends from both sides of the Atlantic. Some guests had already taken to the dance floor where Louis Mitchell and his Jazz Kings— American to the core—provided the music.

As Peter and I made our way to our table, he whispered, "Weren't we meant to arrive with Mother and Father?"

I gave him a dirty look. "I told them we'd meet them here. I only hope Kiki has not put them at our table. I may never forgive her if that happens."

We were in luck. When we arrived at our table of eight, six of the seats were already filled with some of my dearest friends in Paris; chief among them was Frannie Phillips. I could pretend Jean-Christophe wasn't also there. I took great pains to introduce her to Pierre—Peter. As expected, Frannie didn't swoon in the least over him, as did the other two women at the table. I had known she wouldn't. Frannie wasn't like that. Frannie was from London and English to her core, although she liked to pretend she was more French or even American than British. I knew Peter would immediately fall in love with her accent. I immensely enjoyed watching them as they sat down together (after Frannie and I laughed that we were both wearing the same designer, but not the same dress—thank god) and began a deep conversation, much to the very evident displeasure of the pretentious Jean-Christophe Lemieux. Oh, perhaps this evening would not be so bad after all!

Dinner was beyond marvellous—oysters Rockefeller (a nod to the US) to begin, followed by cranberry-orange roast duckling, finishing with cream-filled eclairs (very difficult to eat daintily) and warm madeleines. The champagne flowed, and the crystal and diamonds glittered.

As the dessert was served, clapping started close to the orchestra where a man, resplendent in a particularly well-fitted suit of white tie and tails, was sitting down at the grand piano. There was much whispering at our table: "Who is that man?" The only one who knew his identity was Jean-Christophe. Of course. He was the only one who made it his business to know everyone. I overheard him whisper to Frannie, "That, my darling Frannie," he said, "is up-and-coming American songwriter Cole Porter."

As Mr. Porter began playing, the band's singer joined him. I was enjoying myself when I heard a voice in my ear.

"Charlotte, we need to talk." It was Father.

I looked up to see Father towering above me in all of his six feet and two inches. I looked beyond him and saw Mother, dripping in peacock blue feathers and pearls, her face a mask of blandness. As sour as she often was, she would put on this flat affect whenever in company, lest someone realize the depth of her bitterness.

I looked over toward Peter, but he was asking a woman at the adjacent table to dance, glancing at me with what appeared to be pity. He knew I was in for a parental tirade about my life choices, which we both knew I'd have to face sooner or later. As I was about to get up, I heard a gasp from Frannie, who, until that moment, had been deep in conversation with Jean-Christophe about Cole Porter and his wife. I had been eavesdropping.

"Oh my god, Charlotte," she hissed into my ear. "It's him. He's here."

I looked away from Father toward where Frannie was staring. "What? Who is here?" I followed her gaze across the crowded room to where a man stood alone at the edge of the dance floor, staring—at me.

He was so handsome in his evening clothes, something I never thought I'd see him wear. What was he doing here? Who could have invited him? Then I realized it had to have been Kiki. She knew I would see him. Moreover, she had to know my parents would see him. What was she playing at?

~

I got up as quickly as I could and made my way through the crowd toward the door leading to a hallway where I hoped I'd be able to have a brief conversation with my parents. After that, I expected them to leave me to my own devices once again.

Once we were out in the hallway, Father began. "Charlotte, you look well." Father was a successful businessman and had not taken his company to where it was today by being anything other than congenial with his business associates before going in for the kill. I knew his tactics well and wouldn't be mollified. I knew what was coming next. But before he had a chance to continue, Mother broke in.

"Charlotte Broadhurst, you have been acting like some kind of low-class hussy here in this gaggle of debauchery," she said, with exaggerated distaste dripping from every syllable. I could feel the anger rising as I listened to her, but before I could say a word, she continued her tirade. "Just look around. Look at these people—the drunkenness! The behaviour! The lewd dresses hardly covering anything! This is *not* how we brought you up. You are to become the lady you were always meant to be. I will no longer stand for it, and you *will* come home with us this time."

Much to Father's disbelief over the past few years, Mother had become something of a prudish temperance advocate and often took that holier-than-though attitude. Father, for his part, thought the whole idea of prohibition was preposterous and continued to hide his contraband bourbon and gin in locked drawers and cabinets, but he tried not to argue with her. We all did.

"I am not going to fight with you here, Mother. We can discuss this later. I will come to your hotel."

I put my head down, and as I tried to disappear back into the crowd, I turned quickly and bumped into a tuxedo. I looked up to say how sorry I was for not paying attention and found myself wrapped in warm arms. I looked up. "Auguste," I breathed.

"Charlotte, I have missed you so much." I could feel tears beginning to stream down my face, threatening to take along the black kohl liner I had so carefully placed around my eyes onto the silk of my dress. "Charlotte, what is wrong?"

"Get away from my daughter!" My father's voice boomed through the crowd so that everyone nearby stopped whatever they were doing to stare. I could almost hear their thoughts. "Oh, it's one of those Americans."

Rather than stepping away from me, I could feel Auguste's arms hold me closer. I did not move.

"You heard me. Get away from her, you aging Lothario!"

I stiffened at Father's words, but Auguste did not move or say anything. As my father came closer, the crowd parted. I could now see Kiki at the edge of the crowd, and I wanted to tell her how sorry I was that this was happening at her glorious party. But I could see from the look on her face that she was not the slightest bit concerned. Perhaps she had even hoped it might happen. She had to know there would be fireworks if she put my father in the same room with Auguste again. I only hoped Father would calm down. But he did not.

Father came closer and started to grab Auguste's arm. I looked at the fury in his eyes as he stared into the face of the man he thought had taken away his daughter's innocence—the man with whom he had taken great pains to run off a year ago. I began to feel the rage I'd been suppressing for that entire year since Auguste and I had been forced to part as a result of Father's — and likely Mther's— undertakings.

I could see the last few years flash across my mind from the moment I'd met Auguste. I had answered a small advertisement for artists' models and found myself in his studio with ten of his students. When he asked me to pose for him in his private studio, I had not hesitated because I had already felt an energy between us, and I wanted to pursue it. That I was twenty-one and he was fifty-six at that time was of no consequence to me. The years meant nothing to me, although at first, Auguste had told me I would not be happy with a man so many years older. Kiki had encouraged us—she thought we were well-matched, and it seemed French women had far less difficulty with the concept than Americans. I fell in love. When Father discovered this, he first tried to buy Auguste off through one of his French business associates, but then his tactics escalated to threats. When Father had finally arrived in Paris a year ago, he came armed with a false story that Auguste had raped one of his students, and he was prepared to release the details unless Auguste left me alone. So, Auguste left, and I finally made my way alone again. Kiki had helped, and now I wondered what she thought this confrontation would accomplish. Then I knew exactly what her objective had been.

As my anger bubbled to the surface, I broke away from Auguste, grabbing my father's arm. "Do not touch him, Father. Do not ever touch him again."

Father seemed quite taken aback, permitting Mother to come forward. "Charlotte, you are, of course, making a scene. When will you ever learn some propriety? We are leaving, and you are coming with us—back to America where you belong."

I stood in the middle of the crowd of onlookers, not caring in the slightest what anyone was thinking. I had been so angry for so long that I could no longer stand it. That's when my mother punched Auguste in the face.

~

Later it was difficult to recall the exact events that followed. I blamed Peter's carefully concocted drink early in the evening followed by the copious amounts of champagne I'd later imbibed for the fact that I fainted dead on the floor, coming around only sometime later on a sofa (a fainting couch, perhaps) in the ladies' cloakroom. Kiki was by my side.

"Charlotte? Charlotte, how are you feeling?" she said, her face a mask of concern.

"Oh, Kiki, I am so sorry for that scene. You must hate me for ruining your party."

"Hate you? *Mais non*! Also, I love you as a sister, which would, of course, make that handsome brother of yours my brother too, and that would not do! And, in any case, I had invited that person Louella Parsons to the party, and if we are lucky, we will be the toast of New York in no time!"

"Louella Parsons? What is that woman doing here?" I was shocked. I had heard Pierre—Peter—speak of her with a mix of derision and desire as if he loathed the idea of becoming the focus of one of her columns while fearing he might never be important enough to make it. Perhaps *he* wouldn't be so unhappy about this turn of events.

My head hurt, and I was mortified about what Kiki's guests might think. Then I thought of Auguste. "Kiki, what was Auguste doing here?"

"But of course, I invited him. Why would I not? He is, after all, a great artistic personality, although I wish he would give up that teaching and simply paint again. It had occurred to me that he had given up his art because he gallantly gave up the great love of his life. I must admit that I am a true romantic, so I could not bear this for you."

My head was still fuzzy, and I wasn't entirely understanding Kiki. "The great love of his life?"

"Charlotte, you really are not quite yourself yet, are you? Of course, I mean you. You and Auguste were meant to be together no matter what that fiend of a father of yours says. If you will pardon me, of course." Kiki was sitting on the side of the couch beside me. "And you have missed the best of the scene."

"What? What did I miss?" I tried to sit up.

Kiki examined her nails as if nothing had happened. "Oh, well, Charlotte. It is only that your brother tried to restrain your mother, who had punched Auguste in the face just before you fainted dead away. This caused her to attempt to strike your brother, but instead, she punched a woman who had tried to intervene. It seems your brother has a legion of fans here in Paris, after all. In any case, your mother is none the worse for wear—just a few peacock feathers ruffled. Is she always that unpleasant?" She waved away her last statement. "*Ce n'est pas grave*, never mind, it is not important. It was only, after all, a *petite* brawl." Was she giggling? Was Kiki really so delighted at this misadventure my family had brought to her party? It seemed so.

"I will leave you in the best of hands," she said, getting up from the side of the couch. "Oh, and I did need to tell you that Auguste has painted your portrait in your absence from his life. He has taken it, along with several other of his works, to Frannie for safekeeping."

"Frannie? Why did he leave it with Frannie?"

Kiki shrugged in that Gallic way. "But of course, I suggested it. Frannie is discrete. And Auguste was concerned lest his portrait of you be seen in public and word get back to your father through his Paris friends. He wanted these canvases to remain out of the public eye until he is dead. I do not know so much about these artists and their whims, but *c'est comme ça*—that is the way it is. I thought you should know he has been thinking of you for this past year. Ah," she said, turning toward the door, "here he is."

Auguste entered, and Kiki left us alone.

"Well, Charlotte, my love. What now?"

I suddenly felt well enough to sit up. I raised my arms to him, and he sat beside me, wrapping his arms around me and kissing me more fervently than I even remembered.

"Do you know that writer, Scott Fitzgerald?" he said when we finally broke apart.

"I don't know him, but I know of him. Is he here this evening?"

"He is. We were speaking for a few minutes after the altercation. It seems he was quite delighted when Kiki related to him our story. He said something to me. He said, *There are all kinds of love in this world, but never the same love twice.* I believe we need to heed that observation."

Inspiration

"Wherever you go, you will find your teacher, as long as you have the
eyes to see and the ears to hear."
~ Shunryu Suzuki

I AWOKE TO THE RINGING OF A CELL PHONE somewhere in the
distance. When I opened my eyes, I saw it was beside me. As I
picked it up, I suddenly realized that darkness had settled on this
July evening, which meant it was probably after 9:30. I looked at
the caller ID. It was Evelyn. *Oh my god,* I thought as I turned to
see Patrick fast asleep beside me. *How could we have fallen asleep?*
I picked up the phone.

"Where the hell are you, Charlie? We're frantic here," Evelyn
said, sounding both alarmed and angry. "A few more hours?
That's what you said at five o'clock. Do you know what time it
is?"

When I woke up, I thought only that it must be after sundown
on this long July evening. I took the phone away from my ear for
a moment to check the time. "I'm so sorry, Evelyn," I said, noting
it was now eleven. "We fell asleep." The moment the words were
out of my mouth, I immediately thought it necessary to clarify in
case she got the wrong impression. "We were so tired after the
day we had at the workshop, and when we had a glass of wine, I
guess we just fell asleep on the sofa."

"Charlie, I don't know about that Patrick person. You don't
really know him very well. I think you should get out of there."

I was puzzled by her concern about Patrick, but it was clear it
was time for me to leave. I told her I'd be back to her place as
soon as I could get an Uber, then shook Patrick awake. He was as
surprised as I had been that it was so late.

"Charlie, I think we really need to talk. I had the strangest dream—"

"Dream? It couldn't have been as odd as mine. My head is so full of that Charlotte Broadhurst that I'm not sure I can tell what's the real history and what's in my imagination."

"Charlie, I think we should talk—"

"Of course, of course," I said distractedly as I began stuffing things into my tote bag. "My Uber will be here in three minutes. I really have to go, Patrick. We'll talk."

"When? Didn't you tell me you and Frankie were flying home tomorrow?"

"Geezus, yes, you're right." I checked my phone again for the Uber update. "And I still have to pack." I looked out the window at the street in front of Patrick's house and saw the car idling at the curb. "Sorry, Patrick, I have to go. I'll be in touch."

~

When Frankie and I arrived home in Halifax, Mrs. Conrad, our part-time housekeeper who had been my lifesaver in trying to keep up this big house on my own, had placed our mail neatly in a small pile on the table in the middle of our foyer. I picked up the top two envelopes, one from my insurance company and the other my newly renewed driver's license. Under them was a small package. I immediately recognized the handwriting on the outside and glanced at the return label, which was postmarked London. It was from Tilly.

I was so excited. I knew this had to be an advance copy of her new book—the book Tilly was writing about Genevieve LaChappelle. The magazine articles earlier in the year had been popular and polarizing, inciting many online debates about the honesty or lack of it in creating a persona such as Genevieve had done. There had been many comparisons to Coco Chanel with commenters and pundits on both sides of the debate. I couldn't wait to read it.

Once we were unpacked (not really a major job since we'd only been away for four days), Frankie told me her best friend had invited her to dinner, so I found myself alone in the den, snacking on cheese and crackers and sipping a glass of wine. I opened the package containing Tilly's book and laid it on the table in front of me.

The book was titled *Where Do I Begin?* and the cover image was a stylized, black and white pencil sketch of Genevieve in the same pose as the famous one of Coco Chanel: her body side on while she turned her head and looked directly at the viewer, with multiple strands of pearls dripping down her back. Where do I begin, indeed?

I opened the front cover and saw that Tilly had inscribed it to me.

"For my darling friend, Charlie Hudson, author extraordinaire. May you begin at your new beginning and carry on until the next one. Enjoy! Your dear friend, Tilly."

I started to read.

"Everything begins with saying goodbye to something else. Nothing in life comes from nothing. As political theorist John Schaar once wrote, "The future is not some place we are going to, but one we are creating. The paths are not to be found, but made, and the activity of making them changes both the maker and the destination." He could not have known that his words were more than a political perspective, nor could he ever have imagined the life of a small-town girl who said goodbye, left her world behind and created another one. And it changed her and her destination—nothing less than the world."

I put the book down and sat back in my chair. Tilly was right, and I suddenly believed it. It was time to say goodbye to the phase of my life that was most assuredly over, but I couldn't see where I was going. But wasn't that the point? Wasn't it my job to create something?

I knew what I was supposed to do now. I was supposed to create something—write a new novel. I had been given this gift of characters and a story. I had been bothered by my dream ever since I'd left Patrick alone in his house last evening. I felt uneasy about how real it all seemed, but I brushed off the feeling and went upstairs to my office. I sat down at the desk and turned on my computer. I opened a new file, but as I started to type, "Chapter 1," my email pinged in the corner. It was from Patrick.

"Dear Charlie:

I have spent this entire day trying to figure out what is happening between us. But more specifically, I have been trying to figure out the strange dream I had when we fell asleep on my couch last evening. And I couldn't let this day come and go without sharing it with you. My dream began in Paris in 1923…"

My heart froze as I continued to read his words. There, in black and white, was a retelling of the dream I had experienced. How could this be possible? Of course, it was because we had both been immersed in the story of Charlotte Broadhurst and Auguste Vaillancourt together. Of course, it was because we both had vivid imaginations. Of course, it was because…There was no other explanation.

The email finished with these words, *"Charlie, I would love to hear about your dream so that we can plan a way forward. I have felt so strange since I woke up and cannot shake the feeling that we can't let this go."*

I stopped reading and started typing. "CHAPTER 1."

It felt good to be writing again after such an emotionally charged hiatus. I would begin by drafting a story with characters based on Charlotte and Auguste. It soon became apparent that I'd have to do a lot more research if I planned to pull this off. I had to be able to recreate Paris in the 1920s, and I couldn't rely on dreams and suppositions. I was not someone who wrote historical novels, so I had to figure out how to do this. Although I'd ventured into the past in books like the one I wrote based on my mother's life in the 1960s and my great-grandmother's life that did, in fact, include material on the 1920s in Paris, I had relied almost exclusively on their diaries for background. This book would be unlike my previous ones in one vital aspect: I'd have to plan it. I had never planned a book before; I had just written them. Was that even a legitimate way to write a novel? In any case, I realized Patrick would be my very best source, but I wasn't ready to discuss this further with him yet. I was still freaked out by the similarity of our dreams. I had replied to him with a brief outline of my own dream, and he had called me, but I was too busy to talk. Now I needed him.

By the middle of August, I was so frustrated with how the writing was going—or, to be more precise, not going—I considered ditching the project entirely. I'd scoured the internet for advice on writing historical novels and doing historical research. I'd bought a dozen books as resources—everything from Scott Fitzgerald's novels to books about the history of the so-called Lost Generation in Paris in the 1920s. Everything seemed flat, and as a result, so did my writing. When I sent a few chapters to my agent Pamela, her reply was, "I don't feel you in this book." I was feeling lost.

Patrick and I exchanged several more emails, but I had made it clear to him that I needed to think through our relationship before we could continue. But I was beginning to cave, and he could tell, so he suggested a visit to Halifax the last week in August before his classes started for the fall semester. I finally conceded, and Patrick flew to Halifax for a three-day visit.

~

I had offered to pick Patrick up at the airport. He thanked me but said he'd be happy to take a taxi like a true Torontonian, where few people wanted to fight the ever-present traffic to venture to Pearson International Airport for a pick-up. He texted me when he started into the city from the airport, and as I waited for him at home, I felt myself becoming unexpectedly more and more excited to see him. Why this was so unexpected was a mystery to me since we'd clearly had a connection from the start. Maybe I was just nervous because I'd been putting him off for weeks. I honestly was looking forward to seeing him again.

Patrick joined Frankie and me for dinner on the patio. Mrs. Conrad had insisted on making dinner before she left for the day. When I told her I had a friend coming to stay for a few days, she asked me if it was a man, then insisted she wanted to help. I got the feeling she thought it was high time I started seeing someone again. On several occasions, she had mentioned how I was too young to be alone.

Patrick had met Frankie only once and briefly in Toronto, so this was her chance to get to know him better. If I had been concerned about how he might react to a teenage girl, I needn't have been. They got along famously. Patrick seemed to have a far better grasp of the latest social media platforms than I did, so they had much in common. I suppose that since he had raised a young woman himself and now taught young adults in university, that it went with the territory. Anyway, I was delighted.

Later that evening, after Frankie had gone to bed, Patrick brought me up to date on his own research into Auguste Vaillancourt, now that we knew he had been an art professor. "But he seems to fall off the face of the earth around 1924."

"Perhaps he died?"

"I suppose that's possible. But he was only sixty-one then, and besides, his name should appear in a death registry somewhere. I found nothing."

"What about Charlotte? When did she die?"

"That's the second oddity. There's no record of her death either."

"Did they stay together? Maybe get married?"

Patrick shrugged. "No idea. No marriage record, either." He took a final sip of coffee and put his cup down beside the cake plate where he had polished off a piece of Mrs. Conrad's special chocolate cake. "Charlie, can we talk about something? It's related, but it's a bit bizarre."

"Sure. What is it?" I was nervous since I'd also been feeling bizarre things.

"You remember me telling you about that dream I had of Auguste and Charlotte?" I certainly did remember since it seemed to echo mine. "The odd thing about it is that when I was dreaming, I wasn't just looking in on the scenes. I was looking out at them—through Auguste's eyes. Does that make any sense?"

It wouldn't have made any sense at all except for my own experience. "Patrick, I saw the scenes the same way you did, only I seemed to see them through Charlotte's eyes."

He took a deep breath. "Okay. I know you're even more skeptical than I am about this, but I think we really should consider the possibility that perhaps we knew one another in a previous life."

He was right about the skeptic in me, but I couldn't deny the weirdness of the whole thing. "What do you propose we do about it? We did say we were going to find answers."

"We did," he said. "And I've taken the liberty of contacting an old high school friend who's now a well-regarded psychiatrist in Vancouver. He's almost as much of a skeptic as you are, but he wrote a paper a few years ago on using past life regression as a psychiatric therapy, so he's something of an expert."

"God, Patrick, isn't that some kind of quackery psycho-babble?"

He laughed. "In some circles. Perhaps in many circles, but Robert has a lot of insight. The truth is that I'm not so sure I believe in past lives as much as I believe in parallel lives. And a year ago, I never thought I'd hear myself saying that. What do you think?"

"Are you suggesting we go to Vancouver?"

"No. That won't be necessary. As it happens, he's presenting a paper at the annual meeting of the Canadian Psychiatric Society here in Halifax. And it happens to be this week."

"I see. So you planned this timing?"

"Guilty as charged," Patrick said. "What do you say? Robert has time to see us tomorrow at lunchtime. It could be useful."

"I'm not sure I want to be hypnotized," I said.

"I don't think that's going to happen—at least not yet."

And so, we confirmed our meeting with Dr. Robert Bukowsky for the following day.

~

We met Robert at the Marriott Harbourfront Hotel, where the meeting was taking place. We booked a table for lunch since we all had to eat anyway.

Robert turned out to be a very quiet, thoughtful man with a bright red beard that matched his hair. I knew he was our age, but he looked years younger. His warm smile and eyes seemed to dance behind wire-rimmed glasses. I could definitely see how patients would feel comfortable with him.

We ordered lunch then Robert began to talk about past lives, his skepticism, the evidence and his work teasing out the truth.

"People are utterly fascinated by the idea. Think of the myriad movies made featuring people who come back to earth after death, one way or another. Did you ever see that early 1990s movie *Dead Again* with Kenneth Branagh and Emma Thompson? Well, I cannot tell you how many patients I've been seeing come back to me after viewing that one on late-night television, fearing that they are suffering from a past life experience."

"Suffering? Is that part of the past lives thing?" I said.

Robert laughed. "Not always, but it is the reason so many people look to practitioners for past life regression—or when they've just seen a disturbing movie on the topic."

Robert then went on to tell us about several medical papers denouncing the practice as unethical and how the controversial approach had little support from professional associations, although little outright condemnation. "There is a real risk of implanting false memories."

"So, you think we might feel we've been connected in the past, but we're just developing false memories from the research?" Patrick asked.

"It's possible, even without hypnosis, but you need to know one thing about me. My wife and I had a similar experience to the one you described to me, Patrick. That's one of the reasons I became fascinated with the subject, although I don't focus on it in my practice. I see it this way. Our lives are stories we tell ourselves, connecting and making sense of events that happen to us. Emotions are powerful. When we have conflicting narratives, emotions play an essential part in the one we choose and the story we tell.

"Perhaps it would be easier to think of it this way. Consider a scenario where you're walking through a city with your phone in your hand, much like the Google cars drive through cities and take 360° panoramic views for Google Maps. As you walk, you use your phone to take photos and videos along the way. While taking one video, you are almost hit by a car. When you watch that video later, it will have an emotional attachment. Then you come to a fork in the road, so to speak, and you choose the right fork. You continue down that fork, all the while taking photos and videos.

"On another day, at the same time of day, you return to the same street and take more pictures and videos but notice things you didn't notice before. When you watch these videos later, you may pay attention to other things and thus change your impression of them like we do when recalling our memories. Then, when you arrive at the fork the second time, you take the left fork and continue capturing your surroundings, having a completely different experience. These photos and videos are saved to your phone. You can watch them in any sequence you choose. Let us say the files remain in sequence, but no date is attached.

"If you were to forget these walks, then sometime later find these photos and videos, you might tell yourself the story that they were on different dates to make sense of them within the generally accepted paradigm. You could also argue that you were able to have taken two paths or exist in parallel universes at the same time. What if, like Google Maps' street view, these apparent choices you can make all exist on your phone in the present moment? You could simply choose any path, like the ultimate fantasy role-playing game. The video clip where you were almost hit by the car would have an emotional attachment. This is important because time ceases to exist for events burned into the soul by the fires of emotion. That's the key. Time ceases to exist, so time today and time yesterday—or a hundred years ago—are meaningless concepts.

"Now consider those role-playing video games with which we are familiar. In such games, there are myriad possibilities. All it takes is for you, the player, to make a different decision for the entire game to go a different way. These paths are all present in the computer program. We just make choices. What if our lives were like a video game, and we could make any choice we could imagine? Life progresses, but all those other choices are still here for us if we so choose. It is as if they are parallel lives. We could come back, make a different choice, and follow a different path. And that still does not change the fact that our original path is still there. For this "real life" to work and be a new experience, we would have to forget our previous choices—lives—unlike we do in a video game. Our souls—the players—would remember their prior choices, but we, the characters, would not. We would then seem to play a completely new version. Wordsworth hinted at this when he said: *Our birth is but a sleep and a forgetting*. Seeing our lives this way is difficult for us, but I think it is enormously helpful.

"The present moment is no more than a dot on the microcosm of your life, like the video file on your phone. The truth is that moments could be perceived as leaping forward or back. You feel the future as you live the past. You both know from your own experiences that you can and do relive moments of your life. Both of you have lost important people in your lives, and you can relive these moments. The past is in the present—always. We know this. The question is whether the present is in the past or the future in the present."

Emotion

"Time ceases to exist for events burned into the soul by the fires of emotion."
~ Arthur H Parsons, MD

Paris, 1923

IT WAS IMPOSSIBLE FOR ME TO CONSIDER leaving him again. The day after the party and the day after that, Father sent letters attempting to cajole me into returning with them to America. Their ship was leaving in two more days when he sent me what I hoped would be a final missive through Peter, who was still in Paris.

I was staying with Auguste so that they would not find me. Peter knew where I was but was sworn to secrecy. I could not let Mother and Father see me again. In due course, they returned to New York, and I went on with my life. But they did not give up as I had hoped they would—the letters and telegrams continued to arrive regularly over the next few months.

Within a month, I had given up my apartment and moved in with Auguste. Quite naturally, given Father's Paris connections, he and Mother eventually heard the news that their daughter was now "living in sin," which was the exact phrase noted in a letter penned by Mother herself, something she usually left up to Father. As I read the letter some three months after settling into my new living arrangements, I could well imagine her discomfiture at one of her many dinner engagements, having to answer her friends' inquiries as to my welfare. I could imagine Mother sighing and rewrapping a feather boa around her as she took tea at The Plaza with the ladies, telling them of my

Bohemian life—and perhaps dropping a name or two of famous Americans in Paris. Frankly, I could not have cared less what they all thought of me. I was in Paris, and I was in love.

Auguste and I had settled into a wonderful life of love and companionship. In his presence, I felt loved, adored, and, above all, understood. The gulf in our ages shrank to mere nothingness as we talked about life, love, philosophy, art and the mysteries of other people. We had friends but preferred to spend our time by ourselves. Auguste was still teaching but had recently been exploring the possibility of opening a gallery, an enterprise that interested me greatly. I occasionally still worked in one or the other of the couture houses as a mannequin—most notably for Jean Patou and that Gabrielle Chanel—but I would have happily taken on new duties as Auguste's gallery manager, and I told him this regularly. Throughout that autumn, we met with backers— he always included me in the meeting, so I continued to be hopeful about my future career aspirations. I was often able to smooth the way with several people my father had occasionally dealt with over the years. I was the legitimacy—the stability, perhaps— brought to the table by the artist, or so it often seemed.

When Auguste returned from his class at the university one Thursday afternoon in late November, he found me staring at yet another letter, feeling even more furious about my parents than perhaps I had ever been. I was tired of their tirades and had stopped reading them, so the letter sat on the table unopened in front of me.

Auguste entered the dining room where I was sitting and gathered me in his arms. He said, "Charlotte, my dearest darling, I cannot bear to see you sitting here, staring at your parents' letters, becoming more and more infuriated. But I also know that you would not be so incensed if you did not care." I started to protest, but he silenced me and continued. "As much as you feign complete and utter indifference to their opinion of your life, I believe that it does, indeed, bother you that you have fallen out so badly, especially with your father. Your mother, I cannot comment upon. In any event, if I may change the subject, I have arranged to take the next month off from my university duties."

"You have done what?" I sat up and looked at him. "Is something wrong?"

"No, *mon amour*, there is nothing wrong. Nothing is wrong at all."

I was not so sure. Auguste had an odd look on his face, but he simply shrugged off my concerns and continued.

"As it happens, I have purchased tickets for the train departing tomorrow evening at eight from the Gare de Lyon. If you agree, we are bound for Nice, then Monte Carlo, where we will spend Christmas. And if you further agree, we will be married the moment we can finalize arrangements."

How could I refuse?

~

I was madly in love with Auguste and had never been to the Riviera. I had lived in Paris for four years by this point but had never ventured beyond the city's environs. Paris was enough for me—or so I thought.

The train left precisely as scheduled at eight the following evening. It had been a whirlwind day, deciding what to take and calling Kiki and Peter to let them know I was leaving. Kiki guessed we were eloping, and I had to insist she not get on the train herself to be there for us. I was more circumspect with Peter, although I am certain he suspected what was going on. His only question was, "Are you going with Auguste?" And so, he knew.

The train trip was long but exciting. As Auguste and I settled into our compartment, I noted many British accents. Auguste told me that the train began in Calais, where it picked up passengers disembarking the channel ferry to take the British tourists away from the rain and drizzle of an English autumn and winter to the sunshine of the Riviera.

"This train, it is fairly new," Auguste said. "It had its maiden voyage, so to speak, only last December. Less than one year ago, and now it has become quite popular, as you can see."

I had always found train travel somewhat unnerving, with all that chugging and shaking. Not so for Auguste. He loved the sound and the movement. We ate dinner then he was soon fast asleep. I dozed intermittently but was acutely aware of each stop along the way. First, it was Dijon, then Châlons, and Lyon, before we reached Marseilles early the next morning. After Marseilles, the train turned eastward, making stops at each resort town: Saint-Raphaël, Juan-les-Pins, Antibes, Cannes and finally, Nice. At each stop, I sat at the window imagining the happy holidays the disembarking passengers would have. We finally disembarked, and the train continued on to Monte-Carlo before it was scheduled to reach its final destination, Menton. Beyond Menton was the Italian border.

When the train pulled up at the station in Nice, I was unprepared for how the city would make me feel even as I stepped out onto the platform and felt a breeze so much warmer than in Paris—although to be clear, it was not summer! Auguste had booked us a room at a small hotel just off the Promenade des Anglais, the boardwalk along the Mediterranean Sea. The hotel was small but beautiful with its many tiny balconies and not nearly as expensive as the ones fronting the beach. The room had a small Juliette balcony, and if I stood at the open window and poked my head out, turning it just so, I could see a glimpse of the beach. I immediately wanted to walk along the boardwalk, but Auguste laughed at my enthusiasm, suggesting dinner in a beachfront café instead. I agreed.

While we ate our dinner at the open-air café under colourful umbrellas, I could feel myself falling deeply in love with the ambience of the beach as we basked in the glow of tabletop candles. The sun had set around five, and the temperature dropped as darkness had settled. I pulled the cashmere throw closer and looked across the table at this man who made my life complete. And we would be together forever. I knew this. I was about to say something to that effect when suddenly, standing beside our table, was a couple who looked slightly familiar to me but seemed very familiar to Auguste. As soon as he saw them, he pulled his napkin off his lap and stood to shake hands and share the double kiss.

"Gerald! Sarah! It is so wonderful to see you both here." I was at first surprised he was speaking in English as I tried to remember where I'd met them before. Then he apologized for forgetting his manners and introduced me to Gerald and Sara Murphy, American ex-patriates whom I finally remembered meeting several times over the past year. I remembered something about the brief conversation I'd had with Sara on one of those occasions. Sara, who was at least fifteen years my senior, and I had concluded that we had something in common: both of us were living relationships that were unacceptable to our American parents. They, too, had fled to Paris. And they, too, came from family money. I also knew that Gerald was a sometime painter whom Auguste knew through the university and the artists' circles they frequented.

Sara was dressed like the epitome of autumnal Cote d'Azur style in a dark brown velveteen coat with a stand-up collar, large gold buttons, and a matching hat. I recognized the ensemble as being from Chanel's recent collection.

"What are you still doing here in Nice?" Auguste said. "I thought you would have long returned to Paris for the winter season."

Gerald and Sara both laughed and said, yes, they usually returned to Paris for the winter. This year, however, they were unexpectedly seized by the notion of staying on the Cote d'Azur for the winter. In fact, they gleefully explained they had convinced the proprietor of the hotel where they stayed in Antibes to keep the place open all winter, something that never happened. They were staying for the winter, had bought a villa they were now restoring, and, as it turned out, they were hosting a Christmas party in a few weeks. "You both must come!" Sara said enthusiastically.

As Auguste accepted their invitation, I hoped the party would not be like a French Riviera gathering of clones of Mother and Father's New York friends. Gerald and Sara Murphy might have been in France escaping disapproving families, but they were still well-connected and had their own bags of money. My money was tied up in a trust my grandfather had set up for me—a trust fund my mother and father could do nothing to prevent me from accessing when the time came. The money would be available to me within the year. I hadn't told August this yet but hoped he'd allow me to finance the gallery in due course.

Before they left to find their table, Sara looked at me closely. "My dear Charlotte, you are looking well. I am delighted you will be spending the holiday season here. And, if I might ask," she said, tipping her head to the side as if to see me in a different light, "you two wouldn't by any chance be planning nuptials, would you?"

I was surprised by her candour—and puzzled as to why she might think this other than here we were, far from Paris, alone. As much as I didn't want to share this delicious news with mere acquaintances yet, I fear my face gave it all away. Auguste smiled at me and nodded his head. The cat was out of the bag, so to speak, so there was no point in being coy.

The moment the Murphys figured out that Auguste and I were planning to be married, they began agitating to host the party. They telephoned us at the hotel the following day to beg us to let them host the wedding party at their hotel in Antibes. We didn't want that.

The wedding was at the registry office in Nice a week later. We relented and allowed Gerald and Sara to be our witnesses. I knew that a registry office wedding would not call for cocktail attire, but I did want it to be special and memorable. So, I chose a black velvet suit trimmed with white ermine I'd bought two years earlier with money Father had sent for a ticket home. The issue with black for a wedding notwithstanding, I loved this suit and thought the irony of it all was appropriate. And after all, Auguste hadn't given me much warning. So, I had to improvise from my closet.

"My dear, you look splendid," Sara said when she saw me outside the registry office. "I have always thought white and ivory to be highly overrated as wedding attire. Besides, we all know the hypocrisy of the virginal bride." She winked and took my arm, and we walked up the steps toward the door, followed by her husband and my soon-to-be husband. What a thought. I would soon have a husband.

Following the ceremony, Gerald and Sara's driver picked us up and drove us to Antibes to dine at their hotel, Hotel du Cap. The driver took us along the Basse Corniche, the lower road that snaked along the coast. I had never seen such scenery—beaches and villages surrounding the sparkling azure of the Mediterranean Sea were in full view. The trip took us almost one and a half hours, and I loved every minute of it. Such an adventure! But since it was such a long drive, the Murphys had insisted we spend our wedding night at Hotel du Cap and take their car and driver back to Nice the following day. They said it was to be their wedding gift to us. Once I saw the hotel as we approached, I knew we had made the right decision to accept their gift.

As we pulled in through the elaborate iron gates, we found ourselves facing three stories of white stucco sparkling in the afternoon sun. I was still anxious that Sara and Gerald might have gone ahead and invited others for a wedding party after all but had said nothing. We then had an hour to ourselves before dinner, and I was still nervous as I changed into my Patou cocktail dress for dinner. My fears were alleviated as we entered the dining room to find Sara and Gerald alone at our table set for four. They were marvellous hosts. The food they had chosen for the dinner was superb, and the service was gracious. It seemed all the staff knew them intimately and found their approbation important. We began the evening with a bottle of Dom Perignon and finished it with another after which Auguste and I floated off to bed on a cloud of happiness—and drunkenness, if I am honest.

On the drive home the following day, while nursing a headache of monumental proportions, I found myself staring at the wedding ring that now adorned my left hand. It was a solid band of gold carved with a geometric motif. Auguste and I had picked it out at a jeweller in Nice the day after we arrived. I was now a wife. How did that make me feel, I wondered?

On the one hand, it was a bit thrilling, knowing I would spend the rest of my life with my best friend and lover. On the other hand, it terrified me slightly in its enormity. I had taken on a colossal commitment. I looked at my new husband, who was deep in thought.

"My darling husband," I said, surprising myself with how easily the word slid off my tongue, "is everything all right?"

Auguste turned to look at me, and his face immediately broke into a broad smile, although I detected something behind his eyes. "*Mas oui*, my darling. But of course, everything is wonderful. Why would it not be? I am here with you and have everything I could ever have wished for."

Why did I doubt him? "Auguste, I have been meaning to ask you something."

"Anything, my darling. You can ask me anything at all. I have no secrets from my wife."

Since Auguste had lived a much longer time on this earth than I had, I was reasonably sure this declaration about secrets was not entirely true, but that wasn't bothering me at all. It was something else that had been on my mind since the day he told me he was taking a month-long leave from the university. That had seemed odd to me at that time, but other matters made my concerns fade into oblivion—almost.

"Auguste, why did you really take a month off from your university duties? I have a strong feeling it was not simply because you wanted the time for us to marry. We could have done that on any day of the week in Paris." I hesitated for a moment lest he misinterpret my thoughts. "What I mean to say is that this holiday is a most wonderful interlude for us both, but I wonder at the timing and, if I'm being completely candid, its length does seem unusual at the school." I knew it was strange for someone teaching at École des Beaux-Arts to take an unscheduled month off.

Auguste immediately looked serious. "I am not attempting to keep something from you, my darling. I simply did not wish to worry you." Now I was worried. He continued. "I have been increasingly unhappy that I am unable to spend more of my time as an artist. I am not a teacher in my soul, although the work has had its advantages. And now my superior has suggested I may be spending too much of my time on my own art to the detriment of my students. This is, of course, completely absurd."

"Are your students complaining?"

"They are not. I believe it to be professional jealousy. Nothing more. My work is becoming recognized, and he has had to listen to colleagues praise my work while his own remains unappreciated."

"I don't see how that is your problem, Auguste. If he's childish enough to treat you this way, it's his concern."

"Ah, my darling, but it is my concern since he has made it clear that if he sees even one more of my works on exhibit, not only will he let me go from my position, but he will use his considerable influence to ensure no reputable gallery will show my work."

I could see the anguish on Auguste's face, and it made me weak with distress. "Does he really have that kind of sway in the art world?"

"He does."

"Well then, dear husband, we will simply open our own gallery as you have suggested and display your work."

"You do not fully comprehend, my dear. My desire for a gallery is not simply a vanity project for my work. Indeed, the only way for my work to be recognized is for it to be exhibited by others. I must simply consider complying."

"You'll do no such thing!"

Auguste glanced at the driver, who had looked into the rearview mirror at the sound of my increasingly hysterical voice.

My mind began to race with ideas about how to ensure that Auguste's work would not be lost to history. "Auguste! I have an idea!" I also glanced at the driver, who seemed to be engrossed in our conversation. I slid closer to Auguste and turned to whisper in his ear. "You will simply change your name."

"I will do what?"

"You heard me," I whispered again. "You will paint under a pseudonym. Writers do it all the time. Why not an artist?"

"I am certain this is a preposterous idea," Auguste said without much—if any—conviction.

I could see that he was considering the idea.

He took my hand again and looked straight ahead. I could tell he was thinking about this possibility. I was suddenly enveloped in a cloud of enormous joy and peace. No matter where this remarkable man would be, if I were with him, no matter what he was called, I would be home. I never lost sight of that.

~

Gerald and Sara's party the week before Christmas turned out to be something of a snooze, as it were. They had convinced only a handful of people to stay in Antibes for the Christmas season, so their Christmas party was a low-key affair, and I was particularly grateful for that. Sara kept apologizing, telling me there were many people with whom she would like to acquaint me. On the other hand, I was supremely happy just the way things were.

Auguste and I celebrated a simple Christmas at our hotel in Nice, and as New Year's Eve approached, we discussed my absurd idea. He would change his name, and I would do the same. I had no idea if it could even be done here in France, the master of bureaucracy, although Auguste seemed to think it was a simple matter of changing it. I wasn't so sure the bank would see it that way. I was convinced that if it could be done through legal means, there would be many hoops through which we would be required to jump. But that was for later. There was still New Year's Even ahead of us yet.

On the morning of December 31, 1923, Auguste and I boarded the train from Nice to Monte Carlo. We planned to spend our final night on holiday celebrating the new year in style among the rich and glamorous of the famed Monte Carlo. On the first day of the new year, tomorrow, we would once again board the train and return to Paris.

Auguste and I had decided to splurge for our final night and had booked a small suite at the Hôtel de Paris on the Place du Casino in Monte Carlo next door to the famed Grand Casino. As we stepped out of the taxi that brought us from the train station, I felt like I was walking into another world. I had spent my formative years living in a twenty-two-room mansion in New York staffed by a housekeeper and an upstairs maid (Mother's choice of moniker), but I had not had the chance to travel much until I finally left on my own to live in Paris. So, luxurious hotels were not in my experience apart from the odd gala at places like Le Meurice. I had been a guest in one only once before. It was the Savoy Hotel in London before that ill-fated attempt to return to New York on the Titanic's maiden voyage. It was an interlude I had put out of my mind. In any case, here at the Hôtel de Paris, we were treated like royalty, although that would be something of an understatement.

Our room was small but so luxurious with its smooth, snow-white sheets, fluffy towels, mahogany four-poster bed, and garden view. Given the prices, we couldn't consider a room overlooking the square, but what did that matter? We were here for only one night and would spend but a few hours in our room.

We dined in the opulent hotel restaurant with its gold-trimmed Louis XV décor, glittering crystal and lavish white linens. We had just ordered wine when I heard a voice behind me.

"My, my. What *do* we have here?"

I turned to see the source of the voice and was astonished to find myself looking up at none other than Louella Parsons.

"We meet yet again, Miss Broadhurst, Peter Hurst's sister." Louella, whom I had not actually met at Kiki's fateful party at Le Meurice many months earlier, was staring at Auguste and then back at me. Her eyes fluttered to my left hand, which I quickly slid under the table onto my lap. "Or perhaps it's Mrs. Vaillancourt?"

As expected, Louella Parsons had, indeed, written a gossipy article following the altercation at the party. And it had, as far as I could tell from Peter's letters, boosted, if not his career, then at least his notoriety.

"What are you doing here?" It was the best I could do under the circumstances of my shock, tinged as it was with the terror of publicity.

"I suppose I'm doing what you're doing, celebrating the New Year in this fascinating place. In case you haven't noticed, this hotel is riddled with stars. They do like to keep a low profile, but I can be very discreet in my observations. I do try to get to the continent at least twice a year." She began looking around. "Oh, do pardon me. I see my dinner companion has arrived. Happy New Year to you both," she said as she swept past our table.

I didn't even turn to see who her dining companion was. I was too distressed. "Auguste, you don't suppose she will write about us in her gossip column, do you?"

Auguste laughed. "Us? We are nobodies to her. Even if she did, what difference would it make? Everyone will soon know we have married. Even your parents in America will know once they receive your telegram, as I suggested." He raised his eyebrows a bit. "You have not sent it yet, have you?"

I had not, but it occurred to me that he was right. Everyone would know before long. My only objective now was to ensure my family received my telegram announcing our news before Louella decided to put a line in one of her columns about meeting us in Monte Carlo at New Year's. With that in mind, I shrugged off the encounter and returned to concentrating on celebrating my first New Year's Eve with my new husband. Before long, we had forgotten entirely about Louella Parsons and her gossip column.

As the evening wore on, it became clear that everyone else knew something we didn't.

"What do you suppose they're doing?" I said as I watched each departing guest picking up a champagne bottle and dropping coupes into pockets of fur coats.

Auguste shrugged, then gestured for a passing waiter. "*Que font-ils tous?*" he said, asking them what everyone was doing.

The waiter looked over toward where a red-silk-clad woman who was donning what appeared from a distance to be an ermine stole slid two champagne coupes into her handbag. "*Ils se préparent à aller sur la place. C'est tout.*" Evidently, they were all preparing to go to the square, presumably to celebrate. We decided that when in Rome—or at least Monte Carlo—well, you know the rest.

As midnight approached, we joined the throng of partiers in the Place du Casino. We were shoulder to shoulder with the well-heeled revellers in their tuxedos, evening gowns and furs—so many furs. I had never seen so many dead animals all in one place at one time. Then the countdown began.

"*Dix, neuf, huit, sept,*" and we could see hands slide toward corks, "*six, cinque, quatre, trois,*" and they were ready. "*Deux...un!*" With that, corks began flying into the air, followed by streams of champagne, not all of which was caught in coupes. Then the fireworks began. It was magnificent!

As we joined in the merriment, sipping from the coupes we'd absconded with on our way out of the restaurant (with the approval of the maitre d'), Auguste leaned in close to my ear and said, "I love you, *mon amour*, and we shall do it."

I was puzzled for a split second, then remembered our recent heartfelt conversations.

"We begin a new year and a new life, Charlotte," he said. "Let us make it complete."

That is how Monsieur and Madame Auguste and Charlotte Vaillancourt became Auguste and Charlotte Lejeune.

"Why Lejeune?" I asked Auguste the following day as we sat in our compartment on the train bound for Paris.

"It means young," he said. "As a part of us shall always be."

Convergence

"There is no other space, no other time. This moment is all. In this moment the whole existence converges, in this moment all is available."
~ Osho, *Zen: The Path of Paradox*

ALL THE TALK OF PAST LIVES and parallel lives was making me positively dizzy. The facts were these.

Patrick and I met by chance at a bookstore in Paris. During that briefest of encounters, we felt a connection—not love at first sight by any means, but a connection, as if we had met somewhere before. This situation is hardly an unusual one for two people to find themselves in. Then, Patrick and I met once again by chance. How often does one have to meet by chance for it to no longer be considered chance? I have no idea. This time it was quite odd since it was an ocean away from Paris in Toronto at a grocery store. Again, we shared the feeling that we'd met before.

Also, a fact: we were never able to figure out where we'd met before and yet the feeling never dimmed. Fact: we shared a dream about two historical figures. Is it even possible for two people to have the same dream? I doubt it.

Another fact: Elspeth Savant, historical investigator extraordinaire, found a credible historical connection between Charlotte and Auguste. And Patrick and I were no further ahead in figuring out our connection.

Of course, then there was that meeting with Dr. Robert Bukowsky, although you could hardly categorize our discussion with him as contributing to hard facts. Nevertheless, it added to the intensifying feeling that there might be more to this situation than facts.

These were the dissonant considerations swirling around in my blender of a brain as I sat in my office the week after Patrick's visit, staring at a blank computer screen. It wasn't supposed to be blank. I had sat here often enough now looking at a blank screen to consider ditching the book project entirely since I was no closer to a story about Auguste and Charlotte, historical characters I hoped would be my novel's main characters. All I had was a pile of notes and some computer files. There was still no Chapter 1. I had no idea where the story was going. Then Patrick called. He'd just been to see Elspeth, who had discovered something.

~

Patrick was with Elspeth in her workshop as we spoke. "Charlie, I'm going to send you a link so we can have you on video. You need to see this."

Once I was connected to the workshop visually, Elspeth said hello and excitedly began telling me about what she'd found.

"I knew it was only a matter of time before we would find out some details of Auguste Vaillancourt's life, not to mention the life of an American heiress. I don't have the entire picture yet, but I think you'll see we are moving in the right direction." Elspeth then picked up a piece of paper and held it up in front of her webcam so I could see it.

It was a photocopy of what appeared to be a two-page spread from a government record book. The pages were covered in vintage writing—that kind of elegant cursive style that is all but forgotten these days when no one seems to know how to apply pen to paper. As Elspeth held the page, she used a long, bone pointer like several I'd seen on her worktable when I visited her workshop in Toronto with Patrick. She pointed the tip to a line of writing about halfway down the page. I strained to read the fading cursive handwriting.

"Oh my god," I said when the first name I recognized came into view. It was Vaillancourt, Auguste. I squinted, and Elspeth put me out of my misery.

"Quite, my dear," she said, moving the pointer along the line. "It clearly indicates here that Auguste Vaillancourt and Charlotte Broadhurst were married in Nice, France, on Wednesday, December 12, 1923. It is not much wonder we had difficulty finding it since we expected they might have married in Paris, if at all."

"What were they doing in Nice?"

"We don't know yet," Patrick said. "But Elspeth has discovered an interesting piece of information that might lead somewhere. The names of the witnesses at Auguste and Charlotte's wedding were Gerald and Sara Murphy."

"I'm sorry," I said. "Are they people I should know about?"

"Probably not—at least not yet," Elspeth said, "but Patrick tells me you're considering writing a book set in Paris in the 1920s, so you might well be interested." Elspeth then told me about the Murphys, ex-pat Americans who left the US because their families disapproved of their union—Sara was five years older than Gerald. According to Elspeth's research, they spent a part of each of the years they lived in Paris in Antibes in the south of France, not far from Nice. In 1923, they convinced the owners of Hotel du Cap, their usual home away from home, to remain open all winter, something no one ever did at that time. They then bought and renovated a villa they'd purchased, moving in some time later. The Murphys almost single-handedly turned the Riviera into a year-round playground for rich and famous Americans. "They are such interesting historical figures," Elspeth said.

I agreed that they were interesting and made a note to do some research of my own. But what also piqued my interest was that we now knew Auguste and Charlotte had married. That information, though, seemed to represent the end of the line. Was there more?

"There is one other piece that you might find interesting, Charlotte," Elspeth said. She picked up another photocopy, this time of an old newspaper article. I could see it was from the *New York Morning Telegraph,* dated Monday, January 14, 1924. The byline was Louella Parsons.

"…and just one other tiny morsel from my recent New Year's Eve sojourn in Monte Carlo: I happened upon American heiress Charlotte Broadhurst in an intimate tête-à-tête with new husband, French artist Auguste Vaillancourt dining in style at the Hotel de Paris. You might remember a particular party I wrote about last year featuring young actor Peter Hurst and the punch that was heard around the world when the eternally sour Mrs. Broadhurst (Peter's and Charlotte's mother) punched our Monsieur Vaillancourt in the face. I had expected to see young Charlotte return to America, but it appears we have lost her to the continent forever…"

Monte Carlo. The words started my mind reeling and my heart racing. Although we had talked about visiting, Tom and I had never been to Monaco. We could have well afforded to go, but there were so many other places to visit. Why, then, did the mention of the name set my body into motion?

Patrick sat down in front of the webcam, and I looked at him. "What's going on, Charlie? I can see from that look on your face that something's going on."

Before I even knew what I was saying, I heard my own voice. "We have to go, Patrick. We have to go to Monte Carlo."

~

Patrick and I talked almost every day for months. It was summer before we managed it. Again, Frankie travelled with me to Toronto to spend two weeks with her cousins, and I met Patrick in the lounge at Pearson Airport at six-thirty the following evening for the overnight flight to Paris.

"Mom," Frankie said as I left her at Evelyn's again, "don't worry about me. All my friends are jealous I get to spend so much time in Toronto—you know, the centre of the universe. And I like Patrick. You should get to know him better."

She had no idea.

We landed in Paris to spend three days before we took the train to Monte Carlo. While we were in Paris, Patrick and I both stayed at my flat and spent every hour of every day together, retiring to our separate rooms each evening. Although I knew the city well by then, as did Patrick, we seemed to be seeing it for the first time as we walked the streets together. And each day, as we explored new parts of the city together, I had a more profound sense of déjà vu. He told me he felt the same.

"But it's more than just a feeling of having been here before, Patrick," I said the second evening as we sat across a tiny outdoor table at a bistro three blocks from my apartment.

Before I could explain any further, "Patrick said, "It's as if I'm walking on the streets at a different time, in a different body—and yet it's me. I don't know how to explain it. Sorry, you were saying?"

I laughed. "I think you explained it better than I could because I was going to say much the same thing. I'm seeing places I've never seen before, and yet I have. But it seems to be happening right now. Do you have that feeling, too?"

As Patrick looked at me, I saw deep emotion in his eyes. He seemed to be struggling with something. "Charlie, you know I feel as if I've known you my whole life, don't you?" I nodded and knew I felt the same. "Well, I have to tell you that it feels like something more than knowing you. It feels like a connection—a connection that has always been here."

I wasn't quite sure how to respond, but what was becoming increasingly clear was that this man was important to me—and I could not let him leave my life. That much I knew for sure.

On the fourth day, we boarded the train at Gare de Lyon. As we made our way along the platform toward the first-class section of the TGV—the fast train—I had a strange feeling I'd done this before. Of course, I had not, but Charlotte Broadhurst must have done this. Back in 1923, when she would have made the trip, though, it would have taken at least a day and a half. Today, our train was scheduled to leave in fifteen minutes at eight-fifteen in the morning and would arrive in Monte Carlo at twenty minutes to three this afternoon, just in time for a late lunch.

Patrick and I chatted a bit, but we both seemed to have things on our minds. I spent the trip reading and watching the French countryside go by, wondering what it would have been like to make this trip in 1923—and to know you were about to marry the love of your life. How did I know Auguste was Charlotte's real love? I just knew.

We arrived at the station in Monte Carlo precisely at nineteen minutes to three. I had never been in a train station quite like this one. My experience of trains was not extensive, but what I had experienced consisted of old edifices that had been around since trains started running with lots of old wood and wrought iron. This station was not at all like that.

The Monte Carlo train station was a bright, airy tunnel where the walls and well-thought-out lighting gleamed, and the platforms were so clean it looked like you could eat off the floor. Monte Carlo felt different already.

When we emerged from the cool air-conditioned interior of the station into the blistering heat of the summer afternoon, we found a taxi without any difficulty. Within minutes, we were standing in Place du Casino in front of the Hotel de Paris, where we would stay, as Auguste and Charlotte had done a hundred years ago. Standing there in the sunshine, I knew I had been there before. Otherwise, how did I know that directly to my right was the Grand Casino building which also housed the Garnier Theatre? How did I know I was looking across the square at the Café de Paris and knew what the square would look like from that vantage point? How did I know exactly what this square would feel like if I had never been here before? Then Patrick and I walked up the steps into the hotel, and I knew exactly where I was going.

"Charlie," Patrick said, "why do I feel I know this place? Do you feel it?"

I just nodded, not able to articulate the peculiar feeling.

We checked into our rooms and decided to take a walk. First, we walked through the square with all the other tourists who were gawking at the collection of Ferraris and Mercedes McLarens and Bentley convertibles dotted around the place. Then we walked into the refined interior of the Metropole, a chichi shopping arcade across the square. The moment we walked inside, the feeling of familiarity immediately stopped. Patrick and I looked at each other, knowing we both felt it.

"I don't think this place was here in 1923," he said wryly.

Looking around, I could see that he was entirely correct.

We left the Metropole and headed northwest along the Boulevard de Moulins to find a staircase or even an outdoor elevator to take us down closer to the water—to Larvotto Beach. On our way, we passed the Japanese garden created for the late Princess Grace and the Grimaldi Forum, an enormous theatre complex right on the water's edge. I had read that the main theatre was, in fact, below water level.

We finally reached Larvotto beach, where locals and tourists alike filled every imaginable square inch, each looking for a place to stash their things so they could cool off in the blue Mediterranean. I almost wished I could join them, but I was too busy feeling slightly unglued. My thoughts were jumbled, and I couldn't seem to get a hold of the feeling in my soul. No image crystallized, but I knew one thing. I had been here before—and yet, I was here then and now simultaneously.

Later that evening, Patrick and I dined late and talked about how each of us had felt. He had felt the same tugging deep within him. It was as if we had visited this place before—together. That night, Patrick did not go to his own room.

~

After flying back home to Canada, Patrick and I knew one thing: we did not want to be apart. I couldn't explain it. The only explanation for it was one that my logical mind didn't want to accept, but that my soul knew was the only possible answer. So, Patrick and I embarked on a long-distance relationship and tried to figure out where we went from there. In October, Frankie and I once again flew to Toronto for Thanksgiving. Patrick had asked us to stay with him, but I wanted to be sure his children, as grown up as they were, would be comfortable. So, as usual, Frankie and I stayed with Evelyn and her family, but we would all have dinner together to celebrate Thanksgiving. I don't know who was more excited about this—Evelyn or me.

After settling into Evelyn's guest room and ensuring Frankie was happy with her cousins, I asked Evelyn if she minded if I left to see Patrick. She gave me her blessing, and I arrived on his doorstep half an hour later. Patrick immediately pulled me into the house to hold me tightly and kiss me deeply before releasing me with the words, "Charlie, I've got something to show you."

I followed him into his main floor study and waited for him to turn his computer screen around so we could see it together. He clicked, and the screen was filled with the image of a painting. I peered at it closely. The landscape was very familiar to me, but I couldn't place it precisely. Then he clicked again, and this time, an image of my face filled the screen. But it wasn't me because I could once again see her kohl-lined eyes, something I had never done. And yet, I had. It wasn't me, and it was.

"Patrick, you found another portrait Auguste painted of Charlotte!"

"Yes...and no."

"Is this a puzzle?"

"Sort of," he said, clicking through another six or seven paintings, all clearly by the same artist. I was no expert at identifying works by the same artist, but they looked like the two I'd seen from Auguste Vaillancourt. As I examined each one, Patrick said, "Now look at the signatures."

I peered closely at the screen. "*A. Lejeune.*" Then at the next one and the next. "I don't get it. Who is A. Lejeune?"

"There is no doubt about it, Charlie. It's Auguste Vaillancourt. And what's more, I've found a Charlotte Lejeune on a website chronicling longstanding Parisian galleries."

I was still puzzled.

"They changed their names!"

Now we knew where to look.

Transcendence

*"Life and death are the same thing. When we realize this fact, we
have no fear of death anymore, nor actual difficulty in our life."*
~ Shunryu Suzuki

Paris, 1924-1929

AUGUSTE WAS THE WISEST MAN I had ever met. Being younger
and far more excitable, I wanted everything to happen at once. I
wanted us to return to Paris and plunge immediately into a new
life—with our new identities. As I looked back on this interval of
my life some years later, I realized how naïve I must have
seemed, and yet Auguste never once made me feel that way. He
guided me slowly to the understanding that life unfolds as it
should and that everything that happens to us is a result of
everything that has happened in our past. There was, however, a
part of what he tried to impart to me that I had difficulty
understanding.

Auguste was a firm believer in the transcendence of life—of
the many things all around us that beckon us toward wholeness,
toward a kind of perfection. This deep conviction is what made
him a great artist, but it was puzzling for me at that age. He
believed—no, that is not quite correct—he had a deep knowing
that it was not only his past that affected his current situation,
but it was also his future. *How can that be?* I said to him more than
once. *The future has not happened yet. How can something that has
not yet happened affect what is happening right now?*

Auguste would smile at me enigmatically and say, "The
future is always with us, Charlotte, darling."

It was only later that I understood that we make choices in our lives as we live in the present moment, but that present moment, which seems like all we have, is there with our pasts and futures. It was baffling, but my uncertainty about the veracity of Auguste's words would fade into certainty as the next few years unfolded.

~

We returned to Paris and spent the next few months slowly and methodically devising our plan. Auguste would continue his teaching for the foreseeable future (as Professor Vaillancourt), and I would embark on a search for a suitable space for a gallery. And what about our new identities, you might well ask.

Changing one's name in France wasn't as complex as we might have thought. We simply began using our new surname within some circles. Those with whom we had never before been acquainted merely accepted it, writing it down on any document we cared to sign. My trust fund became available to me in early March of that year. I had some moments of trepidation, thinking perhaps Father might have tried to stop it from coming to me, but the truth was that it had been set up for me by my grandfather. Father's wishes did not enter into how my grandfather, Pierre Senior, wished to treat his granddaughter. And so, on the first of March, I walked into the bank where I had been coming for several years to withdraw money from an account Father wired money into for me and demanded access to my funds. There were no questions asked. Thus, when I finally found the perfect gallery space and offered cash, the current owner accepted our signatures, "Auguste and Charlotte Lejeune," and handed over the key and the deed. The new identities began to take shape.

The gallery space we purchased was located in the eighth arrondissement—a three-story white building with a large, open gallery space on the ground floor and a two-story apartment above. It would be perfect for the newlywed Lejeunes. We would move in as soon as possible. It was next door to a small bistro that seemed to be able to fill its tables both indoors and outside at every moment of their opening hours. We made sure to eat and drink at the bistro as often as possible, soon getting to know the proprietors—Alain and Sylvie Bernard, who also lived above their business—well enough that they always had our table waiting for us. They were happy to know their new neighbours, the Lejeunes.

The neighbourhood was one in which we knew no one; thus, we were able to begin our lives anew. Even our closest friends did not know of our identity change. We simply saw less and less of them. It was so interesting to me to observe how easy it was to move away from a certain life. Kiki and Gaston had a life of their own with their glittering parties and new daughter Juliette to keep them busy. They hardly noticed as we began missing party after party. I quickly learned that social circles were more important to many than deep friendships were. Although I seemed to have moved into a different circle of friends as well as a different part of the city, I happened to run into Frannie Phillips once.

It seems she and Jean-Christophe, the publishing person she had dated and whom I had disliked, had gone their separate ways. I still wondered if she might not enjoy my brother's company, but playing matchmaker for my brother was now in my past. In any case, it seemed she had a new beau—an American—so I did not attempt to offer up my brother! After seeing Frannie on the street that one time, I never saw her again. We travelled in different circles, and Paris was nothing if not a hotbed of cliques. Before we parted ways that day, though, she said something odd.

"Tell Auguste I'll look forward to seeing him some time. " And she was gone.

I never did remember to mention her odd words to Auguste. Seeing Frannie Phillips was the last thing Auguste should do at this point in our lives.

It took us eight months to get the gallery up and running, although we had moved into the apartment almost immediately. The two-story apartment had a drawing room, kitchen and dining room on the first floor (the floor directly above the gallery) and two massive bedrooms and a bathroom on the top floor. Both bedrooms had skylights and high windows with Juliette balconies overlooking the street. We used the largest of the two for our bedroom and transformed the other into a studio for Auguste Lejeune. And so began his new identity as an artist.

By the time we were ready for a gallery opening, we had acquired several pieces from artists we considered the new wave of the art world. We had charmed several pieces from Pablo Picasso, as well as two sculptures and two photographs from American artist Man Ray who lived in Paris. We had also acquired a number of paintings and sculptures from emerging artists, several of whom had been Auguste's students who were unaware that he had an interest in this new gallery. Also interspersed among these art pieces were three new works by Auguste Lejeune. Despite his objections to exhibiting his work in the gallery his wife ran, I had insisted since I expected to be able to entice several art critics as well as others in the arts community to the opening. I believed it was time for Auguste to take his place in the annals of the great Parisian painters, and I wouldn't have dreamed of missing this opportunity.

The day for the opening finally arrived in the middle of November. As luck would have it, the weather was not so perfect—it began raining early in the day. By the time the evening rolled around, rivers of water gushed along the street where Allain and Sylvie's hardy outdoor patrons plastered themselves along the bistro's walls under the awning, watching the rain pelt down while drinking wine. I only hoped the weather would not discourage too many invitees.

We had invited no one from our previous life. Over the past months, as we had acquired our works for the gallery, we had ensconced ourselves into groups of artists and writers who had not known us before. Every once in a while, I would run into someone from America whom I had met through my father. I avoided any mention of being married or what my surname might be now—and they knew better than to ask. There was, however, one American I had pursued.

His name was Henry McBride. I had heard my mother mention his name years earlier, but I was young then—too young to appreciate the potential interest I might have later in someone whose opinions seemed to matter to my social-climbing mother. I vaguely remembered my parents buying several paintings for their New York house simply because of this man, who had written a review of the artist's work in *The Sun*, a newspaper Father read religiously. I never really paid any attention to the artist's name, but what I had noted was his style.

My parents had never been fans of anything remotely modern when it came to artwork for their walls. Their tastes ran more to portraits of dusty old people, still life and landscapes depicting riders on horseback at the hunt. I often thought they would have been better placed in England than New York. These two paintings were different.

I remembered being a young teenager and spending time just sitting and looking at these paintings because they were so very different from any art I'd ever seen before. I once overheard my mother telling a friend about them. She used the word "impressionism," and I realized that the paintings were not really so much reflections as impressions of people and places. I loved them. So began my love affair with modern art.

When I met Auguste, he was painting these impressionistic pieces. I sat for him as a model when I first arrived in Paris, and one thing led to another. I remembered wondering if this was the only kind of art he ever produced, which was when he sat me down and painted my portrait to prove his versatility. It was incredible to see my countenance come to life in oils, emerging from the canvas as if it had a mind of its own—and perhaps it did. However, he had returned to his impressionist roots at the time of our gallery opening. When I heard that Mr. McBride would be in Paris for a week coinciding with the gallery's opening exhibit, I considered that to be too synchronous to pass up.

I contacted Kiki, who would know the details on someone like Mr. McBride, because if there was one thing Kiki prided herself in was her connections to both the financial world through Gaston's banker friends and the arts world through her connections to artists and choreographers. She agreed to meet me for lunch in the dining room at the Hotel Westminster near the Opera Garnier, a location where I expected to see no one I knew in either of what I'd come to view as my two lives.

"Charlotte, you are a sight to behold! Where have you been keeping yourself? Have you been back to America? Why have you not told me where you are now living? How is Auguste?" She kept up a steady stream of questions.

I was purposely vague but gave her just enough information to satisfy her without giving away too much. I certainly did not tell her we were living a double life.

"It has been far too long, *ma chère amie*," Kiki said before launching into details about how wonderful little Juliette was. Once she had come to the end of her description of how little Juliette might well follow in her mother's footsteps into ballet (after all, Kiki had befriended none other than Serge Diaghilev, the maestro of Les Ballets Russes), she turned to me as if she had forgotten. "But you have asked me to lunch, and I have—how do you say it in English?—monopolized the conversation. Did you just wish to catch up, or," and she winked at me, "perhaps you have news?"

I suppose she thought I might tell her that Auguste and I were having a baby—she did know we were married, but that is all.

"As a matter of fact, Kiki, I did want to ask you something."

She was all ears as I told her, in a roundabout way, that I wished an introduction to Mr. McBride when he came to the city. "In fact," I said, choosing my words carefully, "if you would agree, it would be wonderful if you would consider providing me with an introduction before then so I could contact him. Auguste has students, you know…" I trailed off, hoping Kiki would fill in the blanks. But I did not tell her about the gallery opening.

"But of course!" she said excitedly. "Of course, Auguste would want to support his greatest students in any way possible. Yes, I will send him a telegram tomorrow, after which you should contact him to set up a meeting while he is in the city. I would be honoured to be part of the discovery of a new artist in this way. You must tell me how it goes!"

I could see she was about to ask me more questions about the new artwork, possibly even if she could see some of it, so I headed her off and turned the conversation back to Juliette. It worked beautifully. She forgot all about the student work until we were ready to leave when I gently reminded her about her promise to contact Henry McBride. We said goodbye, and true to her word, Kiki provided an introduction for me to Mr. McBride. And that is how I arranged for him to be at the gallery opening in November.

So, on that very rainy night in November, I was more than delighted when I saw an older man I did not know open the gallery door, put down his umbrella and remove his round, wire-rimmed glasses to clean them before stepping inside and looking around. It had to be him. I made my way across the increasingly crowded space to introduce myself.

"Mrs. Lejeune?" he said, extending his hand to me.

I had explained to him in my letter that Kiki would have introduced me as Charlotte Broadhurst but that I wasn't using that name any longer. And since a woman changing her name at marriage was the norm, it would not raise any questions. At least, that was what I was hoping. If he recognized me as a New York

Broadhurst, he didn't let on to me. I was hoping that social gossip would not interest him.

I took his coat and umbrella and then began the tour. Before we had gone more than three steps into the space, he began exclaiming over the Picasso, an artist whose work he recognized at once. Then we moved past pieces by two former students of Auguste's and Man Ray's sculptures and photographs. We found ourselves directly in front of Auguste's latest work, an impressionistic homage to the French Riviera.

"This one," Mr. McBride said, moving toward the piece to get a closer look, then moving away for a long view, "this one is magnificent. You must tell me about this artist."

And that is how the work of Auguste Lejeune made its way across the Atlantic Ocean and into American collectors' hearts, minds and drawing rooms.

~

Over the next few years, Auguste and I were able to carry off what began as our tiny bit of subterfuge but what soon became our very real lives. There was no doubt about who we were—we were Auguste Lejeune, a Parisian artist, and I was Charlotte Lejeune, a Parisian gallery owner. And we loved our life. Then one day, three years later, I received a telegram from my brother, with whom I kept in touch on the understanding that Father and Mother could not know where I was living. I received correspondence from Father only through my banker—a friend of his—a situation I tolerated.

Peter was coming to Paris with his new girlfriend, an actress called Louise Brooks, who had just been offered a contract with Paramount Pictures, where Peter was also a contract actor. There was much excitement among actors in Hollywood at that time as movies transitioned from silent to what people called "talkies," and only certain actors could make the transition. Peter was one of them with his deep, well-modulated voice, and evidently, this

Louse Brooks was as well. I was excited to see him but was still a bit nervous about how he might perceive my new life when he saw it in person.

I had no desire to have anything upset the life Auguste and I had created. We had now been married for almost four years and were more in love than ever. Every once in a while, I could see him looking at me wistfully, and when I asked him about it, he told me he just wished we could have had more years together. I chided him since I fully expected that despite his age, we would have many more. He would then smile and say, "My daring Charlotte, my pensiveness is only for this moment as we have had and will have many more. The future is already here." I wasn't entirely sure what he meant, but it sounded wonderful.

~

Auguste and I were waiting at our table at a small, dark restaurant not far from the gallery when Peter walked in with a ravishing dark-haired beauty on his arm. *This must be Louise*, I thought. *I can see she is going to be wonderful on a movie screen.*

Louise, who I judged to be no more than about twenty years old, had a dark, sleek bob that ended at her chin. Although it was not that different in style from my own bobbed hair, somehow, the dark, shining tresses with the severe bangs across her forehead made her seem that much more dramatic. Perhaps it was also that smouldering look she seemed to have perfected. Whatever it was, I could see why Peter was smitten.

Once their eyes became accustomed to the deep dimness lit only by candles, Peter saw us, and they made their way to our table. He introduced us to Louise, who took off her fur wrap and slung it on the back of her chair before sitting down. She then rummaged in her handbag for a cigarette holder, affixed a cigarette to the end and looked to Peter for a light. He obliged before lighting up himself. Neither Auguste nor I smoked cigarettes regularly, although I could be tempted to puff on a long cigarette holder from time to time. In any case, we demurred when offered. For the next two hours, we ate, talked and laughed in a haze of smoke.

After Peter and Louise (who wasn't quite as gregarious as I had hoped) regaled us with stories of how the Hollywood studio life worked, Peter turned to me. His face was suddenly solemn. "Charlotte, there's something else we need to talk about."

I looked around the table at Auguste and Louise, who had begun chatting about set design as art. I turned to Peter. "Is this about our family?" He nodded. "Perhaps we should find another time when we can be alone, then?" I was also concerned about the copious amounts of wine we consumed. Surely a conversation about Mother and Father would be better held in the cold, sober light of day.

"I think Father is dying," Peter blurted, causing both Auguste and Louise to turn abruptly.

I was alarmed. As much as Father and I had our disagreements over the years, the thought of him dying distressed me. I forgot we had an audience in Auguste and Louise and continued. "What do you mean you think he's dying? Is he ill? What has he told you?"

"He hasn't said so in as many words, but Mother is difficult," Peter said as I rolled my eyes. Of course, Mother was difficult. That was nothing new. He continued. "And I think it's because Father isn't well."

I wasn't thinking quite as clearly as I could have on a cold sober morning, but I wasn't drunk enough not to realize this seemed like double-talk. "Peter, is Father ill, or is he not ill? Is he truly dying, or is he only dying as we all are dying?"

Peter put his head in his hands. "Mother is driving me crazy. She telephones me in California almost every day. She sends long, rambling letters about how she has failed as a mother. She sends telegrams. Whenever she finally convinces me to visit, she spends the entire time crying about how she has been such a bad mother, especially to her daughter. And Father just sits there and listens. He seems defeated by her histrionics. You have to do something."

I was stunned by this. "I have to do something? What do *I* have to do? What *can* I do? I am in Paris. They are in New York."

Then he dropped the bomb. "I think you should move home." I was stunned. He continued. "Father's business is failing, and he needs you."

I sat quietly for a moment, staring at my hands that I held clenched on the table in front of me. This evening wasn't going as I had expected, but we had to finish this.

Auguste, astute as always, stood up, removed his coat from where it was hanging on a wall hook above us, and said, "Perhaps I could see Miss Brooks back to your hotel, Peter, while you two finish this family conversation." He nodded to me.

If I thought I was grateful for this offer, Lousie seemed even more so. She immediately stood up, picked up her fur wrap and said, "That seems like a wonderful idea." She leaned down and pecked Peter on the cheek. "See you back at the hotel, baby." And they left us at the table to work out this family drama.

What I hadn't told Peter was that Mother had also been sending me letters and telegrams through my banker, although I had yet to read a single one. I had told Auguste about them, and he suggested I might want to read them, but I had demurred. Yet I couldn't bring myself to destroy them. So, they sat, unread, at the bottom of a drawer in my dresser.

Peter beckoned the waiter over and ordered two glasses of cognac. I didn't think this was wise, but I didn't say anything.

"Peter, tell me exactly what's going on. You know I can't simply drop everything and return to New York. And you know perfectly well that neither Mother nor Father would welcome me with open arms."

"You might be surprised," Peter said, closing his eyes and sipping his cognac gratefully.

"Tell me why I might be surprised."

Peter put his glass on the table in front of him, keeping his eyes closed as if to savour the golden liquid as it made its way down his throat. Then he opened his eyes and looked at me. "It seems you're the golden child despite defying them." Was he pouting?

"What exactly do you mean? I was never the golden child and even less so the minute they discovered that the man I love is older than I am."

"Old enough to be your father, to be precise, little sister. And let us not forget that he's an artist."

"So are you," I said.

"Oh, no, no. I am not an artist, Lottie. I'm an actor. In Hollywood. There's quite a difference in Mother's mind, at least."

"I thought you weren't going to call me that anymore—Pierre."

"*Touché*," he said, taking up his glass again. "The truth is that I believe Mother has had some kind of a breakdown, and Father cannot handle her. I think it's affecting his health. I discovered that he's changed his will."

"Go on," I said.

"I think he might be just as loony as Mother. He's made you heir to the business. You're to take over as President of the company when he dies."

"What? That's impossible. Father never once mentioned anything about me being involved at all in his business. He always wanted me to find a nice husband, presumably so *he* could possibly take over since his son is an actor."

"Yes, well, he's gotten wind of a few things going on over here on the continent."

"What sort of things?" If we were playing chess, he would just have put my king in check. I was beginning to get a bit nervous about where this was going.

"Well, it seems there's a certain Charlotte Lejeune who is the proprietor of a successful Parisian art gallery. It also seems she has been making a name for herself in the art world here. And what's more, it seems that Charlotte Broadhurst married Auguste Vaillancourt, yet she now seems to be Charlotte Lejeune."

Checkmate. Father knew. He knew everything.

I had to think carefully about where to go from here. "Does Mother know?"

"I don't think so," Peter said. "The truth is that I don't think she knows much of anything these days. She really does seem to have lost touch with reality. She didn't even get out of bed the last time I visited. She just whined about how her baby daughter had forsaken her and should be by her side."

I chose to ignore his last statement. "Then, why did you say *Father* was dying when you started this conversation? According to your story, it seems that it is Mother who is ill."

"Because the last time I saw him, he looked ill and was talking about ensuring his affairs were in order. What else was I to think?"

"Did you ask him?" I was becoming increasingly exasperated with my brother, who didn't seem to be able to get out of his own way. Perhaps it was just as well that he was an actor. Business certainly would not have been his forte.

Peter just shrugged and continued to sip his cognac slowly. I had yet to touch mine.

I had to ask simple question after simple question to get the complete picture of what was going on at home. When I believed I understood the situation, I realized that I cared about it more than I should have after the way I perceived I'd been treated. But when I put myself in their position, I began to understand their objections—not that I would have changed my behaviour, but I understood. I knew I would have to return to New York, at least for a short visit. I had to discuss this will issue with Father, if nothing else. However, the thing I dreaded most about the trip was not seeing my parents. It was the prospect of an ocean voyage. When I arrived in Paris six years ago, I had hated every moment on the vast ocean waves. It seemed I still hadn't gotten over the Titanic mishap completely. Perhaps it was one of the reasons I'd stayed in France. Now it seemed I had little choice.

~

I had hoped Auguste would accompany me, but I was alone when I arrived by train at the port of Le Havre. I was sailing on the new ship Île de France, and although she had made her maiden voyage only some three months earlier, all had gone well.

The ship was beautiful—a floating homage to the new Art Deco—and I noted that my fellow passengers in first class all seemed to be raucous, fun-loving, champagne-sipping party lovers. I spent much of my time either on the deck under a cashmere throw reading books or in my stateroom doing the same thing when it was too cold. I dined at a table with four other people, yet I dined alone. I sat in a crowded bar, sipping a champagne cocktail, yet I was utterly alone. I didn't care to chat with anyone else. When I finally got to New York, I practically kissed the ground, but I had more important things on my mind. And I had only two weeks before I had to return to this wretched ship to sail home to Paris—and Auguste.

Father met me at the pier. The moment I reached him, he took me into a fierce embrace as if I might disappear again at any moment. If that was what he was thinking, he was probably not far from seeing the truth. He said little as we sat together in the back seat of his car while his regular chauffeur, Curtis, whom I had known forever, steered us through the streets of Manhattan to the Upper East Side, where our family home, a sprawling townhouse, sat on a quiet, tree-lined street.

I looked at him as we drove, noting how much he had aged over the past few years since I'd seen him. I wondered if Peter might not have been correct in his assessment of Father's health.

After I had settled into my old room, Father and I talked. The situation was much as Peter had described it. According to Father, Mother was not well. He had arranged for her private physician, Dr. Semple, to visit once a week. Dr. Semple had prescribed rest and not much else. Later, when I knocked on Mother's door, she wearily acknowledged the knock, and I opened the door to find her sitting at her dressing table with her jewellery box open in front of her, trying on rings. She turned.

I had expected her to be startled by seeing me, her errant daughter, here in her New York bedroom after all these years. She simply sat there, placed her hands in her lap and said, "Sit down, Charlotte. I need to talk to you."

She sounded completely normal to me.

"Hello, Mother. I heard you weren't well."

She raised her eyebrows in that way that had been so familiar to me as a child whenever I did or said something she disapproved of. "Reports of my health concerns have been highly over-blown, I'm afraid. She turned back to her dressing table and picked up an object that was sitting outside the large wooden jewellery box. She closed her hand around it for a moment, then took my hand and placed the object into my palm, closing my fingers around it. When she let go of my hand, I opened my palm and looked.

"It is French, you know," Mother said. "It is Limoges. Do you know what Limoges is, Charlotte?"

I did know. Mother had told me often enough about her Limoges vases, not to mention a set of hideous dessert plates she cherished, and I hated. They had filigreed gold edging with tiny pink and green flowers all around the edges and a single pink and green flower in the middle of each one.

"Yes, Mother, I know what Limoges is." I looked at the tiny object in my hand. It did appear to be the kind of porcelain that Mother's Limoges plates were fashioned from, but it was unlike anything I'd ever seen. And I certainly had never seen it in Mother's company. "What is it, Mother?"

"What does it look like?"

Ah, there was the mother I'd known all my life. This was not a woman who wrote beseeching telegrams and letters to her daughter to beg her to come home. This woman was the sour-faced mother who disapproved of everything her daughter had ever done. There were the pursed lips and the annoyed stare that I'd known so well. I almost laughed. I was undoubtedly in familiar territory now.

I looked down at the object in my palm. It was a tiny sewing machine—some two inches long and less than two inches high. Like all Limoges, it was exquisitely hand-painted in black with gold details. I noted a clasp that was fashioned to look like tiny gold scissors, so I opened it, revealing that it was a trinket box. Baked into the shiny porcelain bottom of the little compartment was a miniature painting of a spool of thread. It was exquisite. Suddenly, tears began streaming down my face.

"Ah, so you remember." Mother turned back to her dressing table and stared at me in the mirror behind her in the reflection.

I did remember. I remembered that when I was fourteen, just before we embarked on that ill-fated voyage back to New York, I had seen such a trinket in a shop window in London and asked my parents to buy it for me. At the time, I was desperate to learn to sew. I had made the mistake of telling Mother I wanted to be a dressmaker, a job she thought entirely unsuitable for a daughter of such a powerful businessman and his equally powerful New York wife. She wasn't having any of it. No daughter of hers would ever be a dressmaker and the way she would ensure that was that I not learn to sew or have any reminder of that dream. When I had looked at Father that day, I could see in his eyes that he was prepared to give in to me. Mother took me by the arm and dragged me out of the store.

"Where did you get this?" I said, wiping the tears from my eyes.

Mother stared into the mirror at me and said, "Your father couldn't leave it alone. He returned to the shop later that day and bought it for you. When I saw it, I took it from him and told him I would give it to you in time. When he asked me about it a few months later, I told him I had lost it."

"Why are you giving it to me now?"

"Because I recently read a book, Charlotte. I suppose you might even have met the author in Paris in one of those salons or cafés." Mother waved in the general direction of her bedside table, where three books sat.

I got up and picked up the one on the top. It was called *The Great Gatsby* by F. Scott Fitzgerald. It had been published three years earlier, and I had not gotten around to reading it yet. "I may have met him at a party."

"I thought you might have," Mother said dismissively.

"I'm still not understanding any of this. What was it about the book that made you decide to give this to me now?"

"Do you see that bookmark?" I did. "Go to that page and read the line I have underlined."

"Reserving judgements is a matter of infinite hope," I read out loud.

Mother continued to stare at my reflection, and I at hers. Finally, she said, "Reserving judgement, my dear. It is my gift to you."

Six months later, Mother was dead. But when Father's telegram arrived with the news, I was not even in Paris. Much happened in those six months. I must take a step back.

~

I had much to contemplate on that voyage back to France. I spent hours sitting on the deck alone since no one else was willing to brave the cold Atlantic winds. I felt like I needed them in my face. So, I sat there with two cashmere blankets to keep me warm while I held that tiny sewing machine in my hand and thought about what might have been.

What might have happened if I had pursued my childish dream? What would my life be like now if Mother hadn't taken a firm stand on what was best for me? As much as I hated to admit it, she had done me a great favour. It suddenly occurred to me that everything that had happened in my life seemed to be part of a grander scheme. I seemed to have been on a path that led me to Auguste, which was not something I would have changed for anything else in the world.

When I arrived at the station in Paris, Auguste was there to greet me with open arms. I had missed him so deeply that it hurt.

When the taxi dropped us off in front of the gallery, before we made our way upstairs to our apartment, Auguste looked at me and said, "Have you forgotten what day this is?"

If today was a special day, I had forgotten entirely.

"It is your birthday, Charlotte!"

How could I have forgotten the day I was turning thirty? And yet, I had. It was October 24, and it was my birthday.

Auguste had arranged for a special table at Alain and Sylvie's bistro. After an exquisite dinner of Sylvie's delectable Boeuf bourguignon and a bottle of my favourite Bordeaux, Sylvie and Alain presented me with a beautiful cake topped by a single candle. Then they joined us for dessert. It was a warm and wonderful evening.

Auguste and I settled back into our regular routine—he taught a few classes at the university, painted, and I met with artists and collectors at the gallery. One evening in March of 1929, Auguste sat down with me after dinner and said, "Charlotte, my darling, there is something we need to discuss."

I was all ears, as they say.

As I look back on that conversation, I can say, without a doubt, it was the most difficult of my life. Auguste had not been feeling well for a month or more. I had suspected something, but when I had tried to broach the subject, he waved me off with that Gallic shrug the French do so well. "*Ce n'est rien.*" It is nothing. It wasn't nothing.

Auguste had finally been to his doctor, who suspected lung cancer. An x-ray had confirmed his suspicion. There was nothing to be done about it.

I could barely hear the words as he said them. "Make preparations..." "Perhaps you should consider..." "not much time..."

I did not want to make preparations. I did not want to consider anything. I did not want to hear that we would not have much more time together. And yet, there it was.

"Charlotte, you are not listening to me. I wonder if you have been listening to me these past years. First, you must know that I am not afraid of death. Life and death, they are both the same to me. I have told you before of my deeply held knowing that the past is the present is the future."

"But you will be gone." The tears streamed down my face, staining the front of my dress.

"Charlotte, please listen. I beg you. I will never be gone. I cannot be gone. Please think about this."

And so, I did think about it. Over the next few weeks, the idea began to sink below my consciousness and into my soul. We were as one, and it would always be this way even if Auguste died and I carried on—as a widow. But Auguste did have one thing he wanted to do before he got too sick. He wanted to go to Madrid, a city he had never visited. Thus, six months after I left Mother and Father in New York, I was in Madrid. I was not at home to receive Father's telegram.

~

The trip to Madrid was magical. We travelled overnight on the train from Paris and checked into the Palace Hotel. Built in 1912, the hotel and its décor were more familiar to us than we might have expected. It was done in the Belle Époques style of the grandest Parisian buildings. Were we really in Spain? We were, indeed.

Auguste and I spent a week exploring every nook and cranny of this bustling city. He had spoken briefly with Pablo (Picasso) prior to our trip, and Pablo had been only too happy to provide some suggestions for restaurants and galleries. Pablo himself had recommended the Palace Hotel since he had stayed there some years earlier. He also suggested we have one of the hotel's signature drinks in their bar: an icy dry martini with olives. It was the first time I had ever tasted a martini. I was captivated.

As I might have expected, Auguste's main reason for wanting to visit Madrid was to visit Museo Nacional del Prado, one of the finest art museums in all of Europe. Much of their collection had been owned previously by Spanish monarchs, convents and monasteries. We spent three days in the museum, where Auguste provided me with one of the most comprehensive lessons on European art I could ever have desired, especially in my position as the proprietor of an art gallery in Paris. I suspected this trip was at least as much for me as it was for him.

When the magical week finally ended, we boarded the train for our return trip to Paris. As we sat in our compartment with the Spanish countryside going by, Auguste saw me rummaging in my handbag.

"Have you lost something?"

I was on the verge of tears. "I have, Auguste. I have lost something important." I kept digging. "I had it on my bedside table and was sure I had put it back in my handbag."

It was the Limoges trinket box. I had lost my tiny sewing machine in Madrid.

When we arrived back in Paris, Auguste sent a telegram to the hotel, hoping someone might have found it. If they had, they had taken it for their own. As I thought about how things in life happen, I had a deep feeling that it would end up where it was supposed to be.

~

The next two months were increasingly difficult ones. Auguste insisted that we carry on as if nothing was happening in our private lives, and all I could do was stand by and watch the man I loved as he deteriorated day by day. The day he told me he felt he could no longer sit and hold a paintbrush was when I realized with the greatest certainty that I would have to face the reality of our current life coming to an end.

The events of that final evening are emblazoned on my memory and my soul. I had called Auguste's doctor, who was such a good friend that he left his family at their Saturday evening dinner table to come to our apartment. Some people say that these events are like a blur—like events happening in a kind of fog. For me, they were crystal clear, and I remember them moment by moment. The moment I was sitting with Auguste's head in my lap, and he no longer seemed to hear me. The moment the doctor arrived in our room. The moment Auguste looked up at me and whispered, "Remember, Charlotte, the world will keep on turning even if you cannot see me. We—you and I—are here always." And I remember the moment I kissed Auguste's head as he breathed in then out for one last time.

I closed my eyes and remembered something I'd once read. *"Time ceases to exist for events burned into the soul by the fires of emotion."* That was the moment time ceased to exist for me. And I understood.

Three months later, I sold the gallery, booked a one-way ticket to New York and went home. Auguste had been my home for these past years, and I knew he still was, so it mattered little where I lived. The moment he died, I realized that my home was me.

Father welcomed me with open arms back into his home and business. It turned out I was surprisingly good at overseeing business (with Father's guidance at first) once the men in the company got over the novelty—not an entirely welcome novelty—of a woman in business. At least I had a kind of stature with them. After all, I was a widow.

On October 24 of that year, 1929, I turned thirty-one. Everyone else in the world remembers it as Black Thursday. I was never happier that Father's (and now my) company was still privately owned. The stock market crash did not touch us.

Transformation

"I am no longer what I was. I will remain what I have become."
~ Gabriel "Coco" Chanel

THAT AUTUMN WEEKEND IN TORONTO with Patrick, his children Chloe and Liam, Frankie and Evelyn's family will always be a pivotal one in my life. As I look back on it, I realize I crossed a watershed of sorts—one where everything that came before appears like a reflection of what was to come.

On that first evening of the weekend, when Patrick told me that Charlotte and Auguste had changed their names, we knew this would be a game-changer. And yet, I wasn't sure I wanted the game to change.

After we had spent a few minutes discussing how this revelation might alter the course of our research, he turned to me and said, "Let's put this away for a bit. I am beyond excited that you and Frankie are here in Toronto this weekend and that we'll all get a chance to get to know one another. Chloe and Liam cannot wait to meet your entire family."

I was happy to hear this since I harboured lingering uneasiness that his children, Chloe and Liam, might think I was trying to replace their mother. Of course, I knew that was ridiculous. After all, their mother had been dead for over a decade, and they were both now in university with lives of their own. I suppose I should have been more concerned about Frankie's reaction, but she had already met Patrick and was wholly committed to seeing her mother return to the land of the living, as she put it. Frankie had inherited her father's pragmatism about living life in the moment. I'd had difficulty internalizing that life view when Tom was alive, but I seemed to be learning.

"Charlie," Patrick continued, "we need to meet with Elspeth. Are you free from family obligations tomorrow?" According to Patrick, Elspeth had been working on a line of inquiry with her history professor friend, Donald, from Columbia University in New York once she knew about the name change.

As it turned out, I was free. So, Patrick arranged to pick me up the following afternoon, and we'd head to Elspeth's shop.

When we arrived, Elspeth led us directly up to the workroom. The shop was closed, and Andrea had the holiday weekend off, so it would just be the three of us reviewing her recent discoveries. We sat at the bar-height stools at one of the worktables, where she had neat piles of printed pages in tidy rows.

"We are so lucky," Elspeth said as she arranged her reading glasses to peer at the pages in front of us. "It appears that my friend Donald has become quite fascinated with this story. Who knows? Perhaps he will write a paper on Auguste and Charlotte!" She then turned our attention to the pages directly at her right hand. "As I mentioned when we last met, Donald's particular interest is in the history of journalism, so he has access to the archives of practically every newspaper that has ever been published." She adjusted her glasses and handed the top sheet to me. "Thank heavens we discovered the name change. Look at this story he uncovered when searching for references to Auguste Lejeune."

On the page was a grainy photograph (probably from a piece of microfilm) of a newspaper page. It was dated Wednesday, December 10, 1924, and the newspaper was *The New York Sun*.

"I continue to lament the slow progress of the penetration of modern art into the American consciousness. In this writer's view, it is a tragedy of monumental proportions that we have not embraced the new and more exciting ways of seeing the world. This writer had the very great privilege of attending a gallery opening in Paris last month. It came as quite a surprise as I was introduced to said gallery by American heiress Charlotte Broadhurst, now residing in the great City of Lights

among the bon vivants of that great hotbed of all that is modern and exhilarating about the art world. I cannot thank her enough for my introduction to one whose art will surely captivate the minds and souls of discerning art collectors here and abroad. I introduce to you the work of Parisian artist Auguste Lejeune. With a dreamy eye on his subject, he transports us to the Cote d'Azur, the French Riviera, his work bringing the dream to life. Run, do not walk to your nearest art importer and find his work. You will be the talk of the town…"

"Do you recognize the writer's name?" Elspeth said.

The by-line said, "Henry McBride." I had never heard of him.

Patrick helped me. "He was an American art critic who tried to popularize modern art with Americans. I remember reading one of his reviews from early in his career when he was trying to get Americans to pay attention to Cezanne's work. I actually memorized one of the lines in his review. He wrote, '*The new generation that… seeks for something more subtle, palpitating, and nervously alive, finds it in Cézanne.*' It may be hard to believe, but people just weren't that interested in the nervously alive or in Cézanne's work."

Elspeth took off her reading glasses and left them dangling from a gold chain around her neck. "Donald also told me that McBride had an uncanny ability to spot rising talent. His articles often propelled social-climbing art collectors to purchase particular works they might not otherwise have found. It seems it became something of a contest to see who could find the artist whose work would become most valuable in the future."

"And did Auguste's work become valuable?" I said, trying to keep up with these two experts on art and history.

"It did," Patrick said, "and I knew of his work without the slightest clue about his real identity." Patrick whipped out his phone and clicked on his photos. "Here are some screenshots of Lejeune's works in the Museum of Modern Art in New York."

I took the phone from him and swiped through the images. My heart seemed to skip a beat for a split second as I stared at the third image. It was a dreamy, impressionistic image of a Paris street scene. The building depicted was a three-story, white gallery with two stories of windows with Juliette balconies above. The gallery's front door was flanked by pots overflowing with flowers and greenery. I had the oddest feeling I'd been there before—as if I had stood in that very doorway and walked into the space beyond. Yet I knew it was not a place I'd ever visited when I'd been in Paris on any occasion. I wondered where it was located.

Then I looked at the article again. "So, this Henry McBride was there at the gallery opening when Charlotte and Auguste first started that business?" Something at the back of my mind whispered that it was the gallery in the dreamy painting.

"He was indeed," Elspeth said. She then moved to the next pile of pages.

"So, what happened to Auguste and Charlotte after that? Didn't you say they fell off the face of the earth?"

"That's what we thought—until now," Elspeth said, taking a pile of papers held together with an elastic band. She passed the pages to me. "I think you will find this just as interesting as I did."

I looked at the pages in front of me. They were photocopies of handwritten pages. I rifled through them to get a sense of what I was looking at and noted the pages were dated. The first date was October 24, 1928. "It looks like a diary," I said as a feeling of excitement crept up my spine.

"Yes," Elspeth said. "Indeed, it is a diary. It is Charlotte Broadhurst's—or should I say Charlotte Lejeune's—diary." Elspeth was as giddy as a schoolgirl.

I was incredulous. "Where did you find this? I thought Charlotte fell off the face of the earth and couldn't be found because of the name change."

"We thought so, too," Patrick said. "But it seems Charlotte left something of a legacy."

"Did she and Auguste have children?" This idea made me very excited—and just a bit fearful—although I didn't know where that feeling came from.

"Sadly, no," Elspeth said, "but you will read this and know what happened in the next few years. You two go and enjoy your Thanksgiving weekend," she said. Then she looked at me. "I believe you should read this diary, Charlie. I believe you will know everything you need to know by the time you are through."

Elspeth placed the pages of the diary in a file folder and gave it to me. We said our goodbyes and left her in the workshop. Instead of finding a cab or calling an Uber, we decided to walk back to Evelyn's. The walk back took us almost an hour, but it was a beautiful autumn afternoon, and we needed the air. We also had a lot to talk about.

When we arrived in front of Evelyn's house, I asked Patrick if he'd like to come in. He said no and suggested I might want to spend some time alone reading Charlotte's diary. So I did.

Evelyn had taken Frankie and her cousins to the Eaton Centre, the sprawling downtown mall that was like a magnet to kids like Frankie who lived outside this major metropolitan area. Michael, Evelyn's husband, appeared to be the only one home.

As I closed the front door behind me, Michael called out from the family room off the kitchen, a massive addition to this old house. "Hello!"

"Hello, Michael. It's just me."

"Having a drink here, Charlie. Care to join me?"

I felt obliged to sit with my host for a while, so I agreed, and he poured me a scotch on the rocks. I wasn't much of a scotch drinker, but Tom had been, so I'd learned to appreciate a good one, and Michael had only the best. I saw the label as he poured. It was Lagavulin 16-Year-Old Islay Single Malt Scotch Whisky, and I happened to know that it sold for over $165. So, yes, it was a good one.

Michael and I chatted amiably for a while—small talk, really. He and I didn't have much in common. He was a stockbroker in Canada's largest metropolis, and I was a writer from a small city. After half an hour and a second pour, I took my crystal whiskey glass and excused myself. I sensed he wanted to do some work anyway.

Once settled into the chaise lounge under the window in my room upstairs, I adjusted the thoughtfully placed reading lamp and took the sheaf of pages from the file folder Elspeth had thrust upon me and began reading.

~

The diary began on October 24, 1928, when Charlotte's life took a turn. It was a turn that wrenched my heart because I had experienced the same thing.

"I should have realized there was something wrong. Auguste has not been feeling well, and this has been going on for over a month, but tonight, when he said those words to me, my heart stopped. He has been to his doctor. He has lung cancer. There is nothing that can be done. I could barely hear the words as he said them. "Make preparations…" "Perhaps you should consider…" "not much time…" I do not want to make preparations. I do not want to consider anything. I do not want to hear that we would not have much more time together."

I put the pages down on my lap for fear that the tears that began streaming down my face might blur the writing, and I knew I needed to read it all. I was there with Charlotte as she faced her worst nightmare. I felt it deeply because I had been there with Tom. Her words brought back a flood of feelings, and I suddenly realized that time had ceased to exist—the events were burned into my very soul. There seemed to be no more time or space between us—Charlotte Broadhurst and me, Charlotte "Charlie" Hudson. I picked up the pages and continued.

> *"April 12, 1929*
>
> *Last night we travelled overnight on the train from Paris and have arrived in Madrid, a city neither of us has ever visited before. It was Auguste's wish to see the city before...*
>
> *We are staying at the Palace Hotel, which feels more like Paris than Spain with its Belle Époques style of the grandest Parisian buildings. Pablo himself had recommended the Palace Hotel."*

I looked up from the pages, feeling peculiar. Charlotte and Auguste stayed at the Palace Hotel in 1929? How could there be yet another coincidence? I remembered walking into the Palace Hotel when I was in Madrid on my way to Mallorca and feeling that odd sense of déjà vu. Was this what it was all about? I continued reading.

> *"He has finally admitted that his main reason for wanting to visit Madrid is to visit Museo Nacional del Prado, one of the finest art museums in all of Europe—to see more of the great masters before he dies. I cannot fathom a life without Auguste."*

The next few days of entries detailed the places they ate, the shops they browsed and the artwork Auguste explained to Charlotte in great detail. Then, the entry from the day they returned to Paris...

> *"I cannot believe I have lost it. My special talisman—my tiny perfect Limoges sewing machine. I do not know why it means so much to me except for its connection to my younger, innocent self. I thought I would have it forever. Auguste has offered to send a telegram to the hotel in Madrid to inquire as to whether anyone might have found it. No one will have done so. I know it is lost forever back into the mists of time. Perhaps it will one day find its*

way to the person who is meant to have it for all eternity. I can almost see someone—a woman—finding it and cherishing it. No, I will no longer fret about my tiny sewing machine fashioned from Limoges porcelain. It is where it is meant to be. Of that, I am certain."

I was shaking when I put down the page. The tiny porcelain sewing machine. I looked over to where I had placed it on my bedside table. From the moment the Spanish grandmother had put it into my palm in Madrid, I never left home without it, although I never understood why I was so attached to it. I went over and picked it up, holding it tightly in my clenched palm. I could feel its power. I could feel her—and I knew where it had come from. And now I knew why.

~

The following day was Sunday—the day of the big family Thanksgiving dinner, which this year was to be at Evelyn's house. Although I had offered to help her, Evelyn chose to arrange a catered family dinner—as she did every year except for the one when she took us all out to a restaurant.

Patrick arrived right on time at five pm with Chloe and Liam. I was nervous about the entire family coming together, but I needn't have wasted my time with apprehension. Before half an hour had passed, it was as if we had all known one another forever.

Evelyn pulled me aside as I wandered back to her bar to pour another glass of wine. "They are beyond perfect," she said, her eyes dancing. "This is the best family Thanksgiving since we were kids, Charlie."

She was so right. This felt like family.

Over the next few days, I immersed myself in Charlotte's life. As I read her words, I felt like I was seeing her life through her eyes. When I was back home in Halifax, and Frankie and I were settled back into our weekly routine, I had time to sit and think about Charlotte's words and her life with Auguste. As I sat at my desk the following Friday morning, sipping my coffee and wondering if I would ever write another book—much less this particular one I didn't seem to be able to move forward—I re-read that passage in Charlotte's diary that had brought my world to a standstill much as it had done hers.

> *"Saturday, June 15, 1929*
>
> *I sit alone, staring out the window to the street below. Auguste and I should be downstairs in our gallery, welcoming guests, sipping champagne, introducing new talent to the world. And yet I sit here alone. He is gone. Auguste is gone. And the tears fill my eyes such that I can barely see the page. My heart is like lead. The moment before he closed his eyes for one final time, Auguste whispered, "Remember, Charlotte, the world will keep turning even if you cannot see me. We—you and I—are here always." I sit here alone, and yet not alone. I close my eyes and see the past and not the past. I am a widow and not a widow."*

I laid the diary pages on the desk and wiped the tear from my eye. Widow again. Yet not a widow. How was that possible? I was thinking about Charlotte and Auguste, but I was seeing me—and Tom. Then, the next moment, Tom's image faded into mist, and I could see the photograph of Auguste—the image of Patrick. Not a widow. I was beginning to understand.

~

Charlotte Broadhurst Lejeune had returned home to New York to be with her aging father. According to her diary entries over the next few years, she sold the gallery and, in September of 1929, boarded the SS France at Le Havre on a one-way ticket to New York City. Charlotte's father had chosen her over her brother, actor Peter Hurst as he was known, to take over as the president of his company, Broadhurst Chemicals. Charlotte wrote about how it felt to live in New York during the stock market crash and how she had often felt slightly guilty that her family hadn't suffered as a result.

Broadhurst Chemicals had never gone public, never been listed on the stock exchange, so when the speculation began and stock prices began falling, her family's company was protected. In fact, they were just then on the brink of being able to manufacture a proprietary type of synthetic rubber. This product would launch their success into the stratosphere, so even the subsequent depression didn't have much effect on business. Charlotte was there to help her father at the helm of the company as it went from strength to strength. Charlotte never married again and wrote in her diary only sporadically after her fiftieth birthday in 1948. She had chosen to keep the name Lejeune because, as she had written in her diary, it had a European and, thus, exotic flair. She didn't want people to immediately think she only had the job because her father owned the company. Although this was true, she grew into her position and seemed to have a flair for leadership. By the time she turned fifty, her father was long dead, and she was well-established as the president. Once I discovered these details, it was easy to begin an online search to figure out the rest of the story.

Charlotte Lejeune retired from Broadhurst Chemicals in 1971 at the age of seventy-three. Her nephew, Richard Broadhurst, Peter's son, took over, and Charlotte finally died at her summer home on Long Island in 1979. During the final years of her life, she spent her time developing a foundation to support emerging artists. The moment I found its website online, I began to get excited. There was something here. I just didn't know what yet.

~

It was Christmas Eve, and the snow was falling softly outside. Patrick had arrived in Halifax from Toronto two days earlier to spend the festive season with Frankie and me. Chloe and Liam had arrived a few hours earlier, and they were now downstairs in the basement watching Christmas movies with Frankie on the projection screen television while eating popcorn. It amazed me how well they all got along. We were planning to order pizza later, but in the meantime, Patrick and I sat together in the den in front of the blazing fireplace, sipping wine.

"Isn't this peaceful?" I said as I closed my eyes and enjoyed the feeling of warmth that surrounded me.

"It is," Patrick said.

He sounded a bit abrupt, so I opened my eyes and put my wine glass on the table in front of me. "What's up? You sound…a bit tetchy." That wasn't a word I generally used, but it was the best I could do.

"Yes, well, sorry. I didn't mean to. I was just thinking."

"Okay, I'll bite. What were you thinking about?"

"To tell you the truth, I was thinking about many things. I was thinking about how you and I have clearly known each other somewhere in some kind of parallel universe," he held up his hand to stop me from interrupting, which I was about to do. "As ridiculous as it sounds, I think there's a connection between us and Auguste and Charlotte, and I'm not sure how it happened or is happening. All I know is that it's something real, and you and I have something real, and we need to think about what's happening next and where all of this is leading—"

"Whoa! That's a lot of things," I said, smiling at his discomfiture. I didn't know where he was going with this, but I thought it would be best if I at least helped him to organize his thoughts. "Let's deal with them one at a time. Okay, I agree. It's real."

Patrick picked up his wine glass and took a gulp, something I'd never seen him do before. He was usually a lot more elegant about his wine. "Okay, I'm glad you agree with that part. Now, as to where this is leading." He put his glass back on the table, took a deep breath and turned to me. "Charlie Hudson, we need to be together forever. I think we always have been, and I want to make sure we always will. I need to know the answer to a question."

I wasn't sure what to say yet, so I decided to be quiet and hear him out.

"Have you said goodbye to Tom yet?"

"What?" This was not the question I'd been expecting.

"Have you really said goodbye yet? Because nothing can truly begin until you do."

I wasn't sure how to respond. Of course, I'd said goodbye to Tom. After I'd been to Mallorca, I'd realized it was time to move on, but now that I was confronted directly with this question from a man I—a man I loved—I knew I'd have to be more than sure.

"What does it mean to say goodbye?" I said, finding my way through this carefully. "Does it mean to put someone behind you? Does it mean moving on?" I tucked my legs up under me on the sofa and grabbed a cushion, holding it tightly against me. "Patrick, did you ever read *Peter Pan*?"

"I suppose I did—many years ago."

"I remember a line Peter said. '*Never say goodbye because goodbye means going away, and going away means forgetting.*' It's that forgetting part that scares me."

Patrick smiled. "Well, I guess we'll have to remember that Peter Pan never grew up. Grownups know that saying goodbye often means *never* forgetting. It means opening up a space in your heart for something—or someone—else. And grownups know that hearts are flexible and stretchy. There is always room for more."

I knew he was right. And I knew I could make room in my heart for something more. And I could feel Tom smiling when Patrick asked me his final question. And when I said yes. Now we just had to tell three kids they were about to become a family.

~

Patrick and I were married the following May. Frankie, and her new step-siblings Chloe and Liam, joined us, along with Evelyn and her family, a few close friends and Elspeth Savant, in the backyard of Patrick's house in Toronto, where we exchanged our vows. Patrick and I then flew to Paris, of course, for two weeks. When we returned, our lives began again.

On Christmas Eve, when we had told the kids we were planning to be married, Chloe threw her arms around me. Liam shook his father's hand. And Frankie said, "Does this mean we're moving to Toronto?" Her eyes were shining, and I knew what response she wanted. She got it.

Frankie and I packed up and moved to the big city almost immediately, and the sale of our house in Halifax closed in early August. We initially lived in Patrick's house, but we had decided we needed a new space to call our own for our newly reconfigured family. Patrick and I scoured the city for two months to find a suitable home for our new family. Although Chloe and Liam were both away at school, they still needed a place to feel at home. We finally settled on a large Victorian, not unlike the one I'd just sold in Halifax, but bigger (everything seemed bigger in Toronto). It was six blocks from where Evelyn and her family lived—not too far, but not too close. No one wants to live next door to her sister!

Michael, always the best connected of us, called a friend, who called a friend, and we managed to get Frankie settled into the same school her cousin Katie attended, a private girls' school a fifteen-minute walk away. Frankie even liked their uniform. So, our home life began to settle in. But I had much more to accomplish.

The moment I read about Charlotte Broadhurst's legacy, I knew what I had to do with the money my great-grandmother had left me. From early in our relationship, Patrick knew I had money—more money than any art history professor could be expected to accumulate in a lifetime—and he was slightly uncomfortable about it. I rolled my eyes and told him we should just enjoy what life had given us. That being said, I still knew the money that was sitting in my investment portfolio didn't all need to be there for me or even for Frankie, Patrick, Liam and Chloe. It needed to find some work to do, and I knew what it was.

The minute Patrick's classes started again in the fall, I began looking for a gallery space. I wanted to find something with a prominent street frontage, storage space, several offices and a studio. I wanted this gallery to emulate the one Auguste and Charlotte had owned in Paris, so I found myself looking for something that reminded me of Auguste's painting of their gallery. The day I arrived at a vacant gallery space to meet my realtor and looked up to see a three-story white stucco building with two floors of windows above, I knew I'd found the perfect space. And I could even add the Juliette balconies.

The gallery's mission would be to seek out and showcase new talent. The gallery owner (me) would need to travel periodically to other major cities to find that talent. Paris, London and Vienna were first on my list. I also needed to cultivate relationships with various art colleges and universities. That's where Patrick's connections became very useful. It wasn't long before I realized I'd have to find someone to do publicity for the gallery—the gallery would not succeed strictly by the idea's osmosis into the zeitgeist. That's when I found Amy Albright.

Amy had graduated from a public relations degree program at a local university a year and a half before I met her. She had spent the last year working for the Art Gallery of Ontario as a publicist. Amy was a petite blonde with a bouncy ponytail balanced by large horn-rimmed glasses. She was at once perky and serious. It was an oddly appealing combination. When she appeared at the gallery for her interview dressed in head-to-toe black in stark contrast to her light blonde hair, holding her tablet at the ready for notes, I knew she was the one. It turns out I have considerable acumen in hiring the right staff!

Once I had finished filling out my staff—in addition to Amy, I hired two young art curators to staff the gallery and two office staff—and I began to acquire pieces from art colleges and street artists, Amy went to work on a campaign to put *Convergence Gallery* on the world map.

Amy and I sat in her tidy office behind the gallery. She told me she couldn't move ahead with creating the publicity magic, as she put it, until she understood the gallery—and me—better. As usual, she was dressed in all-black and wore her blonde hair in a ponytail. She had taken off the glasses, and I saw that she had very blue eyes that crinkled attractively at the corners, belying her age. She was one of those people who could have been twenty or thirty-five. It was the first time it had occurred to me that she didn't need the glasses at all—they were merely a style statement. I was ready for my interview.

"First, I need to hear about your background."

Hmm, I thought. *This is going to be interesting since she doesn't know anything about me. She thinks I'm a wealthy married woman looking for somewhere to put my money. She has no idea about my background. This could be fun.*

I had deliberately not told Amy much about my background, fearing she would have different reasons for wanting to work with me. As a writer—even a bestselling one—I was pretty unknown as an individual. Unlike actors who made their living from being in the public eye, a writer could be famous in name only. No one had to know what you even looked like. Frankly, that was preferable as far as I was concerned. I also knew that many young men and women who studied public relations and communications at university wanted to be writers. The fact is that for them to be able to do the job well, they did need to write well, but many of them wanted to write books. I didn't want to hire anyone who wanted the job simply because she thought I might introduce her to my agent or send a manuscript to my editor for her. But now, I was the face of the gallery and our mission to uncover emerging talent in the art world.

"What would you like to know?" She may have rolled her eyes slightly at that. How dense could I be? She had no idea.

"Who was your family? What did they do?" So, she thought my money came from my family. She was in for quite a surprise.

"My mother was a designer, but you've probably never heard of her. My father was an accountant. Not too exciting, I know." I must admit she did look a bit disappointed. She probably thought my family was on some list of the wealthiest North Americans or something.

"Well," Amy said as she seemed to struggle for the right words. "Did you ever…well, did you ever work in a gallery before? Yes, what's your background in gallery work?" I was sure she wanted to ask me if I'd ever had a real job or if I was just a kept woman. (Does anyone ever use that term these days? I have no idea, but it was fun to watch her try to be less Gen Z and more Millennial, a stretch for sure.) She seemed quite pleased with herself that she'd found a way to wade into my background without insulting me.

"No," I said, "I've never worked in a gallery before." I knew I was being deliberately obtuse, but this was fun.

"So, what kind of thing did you do before?"

She seemed to be purposefully avoiding asking me about what kind of "work" I'd done. I was getting close to putting her out of her misery, but I wanted to stretch it out. "I have an MFA in writing."

Amy brightened considerably with this news. "Wow, so you wanted to be a writer. Have you ever written anything? I mean anything I might have read."

"Possibly," I said. "It depends on what kind of books you like to read."

"So, you're a published author."

I held myself back from correcting her by telling her that the term published author was redundant. If you were published, you were an author, but I let it go. "As a matter of fact, I've written several books." I stopped for a beat to let that sink in.

"You might be familiar with my *nom de plume*. I write as CK Hudson."

Her eyes widened and I thought she might swallow her tongue. I guess she had heard of CK Hudson after all.

"I love your books. You know, I've always wanted to be a writer." And there it was.

I was proud of myself for not mentioning this before because I might not have hired her if she'd told me that at her first interview. Now, I knew her better, appreciated her skills and felt strongly that she wanted the job because of the job and not because of me and the doors I could potentially open for her in the writing world.

"So you really didn't recognize me from the back cover of my books?"

Amy looked at me as if she thought I might have two heads. "The back cover?" Then the penny dropped. "Oh, you must mean an actual book thing. I don't read those. I only read eBooks. No back cover, so, no, I didn't recognize you, but I wish I had!"

I was delighted she had not—like Bella, who had also only read my eBooks. We then moved on to why I was doing this and where I wanted the gallery and its work to go.

"There is one thing you've never told me," Amy said as we concluded the interview. "Why is the gallery called *Convergence*?"

It was a great question whose answer should probably be the first thing on our website. I thought for a moment to figure out how best to explain this to her since it was intensely personal.

"In the early twentieth century, there was an Indian mystic who wrote that '*there is no other space, no other time. This moment is all. In this moment, the whole existence converges; in this moment, all is available.*' For Patrick and me, convergence is a true coming together in the moment, knowing that art and artists have always been part of our convergence, no matter when or where."

Amy looked slightly lost in my explanation, and I didn't blame her. It was as simple and clear as it was complex and opaque. I was okay with that. At least she took notes (I expected her to return for more clarity at some point, and I'd be ready for her.)

A week later, Amy Albright presented me with her PR strategy. It was beautiful to behold. Her main focus was to get me—CK Hudson—to be a guest on several popular talk shows in Canada, the US and England. She wanted me to use my authorial fame to promote the gallery. She called it synergistic. I called it dangerous.

"Amy," I said as we sat in her office again the following week, "I don't want my writing to be a distraction. I have no desire to get on one of these shows and have to discuss my books. I've done that, and this is strictly for the gallery's publicity."

"No problem. I'll make the brief crystal clear to the producers. But your name is going to get us in the door. No one will turn down the chance to have CK Hudson on a show, no matter what the reason is. Don't worry about it. I'll make the media kit so fascinating they'll be afraid to pass on it in case it's the arts story of the century—which it will be."

I did not doubt that the media kit would be outstanding and irresistible, nor did I doubt that if anyone could make this the arts story of the century, it was this young woman. But I was less enthusiastic at her next suggestion.

"We have to get you on TikTok."

I held my ground. That wasn't going to happen. Then I had a thought. "Amy, what if I could get you a few young people to front the gallery on TikTok?"

Her eyes opened wide, and her smile showed her dazzlingly white teeth. And that's how Chloe, Liam and Frankie became the TikTok face of *Convergence Gallery*. I had never been more sure that I'd chosen the gallery's name well.

~

It took Amy only a few weeks to get the interview machine rolling. She thought we should start close to home, so she scheduled my first interview on a popular afternoon talk show that was filmed right here in Toronto. It had a North American reach, having recently been picked up by ABC in the US. Amy was ecstatic. This was entering the big leagues.

The show was called *Outlook on Life*. It was one of those women's talk shows—a bit like the American show *The View*—with four female co-hosts who all sat around a table to chat and interview many and varied guests. I'd never really been a fan, mostly because I never watched television in the afternoon, but Amy assured me that this show had a significant following. Arts and culture were two of their favourite topics. Who knew? Anyway, my main connection with it was that one of the co-hosts, Erica Flannagan, was a friend of Evelyn's. As far as I knew, they played tennis together and lunched occasionally. I'd met Erica once or twice at Evelyn's various parties over the years, and I can't say I liked her that much. She was the resident curmudgeon on the show, or so she had proudly told me a few years back as I stood in Evelyn's family room balancing a glass of wine and a plate of *hors d'oeuvres*. The rest of the on-air panel consisted of two other forty-something women like Erica and a token twenty-something Gen Z representative to keep the rest of the oldsters on their toes.

The show was filmed in front of a live audience every weekday afternoon between three and four pm. Of course, Frankie and Evelyn wanted to be there, as did Patrick. I left it to Evelyn and her contact—Erica—to get tickets.

I arrived at the studio forty-five minutes before the show, as directed by Amy and the producer. When I arrived in the Green Room—where guests on TV shows sit and wait their turn—to wait my turn in the makeup chair, there was a commotion outside the hall. *Dear god*, I thought. *Don't tell me they're excited about a bestselling writer arriving.* Well, I was partly right.

They were indeed excited about a writer, but it wasn't me. When I turned to see who was in the middle of the fuss in the corridor, I could see the one and only Tilly Foster-Matthews standing in the middle of the crowd, signing copies of her most recent book. She had moved on from revealing the hidden backstory depths of a wannabe Coco Chanel (with her blessing, of course) to a lascivious, unauthorized biography of Prince Harry—yes, another one—but Tilly's version speculated about his past lives as the Duke of Westminster (Coco's famously wealthy lover) and a composer who was the contemporary of Mozart. Evidently, the composer also had the audacity to leave his family in the lurch. I had yet to read that one. Anyway, I was flabbergasted that she hadn't told me she would be here at the studio or even in the city.

Tilly looked in my direction, and her eyes widened as soon as she registered that it was me. She excused herself from the crowd and elbowed her way through, making a beeline for me. She enveloped me in a bear hug.

"Darling, Charlie! Are you here to see me?" Classic Tilly.

I smiled and shook my head. "Not exactly, but I'm delighted to see you. I'm actually a guest on the show as well. Why didn't you tell me you'd be in town?"

Tilly went on to tell me that it had been arranged at the last minute and she had planned to call me as soon as she was off the air and wasn't it wonderful we would be guests on the same show. When I told her the reason for my appearance, she was her usual excitable self and promised to gush about my project whenever she had a chance. "You know I am an inveterate name-dropper, darling. I will do my utmost from this moment!"

I suddenly realized how well-connected Tilly was with the UK press. This was, indeed, fortuitous.

That first appearance to talk about the gallery and the foundation I'd established to support up-and-coming artists turned out to be fun in a way I hadn't expected. The hosts were delighted with the idea that someone would support new talent, and the youngest host even took the opportunity to show clips from our new TikTok channel. When we got home after the show, Frankie couldn't stop talking about Jennifer (the young on-air host) and how she'd shown Frankie's TikTok reel. Frankie now saw her future as a television presenter. I just rolled my eyes. Whatever worked.

After the interview, as I picked up my things left in the Green Room, Erica Flannagan appeared in the doorway. "Knock, knock. Charlie, it was nice to see you again. I've been meaning to try to get you on the show to talk about your books, but my producer says you haven't written anything recently."

I bit my tongue to keep from saying something snide like, "If you had ever read any of my books, you wouldn't need a producer to tell you that." But the truth is that a response like that would have said far more about my unease about being a writer who isn't writing than it would about Erica's lack of sensitivity.

"It's true, Erica. I haven't published anything in a few years. But I'm working on something."

I'm working on something? Where in the world did that come from? What, precisely, am I working on?

Erica then chatted briefly about Evelyn and tennis and how we should all get together (like that was ever going to happen), then her phone rang, and she said something about having to take it and turned, making a quick exit. But I was left with the feeling that I was working on some piece of writing—I just didn't know what it was.

I was still thinking about the writing I was doing but wasn't doing when Tilly came for dinner the following evening. The four of us—Tilly, Patrick, Frankie, and I—had a marvellous couple of hours at the dinner table. Tilly had Frankie in stitches talking about her adventures as she researched her "biography" of Prince Harry's past lives. Then it was time for Frankie to do her homework, and Patrick, sensing Tilly and I would enjoy a girls' *tête à tête*, offered to clean up before retiring to his office to mark some student papers. He knew me so well.

"Patrick and you are wonderful together," Tilly said as we settled into the family room with our tea. "I can sense something extraordinary between the two of you. He's the one, isn't he?"

"Of course, he's the one," I said, sipping my tea. "I wouldn't have married him otherwise."

"That's not what I mean, and you know it, darling. He's the one you sensed you knew. He's the one you, in fact, have always known. Am I right?"

I couldn't argue with her there.

"Not to change the subject—and perhaps it's not a change at all—but what are you writing these days?"

"That's the funny thing, Tilly. I'm not writing anything, but I feel I am writing something."

"Ooh, I do love a riddle. What are you writing when you're not writing but you are writing?" Tilly walked over to the bar where Patrick had left the half-full bottle of the pinot noir we didn't finish at dinner. "May I?" I nodded, and she filled two wine glasses Patrick had conveniently left beside it. "Now, back to your riddle. What are you writing but not writing?"

"I wish I knew," I said, taking the offered wine.

Tilly settled back into her chair across from me. "I think I may be able to help you with this one." She sipped her wine daintily before continuing. "Do you remember several conversations we had—you and I and Bella—after we left Mallorca?" I nodded. "Well, if you will recall, the subject of past and parallel lives was one of considerable interest to me for obvious reasons. What I now know is that it doesn't matter if you believe in any of that. Your belief in a thing is rather irrelevant. That American philosopher fellow Emerson once wrote, *The mind, once stretched by a new idea, never returns to its original dimensions*. I believe, Charlie, that your mind has been stretched, whether you see it or not. I believe you are writing your own story. I believe that some version of CK Hudson is constantly writing. All you have to do now is sit in front of your fancy computer and let that CK Hudson talk to you. She is, after all, writing her life. Just listen."

And so I started listening.

~

Over the next few months, whenever I sat down in front of that blank screen, it was as if something—or someone—had taken over my fingers. They flew across the keys, clicking away as page after page emerged. I was sitting back, reading what was on the screen one Thursday afternoon, when Frankie came in to tell me her school was planning trips and asked if she could go. When I asked where they were going—fully expecting it to be New York or maybe even London, both of which would not be new places even for young Frankie—I was astonished at her answer.

"Istanbul, Mom. Can you even imagine! Istanbul! I can go, can't I?"

My first thought was to wonder what kind of school trip heads to Istanbul. Wasn't there political unrest going on there? I wasn't sure, but it seemed to me there usually was.

I'd travelled extensively throughout my adult life, but one place I'd never been was Turkey in general and Istanbul in particular. That was probably why I was taken a bit off guard by the idea that my little girl (who was at that time almost fifteen) was going without me.

So, we sat down as a family (Frankie had already convinced Patrick to plead her case, so I was already outnumbered if I had any objections), discussed the parameters of such a trip and signed the forms. Of course, we also paid the bill, and in June, as the end of another school year loomed, Frankie jetted off to the other side of the world for her adventure.

There is an eight-hour time difference between Istanbul and Toronto, a time difference that didn't seem apparent to Frankie. One morning at four am, my phone, which was sitting on my bedside table, rang. As I groggily reached for it, I saw Frankie's name flash up on the caller ID and was immediately awake.

"Frankie! What's wrong?" Because, of course, there would have to be something wrong for her to be calling me at four am — even though it was noon in Istanbul.

"Mom," Frankie said excitedly, "you'll never guess where I am!"

She was right. I could never guess. "Frankie, what's going on?"

"Mom, I have to meet everyone for lunch in a minute, but I just had to call you. I'm at a place called Dolmabahçe Palace. Have you ever heard of it?" She didn't wait for an answer. "It's one of the sultan's palaces. It's incredible! Anyway, this palace is on the Bosphorus River, and I'm standing here looking at the water, and the sun is shining, and it's like I've been here before. And when I walked into the palace and we walked up that staircase on the red carpet under this huge crystal chandelier, I knew where I was going. I knew what rooms were at the top of the stairs, Mom. I had been there before! Have I ever been here before, Mom?" Again, no waiting for an answer. "I know I was there. I know I walked up those steps. Mom, has that ever happened to you?"

I took a deep breath and said, "Yes, Frankie. It has."

Denouement

"I take pleasure in my transformations. I look quiet and consistent, but few know how many women there are in me."
~ Anais Nin

Long Island, New York, 1979

ELEANOR CAME TO VISIT ME THIS AFTERNOON. As usual, the moment we finished our tea and Susanna, my housekeeper, was out of sight, Eleanor found the scotch and set about pouring each of us several fingers, as they say.

I have never found American women particularly appealing as friends. Perhaps it was one of the reasons I moved to Paris all those years ago. However, my grand-niece, Eleanor, is perhaps the most remarkable woman I have ever known, and she has lived her entire life on the east coast of the United States—first in Boston as a child and now in New York. She isn't especially pretty in conventional terms, with her grey-pinstriped suits and white silk blouses with those big bows at the neckline—although the pants do have those trendy wide legs—yet she manages to have suitors falling all over her on a regular basis. My nephew, her father, Richard, who took over the company when I retired, has been trying to convince her to join him at the helm of the family business, which is an enormous global enterprise these days. But she has told me—and him on many occasions—in no uncertain terms that her passion lies elsewhere. Indeed, she is a talented literary agent with her own stable of writers. As it turns out, much to my surprise, I am one of them.

"Aunt Charlotte," Eleanor said when she had taken her first sip of the golden nectar, "I am astonished at this story." She picked up the sheaf of type-written pages she had laid beside her on the couch and looked at the title page. *It All Begins With Goodbye*. "It's extraordinary. It reads as if you're writing the characters in the future, and yet I cannot put my finger on why that seems to be the case. I've never read anything like it. I am very curious, though, about where you found inspiration for the story and the characters."

I wasn't certain even I knew how that process occurred. I only knew I did not appear to be in command when writing. The fact that I was writing at all was enough for me to question who or what was in control. I was no writer, although Eleanor argued to the contrary.

Over the past few years, as Eleanor and I got to know one another as adults—of course, I had known her all her life—she had begun to ask me questions about my life before I began working with my father all those years ago. I was at first hesitant to share the world I had inhabited back then, frightened that she might draw incorrect conclusions about her great-aunt, who had seemingly turned her back on her family for so many years. In all honesty, though, I also felt that looking back on my life in Paris was like looking back at a different person's life. I sometimes felt as if I inhabited a different body then, or at least a different persona. And perhaps I did.

My brother, Peter, her grandfather, had died before he could relate any of this background to Eleanor—indeed, before he even knew he would have a granddaughter. Peter had died as he had lived: in the fast lane. One evening after a particularly rowdy Hollywood party to which he had not taken his wife, his car veered into oncoming traffic. Peter was at the wheel of his cherished Porsche 911, drunk and driving well over the speed limit and had killed only himself—everyone in the car he hit was fine, thank goodness. He never lived to see old age or the granddaughter who sat with me now, sipping scotch.

When Eleanor, an inquisitive teenager, had asked me why I had never married, I told her that I had, in fact, been married but was now a widow. She knew a few pieces of my life with Auguste and our life in Paris, but I must admit I had been somewhat circumspect.

I had tried to explain to Eleanor that the characters in this piece of writing were, in fact, Auguste and myself, and yet they were not. It was difficult for her to understand the depth of the connection we had experienced since she had never been so fortunate. She had less difficulty with the story I'd told her about following my heart and not doing as I was told. That resonated with her, a modern woman of the 1970s.

"But you've written them as if they are in the future, Aunt Charlotte, and yet not in the future. They seem to be stories that have not yet happened. How do you see things that way?"

I was not at all sure I could explain any of this to her in a way that she would understand. All I knew was that she might one day have a similar experience and come to know herself as I had come to know myself.

"I cannot wait to read the ending," Eleanor said as she tidied the pile of pages.

I nodded as I thoughtfully sipped my scotch. I was of much the same opinion. I could not wait to read the ending, yet I was supposed to write it.

"It is oddly synchronous, though, isn't it?" I said. I could tell from the frown on her face that Eleanor clearly had no idea what I was talking about, and I was not much further ahead of her in even knowing what I was about to say. "The way lives proceed in parallel."

She shrugged. "I suppose. I think about the way some of the women in my class at NYU have lived their lives. We almost seem to be on parallel paths and almost connect with one another from time to time, then veer away."

I smiled. Eleanor had no idea what I was talking about. She had no idea I could think of only one reason whenever I tried to determine why I was even writing this story down on paper. It was not fame, fortune or the need to leave a legacy. The one reason I had for writing this book was that I somehow knew it would find its way into *her* hands sometime in the future after I had left this earth. I did not know who she was. I only knew that when she finally found this book, she would know.

She would inhabit a different time and place, a time and place she inhabited even now as I lived my life. She would have her Auguste as I had mine, as brief a time as it was. And she might understand that *It All Begins With Goodbye*.

Then I remembered the moment I finally said goodbye to Auguste. That was when everything else began because I knew it was only goodbye in that time and place. From that moment on, I realized he and I were living a life somewhere in some time, and that would never end. I only needed to pay attention.

About the Author

PATRICIA J. PARSONS started her writing career as a freelance health and medical writer and has written more than twenty books, including health and business books, a memoir, two historical novels, and now women's fiction.

She has been a fashion design and sewing fanatic for most of her life, a passion she writes about online at *The GG Files*, which you can find at www.gloriaglamont.com.

She lives, writes, designs and sews in Toronto.

Connect with her on Instagram
@patriciajparsons or @pjparsonswriter

Join her on Facebook
@patriciaparsonswriter and facebook.com/groups/12dresses

Visit her website
www.patriciajparsons.com